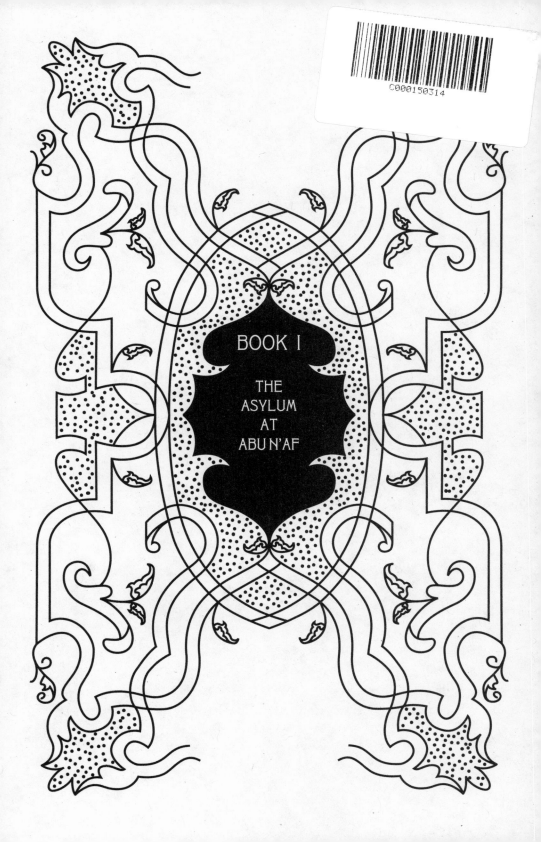

BOOK I

THE
ASYLUM
AT
ABU N'AF

THE FIRST MORNING

René Laforche, the Administrator of the Asylum at Abu N'af, is a small man with gleaming black hair, toffee-coloured teeth and a row of shiny medals pinned to his grey suit. His Anjou Rose medallion for public service has white polish clumped like beetle rot to the silver. He keeps running his thumbnail around the grooves, trying to shift the polish, frowning at me. I sense a breakdown in communication which Mitch's solution for problems like this – the fat envelope filled with dirham notes sitting in my briefcase – will no doubt exacerbate.

Laforche flicks out what he thinks is the last bit of polish – it isn't, and he will dislike me even more when he realises – and sits up straight.

'I'm sure you are aware, Monsieur, that the Asylum is where they brought Rimbaud in from the desert.'

So this is the game: humiliate the hick foreigner.

I assume my blandest expression and say to the irate puffball opposite, 'Rambo? The American action man with the red headband?'

The puffball swells further. 'The famous French poet, Monsieur! *Le symboliste*, follower of Baudelaire, *un ami du Verlaine*. He came to the desert to die.'

I nod as though I am pretending to know what he is talking

about, even though I do know what he is talking about and am just pretending to pretend to know.

I eat a date – and another two – and drink the mint tea. Dust irritates my ear drum.

'So Monsieur Deviling – '

'Devlin.' I extract my business card. 'John Devlin.'

Laforche holds the card by one corner, away from him. 'Our doctors – '

' – are very, very qualified.' I reach for my briefcase. 'But – '

He raises his voice. 'Monsieur, how can you talk to this poor disturbed woman? A woman who runs into walls because she says she wants to climb inside a pebble? She is in the hospital now.' He shakes his head.

I look at Laforche's gleaming hair. Is it dyed? Maybe not. He is in his middle fifties – the same age as the husband of the woman – but older than me by a decade. I wonder if he is in love with her.

'What she did to her face . . . ' His voice is actually fading.

I bite my lip as if shocked. It is not completely an act. I did see the photos.

'How you can talk to her if you do not even know who Rimbaud is?'

Baffling. I am ground between two intractable ways of thinking: the hard, cutting lines of the stars and bars of the great US of A, with its aisles of pills in neon-lit mega-stores, and this land of endlessly shifting curves and veiled ambiguities, of ancient herbs in tiny cut-glass bottles. I imagine living in a world of sand where footprints are constantly erased. I suppose our symbol would be the moon's crescent too. Something that reshapes itself. Disappears.

I pat the briefcase. 'Monsieur.' It sounds like "mon sewer". I say, 'Her family authorises – '

'How do they know who she is?' he says. 'She does not know. We do not know.'

'Well, the people who are interested believe they know.'

He looks through the window, past the helicopter parked in the shadow of the high stone walls, to the Kabir Massif. Sheets of sullen orange hang over the stubby peaks and tremble there. The pilot is rubbing furiously at the smears of marmalade dust dulling the chopper's shiny panels. He is having to go over the same spot every few moments.

'Abu N'af is famous for its storms,' says the Administrator maliciously. 'A grain of sand will bring down your fine machine.'

'Not a grain, surely.' I hunch lower in the chair, try to look like a dutiful messenger, a low-rung grunt. 'Monsieur, you must see what is at stake here. The smuggling of priceless artefacts. Heinous traffickings. Lootings of culture by the father of the Australian woman you are sheltering.'

Laforche smiles. 'Usually it is the French who are considered the looters. The books taken from Danang and Hanoi. Napoleon's foragings in Egypt and Spain.' He examines his thumbnail and frowns. 'You are here to arrest the woman.'

'No.' My voice is over-emphatic; above my supposed pay grade. 'But she has information that is very important to certain people.'

'And you?'

For the first time, I am not sure what to say. 'I won't judge the poor woman.'

'It is just a job to you.'

I do not answer. I open the briefcase, place the envelope in front of him. His shoulders droop. He takes the money. I knew he would.

Laforche insists on finishing his tea. To punish me. I make myself take another date. I chew it slowly. The time on my watch clicks over: another minute gone from forty-eight hours. And I've lost an hour in the flight from Casablanca. I try not to think of the time lost after I heard the news, time spent on my knees retching over the chipped toilet bowl recessed in the floor of the shabby bathroom in Hafid Street.

Mitch is sure to have started the countdown from the moment he told me her whereabouts. There will be no extensions, no excuses.

Laforche is offering me more of the local dates, unappetising papooses in a particularly malevolent yellow. I force another one down. More seconds tick over. Now he is wandering away. For God's sake. I try not to think about Mitch and his goons coming in. Hurting her.

I can feel the steady thud of the generator through the tiled floor. Sand is itching under my collar, my watchband. There are grains of sand under my fingernails. 'We don't get tea-breaks like this at the Embassy, I can tell you.'

'You Americans,' he says. 'Always in such a hurry.'

'Actually, I'm Australian.' More seconds. Dust catches the back of my throat. I worry that grit will ruin my satellite phone. I check it on my belt, the red light is still winking. Next to the chair is my briefcase, a reassuring sentry. I swear there is more dust on the shining steel clasps than there was a moment before. I take out my handkerchief and dust its cool solidness: pure titanium, able to withstand being run over by a tank.

Laforche is bent over the stereo system on the long mahogany side-board. There is a clicking noise and he mutters about the generator. The watch ticks on.

I am like a man going to the guillotine. I just want it to be over. I avert my gaze from the low window, the spackled sky, the Martian-red plain spread out behind the helicopter. The desk in front of me is almost bare: a few files, the embossed silver tea tray and teapot, a black and white photograph of a couple kissing in a very Parisian-looking café. The couple is seated in front of a mirror, in a booth, the seats covered with some dark lush material. The girl's head is thrown back, lips parted, eyes half-closed. The man is not Laforche. I imagine a photo like that on my desk in the Hafid Street office or even in Canberra. There would be a moustache drawn on the girl, tits on the guy, within a day, within hours.

There is glass over the photo. As I shift in my seat, I see myself reflected. I move immediately but it is too late. There is no sign of the happy, fleshy lover in Sicily; only a tall man whose cropped dark hair and designer suit and immaculately knotted silk tie can't disguise the wary eyes and the tense jaw. The muscles chipped beyond health, the body turned wolfish. A once-sleek man teetering on the edge of gauntness, a physically strong man ravaged by darkness. By lack.

I open the briefcase, take out my colour-coded schedule for the next three days. I have allotted three hours for the first interrogation.

Once she knows she has been found, she would be a fool not to co-operate. Not to ask for mercy.

Laforche has drifted over, a vinyl record in his hand. He stares at the chart with interest. He points to the few small green squares in the brick wall of red.

'Leisure time,' I say.

He gives me a pitying look.

I wonder what she will do when she sees me. Scream, try to run away? Or the shock will make her fall, ashen and trembling to the floor. Or she will be haughty. Maybe she will cry, 'Thank you, thank you'. Maybe she will fling her arms around me. When I think this, I get the familiar pain beneath my ribs; acid washes through my stomach. Mitch thinks these are symptoms of the detoxification after Sicily. But I know they are not.

The gravel purr of Edith Piaf climbs through the dry heat, wrestles with the slowly turning fan.

Laforche says to me, '*Chanson réaliste*: all about the misery of life and love. But like Piaf, we must regret nothing.' The song swells, filling the room like clouds.

He glances at me. 'But maybe you do not want a love song? Maybe this . . . ' He changes the record. A tremulous note begins, not a flute, some kind of pipe, and a woman's voice, talking half in French, half in Arabic, her words grinding out to meet the eerie notes. Laforche watches me and I think of snake-charmers.

'*Les heures et les fois*,' he says. 'The hours and the times.' He begins to sing along, also in that dragging style, '*Dans le noir, je me réveille, seul et silencieux à la page blanche du désert*. In the dark, I wake, alone and silent on the white page of the desert. *Dans le noir, la solitude est sainte*. Solitude is holy. That is you, yes?'

He doesn't wait for my response. 'When I was allowed to run the generator at night, I swear the camels would come right up to the window to listen.' He sways in time with the song. He asks me what music I prefer.

'I'm a Beethoven man myself.' I look at my watch.

'Very correct.' He sighs. 'It is horrible not to be allowed to play music at night in the desert. It is like being without family. Or a woman.'

'Maybe,' I say indifferently. 'I can do very well without women.' I try not to think of the man on the surveillance tape who said, his voice breaking, *Ravenous*.

Laforche raises an eyebrow.

'No,' I say. 'I'm not. But the personal and this job don't mix.'

He shrugs. 'I have a wife and five children in Casablanca. But, yes, I suppose. Go on.'

'Well . . . ' I don't know what to say next. There is danger in talking about this. 'You don't need it, that's all.'

'There is always *une prostituée*.'

'I would never visit a prostitute.'

'You are a romantic,' says Laforche.

I can't bear it any longer. My chair scrapes as I stand.

'Yes, yes,' says Laforche. He switches the record off, comes back to the desk, opens a folder and passes across a slim pile of black and white photographs.

The photos are of clouds of sand, piles of dust. The light has an odd intensity, making shadows where there shouldn't be shadows, the dark grey sky flaring into white. There are strange swirls like the imprints left in water by a trailing hand. The photos look like shots of an anti-land, the negative of a positive. I think I see my own face in some of them, distorted, like a beast.

'Mirages,' says Laforche. 'She had been photographing mirages. The nuns think she has photographed ghosts. See – don't you think that is a man on a horse?'

'Heat distortions,' I say. 'The combination of light and hot air distorts the natural perspectives.'

'Ghosts,' says Laforche.

I look at my watch. I swear the glass is dusty.

'Yes, well.' My voice booms over the tiles. 'There is nothing that can't be explained rationally. The Bermuda triangle? Nothing but the earth spuming methane, disorienting plane sensors, overturning yachts. Giant farting, that is all.'

I say it again, louder. 'Giant farts.'

I take out my notebook in its titanium cover, uncap the zero-gravity pen from NASA.

'She came walking out of the desert,' says Laforche. 'At first she was a speck on the horizon, like a black spot in her photographs, a piece of sand.'

'She came walking out of the desert,' I say, scratching uselessly against the page, 'because she had escaped custody.' The pen won't write.

The Administrator folds his arms. 'We are all specks in the desert. When we look so far out into the landscape, we become the landscape. The desert imprints itself on our retina, enters us.'

I stare at him. He could be a talkative man, a lonely man. But I don't think so. I think he is punishing me for humiliating him. This is the Arabic equivalent of a stoush behind the pub. Melee by metaphor.

'I'm not here to study the desert,' I say. 'I'm here to do my job.'

'You won't last long,' says the Administrator, 'if you ignore the desert.'

I jab at the white plain of paper. 'You found her wandering in the dunes with no possessions, no documents?'

He hesitates. 'Sister Antony would know if she had anything on – on her person,' he says delicately. 'All I saw was the camera.' He nods at the photos. 'Meersun, the daughter of Betsoul, a protégée of the Sister's, found her first.'

I jab at the paper again. 'So the woman was brought in and then – '

Laforche is still. 'We were told that an Australian called Devlin was coming. And she placed a scorpion on her face.'

I am ravaged beyond the pit in my stomach, the permanent pain below my heart. Beyond darkness.

Laforche looks away. 'She was lucky. It was an old scorpion, scarred and weary. No longer as potent.'

The point of the pen is breaking through the paper.

'This is a region,' says Laforche slowly, 'where the women hide daggers in their hair. The girls have poison necklaces, for times of war. Maybe that is what the woman was doing. She picked up the scorpion by one leg, how I don't know, and she draped it around her, like a necklace.'

I flinch but he doesn't notice.

'She said, "I'm going home". And then the scorpion moved all over her. Who would have thought it would move so fast? It stung as it went, stabbing again and again with its devil tail. As it crawled over her eyelid, she fell slowly, like someone falling through clouds.'

We stare at each other. This was the tipping point, as Mitch would say, with his usual trite way of reducing calamities; the moment when I should appeal to Laforche's gallantry, his pride, whatever drove his feeling for the woman.

I think of asking him for help. My stomach heaves. I scribble around the pockmarks in the paper and say, 'You don't know what she is capable of.'

Laforche says, 'I do not know what you are capable of.'

The pen still won't write.

'It's the dry air,' says Laforche.

'It's a NASA pen,' I say. 'Specially designed for extreme conditions.'

He pulls out a drawer. The knowing eye of the girl in the photograph gazes up at me.

Laforche gives me a pencil. I sigh, acknowledge my defeat. I take the pencil and write.

There is a small smile on the Administrator's lips.

The Asylum has two levels of deeply recessed arcades on all sides of a wide courtyard. The sick bay is located directly opposite the Administrator's office. It is 11 am when we step out into the shuddering air.

We skirt the cracked fountain in the centre of the courtyard. Its square-headed lion gapes dry-mouthed at us. Chickens scratch at tufty plants growing around the chipped base. The heat falls on me like stone. I can barely see in the searing light, even with my sunglasses on. Along the upper arcade, female patients sit between the washing hung in the stone arches. I squint and count five: thin, slack-jawed, mostly dark-skinned, with cropped hair.

'We only take special cases,' says Laforche. 'Only what the Church sends us. So if we are not sent . . . ' He points to a rusted iron grate in the compacted earth. 'After the old monastery burnt down in 1408, the new one was built around the well.' He made it sound like yesterday.

'Rimbaud used to write in . . . ' He turns, almost stepping on a chicken which was pecking at his trouser cuff. He points to the nearest stone turret, one of four, each tulip-shaped. 'There. We have his diary.'

I am startled. That wasn't in my files.

He laughs. 'Maybe it is a forgery. For the tourism, Monsieur Devlin. In winter and autumn, we charge for visits. On Tuesdays.'

'The Church doesn't mind?'

'The Church wants to spend even less. We are all thankful for the crowds who pay to visit one of the great outposts of French exploration. The diary of Rimbaud might condemn us to coach tours at Christmas but Sister Antony would say it has been our saviour.'

He absorbs my expression. 'You really know nothing about Rimbaud?'

'I really don't.'

'They say Arthur Rimbaud never wrote poetry after the age of nineteen,' says Laforche. 'Imagine – the shocking, outrageous poems about sex and death and madness, the revolutionary work that will begin modern poetry, it is all done between the age of sixteen and nineteen. Sixteen, Monsieur. Think of what you were doing at sixteen. Then Rimbaud goes to Brussels, the final break with Paul Verlaine, he comes to Africa, to travel and run guns. After Africa, nothing. No more poetry.'

'Do you believe that?'

He glances at me. 'I do not believe it. I think, in the beginning in Africa, it was true. He was emotionally exhausted, he felt he had failed in Europe. He had wanted to be a prophet, famous among all men. A wild, reckless youth: if he said a thing, then he couldn't take it back. But I think once he walked out of the desert, he became the seer he always wanted to be. He started writing again.' Laforche closes his eyes for a moment. 'He must have,' he says, almost to himself.

'Where did he walk out to, after the desert?'

'Here. The first place Rimbaud came to after the desert was Abu N'af.'

'Just like . . . '

'Yes. Like the woman.'

We cross into the shade and turn into a long room with white-washed stone walls and large windows. There is a row of empty beds and a silhouette by the farthest window.

A thin nun in a white pinafore over her black habit sits, reading, in a chair next to the last bed.

This side of the Asylum is on the edge of the plateau, with a sheer drop to the pitted plain below. I take a good look around the room, searching for possible exits. There is only one door. At the far end are six windows fitted with wooden shutters, half of them hooked back against the outside wall. The fierce light is muted here, away from the morning sun.

The door is behind me. There is no escape if the door is blocked.

I straighten my tie. It is 11.05 am. Laforche, halfway across the room, looks back at me.

I scan the room again, note the plain dresser with two hurricane lamps, both full. On the nearest wall is a faded photograph of a series of fountains falling down a steep hillside, the sun catching chips of colours in the water sprays below an iced-white chateau. People in mini-skirts and stovepipe trousers pose, smoking. I read the title: *The Singing Fountains At Villa d'Este*. On the far wall is another photo, of a luridly coloured oil portrait of a glum man in white robes. The current king, Mohammed VI.

I move closer, put the briefcase on the next bed. My fingers slip on the silver clasps. Another look at my watch. Execution hour. I open the briefcase, lift up the files on top, feel the micro-camera, the finger-thin laptop computer. The gun is there, next to the burnt diary held together by the red silk ribbon. I touch the ribbon and the gun and take out the tape recorder.

The woman lies on her back under the misty cloud of a tethered mosquito net. Her arms are by her sides, her palms up. I brace myself for the turn of the head, the sudden cry. But nothing happens.

Laforche beckons.

She is blurry – I think it is my eyes. But as I draw nearer, I see the figure is bandaged from her head to her palms. Welts creep like red vines from under the white bandages at her wrists. Her hands are swollen starfish.

I step closer still. Her entire face is bandaged, apart from gaps for her eyes and her parted lips. Her eyes are closed, lashes in a dark half-moon over purplish bruises. There is a low funnel of escaping air, like the sea turning over. Her nose must be so swollen that she is breathing through her mouth. There is a twig of some kind – lavender – pinned to the pillow above her right temple.

Closer. A light breeze strokes my cheek and a shutter rattles. At any moment she will look at me. Her face will change, contort. My career could be over in a few words. There will be a trial, a secret military court, no hope of escape. Prison. This is what I must focus on: everything I had worked for, gone. All the sacrifices. The loneliness.

After so many months, I can reach out and touch her. I don't understand why she still has her eyes closed.

I take a deep breath. 'Madame, I need to question you about Sicily.' I sound tentative. 'I must question you about your husband.'

Now. Now she would turn and look at me. I wonder what to do if she is angry enough to spill details in front of witnesses.

I know what Mitch would say.

The Administrator and the nun stare at me.

'Madame . . .'

'She can't hear you,' says Laforche. 'She's unconscious.'

'She's faking,' I say immediately.

Sister Antony holds the book before her – it is the Bible – and stands, her head bowed. She is tall and, with her back to the window, her face is an oval of darkness.

'How do you know?' Her voice is flat, clamping the faint accent. I visualise my files. We had focused on Laforche; there was only sketchy information on the rest of the staff and only hearsay details on Sister Antony: her arrival in Casablanca in 1959, the years of drug-taking, the break-down after the German boyfriend left, the volunteer work at the Catholic Mission, the disastrous interference with the young Arab girl, the withdrawal to the desert in '78. I had searched her last home in Casablanca but her constant changing of names during the drug years made Mitch impatient. He stopped me investigating further; her life before Abu N'af was not relevant, he said.

I dismiss the files and point at the figure in the bed. 'I know this woman,' I say, trying to sound disinterested; a man married only to his job.

'How do you know this is her?' says the Sister. Again that flattening of the explosive consonants. Of the old Central European accent.

I look at the nun blankly. Her only adornment is a wooden cross strung on what looks like a long plait of camel's hair around her neck. A slender gold crucifix has been nailed into the wood. The stem of the cross is rubbed down.

Laforche says, 'Sister Antony has spent the most time with – what do you call her?'

The nun dips her head. 'Madeleine, Monsieur.'

'Monsieur Devlin thinks he knows who she is.'

There is a gleam of light as the Sister lifts her head but she is silent.

'You undressed her, washed her?' I say. 'You found no documents?'

A slight hesitation. Sister Antony shakes her head.

'And she has been unconscious all this time?'

Another hesitation. A nod.

I take out the diary with its pale scorched cover and its torn and burnt pages. I watch the nun carefully as I untie the red ribbon and select a less-singed page.

'Do you recognise the writing? Has she written anything like that?'
'No.'

A shutter rattles in the pause that follows.

'I must question her. You know your government authorised this,' I say to Laforche.

'The same way you authorised me? I'm sure,' he says. 'But as you must oberve, she is not fit.'

I wave a hand. 'I have something to wake her up.'

'No.' The nun's voice is harsh, like dried twigs.

A curl of dark hair cups the woman's ear, rising and falling with her steady breath. But I know she is awake. Watching me.

I want to look for the scars I know are on her inner arm but bandages hide the older misdemeanours. Useless to ask for a DNA swab or a hair sample; Mitch won't give me the time to get them analysed.

'I need to see her face.'

Laforche looks at the Sister. My fingers grip the ampule in my pocket.

The Sister's gaze drops to my wrist. She crosses herself.

After a long pause, she steps forward, slips a hand under the woman's neck, raises her head and slowly unwinds the bandages. The creamy cloth comes off, round and round, an endless white tongue.

The woman's forehead is visible. I see welts as long as my fingers dissecting her cheeks from forehead to chin, shining like burns from the lotion. Her lashes tremble against the shadows under her eyes.

I stare at the smattering of freckles over her skin. The desert sun must have brought out the freckles. I tried to remember whether I had seen them in Sicily.

I replay scenes like photographs. No, I couldn't remember freckles.

I look at her face.

For the first time in eight months. Thirty eight weeks. Two hundred and forty days.

I look at her.

And look.

Her eyelids tremble. She's awake, I'm sure of it. But she remains still.

The Sister steps back. 'You can make your identification now.'

'I need to talk to her,' I say. Laforche raises an eyebrow at the note in my voice.

The Sister says, 'She is beyond sleep, Monsieur. The poison will soon make her skin hang from her bones like flags.'

I shrug and look to the door as though someone is entering. When the Sister and Laforche turn, I lean over the woman and break the ampule under her nose.

The bitter smell of amyl nitrate fills the room. Laforche curses and comes forward.

'I'm authorised,' I say to him.

The woman jerks like a marionette and her eyes open. I draw back out of her line of sight. She is staring at the ceiling. She shudders; her eyelids begin to close.

I wave the ampule under her nose. 'Look at me.' I lean over her. She is still staring straight up. I bring the ampule under her nose again but quickly; any more and she will be sick. The smell is making even me gag.

'Look at me.'

Her eyes are all blue, like light hitting shallow water at noon, the pupils contracted from the pain. I want to tell her she looks like the heroin addict she once was. I want to remind her who's in charge here, who's in control. I know that fear is driving my anger. The pain is beneath my ribs again, the hollow feeling, the void needing to be filled.

Laforche throws back the remaining shutters to let the smell out. Light floods the room. The welts are livid, distorting her face.

'Do you know me?' I say.

She starts to shake her head, stops; it is too painful. Her eyes are a clear unflinching blue.

'No,' she says in a thickened voice. Then, 'Police man. Government man.' No recognition in the swollen features.

'We've never met?'

'No.'

She blinks. Her mouth relaxes. She is losing consciousness.

'Wake up!' I shout.

'Move away from the bed.' Laforche stands opposite me. Any cordiality he felt – had begun to feel, towards me – has gone. He is furious.

'It's her.' I can barely speak.

'She says she doesn't know you.'

'Pretending.'

Laforche snorts. 'Is she?'

It is too enormous a question to lie about. 'I don't know.'

The Sister slips past me, bends over the woman, listens to her breathing. 'She's unconscious.'

'Faking,' I say. 'Lying.'

Laforche says, 'For God's sake, have some pity.'

I can't meet his eyes.

'There was – she made mincemeat of one of our men,' I say. 'In Sicily. A stupid man. There was an opportunity but she slipped away with crucial information. He let it happen. The stupid man.' All I could think, once the words slipped out, was that I was under pressure, rattled, not my usual self.

Laforche looks at the Sister who places her hands inside her wide sleeves and withdraws into her oval of darkness.

Laforche says, 'You can't question her any more.'

I had been expecting that. 'Later – '

He glares at me. 'Never. It is too much for her.'

The Sister says, 'Monsieur Devlin should talk to her again.'

We both swivel to face her. Her expression is stern. 'If Madeleine doesn't know who she is, she needs to know before she dies. If she does know, then she should tell us.'

I trudge out into the gritty air to talk to the pilot, a stocky man with a moustache wider than his chin. He leans into the shade of the walls, flirting half-heartedly with a thin dark woman who oozes away when she sees me, her strangely marked heels kicking up small puffs of dust.

The pilot looks at me expectantly and taps his watch, a cheap stainless-steel knock-off. I tell him I have to stay the night. He breaks into a passionate speech about why we should leave immediately: a speech involving his family, his health, undisclosed tax reasons and the presence of too many amorous women barely contained by these puny crumbling walls.

I stare at the shadow of the rotor blades cutting like a crucifix into the hard ground and feel the machine's metal body pulsing with heat.

The helicopter had been a mistake. I should have come by car, an old Jeep or trader's truck. The time in Sicily turned me reckless. I should have kept my temper under control, been drabber, inconspicuous. My vanity made me wear my best suit – so she would wish she never left me. I should have worn jeans and a Hawaiian shirt; everyone thinks Australia is an outpost of America anyway. I should have been a walking cliché; clichés make people relax. They stop asking questions. They assume they know.

The pilot is trying to cross himself: he is a good sub-contractor and has learned gestures to please his Western clients, but his hands won't stay straight and soon drift into the undulating gesture of the salaam.

'May God be with you,' I say sardonically; the Arabic equivalent of *You're fired*. He deflates into a mumble.

'Shut up, will you?' I say. 'I'm staying but you can go.'

In my experience, people never mind rudeness if you are telling them what they want to hear. In their relief, they often reveal more than you ever expected.

The pilot is no exception: the dark woman, he says, is called Meersun. She helped care for the woman after she was bitten.

I feel better. Away from the sick bay, the office, in fact away from everything inside the Asylum, I feel clearer, more in control. Energy surges back through me. One way or another, I will get results. I always do.

I am confident enough to take my first good look at the countryside. I see desolation. The fierce light bleaches the red sands into baked tan, a granite world. The sky faints into a leached blue, the sun reduced to pale yolk by its own brightness.

Lethargic clouds ridge the sky like a half-opened shell. The only sound is the wind's breath, turning ragged now. Maybe there is the echo of far-off dogs. But that could be my imagination. I have developed a distaste for dogs ever since Sicily.

The Asylum's road is just gravel overlaid on a scraping apart of the sand and rock. It falls down the hillside like an exhausted tongue, rolling out across the plain below, to the squat brown outcrop in the distance. The Kabir Massif.

I take out my binoculars. Primordial rock gapes through the deep grooves left by the retreating ice. How ironic that for most of its forty-million-year history, the Sahara was a place of seas. That what turned Europe into a wintry hell for a millennia made the desert cool and lush and green. Rain for a thousand years – until the dry spells became longer and longer. No wonder everyone in the desert talked in terms of water: a sea of sand, waves of dunes. A form of nostalgia, of dreaming.

I scan. The land is folded and squeezed into the distance. The heat haze makes the plain shimmer; the lonely road trembles. It doesn't matter how much I adjust the binoculars' lenses: the tough pale plants and small outcrops of grass stand in focus only briefly. Then the earth shifts.

I am not a fanciful man. The most logical explanation is usually the right one. But all this airy fairy talk about deserts is distracting me. It is impossible to get anything done – and I'm on the clock. It's stress, I say to myself. And the sun. I'm used to the heat after Iraq and Borneo; but this air is too thin or dry. I think I see an immense beast with the head of a vulture and the paws of a lion, moving its slow thighs, shaking its head, beginning to rise from the sands.

I see black specks coming out of dust clouds. I see helicopters.

A sound claws into the great bell of silence. My watch is beeping. It is time to call Mitch.

'For fuck's sake,' says Mitch, static eroding his words. 'She's obviously not sane. Wave more amyl under her nose. Find out where she hid the stuff.'

'The Administrator – '

' – can see the writing on the map. The desert is a busy place these days.'

I roll my eyes at the brown void below.

'I know you didn't want this job,' says Mitch. 'You must hate my guts for sending you . . . ' He pauses expectantly.

'No, Mitch.' I grit my teeth. 'I appreciate the opportunity – '

' – the opportunity not to go to jail for letting her get away. So you'd better nail her good this time.'

'Yes, Mitch.'

'You're on probation until then, you know.'

'Yes.'

I stare at the gravel grimace, hear the endless silence. Always we try to make our little marks on this vast page, digging out roads, reshaping mountains. It is a compulsion, this constant remaking. Like reaching out in the middle of the night to cup a hand around a woman's calf and, very softly and gently, move her leg a fraction.

I catch my breath.

'What's that sound?' says Mitch.

'The wind's coming up. People go mad in the dust storms here, apparently.'

'Madder,' says Mitch. 'Well, you've got one day – '

'Two,' I say.

'Dude, if you can't get her talking by tomorrow night, dump her in the desert. We could pick her off from the air. Problem solved.'

Static eats the humour in his laughter.

'Joke, Devlin,' says Mitch. 'Like your Hollywood name.'

'Yes,' I say. 'Joke.'

He says, 'You field guys. You all think too much.'

Laforche had refused to wake the woman. Instead, he told me a long pointless story. An old tale of the desert, he said. Two friends are parted for years by various malign fates, the weather, new loves. Then, after many more contrived circumstances, one finally sends the other a letter which contains only the words, *This morning I pruned my rose tree.* After many more malign circumstances (bandits, failing carrier pigeons and so on), his friend replies, *This morning I too pruned my rose tree.*

Whole minutes went by while I stared in despair at the photo of the kiss in the café. The wooden fan overhead creaked into my silence.

'You see?' said Laforche.

Now I am being given a guided tour of the property by Sister Antony. The condemned property. I wonder if Laforche knows. Maybe he thinks it will help, if he co-operates with us. Maybe he doesn't care; it is another game to him. A game putting me behind schedule.

I am standing in the room where the woman slept when she first arrived. It is a windowless cell, one of the summer sleeping rooms burrowed into the earth, taking advantage of small caves and natural pockets in the rock. But even here, some indecisive murk of sunlight falls down the curve of the rubbed-shiny stone steps and sidles exhausted, the colour of grey felt, around Sister Antony, who waits for me in the cool corridor.

Dust is still itching my ear. I am annoyed enough to want to take off my tie and jacket but I refuse to lower my standards. I sit on the cot in the corner which, surprisingly, takes my weight without protest. A white sheet covers a lumpy pallet made from tough calico. I scratch a thumbnail against stubby stalks. The pallet is filled with straw. I feel the weight of the satellite phone on my belt, the solidity of my briefcase, the fine weave of my suit. Straw.

The nun is stationary, her face shadowed above her impossibly white pinafore. She is wiry and tough; a desert plant. But there is light below her heart. She traps light in her slender gold cross.

I contemplate her. I have already tried my panting-puppy routine, complaining about the heat, admiring her fortitude. I have grumbled about the Casablanca traffic on Haussmann Avenue, the endless parking notices – 'To be paid in cash! Always worse on a Monday! Lottery night, it's a scandal!' – to show that I am on her side, an oppressed worker. But all she gives me is a tightening of those thin lips. The only time her jaw relaxes is when I slap the thick stone walls and, in a blurt about medieval architecture, praise the Church for maintaining buildings like these. For a moment I think she is about to speak but then she bows her head again.

I play my torch over the walls. The back wall is pitted rock, shifting like deep sea under moonlight. There are glints of grey; tin maybe. Last week's satellite photos showed new mining to the south, in the blood-stained sands of the Western Sahara.

The rock is cool to the touch, a relief from the gritty heat upstairs. Down here, you could fool yourself you could beat the desert. That you would win. The torch light ripples over the rubbed floor stones, catching odd marks; writings in French and English. I stare at the hopeful postcards. Brave little sign-posts: *Pierre was here*; *Silvana was here*. I have no sympathy for them.

I kneel on the cool floor and lift the cot away from the wall. There is something scratched in French in the corner:

Je suis Rimbaud, l'ange déchu de Paris.
Je suis allé dans le desért sacré.
Maintenant, je suis un autre.

She's likely to do the opposite of what her father wants, I told Mitch right from the start. Of what we want. Out of spite. Out of revenge.

The mother, of course, was committed years ago.

I stare at the rock. My watch beeps again. By now I should have finished the first interrogation. Should know where I stand.

I think of the man who said to her, 'The light from the moon spills into your shoulder.' A less haggard man. A man proud of his strength, his ability to catch her in his arms and raise her above his head, up to the moon. A man who could make her laugh. A happy man.

It was probably on the surveillance tapes. Somewhere, waiting to be found.

Stupid man.

The cell is airless, the only sound a rustle: a small black beetle picks its way painstakingly along the side of the wall, lifting its long thin legs as though there was an art to walking. An art to walking. Ridiculous. I lift my foot. The beetle stops under the sudden increase in gloom. I lower my heel, wanting to grind, to smash.

'No!' says the nun by my side. The beetle lurches forward, turns as though it wants to run into the wall – *she wants to climb inside a pebble* – and disappears.

'Tunnels,' says Sister Antony. 'They make tunnels between the stones.' She bows her head. Her lips move. I tug at my tie. I am surprised to find that I am breathing heavily. I can see how emotions become muted in the desert. Nearly nothing is worth the physical toll.

The nun kisses her crucifix. Her hands are like the stone floor: a smooth, deep brown, crisscrossed with lines, a blue vein travelling like a river through this country with no boundaries.

I tighten my tie. A country with no boundaries. Ridiculous.

I ask for a translation of the French scratched into the corner.

She says, 'I am Rimbaud, the fallen angel of Paris. I went into the sacred desert. Now, I am another.'

'The Administrator said that he came to the desert to die.'

She smiles, her mouth turns downwards. 'Monsieur Laforche was born in Paris, the metropolis of red roses. The desert frightens him.'

I make an encouraging noise, nod thoughtfully.

'He sustained him in a desert land,' she says, 'in a howling wilderness waste. He shielded him, cared for him, guarded him as the apple of His eye. Deuteronomy.' Her voice is no longer like dried twigs. 'Rimbaud did not come here to destroy his body but to transform it.' Her words ring out like bells. I swear I hear an echo. 'Like Jesus, he wandered in the desert, and when he came out of the desert, he built a community.'

I stare at her. 'Did Rimbaud begin a church here?'

She withdraws her hands into her wide sleeves. 'He saved Abu N'af.' Her hands move beneath the material. 'When the Church would have closed us.'

I recall the report. Once Abu N'af was crowded, with waiting lists of two years. It was a retreat which imitated those of the Italians who, in the 1970s, opened their convents and monasteries to the newly distressed as well as the faithful, as long as they paid. But in these days of terrorism, the Moroccan desert and Rimbaud weren't the drawcards they used to be.

'You need another poet,' I say to her.

I open my eyes on darkness as smothering as a cowl, with black wind in my mouth and sand under my cheek on the pillow. I think I hear a helicopter, Mitch arriving. But it must be the upper shutters clicking like bones against the wall. My watch says 3 am.

I feel woolly-minded; the familiar pain grinds below my ribs. It is like the shame I used to feel about my addiction to alcohol. When I was drinking, all I thought about was drinking. It is hunger but it is not.

I see freckles. There is only one person who ever took the pain away . . .

I am in the room she slept in: Rimbaud's room. I turn on my torch, pull on my trousers. I am halfway to the door when I remember my briefcase and my shirt. I put on my shirt, take the briefcase.

The steps are smooth and cool under my feet. My bare feet, I realise as I step into the courtyard. The air is swollen with pine nuts and diesel oil and warm musk. A breeze slaps my face. It reminds me of Sicily. But seeing her, I say to myself, would remind me of Sicily.

The lion stares at me black-eyed under the swollen and bruised moon. I need my shoes. Only the thought that I will be quieter without sends me on.

I switch off the torch. There is enough light to see by. I am still not accustomed to how low the moon rides here. A yearning for home shakes me: wattle on the breeze, jacaranda trees dripping purple on the stone, the southerly buster at dusk chasing the heat away. The high moon.

The door to the sick bay is ajar. I slip into the darkness and feel my way along the wall, past the sideboard, walking my fingers over the gravelled metal surfaces of the hurricane lamps to the first window. I ease the shutters apart, latch them back.

Slowly dissolving verticals of moonlight fall over the black desert, trailing breaths of cloud, tendrils which reach down to the dark ground. Then I see that it is the ground reaching to the sky. The sand is rising: the moonlight catches the glitter of a thousand fragments in the slowly turning dust spirals; the echoes of a thousand sounds are held in the heart of every spiral. A thousand faces are out there, breathing.

The room takes on a hushed, waiting quality. I feel as though I have walked into an absence of sound, where I won't be able to speak, no-one will be able to speak. I sway. I am falling through all known points of contact, falling through a void. With sheer force of will, I make myself walk towards the bed. At the back of my mind, a voice says, *Stupid man.*

The woman lies under the mosquito net. She is an effigy; the welts blue in this light. I unlock the briefcase, the sound as loud as rifle fire. I take out the gun and put it beside the briefcase, on the floor.

The net comes up like foaming sea. I know it is made of some rough thread, camel hair or hemp. But it shimmers around the woman. She moves like the tide as the net comes up. She is diaphanous.

I throw the net back, reach out and run my fingers through her hair. I feel grit, tiny pieces of coral, metal flecks. A small triangular object, flint maybe, the tip of an arrowhead or a hook. Old weapons, old seas.

Her breathing is steady.

I bend over her, put my cheek on the pillow, feel my eyelashes an eyelash away from hers, smell the lotion on her skin: a flat antiseptic smell and some scent known only to this part of the world.

Her breath catches, her eyelashes lift.

I straighten. Her eyes are deep water.

I say her name.

She raises her right hand and traces in the air. The light streams between her parted fingers.

'Is that a sign?' I say. 'A map?'

She ignores me, keeps tracing. 'We must talk,' I say loudly. 'Before Mitch gets here.'

Her hand is trembling, slowing. Her lips are moving; I catch the murmur of a strangely familiar song. It reminds me of the moon behind black branches. I can't place it. I dismiss it. It is not relevant.

I say, 'If you don't help me, you're against me.' There is a shifting of shadow behind me. But I ignore it, bend down, grope for the briefcase, the gun.

'Fuck you then,' I say.

The Sister comes up beside me in a pool of yellow light, catches my arm.

'She's dying,' says the Sister.

'She knows who I am.' I say to the woman in the bed, 'You know me.'

Her hand stops.

'No,' she says in that swollen voice. 'I don't know you.'

'You can't lie about this. It's recorded. You worked for us.'

Her hand resumes its slow tracings.

'Stop that.' I grab her hand. Her fingers are still, quiescent, like water, slipping away from me as I release her. I feel burned.

The Sister says, 'Go now.'

'She's lying. Don't you understand? The whole family is rotten.'

The Sister shakes her head.

I say, 'You know I'm right. Otherwise you would have called for help.'

I see the three of us, caught in the pool of light.

The woman in the bed says, 'My mother has someone else's body.'

The Sister looks down at her.

'The chauffeur took me back to the Manse,' says the woman. 'The Mausoleum, my brother called it.'

'Wait,' I say. 'I know that.' The Sister tenses as I open the briefcase and take out the diary. I move closer to the hurricane lamp and undo the red silk ribbon, turn the pages.

The woman watches me, unblinking. I hold a handful of pages in front of her. 'You recognise this, don't you?'

'No,' she says and turns her face away.

'Yes.' I select a page and read it out, skimming. '*August 19. The chauffeur takes me home to the Manse . . . My mother said the black wrought-iron draped around the house was black lace but my brother called it iron spider webs.*'

The woman closes her eyes.

'This is your family,' I say, turning pages. '*Usually I make allowances for my mother . . . for duty's sake, for the sake that I really don't care. But today . . . I overhear the nurse . . . We found the blood in Anna's room.*'

The woman doesn't move. I skip down, raise my voice, 'This is what you wrote about your mother: *Misery is making her sag, despite all the plastic surgery. I'm sick of you kids, she says. Kid, I say. There's only one of us left now.*'

I close the diary.

The Sister grips the base of her cross.

'You recognise that, don't you?' I say to Sister Antony. 'From her ramblings.'

'Is she Anna?' says the Sister. She lifts the cross and holds it at me – to keep me at bay – and says, 'Don't tell me. I don't want to know.'

I see myself as she must see me, leaning over the woman in the bed. I am a black cloak, an anti-presence. The woman's head is always turned away, her neck always exposed.

'You let people down,' I say to the woman. 'They trusted you. It was important what you were doing. It mattered. You ran out on them – '

Before I can stop, the word slips out. The unsayable word. It hangs in the air, gaudy with flies. The force of it, the way I meant it, was like a slap. I see myself advancing inexorably from behind, enveloping her, holding her down, biting her shoulders, her back, her buttocks, leaving bloody teeth marks. Being the man we both always thought I was.

I am already falling back exhausted from the weight of the word when I say it.

'Whore.'

Time passes. A shudder runs through her body but she doesn't open her eyes. She slowly raises her hand and gives a small but definite flick of her fingers, the Italian gesture of contempt, her nails catching the light as though she has handfuls of stars. She flicks again, her arm shakes and drops. She lies still, palm upwards.

The Sister is at my side, gripping my arm. 'Enough.'

I back away. 'She's not – is she breathing?'

'Yes.'

'I've killed her.'

I would have fallen if Sister Antony hadn't held me up. I shout and my voice is louder than the banging shutters, 'Oh Jesus Christ, I didn't mean to – '

I pick up the briefcase and throw it with all my might against the wall. 'Why did you let me?'

The Sister slides the sheet from the woman's legs. There, on the inner right thigh, above the curve of the calf and the knee-cap showing ivory, is a small patch of light and dark.

At first I think it is a tattoo, a decorative pattern in the Arabic style, heavily inked swirls and lines. But there are strange verticals of light running through it like a bad photocopy. The Sister brings the lamp closer. The lines sharpen. It is a photograph. A black and white photograph developed directly onto her skin.

The shutters are banging furiously.

The moon sits brooding in the window frame.

I look closer and closer and see that the photo is of a man.

A man's face.

My face.

THE SECOND MORNING

Iwake into *l'heure bleue*: the blue hour, the French call it, the moments between darkness and day, night and redemption.

Even deep in the earth, in Rimbaud's cell, there is the sense of gloom lightening.

I am naked beneath the rough blanket. I grope for my briefcase. The diary and gun are inside. I take out a new shirt, still in its wrapper, and clean underwear. Someone has removed yesterday's shirt and underwear and left a folded robe on the end of the cot. I stare at it dubiously. Laforche wears a suit. To be less dressed than Laforche seems to be a sign of weakness. I wonder who has taken my underwear. I don't like the thought of someone washing my underwear and make a note to find out where it has gone.

My organiser pings, the screen glows green. A reminder to write up my notes from yesterday's interrogation. The failed interrogation. I slump on the cot. In another day, Mitch and his thugs would arrive. If I didn't have some answers for them, they would go to work on her – the woman – and if they didn't get what they wanted, they would go to work on me. I have an image of my body being ground down into sand. Grated.

I suppose it doesn't have to be the right answers. Any answer that sounds plausible will do.

I haul myself up, put on my clean shirt, my trousers, my tie, my jacket. I am unassailable in my clothes. My hair is cropped short: no chance of the wind messing with that.

I take a deep breath, pick up my briefcase and prepare to face the day.

I find Laforche in the courtyard. He is dressed in a short-sleeved white shirt and tie and dark trousers. I note the absence of a jacket. He holds a small cup of very black coffee and a silver plate heaped with grapes and mango and thin slices of ham and cheese.

He stares at a tufty plant nudging the archway to the office.

'So, American,' he says. 'Did you sleep?'

I nod and adjust my sunglasses to hide my puffy eyes.

He offers me a bunch of grapes. There is a small smile on his lips. 'You didn't hear the drums from the mountains?'

'No.'

'Or the howls of the wolves?'

I spit out a pip. 'There are no wolves in this part of the world, Laforche.'

'Only the human kind.'

'I didn't hear them either.'

'Then you must have slept well.' He raises a forefinger. 'We should see the desert before it gets too hot.'

There is a spiral staircase inside the far turret. We climb up past the second level and come out on a broad flat walkway which I realise is the roof of the arcade below.

Laforche leans against the chest-high wall on the outer edge. There are gaps in the red bricks for the archers. At this hour, in the coolest part of the day, the Kabir Massif is metallic blue. The wind has dropped – it is not even a whisper – but it will rise through the morning, says Laforche, from a caress to a high-pitched whistle, like the echo of a falcon's scream as it falls through the clouds from the mountaintop.

I say, 'Have you ever heard a falcon falling from a mountaintop?'

'A little imagination goes a long way in the desert.'

I pass the binoculars to Laforche. 'I have never seen it like this.' He says, half to himself, 'I am stationed at the wound. Beings who are nothing come to be nothing here.'

Beyond the Asylum, he says, there is nothing. The desert stretches east, mile upon red mile. He looks at the white hole of sun. 'That is what she came out of. She looked like a mirage. It was a . . . ' The word hangs in the air.

He says, 'How did she come across the sacred empty, a white woman on foot? The only other white person who has done so and lived is Rimbaud.'

I point back to the Massif. 'There must be water?'

He hesitates. 'None that has been found. The Massif is solid rock, impenetrable.'

I scan the horizon. 'So the Asylum is the only watered spot until Kabir proper. Very handy for visitors from Algeria who wish to slip into Casablanca quietly and avoid the port and road checkpoints.'

'You're thinking of the Groupe Salafiste, Algerian Pour Le Combat, those killing gangs,' says Laforche smoothly. 'But it is too far to reach here on foot. They would have to carry water. That means camels or trucks. Which your hi-technological satellites would be sure to find.'

'Satellites can only see what they are pointed at. A group of men on foot might pass undetected, travelling by night, buried in the sand by day.'

Laforche shrugs. 'You are not the only one who wants information.'

I am alert. 'Meaning?'

'My government graciously allows you Americans to question the woman first. But after that – well, our police are interested.'

'This is a civil matter,' I say. 'Private lootings by the woman's father. Trafficking of goods and other cargo.'

'Other cargo?' says Laforche.

'It is not military, Laforche. There is no question of a security risk to Morocco.'

'Really? We shall see.'

44

The sun is high over the horizon, the cracked face of the moon is slipping away. Up on the roof, the heat wraps around the body like a cloak.

Laforche says, 'A walled city is worse in summer. It becomes Rimbaud's city of black roses.'

'Your English is very good,' I say. 'Better on some occasions than others.'

'It's the Arabic way,' he says. 'I know how much that infuriates you Americans.' He spits out a grape seed. We watch it land in a minute puff of dust on the red earth. He says, 'You sit in your offices on Hafid Street. Or the Hilton on Haussman. Anywhere there is air-conditioning. And a mini-bar behind the wood panelling in the bedroom bureau.' He smiles. 'The CIA quarter. We all know it.'

I pretend to rub dust off my cuff. It is no pretence. There is dust on my cuff. Even though there is no wind that I can detect.

I ask Laforche what else is on the second level.

'The patients' rooms, you already know,' he says. 'The dry goods storeroom, the recreation rooms. Then, on what you Americans call the ground floor, my office, the infirmary, the winter kitchen, showers, laundry, generator and mechanics' workshop. Below ground are the nuns' cells, the summer kitchen, the well and water storage, the pantries. We only get supplies once a week at most.'

Ahead of us, the stone turret rears. This stone is a different red to the rest of the Asylum.

'Built in 1890, when Rimbaud came to stay,' says Laforche. 'Built for him, they say.'

Rimbaud came up the coast of the Western Sahara and Morocco, Laforche tells me. Riding with the caravans of the North West Africa Company. They said he travelled with a dog, a cat, a chimpanzee and a hyena. This was after his years of teaching, his time in the circus, the time spent working for a coffee company. He was older; it was nearly twenty years since he had written his last poems. He was running guns by that time and hunting. He traded the leather and ostrich feathers for tea, sugar, cloth. Being a Frenchman, he had to be careful. Tensions were running high. The Spanish were trying to take over the caravan routes, fighting bitterly with the French whenever they found them. Forts were being built all along the coast: Cap Juby was half finished, Villa Cisneros was being constructed. The soldiers were hot, restless, bored. They would frequently leave their forts and go on hunting parties; hunting for enemies.

'Everyone hates the French,' I say.

'Yes, in Africa we were like the Americans are now, everywhere,' says Laforche. 'When the air routes to South America were opening up, and the Germans were competing, they would give the locals Mauser rifles to shoot at French planes.

'We are a nation of solitaries,' says Laforche. 'Of travellers. The French are made so that nothing contents us. Not standing still is a form of survival. Writers, con-men. André Gide, Pierre Loti. Men who travel dressed as women like Michel Vieuchange. Women who travel dressed as men like Isabelle Eberhardt. Restless spirits.'

'Suicides,' I say.

'People who cross the frontiers are always fools and madmen. They are drawn to the desert. The desert is the shape of their death. It is the death they carry inside them. One addiction among many others. To sex, to kif and other drugs. To the dice.' Here, he pauses. 'They could turn back at any time but they never do. They go on towards the mirages. Towards death, to cheat death. Rimbaud said that he wrote to outwit the evil clock of time.'

'Did he?'

'No,' says Laforche. 'He got an ulcer in the leg which turned to gangrene. He was carried to Marseilles in agony. His body eaten from within, trying to find a way back.'

'Back home?'

'Back to peace of mind. To poetry. To feeling. Because he had become fire shut up in stone.'

Below, a nun dawdles across the courtyard, followed by three women in robes and hoods. They carry platters covered by muslin cloths.

The smell of hot chocolate and bread drifts up. The women talk, peer into the dry pond, pull up a thistle.

They see me and make signs in the air. One spits. They say nothing yet there is an aura of furious words around them, like grasshoppers swarming.

'They think you are American,' says Laforche. 'The Asylum had a certain reputation during the Algerian uprisings. It was used by the French military. Sometimes the CIA. They needed a discreet place.'

'Torture,' I say.

'Yes. And not just for foreigners. The locals were sent here, too.'

It is 6.30 am. I have been here for twenty hours and accomplished nothing. I have a moment of anger so intense that I feel dizzy. I grasp the stone wall. It would be fatal to be too direct. Laforche is obviously the kind of man who likes to fence, who has nothing else in the world but time to talk.

I want to shout, A woman's life is at stake. The effort of not shouting takes as much energy as doing it. I lean heavily on my hands, slow my breathing, pretend to look at the Massif. Sand grates under the sweat on my neck. If he says the wrong thing, I tell myself, I am going to punch him.

Dirty tattered chickens are moving across the cracked courtyard. From here I see the faded mosaic of a lion on the bottom of the empty fountain, coloured in weak yellow and traced in chipped black.

Laforche says, 'Animals have always been our others, no matter what the Church instructs. In battle, wherever you saw lions rampant on silk parasols, you saw a king.' He gestures at the courtyard. 'Once this was a garden with fabled greenery, an oasis in the desert. Did you know that a garden appears in nine hundred of the one thousand and one stories of the Arabian Nights?'

He looks at the dry plain, his eyes half closed. 'They say there were oceans filled with fish. Then savannas with animals. The gardens of Abu N'af ran in terraces all the way down to a vast lake. Orchards to the horizon, with the finest apricots and dates and oranges.'

'Fresh water?'

'Fresh water.'

We are silent, awed by the richness of the image. Near the shadows of the chicken, I see paws moving under the dirt.

'In the desert,' says Laforche, 'there is no greater wealth than water and flowers. Loss of the oasis is banishment from the garden paradise. Homelessness.'

'But this isn't home.' I rub my neck. 'It's dust.'

He turns quickly, the fastest I have seen him move. 'It is an entire country underground. Everything in the desert buries itself to survive: animals, plants, people.' He puts down his coffee. 'We have always buried our art: relics and statues, the locations passed down from father to son. We buried libraries in the sand. Any person could pick up a handful of sand and feel knowledge trickling through their fingers. There were families who, even though they had nothing, walked with the arrogance of those who were rich in treasure.'

He raises both arms, as though he is holding the desert and the sky. 'Returning travellers fell to their knees and kissed the earth. They knew the desert is a secret life waiting to be found.'

'I don't have time,' I say. 'Don't you understand?'

His arms drop. 'Maybe it is beyond your control. Maybe you don't have the right to make decisions about – ' He pauses.

'About her?' I step forward. 'And you think you do?'

'Take off your tie, Monsieur,' he says. 'That would be a start.'

The generator begins its steady thudding beat. Laforche shakes his head irritably but somehow, in between the dulled strokes, I am more aware of the silence of the desert, how far we are from the city, from Mitch's bullet-point memos and deadlines. Even the word "silence" is misleading. I hear whispers inside the sky; I imagine the wind pressing down on lost civilisations, solitaries, map-makers. Criminals.

The Asylum has ten patients, Laforche says, all women. Six novices at the most, instructed under Sister Antony. 'This from a century ago, Rimbaud's time, when a hundred, two hundred, would be cared for here. Travellers, leprosy sufferers, French soldiers with the usual desert sicknesses: syphilis, opium addiction.'

He takes out an immaculate white handkerchief and pats his face although there is no sweat that I can see. I shift uneasily; my shirt is sticking to my back.

'The good Sister thinks prayers will be enough to save the Asylum,' says Laforche. 'The Church, of course, hears so many prayers it has become immune. "Asylum" is not a friendly word.'

'Sister Antony will go?'

'To a bed in a less desirable convent. She made enemies thirty years ago with her criticism, her attempts at improvements. True solitaries are always feared. And the Church has a long memory. She will be working until the day she dies.'

We walk through the archway, climb two circles of broad stone steps and come out into a hexagonal room. There are narrow windows set in every wall. Light pours in yet the stone keeps the heat out, so far. The shutters are clipped back and here, finally, is the wind. It flows across the room, pressing sand flecks into my cheek.

There are two long desks piled with books and papers, a feathered pen in an inkpot, a decanter filled with red liquid, a half-full glass, more books in an open chest on the floor. A smaller table with three chairs, a rug, a chunky wooden bureau with an ornate silver lock. A low divan in the corner is covered with an unexpectedly rich sapphire blue velvet quilt and long silk cushions embroidered with flowers and peacocks.

'This is where he wrote,' says Laforche. He points at the divan. 'And lay there, for times of reverie. Not the same divan, unfortunately. Although we let people think it is.'

A book with a cracked red wooden cover is open on the nearest desk, its yellowing pages covered with large meticulous writing in ink. The date at the top catches my eye: *Abu N'af. September 30, 1890.* I read:

When I was lost in the desert, among sands the colour of saffron,
I raised my head and saw on the horizon, monks moving in the spaces

*between the dust spirals. These travellers were frail, their robes full
of wind. By their presence, you see the wind. They walked backwards
against the furious air, their heads down. Clouds swirled around them,
the sun glinted off the metal crosses of the novices, the gold cross of the
abbot. I thought they were a mirage until I came to Abu N'af.*

A silverfish or some creature has crawled across the right-hand page
and expired. Its body is long gone but there is the faint spiky outline
of brown bones pressed into the yellowing paper.

'Rimbaud wrote in English?' I say.

Laforche grins. 'You would be astounded, Monsieur, how few of
our tour groups ask that question.'

'So this is – ?'

'A translation,' he says smoothly. 'For display, since the late 1970s.'

The page has scorch marks, as though made by a candle. I touch
the skeletal stain with my finger. 'The silverfish is a nice touch.'

'Sister Antony is very dedicated.'

'Sister Antony did this translation?'

'Sister Antony did all our translations. She could already see the
benefits of the never-ending curiosity of the English tourist.' He
half-bowed in my direction. 'And American, of course.'

'Of course.'

I turn the page, reading at random:

*Entering the desert is like entering the ultimate book, in which the
voice is that of ourselves, alike but different, a radical stranger . . . In
the desert madness is an asset . . . It is tedious when a journal is filled
with doom and premonitions. Who's to say that gaps weren't left in
the beginning and filled in later, to retroactively forecast momentous
events, national disasters? There's no point spinning elaborate scenarios
about loneliness and rage and revenge. Just say it plainly. Just say:
I frequently dreamed that my hair was a cold flag of rain and my
hands were coated with tomb dust.*

'Your tour groups would appreciate it more if they couldn't touch
it,' I say. 'Human nature.'

'That is why,' says Laforche, 'reluctantly we show them this.' He goes to the bureau, takes out a large key and fits it into the silver lock. He lifts out a silver box studded with small rubies. The hinged lid is elaborately patterned. Laforche raises it and carefully takes out a book wrapped in ivory silk. On top are two gloves of white kid leather. Putting on the gloves, he delicately opens the book.

The cover is made of black leather, cracked now in places but still supple enough to show it is of the finest quality. The pages are almost translucent. I am reminded of onion skin; there are faint lines running through the waxy surface.

'Wax weave pressing,' says Laforche. His voice has a hushed quality as though he is speaking in a church. 'A very old process. Very slow. Traditional.'

I bend. The pages are covered in black ink. The writing is in French.

Laforche says, 'Arthur Rimbaud's diary.'

'He left it here?'

Laforche hesitates. 'It was gifted to us, by a relative of the last owner.'

'And the English one, the one translated by Sister Antony, is an exact copy?'

He hesitates again. 'Yes.'

I point at the French writing. 'Does he write about his journey across the Sahara?'

'He writes about everything, Monsieur.'

The writing is bold, impatient, forward-leaning. 'I can't read French,' I say.

Laforche turns the translucent page, slowly, and reads in English:

To be born intelligent is one thing. To be born reckless and stubborn is too close to madness. In the desert, madness is an asset. Once your mind has split and peeled backwards, once the smallest sounds thundered in your ears, you can cope with the nothingness of it all. I see the long line of events beginning with the muddy-kneed boy in the farmyard shouting at his mother, see all the way to this magnificent

blasted land. In the end I had to come to the desert. It was perverse.
It was inevitable.

'That sounds like you,' I say.

'But not you.'

'Never me.' We look at each other and laugh.

He touches the page, lets the tip of his white glove rest there.

'Why do you like Rimbaud so much?' I ask. 'A guy who failed as a poet, couldn't hack the competition, who ran away.'

'Rimbaud left the map,' says Laforche. 'In his writing, he was a true explorer. All writers are explorers and guides. But he changed the world. No-one could enter his country afterwards without acknowledging his footsteps.'

'His country?'

'Poetry.'

'Poetry.' I sigh, suddenly weary. 'There is too much poetry in my life. I never wanted it. What is it good for anyway?'

'Compression,' says Laforche. 'Communication. Reality. Intensity.'

'I have a problem with intensity already.'

'We noticed. Yet you say you don't care what happens to Madeleine.'

I kick the briefcase. 'Don't call her that.'

'Madeleine is the symbol of France.' He shrugs. 'The woman, then.'

'Laforche, there is no big conspiracy. She has information, she needs to share it. Then she can disappear back to wherever she came from.'

'Back to the desert,' says Laforche. 'You want to punish her.'

I try not to think of the gun in my briefcase. I say loudly, 'I just want the information.'

'Or?'

'It will screw my career.'

'And this is so important?'

'It's all I've got.'

The doorway darkens. It is the thin woman who had been talking to the pilot. She looks me up and down and puts her hands on her hips. There are blue inked flames curling around her wrists. She says to Laforche, 'M'sieur, you must come.'

I step forward. 'Is it the sick bay?'

She ignores me. 'A message from the city,' she says to Laforche.

He looks at the two books on the table.

'Don't worry,' I say. 'I'm not interested in your precious French book.'

Laforche takes off the kid gloves. 'Be careful,' he says to me.

The minute they have gone, I take the camera out of my briefcase. From the top of the steps, I hear Laforche's voice, receding.

I set my watch for two minutes and go to the book of French writing, leafing through it as quickly as I can, looking for anything that seems relevant: to the woman, to Sicily, to Koloshnovar. I try to be delicate. God forbid I should tear a page. But there are only fragments of writing with dates, words clumped in lines, sketches of camels and lumpy mountains and men on horseback. I want to find a map. It would be a solution of sorts.

I see nothing. I leave it and turn the pages of the English book. I try to absorb whole paragraphs, to commit them to memory.

By the very act of walking, the sand under our feet changes. Reaching for a book is like walking into the desert: we are surrounded by alien voices, the voices of ourselves. The way ahead seems clear and fixed but that is a mirage. Instead, we are going deeper into ourselves, deeper into our own long-buried subversions. The white page is the desert; the words are trails of our own lives.

Ramblings. I am impatient.

On the third night, I see a light far away as though a candle is held above a night sea. After a while the light moves. Bedouin travellers maybe.

I turn pages, faster.

Look at the soft edges of mirages, nothing is finite. The opposite of our cities, all those hard lines, those sharp edges which confine us but never touch our soul. Your mind is unfettered in the desert. You go out into the void and the void goes into you. The void is in yourself. We are made so that nothing contents us.

I stop. Now I see where Laforche gets his ideas from.

I am like the great writer who, when he was sick, called out for a fictional doctor, the character in one of his books. I call out for mirages to save me and in the end the desert did. But only when I began to believe.

A noise outside makes me go to the window. A woman is draped across a balcony on the second level. The red stone under her dark robes makes it look as though she has already fallen, is bleeding. One of the younger nuns is trying to coax her back.

I turn pages faster, feel them tear at the binding, have to slow down. I turn and turn, stopping every now and again, an ear to the stairway.

In my delirium, I saw antiquities in the sand: the giant hand of the Assyrian god of war clawing out of the desert; nearby, the dagger from the great statue at Ur used in the King's battle with the panther beast.

I take a shot of this page, keep turning. More on being lost in the desert:

Can you hear all I feared and never dared to write? . . . the darkness above me reels with hovering birds . . .

I turn quicker, barely seeing the words, until finally a heading catches my eye. Abu N'af.

On Sitting With The Polish Traveller At Abu N'af. The watch beeps. In desperation I take three photos, pages at random, because some word I haven't even fully processed has caught my eye. I pick up the book with the black leather cover and my nail catches on a thicker page, at the end.

It is two pages, partially glued together, with something inside: contrasts of light and dark. A photograph. I run my nail along the gummed edges; there is only room to slide in my little finger.

A noise, close by. I hold my breath. Laforche is coming.

I can almost make out the image although I can't quite believe what I am seeing. It is a man standing next to a line of other smaller shapes. The smaller shapes are attached to structures which I feel are made of wood. There is writing on the shapes. *Les fugitifs*. I am beginning to guess what the wooden structures are. My brain can't process the image. 1890, I thought. That is impossible. It is impossible that there would be a –

Footsteps on the stairs. I just have time to put the book down and slide the camera into my pocket as Laforche comes into the room.

'**A** message from Casablanca,' Laforche says. 'From Hafid Street.' He looks carefully at the desk. 'Imagine being stationed out here, a century ago. Many times Abu N'af was used as a garrison: protecting the well, you see. Then it would take weeks of hard travelling to get back to Casa. The soldiers would sit with nothing to do but play cards, dice; their uniforms crusted with sand, wet rags wrapped around their heads, enduring the flies, the scorpions. Knowing that you couldn't leave would make it worse. But a roll of the dice never defeats chance.'

I should be used to it by now, his techniques. I should know that all I can do is wait. It is pointless asking questions.

But of course I can't help myself. 'What message?'

He says, 'Your friends are coming.'

The shock opens crevasses under my skin. Mitch is coming early, just as he threatened. To show me who's in charge? Or because of new evidence from Sicily about her husband's death?

I have to get to the roof and call Mitch. There is a thudding in my ears. The sound of my pulse. The sound of helicopters.

I bite down, hard, and say steadily enough, 'What time?'

Laforche smiles. 'Maybe right now, they are climbing into the helicopter. Maybe the blades are turning. Now they fly over the desert,

56

watching their shadows fall distorted across the dunes.' He takes out his handkerchief and delicately wipes his hands. The smell of lavender wafts past me. 'You know them better than I do, Monsieur. Your friends from Hafid Street.' He begins to fold the handkerchief precisely. 'What do you think they will do? These Hafid Street men. These CIA men.'

'For God's sake, Laforche, I keep telling you I'm not CIA.'

He puts away the handkerchief and wraps the French book in its ivory silk. 'If you have offices on Hafid Street, you're CIA. Maybe you are just a lapdog of the Americans. But don't keep telling me you are a lowly worker at the Australian Embassy.'

'I can hardly admit to anything else, can I?' I say.

He thinks for a minute and nods. 'But I still have jurisdiction here, you see? So if I decide that the woman is too sick to be questioned, then it does not happen.'

I put the briefcase on the desk. 'What do you want? Money?'

'You've already given me money.' He eyes the briefcase. 'Do you have a gun in there?'

'I'm a pencil pusher, Laforche. I sit in my back room – with my Scotch, as I'm sure you've guessed. I organise, I collate my facts. Everyone thinks this business is all guns. But I've barely handled one.'

I want to say: I live in shadows. I've played a part so long I've atrophied into it. I am the job.

'I think,' he says, 'you are telling me what you were.'

I spread my hands, try to look casual. It is an effort. I realise how much I have let him rattle me. But then I wasn't in good condition when I arrived at Abu N'af. Right from the start, I was damaged.

I say, 'If I tell you anything else I put her life in danger.'

He snorts and eases the book into the jewelled casket, places it in the bureau and turns the key.

I say, 'You think I can tell you she is innocent. But it's just the opposite.'

'Why do you think I need answers and definitions? You Westerners are in love with endings.'

I stare at him. 'You must need to know guilt or innocence.'

'Sometimes silence is the truest form of affection.' He sighs. 'Anyway, who decides guilt and innocence? You? Why should I believe your judgement?'

'Because,' I say, 'I was there.'

He raises an eyebrow.

'All right then,' I say. 'Because I'm as guilty as she is. That is why you need to let me talk to her again. Before the others get here.'

'This so-called interrogation is an excuse for something personal.'

'You're wrong,' I say, 'if you think this is a story about revenge.'

'Not revenge.'

'You think this is a story about love?'

'I think,' says Laforche, 'it is a story about maps.'

'Maps?' I stare at him. 'That's crazy. What have maps got to do with it?'

'Everything is a map. These diaries can be a map. Our bodies are maps.' He goes to the top of the stairs. 'If Sister Antony agrees, you can talk to the woman. But I will be present.'

On the walkway, I sit down in the shadow of the wall and plug the camera into my laptop and download the shots of the English translation of Rimbaud's diary. Supposed diary, I remind myself. I still think of the diary as something forged by Sister Antony.

I loosen my tie. The shutters rattle occasionally. No-one else is on the walkway. I take off my tie. It is dark blue. Office blue. All my ties are plain colours. Usually dark. I let it fall to the ground. After a minute I pick it up, fold it neatly away in my briefcase.

The laptop pings: the photo of the pages grows on the screen. I read.

Abu N'af. October 1, 1890.
'I hate the desert,' said the Pole, staring with dark unhappy eyes at the red landscape. He waved a small whip of knotted ropes at the flies. The knots caught him on the cheek and left flecks of blood. There were tiny iron nails tied into the ends of the ropes. He closed his eyes, waved the whip again, his mouth quivering when the nails caught his cheek.

'Why come to the desert?' I said. I was bored. Contrary to what everyone always thought about me, perversion doesn't interest me. I am already too wracked by my own personal demons to ever want more than the most straightforward connections in other areas. Ironic, but there it is. The number of publicly adored poets, proudly scandalous poets, poets who boast of deranging the senses, who adopt exactly the same position every time – Mallarmé told me he found it soothing – is incredible.

Incroyable, I should say. I feel my French slipping away like a mirage here. My language is becoming a jumbled mix of Arabic, French and English and, now that I have a Chinese valet, some Mandarin as well.

I imagine the world using one language in future. It would be made up of words that sound like their meaning, evoke their emotion. Every word has an emotion, a colour. Amigo. That's blue. Peace: a soft green. Butterfly: jade at its lightest, like the crest of a wave turning over in the shallows near the shore.

Language would be simpler, no more than the basics in trade. Direct, unpretentious, egalitarian. The new slang. Elitist language would be reserved for the writers, the poets, whose work would become more and more ornate.

I shuddered. I could already see the laborious Alexandrine making a return.

'. . . easy enough to carry away,' the Pole was saying.

'Pardon?'

'In war it is easy enough to carry even sizeable pieces away. If one is organised.' He saw my look. 'Of art, Monsieur. Pieces of art.'

'Art? What is left? Napoleon took everything he could lay his hands on. The English did their damnedest to remove the rest.'

'In Europe, yes.' He pointed the leather butt of the whip at the white sands, the white hole in the sky. 'But not here. Not the Orient.'

'Here?' I looked around at the stone walls, the camels dropping turds in unison under the lone palm tree. 'They're welcome to the flies.'

'No, no.' He pointed the whip away, to the west, to Casablanca.

'They'll shoot you before you go a camel-length.'

'Usually, yes,' he said. 'But in war, matters get confused.'

'They'll shoot you even more then.'

A clink of bracelets. The dark woman who brought Laforche the message has returned. She stands in the archway and stares at me without blinking. Flames are painted in henna on her feet. Her dark pupils are ringed in a ghostly grey.

She puts a wool blanket and a cloth bundle on the stone floor and marches across, grabs my hand. When I try to retreat, she tightens her grip. She is surprisingly strong.

'I can read it,' she says. 'I tell good fortunes.'

'I don't believe.'

'You should.' She presses a blunt thumbnail into my palm, staring at me with her fearless eyes. She says, 'You were born with a map of calamity in your hand.' She takes the bundle, kneels on the floor and spreads out the blanket. There are minute leather bags hanging on plaited ropes, a few dark wooden bowls, a clatter of thin gold bangles, small woollen mats in clashing reds and purples.

'Before I tell you what I heard, you choose,' she says with a sweep of her hand, sitting back on her burning heels.

'I don't want – '

'First, I tell you a little about each precious gift. A gift for your lady friend.'

'There's nothing – '

She ignores me and begins to relate the history of each object. 'The three camels on the lid are the three mountains of Mahtouf,' she says, picking up a small painted box. 'This is the emblem of my mother's tribe, the tribe of Betsoul,' pointing to a mat. 'This bracelet shows fires and plagues; this bowl is useful for eating chickpeas and onion.'

I think, Someone at Abu N'af sent Mitch the photos of the woman. I had thought it was Laforche. Now I wonder if this woman is on Mitch's payroll.

She puts down the last bowl and says, 'You can pay me in wheat flour.'

I look at her helplessly.

She points at my watch. 'You pay me with that.'

I instinctively cover my watch with my left hand, as though she could levitate it off my wrist. 'I need information about the woman in the sick bay.' I add hastily, 'The truth.'

'My fortunes are the truth.' She sits, cross-legged, the flames on her heels merging with the red-sand colours of her skirt.

'I don't think you know anything to help me,' I say.

She rolls up the blanket. Her bangles clank, muted and resentful. 'The Nazarene talked in her sleep.'

'I need more than babblings.'

She gathers the blanket and rises gracefully onto her toes, stretching, and stands, flat-footed and flat-backed.

She says, 'I carry your heart with me. I carry it in my heart.'

I give her the watch.

'My name is Meersun,' the woman says, sliding the watch into a pocket in her skirt and squatting on the stone floor.

'I won't weary you with my story . . .' Here she shoots me a sly look as though she senses my lack of interest. 'Enough to say that my mother Betsoul suffered horribly at the hands of the Nazarenes. My grandfather cast me out when I refused to marry the man he chose for me. A man who had already beaten two wives to death' – her voice rises indignantly – 'who took little boys into back alleyways. Women are for babies, he would say to me. Men are for fun. A soldier, of course.

'Sister Antony took me in. She owed me a great deal.' She raises her broad palms. 'No-one can operate the rollers in the laundry as well as I can.'

I wait. She gives me another sly look. 'Your woman said you found her when she had left her home.'

'So she remembers.'

Meersun takes the watch out of her pocket, holds it to the light, turning it this way and that so the glass face becomes a bright disc in the room.

She says, 'I had to sit with her. Even Sister Antony must rest sometimes. I think she is angry God does not give her energy to work day and night.' She slips the watch on, up to her forearm, admiring it. 'The woman told me lots of things. True things.'

The thudding is back in my ears. 'Only I can judge what is true.'

Meersun comes towards me. I hear the swish of her skirts, the slap of her feet on the stone.

She says, 'The woman didn't look at mirrors but watched herself in bowls of water she shook, to make ripples. Then she drew herself like that.' She waggles her tattooed hand so the inked flames shift and blur before my eyes.

'Distorted,' I say, turning.

Meersun says, 'I think she made the scorpion bite her, so she looked like what she saw in the shaking water.'

A cloying musky smell comes off her as she stands behind me. Metal rattles and pauses, rattles and pauses. She is tossing the watch up and down in her palm.

'I like this watch,' she says. 'Do you have another?'

'No,' I say. The thudding is louder. There are specks in front of my eyes. I rub them angrily.

The musky smell is more intense. She whispers, 'No-one else knows this.' She is right behind me. 'The woman told me you killed her husband.'

The thudding is louder. Closer.

'That's a lie,' I shout, turning so fast that my elbow catches her shoulder. She backs away. 'You're lying.'

Meersun stares past me. I hold out my hand. 'She wouldn't have said that.' But I think, *Would she?* I raise my voice over the increasing noise. 'Give me the watch back.'

My words disappear in the roar that sweeps over the Asylum. A black helicopter swoops past the window. It rears upwards, out of sight, the noise wrenched away.

That bastard Mitch. He had no intention of waiting for me to find something.

I push past Meersun and shove the laptop in the briefcase. My hand touches the gun and I wonder whether it is just Mitch and the pilot.

I head for the stairs. Meersun catches my arm.

'You'll never prove it,' I say as I pull away.

She yells into the spiralling light. 'She said it was the poem you learned for her. *I carry you in my heart*. It was you.'

'You're wrong,' I shout. 'I hate poetry.'

I blunder down the steps, slip on the rubbed smooth stone, and hurry past the fall of stronger light at the archway on the second level. I come out into the ground arcade, nearly tripping over a chicken sleeping against a pillar. I run through the main gateway. I run, head uncovered, clutching my briefcase, a ridiculous man running out into the noonday desert sun.

The cleared circle where my pilot had landed the day before is empty.

Away from the shadow of the walls, the air is gasping with heat. I am gasping. I can barely see. I shove on my sunglasses and run to the edge of the plateau.

Almost immediately I stumble. I slow to a fast walk, then a stroll, then a careful plodding. The ground here isn't red or even brown. It is a pitted grey landscape of nothing but stones.

I reach the edge and look down to the plain. The helicopter sits half on the road below, at an angle, as though it has been carelessly parked. Some malfunction?

A man gets out of the helicopter. White shirt, black tie, black trousers: Mitch's uniform. I open my briefcase and use the binoculars to scan the body of the helicopter. Arabic markings, unsurprisingly. Officially, the Hafid Street office is a small import export firm, tight on money, forced to charter from the local businesses.

The windows are tinted. I calculate: twenty minutes to walk to the plain. Mitch would have water there.

I hang the binoculars around my neck and set off.

The road is steeper than it looks and roughly cleared of the larger stones. I try to keep an eye on the helicopter but if I don't watch my step I slip on jagged pieces of flint.

A row of white pebbles edges the road. There seems little difference between the stony ground of the road and the stony desert next to it. But it is a valiant gesture. I plod on, feeling my tongue swell in my mouth, checking every now and again that the helicopter has not moved. I begin to see patterns between the rocks; the glaze of lizard tracks. Fragments of pottery, red and crumbling. The dust has coated my shoes; there are big smears on my trousers. I slap some of it off but it seems to settle again almost immediately. The heat is pushing into my bones, my knees feel disconnected. The briefcase is heavy in my hand. I am almost tempted to put it down and come back for it later.

I am walking into the sacred empty, I tell myself, leaving behind the technological marvels of the world.

That sounds right. That sounds like something Laforche would say.

Desert speak.

I stop. I have almost reached the bottom. Behind me, the road slopes up steeply. The Asylum is pugnacious against the white sky. It is bigger than it looks from the inside. The turrets rise like buds, holding the Asylum's secret stories. Stories within stories; lives flowering within. Rimbaud, the nomad poet, could well have thought he could create here.

I stumble over a large stone and another. Not stones: two blood-stained goats' hooves. They are cut raggedly above the fetlock, the white hair pink-tinged, the split hooves as grey as the desert soil. I back away but it is too late; a scarlet splash is thrown over my shoe.

I plod on. I think I am moving quicker now that I am on level ground but the helicopter is no nearer. I look through the binoculars.

On the ground next to the man in the white shirt is a small black briefcase. Beside him is a man dressed in the immaculate white robes of the Sahara. They both have their backs to me. As I look, the second man jerks his wrist. Something dark flies into the sky. I tilt my head but the sweat runs into my eyes.

The ground shifts.

The desert is the true seer, I see that now. I recognise the immensity of the landscape. It has a kind of purity: the ultimate truth. But do I want it? I shake my head. I want the sweat to run into my dry mouth. But all I taste is salt. When it rains in the desert, the sand must smell like the sea.

I re-focus the binoculars. White clouds billow behind the Massif. I find the dark bird – a falcon – tearing at the wispy gauze of sky. The bird plummets to the ground, turning as it goes. A hand's length from the ground, it swoops up again.

The robed man raises his arm. The bird drops out of the white air, extending its clawed feet. It slows and sits on the man's forearm. I see the tracking bracelet around its left ankle. Pain – as sharp as it ever was in Sicily – stabs me.

The man with the briefcase takes out a small black box, extends an antenna and sweeps the horizon. I adjust the binoculars. He has a solid gold watch on his right wrist, a heavy signet ring with a large ruby on his finger.

The falcon is thrown up again. It soars into the skies, a dark rose thrown off a snowy bough.

To touch the very face of God, I whisper to myself.

Sweat runs like an animal down my cheek. The lines of the helicopter are distorting.

The bird returns. The man with the scanner commences another sweep. He finishes, lowers the box and the falconer eases a leather hood over the bird's eyes and they walk back to the helicopter.

The Asylum is far away. On the road, the black metal blades are turning. I could leave now: hitch a lift to Casablanca, bribe my way out, disappear. Back to Borneo.

At the thought of Borneo I drop to my knees. Stones dig into my shins. I open my briefcase, take out my tie, put it on, search for my spare watch, slide that on, set the alarm for three o'clock. Interrogation hour.

Closer to the ground, the plain doesn't look so much like rubble. I see distinct hills and valleys, a landscape in miniature. A small pale cactus, the length of my forefinger, pokes out from a rock in a strange deep groove. When I sit back on my heels I realise I am in the remnants of a water track.

Now I see there are myriad variations of colour in the earth. A million versions of brown.

I raise my face to the sun. I don't feel thirsty anymore. My mouth tastes metallic. The light presses against my closed eyes. I could imagine that in the desert you only dream in light. Even your nightmares would be in light.

I look at the watch. Noon. The seconds seem to slow on the panel. Fifty-seven seconds. Fifty-eight. Fifty-nine. The small numbers flicker. Finally they stop – 12.01. Minutes go by. The panel does not change.

The helicopter lifts, its blades bending in the hot air. It hovers and turns west, following the road to Casablanca. Soon it is a speck in my eye.

I stay on my knees in the desert, staring at the shadow my body makes on the ground. This seems like the only shade so after a while I try to crawl inside it. Lying on my back, I see a large black bird. It has a hooked neck and long narrow beak. Another bird appears. They circle lazily. I want to recall the helicopter. I open my briefcase to write a message: *Here are your birds*. But it seems easier to lie still, grit in my eyelashes.

After a while, I feel myself moving into shadow, into black water. Back to the black lake in Sicily.

'Water is a kiss.' Who said that? I knew; I just didn't know her identity. 'We dive into rock pools like lives we never thought we could enter. We shed our old skins in water, we take on a new skin. Water passes into us. We want new masks, new identities, but all we can do is take in water. Like tears, like pulses.'

The light is blotted out. Sister Antony kneels, tugs me upright. Her hood is drawn over her head and her palms are cool. As though night is somehow trapped in her body, like the pockets of darkness trapped in the ground at the end of night.

'When I . . . interrogation, what . . . say?' My voice disappears into some words.

Sister Antony raises my head, puts a metal flask to my lips. I choke on the sugary water, feel a sharp aftertaste, like thorns in honey. I twist my head so the sourness runs down my chin but she says, 'Drink this and I'll tell you.'

The grit in my throat is washed away. The terrible heat lessens.

The Sister tips the bottle higher. 'You need to bring her to life like the desert is brought to life with rain.' I can barely hear her over the sound of falling water in my ears. She says what sounds like, 'You need to bring her to life with words.'

'Nothing . . . she listen to.'

'You're wrong. We die always of a frustrated word.' Her lips do not seem to move but her voice says, 'The woman sings songs to the disappeared. I say prayers to God. Laforche looks for poems that will conquer the desert. We are like cactuses sending out shoots, placing our hard thorny side to the world.'

I finish drinking and hand the bottle back. After a moment, I am able to sit up.

'You want . . . me to talk to the woman,' I say slowly.

'Yes.'

'Why?'

She hesitates. 'Every time the Asylum has been on the verge of extinction, a woman has arrived to save it.'

'But it can't be this woman. Maybe it's you.'

Her face hardens so the sun traces the flat planes of her chin and right cheek in fire. 'I hid from Him through the longest night and the brightest dawn.' She closes her eyes. 'There is a famous story of the desert. Maybe it takes place in Abu N'af, maybe not. It concerns a religious community long ago, one grown vain and complacent. Trading for silks and ivory idols from the south had replaced contemplation. The community fell on difficult times: years of sandstorms which blocked supplies and left the nuns and monks near starvation. A serving girl appeared among them: a bedraggled thing, barely able to speak, filthy. She was treated roughly, given only crusts to eat, but she never complained. One day she disappeared as suddenly as she came, taking the dust storms with her. The community prospered. Years later a lion was seen digging a grave in ground near the Kabir Massif, ground so hard that no shovel could break it. The lion was burying a woman, uneaten. The body of the serving girl who went into the desert.' She opens her eyes.

'Storing left-over food,' I say, holding up the watch, shaking it.

'The body was untouched, the women said.'

'Why didn't the nuns dig up the body?'

Sister Antony looks at me as though I am mentally deficient but she answers politely enough, 'No human tool could break the surface.'

'Right.' I shake the watch again. The numbers are still frozen.

I can't decipher her expression. Later, I realised what it was: acceptance. She could accept my sneers because I had caused someone to be brought to Abu N'af who more than compensated for my lack of faith.

'A mirage,' I say, sliding the watch back on. 'They imagined the whole thing.'

'All of them?'

'Mass hysteria. Common among solitaries, I would have thought.'

'Maybe.' She says, 'Two nights before your woman arrived, lions were seen on the grave.'

'Oh, no.' I slap at the dust on my legs, punching to the bone. 'None of us are saints here,' I say loudly. 'It's different after thirty-five, after forty. There's a sense of regret. Everything is ruled by time. By calculations. This isn't a story about a winsome girl. She would be the first to tell you she is no saint. There's a sourness. A melancholy. A sarcasm.'

'In the desert you only reach your goal by zigzagging through the wind.'

I have to restrain myself from swearing. 'Did she tell you her real name?'

'We don't use our names here,' says Sister Antony. 'We take on other identities in the desert. Other lives.'

She closes the briefcase and stands. There is no dust on her robe. She leans to help me up. I sway and she grasps my wrists. 'Your watch has stopped.' She taps it with her fingernail and the numbers tick over. The alarm setting comes up.

'Three o'clock?' she says.

'I must talk to the woman then. After that it will be too late.'

'For you?'

'For her.' I hesitate. 'For both of us.'

She still has her hand on my wrist.

'You won't allow it,' I say. 'Like last night.'

'Last night, it was 3 am when you tried to talk to her. That is the devil's hour, when Christ died on the cross. 3 pm is the opposite; 3 pm is when Christ was born.' She releases me. 'Today is your last chance to speak to her.'

I take a step and tremble. 'How long was I out here for?'

'Twenty minutes. You were out in the desert for twenty minutes.'

'Who would want this land?' I say as we walk.

'You would be surprised, Monsieur. The Saudis come weekly for their hawking – '

'But the land is dead.'

Sister Antony points. 'See the life around you.' She digs her fingers into the sand and comes up with a small shrivelled date the colour of faded parchment. 'This is still sweet next to the stone. You can grind it into flour. And that small plant – ' she touches the tip of a straggly thistle of a green so faded that it looks almost white – 'can be used for headaches, but only in the right doses. Anything bigger and it becomes a poison.' She picks up a tiny black seed with her fingernail. 'This helps digestion but in small portions or you hallucinate.' She lets the seed drop. 'Everything must be judged to proportion in the desert. Take too much and you die.'

Instead of leading me up the hill she turns off the road and walks east, away from the Massif and Casablanca. She points across the flat country. The grey stony ground gives way to the sand dunes rising and falling to the horizon in waves of burnt sand, the flames showing even in the fierce noon light. She points to the most desolate spot in the middle. 'That is where we found Madeleine.'

I can't believe it. There is nothing there.

'Laforche thinks she had maps,' I say, 'of some system of old wells.'

Sister Antony shakes her head.

'If Madel – the woman told us of a way across,' I say, 'that would make it better for her.'

'She didn't have maps,' says Sister Antony.

'No water? No protection?'

'No.'

I look down at my dirty hands: the small cuts on my palms, the skin already turning a dull red.

'That's impossible,' I say. 'She must have had help.'

'She did.'

'Who – oh, no. I'm sorry. I can't believe in divine intervention.'

'What other explanation is there?'

'There must have been someone else with her.' I try not to think of Pietr. Pietr is dead.

Sister Antony says, 'There were no camels, no cars. She was alone.'

'What did she look like,' I ask, 'when you found her in the desert?'

'She was hunched over,' says Sister Antony, 'as though in great pain. She was trembling, there were stains across her tunic, across her heart.' She gestured across her chest. 'But there was not a mark on her. No sunburn, no cuts on her feet, although the ground between the dunes and Abu N'af is harsh, filled with small stones, cactus, old shells, bleached bones. When I put a hand on her shoulder and asked her what she was doing, she said, "I am eating my heart. It is bitter but I like it because it is bitter and because it is my heart".'

I stare at the dunes falling away into Algeria: no trees, no roads, no shade.

'Imagine the first people here,' says Sister Antony. 'Even the hardiest must have quailed at what was before them, those black people from the south. The drought would have weakened them. After them, invaders who rode horses and had weapons made of iron: the Berbers. Then, centuries of fighting with clans, the Masmouda in the Rif, the Sanhaja. The Vandals controlling everything until the time of Idris. More clans until the Alaouit ruler Moulay al-Rashid. No real enemies but each other until the French came and divided it all up with the Spanish. And so it goes on. We ousted the colonists. Now we fight, to annexe the Western Sahara, with help from Algeria, of course. And the Americans when it suits them.'

'My employers have some wild idea that arms from Algeria are being funnelled through Morocco and Tunisia,' I say, 'and on to Sicily, just a boat ride away.' I watch closely. She is impassive. 'Then on from Sicily to bomb targets in Europe.'

'And elsewhere,' says Sister Antony.

At the base of the hill with the Asylum directly above us, she faces what looks like solid rock; I think she is going to walk straight into it. But at the last moment she turns sideways and disappears through a narrow opening.

I squeeze in behind her. Almost immediately the gap widens into a shallow cave. The roof presses down on me. The temperature drops ten degrees.

Ahead is a doorway: reinforced wood with metal brackets and hinges hammered into the rock. The Sister takes out a large iron key and heaves the door open, revealing stairs cut into the same dark rock that I had seen in the underground bedrooms.

We climb through the dusky light to the next level. The wall is cool, even slightly damp when I touch it. I smell salt.

Sister Antony takes a torch from her pocket and points to a passage running off to our left. 'The well,' she says. She opens a door on our right. Meat on hooks is hanging in rows; chests filled with ice line the whitewashed rock walls. There are lanterns by the door and stacked candles. In Casablanca, the hanging meat is coated in flies, turning a dull green. But there are no flies here.

Sister Antony points to the wet sheen on the flagstones. 'The well is drawn off a channel which runs under the Massif to the Kabir mountains. Somewhere deep below the rock, they think there is an underground lake which feeds the channel.' She draws a breath. 'To find that . . .'

'You could irrigate the desert.'

'Then the people would come.'

'Businessmen,' I say. 'Non-believers. Americans.'

She refuses to be drawn. 'Abu N'af will always be a refuge for solitaries, hermits, people who cannot survive in the noisy world.'

We climb the stairs. Light comes down to meet us and I see the numbers on my watch. The old sickness is back in my stomach. It is as though it has never left me. It has only vanished briefly, during that time in Sicily. With her.

I sway against the rock. Sister Antony grips my elbow, hard.

'Everyone plays their own games in the desert,' she says. 'For amusement, for money, for revenge. Laforche knows exactly when the Saudis come hawking; they radio ahead.' She lets me go, steps back. 'The desert will send you crazy with suspicions, with mirages.'

'Crazier,' I say.

'Remember,' says Sister Antony, 'you can always make a fresh start with your next breath.'

We are at the door of the infirmary. Laforche stares at me. 'You understand this is your last chance to speak to her. After this, she says – '

I snort. 'She doesn't have a choice.'

'But I do, Monsieur. Remember that.'

We go in.

Through the half-closed shutters, the fierce light is already fading. Grey is soaking up the sky. The wind whines against the hill.

'It will storm tonight,' says Laforche as we walk across the floor, our feet hitting the tiles like castanets.

'Rain?' I am trying to breathe slowly, clear my mind.

'Dry lightning.'

We reach the bed. Again, Sister Antony is sitting, her head bowed. Laforche stands at the foot of the bed, arms behind his back.

'You look different,' says the woman.

I put my hand to my open collar, to where my tie should be. 'Not the office boy.'

'No.'

'Not the patsy.'

'That's your interpretation. Not mine.'

I pull a wooden chair out from the wall, sit next to the bed, my briefcase on my knee.

'Still got your beloved case,' she says. 'Your identity.'

'Always.'

'You can't keep files on everyone.' She presses her lips together, her back arched. I half rise from my seat. She continues, in gasps, 'Ashes to ash.'

'Don't.' I stop myself from cursing her. 'Do you want names here? Should I call you Ophelia? Yeah . . . Ophelia and her brother, of the tragic house of – '

She forces herself up. She shouts, 'Don't you dare include my brother.' Her face drains white. The welts are as dark as scars. Sister Antony lowers her onto the pillows. The sound of the woman's breathing fills the room.

'I'm sorry.' My fists clench. I feel the tendons standing out in my neck. 'Your brother wasn't – '

She sits up again, clutching at Sister Antony. 'You bastard!' she says. 'You told me my brother was alive. Getting me to help your demon friends.'

'Enough,' says Sister Antony. The woman falls back, staring at the ceiling.

Laforche clears his throat. 'I think – '

'Not yet,' says Sister Antony, and to me, 'Ask your questions.'

I look at the crumpled figure in the bed.

'Now,' says Sister Antony. 'Or never.'

I sit by the bed. The only way I can look at her is to think of her as a map, not a person. She is a map to recovery with all the answers. She is a country of red and white, of smooth planes and festering welts. I think of the smudged Sicilian afternoon light falling on the gleam of a wrist bone, the curve of her right ear. The lower lobe. Lobe. I almost thought "love".

'We need to know.' I raise my voice so Laforche and the Sister will remember when Mitch asks. 'What did Pietr tell you before he died? Where did he hide the Baghdad statuettes?'

'Isn't it odd,' she says dreamily, 'that at any moment of tragedy in the world, a horse is rubbing itself against a fence or sailors are looking the other way when Icarus falls from the sky?'

'Don't play the fool,' I say. 'You'll only hurt yourself.'

She is silent.

'If you don't tell us your movements on the last night,' I say, 'they will charge you. Someone disabled all the surveillance in the house.'

'You,' she says. 'We both know why.'

'Pietr must have told you something.'

She closes her eyes.

I say to Sister Antony, 'You think all she's facing is a slap on the wrist, some jail time. But if you don't take my help now, Mitch will be here soon, tonight even. I'll have no power then, do you understand? She'll be gone, charged as a terrorist and gone to a CIA prison. Off the books: Poland, Afghanistan. It'll be like she never existed.'

'That's like saying Saint Antony never existed,' says the Sister, 'because he tried and failed to build a community in the desert. Yet here I am.'

I stare at them. 'Don't you see? She's the woman at the centre of a web of survivals.'

I say to her, 'What have you been doing all these months?'

She won't open her eyes.

'Who have you been seeing?' The moment the words are out of my mouth I know they are wrong. They give too much away. Words destroy. I always knew it. They had ruined the two of us.

The woman opens her eyes but she doesn't look at me. She looks at Sister Antony. I feel some communication pass between them. The woman says, 'I'll never tell you.'

The afternoon sun struggles through the clouds. The dunes fan out in wrinkles under the sullen sky. The ground is moving as though horsemen are rising out of the sand. The riders have been hidden in pits underneath, sand laid on cloth laid over branches. They will ride up the slope of the pit and attack the attackers. Victory by hiding yourself away; the way she has done for the last eight months. She has hidden but I am the one who is stuck in the pit.

I say, 'How did you come through the desert?'

'I had Rimbaud's diary,' she says. 'I followed the landmarks in it like a map.'

I look at Laforche. He frowns.

'That's impossible,' I say to her. 'The only diary is here.'

'I had a copy, made thirty years ago.'

'Where is it?'

'It's been given back to the last surviving relative of its last owner. It's not part of your big conspiracy. You and Mitch will never get it.'

The wind swells. Sand sprays onto the floor. Laforche and the Sister go to close the shutters. I glimpse the clouds wrenched apart, the moon rising like a half-developed photograph, an apparition sitting low over the horizon. A lightning flash tears through the image, more sand lifts, veiling the plain. Goats cry in the courtyard and dogs howl in the distance.

'How much do you remember about your career as a spy?' I ask the woman, leaning towards her.

'My short and disastrous career as a spy.' She is tracing the welts on her left hand with her right. I see the lighter line where the skin hasn't been tanned, where her wedding ring had been. So she has been wearing it all these months. Despite her husband dying the day they got married.

She says, 'Your spy.'

'But not my assassin.'

She stares at me. 'You think I killed Pietr?'

I have to get my story right. I am exhausted by all these double acts. I say, for the witnesses, for Mitch, 'Mitch says they found two bodies in the fire, both shot.' I say, as though I don't know better, 'Maybe you killed Pietr in defence. Maybe Rosza was attacking you.' Ambushing you, in the house I sent you to.

She says, 'I didn't kill them.'

'Evidence – '

She laughs, almost without sound. 'I know what evidence Mitch can come up with. And if you lied about my brother, why couldn't you be lying now?'

I grasp the briefcase. 'I've got photos, of Pietr.'

'No.' Her eyes fill with tears. 'I don't want to see.'

'You don't want to see what happened to your husband? Unless you already know what happened to him. To your husband.'

'Yes, husband,' she shouts. 'Husband. That just kills you doesn't it? I can hear it in your voice.' She puts her hands over her face, says, low, 'You've only yourself to blame. That I married him.'

She lies back in the bed. Her face is tinged grey, as though swept by sand mist. 'I have been dreaming about hearts,' she says. 'The worst thing about being medicated is that you feel as though you have no heart. The empty space fills up, first with water, then with clay, then glass.

'I have been reading about poets and thinking about hearts. After Shelley drowned, and his body was washed up on shore, he was identified by a volume of Keats' poetry in his pocket. They tried to cremate him but his heart refused to burn. Byron insisted it be taken out of the fire, out of his poor burnt body, and given to Shelley's wife Mary. When she died, years later, they say she still had the heart, in a gold casket next to her.'

'Drowning,' I say. 'You've been thinking about drowning again.'

She looks at me steadily. 'If you scar even the smallest part of the heart, you have a scar forever.'

'You knew it was me the instant you saw me,' she says. 'Why are you even interrogating me? You'll get your promotion.'

I think of all the times I had told her she was just the job. I can't speak.

'He was frightened of what you had told us,' says Laforche. 'But it is too late now. His friends will be here in a few hours.'

She turns dark eyes to me. 'Mitch?'

I nod.

'Then you're ruined,' she says. 'He'll show no mercy. I told you that in Sicily.'

I force myself forward. 'Where are the two statuettes? Say it for the tape. Appear to co-operate.'

'You want me to trust you?'

'I – yes.'

She blinks. 'You'll help me, even though you think I'm a murderer?'

I hesitate. 'You were the only one in the house.'

'I went back to get Rimbaud's diary,' she says. 'But I didn't go into the house, I went up the tower steps. What about you?'

'I know I didn't do it.'

Laforche stirs. 'That's hardly evidence, Monsieur.'

'I needed Pietr alive.' I hear myself: hesitant, resentful. Lacking conviction.

'What about Mitch?' says the woman.

'Mitch wouldn't – ' I stop.

'Of course he would,' she says.

'How do we even know this is the woman you're looking for?' says Laforche. 'It's only your word against hers. If we refuse to release her . . .'

'They'll take her anyway,' I say.

'Not if we negotiate with them.'

'To negotiate you must have something to trade,' I say. 'If she won't swap information, what do you have?'

'Her diary,' says Laforche. 'It has all the details does it not?'

'Not what they are looking for,' I say. 'Not about the art.'

'But it has other things,' says Laforche. 'Things we could trade.'

'We?' I look at them. Sister Antony folds her hands.

'The diary is of more use than you think,' says Laforche. 'Why don't you see?'

'Stop it,' says the woman. She looks at my open collar, my tie-less throat. She says, 'Stop taunting him.'

The clasps on the briefcase crack as I unlock it. I stare at my worldly possessions. Twenty-five years working and this is all I have. I feel nauseous.

I lift up my files, the camera, the tape recorder. I see the inevitable absences. The diary is gone, and the gun.

'He has a streak of cruelty in him, I see that now.' Laforche's voice rolls through the room. He is standing, bent over the book in his hands, reading from it. I see a flash of red. 'Sometimes he will pin my wrist to the table in Café Flora, watch me with those black eyes, to see whether I will pull away. He is constantly furious, constantly talks about death and killing. Killing Pietr.'

Laforche holds up the diary. The red ribbon is a flame between his hands, like Shelley's heart in the hands of his wife.

Laforche reads from the diary, 'He sat opposite me in the café, this man with the closed face. He has the blackest eyes of any blue-eyed man I ever met. When I first saw him I thought he was ill. He is intensely angry at times; he radiates anger. I work from rage, he said to me. I work and work. I keep waiting for my life to start.

'I know that I should say that his life has started, with me. I want to heal him, it would make up for everything. We are bound together by our individual guilt, I saw that the moment I met him. If he were whole . . . If I can make him whole . . . But I am angry myself, about his lies. I let him mark me, I want him to be guilty. He pins my wrist to the table, he leaves bruises on my inner arm, my inner thigh. Bruises hard to explain away, bruises he wants Pietr to find. He is a traveller in a strange country. He has never been in this place before and he is testing to see how far he should go.'

'A cruel man,' says Laforche.

'A man in the conflict of inner darkness,' says Sister Antony.

'An enraged man,' says Laforche, turning a page.

He reads, 'This man, the man who calls himself Devlin tells me, You know what the recruiter's greatest tool is? Inspiring self-delusion in others. I never got you to do anything you didn't con yourself into doing, he says, you believed what you were doing. You told me you would help me find my brother, I say to him. I'm not a kind man, he says. I don't do anything for free.'

'A manipulator,' says Laforche.

'A man not knowing whether he wishes to live or die,' says Sister Antony.

'A liar,' says Laforche, turning the page. The next page is blackened; I smell fire. I am back in Sicily, running into Pietr's house. I am calling her name, trying to part the smoke clouding the marble hallway.

Laforche reads, *'Whenever he talked about the past, his eyes refused to accept the light. He told me that his grandfather was an inveterate thief. He said that to compensate, his father Czeslaw wanted to be a monk. He told me he thought his grandfather, Czeslaw's father, had endured a childhood so devoid of affection that he stole anything he could find; objects of beauty as nourishment. He said, My grandfather stole wherever he went: Poland, Italy, Africa. I asked him how he knew. He said it was because his childhood was the same.'*

'A thief,' says Laforche.

'That's not me she's talking about,' I say.

Sister Antony is silent.

I say, 'That's Pietr, the man she married.'

'The man she married instead of you,' says Laforche. 'You, the jealous man, the enraged man. The man who says – ' he reads from the diary – *'You make me feel like a beast.* A man desperate for clues to himself, she says, for signposts, bearings. A man who admits: *I tear open letters about you and lick the seal for any trace of you.*

'Tell me,' says Laforche. 'Why should we trust a man like this?'

I want to shout at them to stop. But I can't speak. Laforche reads on, remorseless.

'The thing I always liked about him was that he had no honour. I am so sick of men talking about their honour. It always precedes some appalling act. Or a way to judge the world – women of course – by a set of rules they have made up. Like people who moralise about religious virtues because they have to keep reminding themselves. But he never had any honour, he told me. He always believed the worst. That is what I most like about you, I said to him.'

'No honour,' says Laforche. 'A violent man. A jealous man, as we've seen. Who will the police believe?'

'Police?' I find it hard to process the word.

Laforche says, 'You are the only person saying who she is. Why couldn't she be someone else? There is another woman in this story:

the same age, dark-haired. Anna, the daughter of Pietr by his first marriage. Why couldn't this be her?'

I stand. Sister Antony rises slowly beside me.

'I know it's you,' I say to the woman in the bed. I see her lashes droop against her smudged skin. I shiver. The temperature is falling. 'You know how I know.' I put my hand on her leg and look at Sister Antony. 'You know how.'

I throw back the sheet, looking for the photograph printed on her skin.

'You devil!' shouts Laforche.

Even before the woman points her finger at me, I know what I will find.

'I erased you,' she says, low. 'You deserve to be erased.'

There is nothing, no mark on her thigh. Nausea wells inside me.

She says, 'The minute you lied about my brother, you went into uncharted territory. You took us both there. And Pietr.'

'I never killed him!' I shout, but the effort makes me sway and I have to lean against the wall.

'He's sick,' says Sister Antony to Laforche. 'You put too much in the sugar drink.'

'He will survive,' says Laforche. 'Once she has gone.'

'Where is she going? The desert?' My jaw hurts. 'She won't last twenty minutes.'

'She did before,' says Laforche.

'A fluke,' I say.

'Intervention,' says Sister Antony.

'Suicide,' I say to the woman. 'It'll be – '

She says, 'Like putting a scorpion on your face?'

'You can't leave me. I came all this way to find you.'

'To catch me.'

'No.'

I see her eyes, as blue as the lake in Sicily. A current moves deep below. She is remembering those hours in the hut above the lake. For a moment, I have her between my hands, I am pulling her towards me, wrapping my arms around her, wrapping my leg over her leg, my hands at the small of her back, pulling her into me –

I touch her wrist and she flinches. 'You remember Sicily,' I say as clearly as I can. 'Don't tell me you don't.'

She stares at me, her mouth open. I bend and kiss her on the wrist, let my head rest on the side of the bed. An enormous heaviness rolls over me. Her hand touches my cheek, her fingers travel gently along my jaw, my ear, trace upward, smooth the lines between my brows, slowly stroke my hair.

Far away, I hear Laforche say, 'He came here to catch you. Remember that.'

I try to lift my head, to tell him he is wrong but it is too much effort. Her hand is still stroking my hair, my shoulders are dropping. The terrible burden I always carry slips away.

'You were the only one,' I try to say, 'I could ever relax with.'

She holds my face, her lips are in my hair. She says, 'Sleep now.'

The black sky is lit by flashes. Broken silver spears part the curtains of purple-black clouds and batt away the dirty yellow moon. The Massif is a frowning profile. Lightning flares over the plain like tracer fire: the smallest plants become gigantic black roses, hollows become lakes, stones grow to boulders. Shadows that might not be shadows move between the enormous cactuses. The barking of dogs is carried for miles through the racing wind. The air shudders and hums.

A fine rain falls on my cheek. It burns me and it is cold. There is sand in my mouth.

It is dawn when I wake. The shutters are open and a flat blue sky is growing. I feel salt on my cheek and a crick in my neck. I had fallen asleep with my head on my folded arms, leaning on the side of the bed. When I stretch out a hand, the sheet is cold and stiff.

I sit up. The bed is empty.

Sister Antony is standing by the window.

I look around the room for a hiding place. It occurs to me that nobody had said she couldn't walk.

Sister Antony pushes back her hood and it is as though I finally see her clearly. She has a scar like a river of ill luck running down her left cheek. Her dark grey eyes are clear and hard, polished pebbles reflecting the light. Her hair is pure white.

She says, 'Jesus walked into the desert. It was a surrender in the tradition of the Desert Fathers. Like Saint Antony. Absolute poverty is absolute nothingness. You must make yourself as blank as the desert, as the page. To be written on, by God.'

I heave myself up and stagger to the window, stare across the stony plain. The sun surges over the horizon, the dunes are blood red in the early light. I feel the heat coming.

'She's gone,' says Sister Antony, 'into the desert.'

She comes to me, presses something into my hands. A sheet of paper.

It is a note in the woman's handwriting: *When I look at you, I know the people I loved are gone. Five deaths are too much for one person to endure.*

I crush the paper between my hands. But even as I shred it and the fragments fall like snow, I am kneeling. I gather them up and hold them in my cupped hands and stand, looking at the desert.

The land falls away, remorseless. The sun rises in the blue wall of the sky.

I wait.

It is only a little while before the black helicopter comes out of the west and swings in a low circle around Abu N'af. It beats its way past the windows, closer and closer, louder and louder. Mitch is sitting in the passenger seat.

He sees me, raises a thumb and forefinger, aims them and cocks them like a gun, firing at me.

The helicopter thuds past, the beat steadying as it drops to the ground. The noise slows, and stops.

I put the fragments carefully in my pocket.

I go out to meet Mitch.

BOOK II

THE WOLVES
OF
SANTA
MARGHERITA

Czeslaw pulled out his map, wrote the day's date – 19 August – in Polish at the bisecting co-ordinates of 13 degrees longitude, 37 degrees latitude. A guess, of course. He had no idea exactly where he was.

Sicilie Pars, the map read, next to the black boot-shaped island below the Italian mainland. He spread his hand against the rich indigo blue of the Mediterranean. The grease in the cuts from yesterday's breakdown made fine black rivers and tributaries across his palms. Sand grated under the sweat on his back and he was light-headed from fasting. He had only had bread and water today.

He pressed a painted fibre lifting off the map. He was closer to Trepani than Palermo, he thought, but last winter's flooding had carried off the road signs and it seemed no-one had bothered to replace them. The wolves took them, the villagers in Siracusa had said, crossing themselves and spitting on the worn stones of the taverna. Wolves? There were no wolves left after the war, surely, when everybody ate them? The locals spat again and muttered about the sea crossing from Albania and animals which leaped through the night as the moon turned the crests of the waves to silver.

He put one fingertip across the calm eyes of the Jesus painted in lustrous oils at the top of the page, traced a path back up the Italian coastline, past the words and figures written there: notes on his fasting, the times he had whipped himself, the amounts of money distributed to the villages on his route. He traced his projected path across the map, from Koloshnovar straight through Czechoslovakia and Austria, down the Italian coast, up to France and the home of the rightful owner of the Frenchman's book. He avoided the shining palm leaf, cut from sheet gold, which marked Rome.

As he drove across the flat plain, dust was channelled up to the sky. The echo of shouts grazed the wind and the clouds seemed to quiver. He heard the ragged engine and the back of his neck tightened. He had learned not to ignore those feelings. He shifted down through the gears and steered toward the jagged hill, an outcrop of the mountain range proper, black against the sun.

At the base of the hill, he eased the car across the rougher ground. The suspension groaned over the chips of flint and slate and odd scattered objects: a water canteen, a picnic basket, a tyre crumpled like the skin of a dead animal. When the rocks became blunt boulders, he switched the engine off and pushed the goggles back. The pistons stamped down, the fan ticked unevenly to a close. The wind prickled his forehead with dust and pine tips.

He used the metal base of his compass to ease out the panel in the driver's side door, put his hand on the oiled leather bag wedged there, hooked his finger through the gold silk draw-string, gripped its dark sliminess, smelled the escaping sea. He closed his eyes, listened. No shouts, just a far-off hawk crying over a moving shadow.

He would rather have made it to the other side of the plain. Landslides were not uncommon in this region. And bandits.

The sun bleached the ground now but the grey haze staining the horizon meant a storm. Maybe he should put the roof up. He got out of the car, folded back the front side panel of the hood and tugged at the limp fan-belt.

Number one: change the fan-belt. Check the water, number two. Number three – he looked up and saw the children, a boy and a girl. Their hair was a muddied blonde, not as light as his own, but still unusual this far south. Maybe closer to the Austrian border, yes. Even for the villages in these parts, they were dressed in a very old-fashioned way. He took a closer look. Was she holding . . . ? Yes, it was a bonnet, with a fringe.

The girl came forward. She was tall and slender with pale blue eyes. She stared at him, unblinking.

Czeslaw had a working knowledge of Italian, picked up from the mechanics on his mother's estate and at the annual Torino races. He had mostly forgotten his schoolboy Latin, which was ironic, he thought now. He had always been an indifferent student, always yearning through the window.

He asked the children where he was, who they were. The boy hung back, glowering at him: the bad foreigner; the seducer. He felt like laughing. If they only knew.

The sun on his head was making him drowsy. He wanted the breeze, wanted cool weather, poplars straight as spires down the long avenue at Koloshnovar, elegant emerald sentries, tipped with blue. Not this hunched and leached green, these crooked fingers scratching a sullen sky.

The girl edged forward, slowly. She was older than he had thought. For some reason, he wanted to retreat. He moved to his right, keeping the car between them. He could see the inside door, the missing panel, the light sliding off the leather bag, the drawstring protruding like a hangman's rope.

She turned and waved. Two more children – teenagers really – appeared from behind the rocks: a plump girl, another boy, both with the black hair typical of the region.

They must have been waiting there. Hiding.

Czeslaw picked up the wrench.

The blonde girl beckoned but only the plump girl came forward, mouth open, staring at him.

The blonde girl raised her voice, was saying to the boys what sounded like, 'Now. What are you waiting for, Paolo?'

The blond boy shook his head. 'The parents never take two in two days.'

'Useless,' shouted the blonde girl. 'How will we ever get out of here?' She swung back to Czeslaw so violently that the cross around her neck tumbled out from her collar. The gold caught the sun like shook foil, the light piercing him. She came closer, smiling in a way she obviously thought was seductive. The boys still hung back but Paolo had picked up a large rock, was holding it by his side.

The girl said something about the next village, needing a ride across the plain. Czeslaw knew they meant to rob him – or worse – but he couldn't turn his back on the beam of gold light from the crucifix.

He said, 'Do you have a priest in your village?'

The plump girl crept closer.

'There is no-one here,' said the blonde girl sharply.

'You said the *next* village,' said Czeslaw. He traced back from where the children had appeared. Now he saw a faint line through the rocks, a clearing of boulders and scrub, a trail of disturbed bushes which zigzagged to the black summit.

He reached into the car, slid the leather bag into his satchel. It slipped beneath his fingers, wanting to escape him. He said, 'I'll see for myself.'

'No,' shouted the boys but the plump girl skipped past them and said, gazing up at Czeslaw, 'I'll take you.'

The blonde girl said, 'You're not the boss of this, Rosita.'

Rosita hesitated. She pointed at Czeslaw. '*Bel ragazzo.*'

The boys sniggered. Red washed up her doughy cheeks but Rosita stood firm. She pointed at Czeslaw's hair. 'Like the moon in well water at midnight. In the books – '

'Fairytale books,' said the blonde girl. 'Go back to the rocks, little mayor's piglet.'

Czeslaw heard the words through the sound of wind rushing through the forest. A Polish forest. Maybe he needed to break his fast. He leaned against the car for support.

Rosita put her fingers in her mouth; her nails were rimmed with dirt. She moved slowly, sideways, towards Czeslaw. She had round black eyes as shiny as a doll's. She said, 'There is a priest.' She pointed at the summit. 'And food.'

'A priest.' But even before he looked up the hill, he knew he would go with them. The urge to confess was too strong. After that . . . Whatever happened to his bodily self was pre-ordained.

The plump girl moved closer. She said, 'You must be . . .' and covered her eyes with her hands.

He insisted that the blonde girl and the two boys be in front. He took only his satchel with the maps and the compass. He debated hiding the leather bag in the car; if they attacked him, they would find it. But he couldn't bear to be parted from it. At the last moment he shoved it into his satchel.

They tied a red scarf across his eyes. For the first few hundred feet, all he could do was concentrate on not falling. Rosita stayed by his side, keeping up a running commentary about boulders and loose gravel, clutching his arm even on the flatter ground. He smelled hay on her and manure and, occasionally, a faint sour trace of urine.

At the steepest patches, he had to bend and grab at tufts of grass to pull himself up. If he looked straight down, he saw grey dirt and broken rocks through the quarter moon of his vision. Rosita went ahead but he sensed she was turning almost every other moment to look at him. Soon he had to crawl which, perversely, he found easier; the dirt under his hands steadied him. He felt moulded black ovals, smooth against his thumb and forefinger, like the detritus from a glass blower's forge; beneath the dry topsoil was damper earth. Snatches of schoolboy history came back to him: Sicily, the Mediterranean's granary, a land so rich it was once coveted by the entire world.

He felt less dizzy, not standing. He got into a rhythm of pulling himself forward and up by the small, stubby bushes.

The next time he stumbled, he shoved the blindfold off. Rosita touched her thumb to the outside corner of her eye, pointed at the grey sky. 'Your eyes,' she said.

They were moving among thicker scrub, shrubs which grew out almost horizontally from the slope. The temperature dropped suddenly. He slipped on something too smooth to be rock, landed on all fours, dropping the satchel. The oilskin bag slid across the loose stones, gathering momentum, a mini-avalanche rolling down the hill.

Gold coins spilt but he ignored them, threw himself after the bag, grabbing it, grazing his hand, spots of blood welling up, sitting in trembling drops on the rubbery black material. The drawstring slipped, the bag opened. He saw a pale gleam inside – pages the colour of bones – and shoved the bag inside his shirt. It lay against his heart, the cold seeping into him.

He crawled back to the satchel and a flash of yellow and black: an unusual rock formation? As he began sweeping with both hands, stones tumbled past him. The blond girl and boy had stopped above Rosita. The other boy, the dark-haired one, was further up, sitting on a rock, using a large square-bladed knife to trim the knots from a thick branch.

Czeslaw craned his head. Chips of fast, angry Italian fell down the hillside.

'What are you waiting for?' the blonde girl was saying.

'We can't do it now,' said Rosita.

'You're not the boss of us.'

'My papa is,' said Rosita.

The wind curled into the silence with a soft sigh. Czeslaw moved his hand and saw a cracked eye rolling into the dry earth, a gleam of light and curved yellow fangs veined with black.

Dirt fell on the picture in the ground. The dark-haired boy was descending. He carried the branch like a club over his shoulder.

'No, Stefano!' screamed Rosita.

'Sophia's right.' The dark-haired boy pointed the club at Czeslaw. 'He puts all of us in danger.'

'No.' Rosita pressed her hands to her burning cheeks. 'There's a new plan.'

'What plan?' said Stefano. 'Did you know about this, Paolo?'

The blond boy shook his head.

'She's lying,' said Sophia. 'Do it now.'

Czeslaw looked down. He could run and risk a broken leg. He rose slowly, the incline of the hill tugging at him.

The blond boy, Paolo, held up a flat piece of grey shale with a side as sharp as an axe. Czeslaw could almost feel it slicing into his temple.

Rosita moved so that she was between Czeslaw and the others. She shouted, 'You can't do this without checking with my father first.'

'Get out of the way, mayor's piglet,' shouted Sophia. 'No-one listens to you.'

'The signori decided,' shouted Rosita. 'No more stopping the cars. If the parents don't do it any more, we shouldn't either.'

'Liar!'

'How would you know?' said Rosita. She frowned at Paolo. 'Who is more likely to know what the signori decide? Her? Or me?'

'The signori,' said Paolo in a considering tone. He glanced at Stefano, who shook his head and turned. Paolo dropped the rock.

Sophia shouted 'No!' but Paolo was already climbing.

Rosita raised one arm, pointing. 'Go,' she said to Sophia. Only Czeslaw was close enough to see that her hand was trembling.

Sophia looked at her. Then she spat and began climbing.

The cold ate at Czeslaw's knees. He saw thin lines of black painted stones: a mosaic of a deer, head twisted away from the beast which rode its back, paws wrapped around the slender neck. There were words in black at the top of the picture: *Cubile Omnium Bestiarum* – The mosaic broke off into jagged triangles.

Cubile omnium, thought Czeslaw. His schoolboy Latin wasn't enough. Another month and he would have started his training. *Cubile omnium*: The lair of – ?

A pebble clattered. Rosita extended her hand. 'They won't harm you,' she said, 'as long as you are with me.'

He picked up the satchel. Maybe this was God's will, he thought. The journey wasn't the penance. Maybe the Frenchman's book was meant to stay here. He rubbed his forehead.

'Food,' said Rosita. 'And the priest: up, up.'

He saw the wolf in the ground clearly now, the huge yellow fangs ripping into the slender neck, the blood cascading from the white fur of the deer's chest. A hunting scene.

Rosita pointed to shiny black rivulets on the cliff face. 'The black tears.'

Light was trapped in narrow slivers along the spine of the shiny ridges. He scraped with his fingernail. No flecks, no splinters. Lava.

'Tears from the black faces,' said Rosita. 'Over to your – ' she hesitated as if she couldn't remember. 'To your right.'

He saw a dark brown face painted on the rock: a pre-Roman face with white hooded lids, slits of darkness for the eyes, a black rectangle for the oiled beard and yellow lines for the gold clasps tethering it.

The coldness at his heart expanded. A remorseless face from across the sea. Africa.

Shouts fell from the summit. Rosita tugged at his arm. In a reverse of nature, the taller trees started here. He heard the breeze through the branches, a sound like rolling surf. Rosita seemed to have gone through a clump of bushes. He plunged in; bony dried branches scratched him, grey nails caught his clothes. His feet hit stone, a small ledge, a step. More steps. An old wall rose out of the ground, decayed but recognisable. And a cracked stone base, a fallen column, hieroglyphics smudged in the crumbling stone, the bearded profile of a man.

The ground flattened, the steps became a path. He was still bent, weighted by the thick cold air; the tendons behind his knees ached. He held his hands against his heart to make sure the bag didn't slip. Mist seemed to be swirling around his feet. More steps then a cave – no, not a cave, a natural arch of rock, daylight immediately ahead. Rosita and the others had disappeared. The path broadened into a road of flagstones, the start of buildings, squat cottages. Beyond, the clouds low and swollen. The sky was darkening fast; lightning ripped, rain fell in flat panes. He saw an opening: a building to his left, a barn. He ran to it.

As he was about to step into the darkness, someone grabbed his hand. Or was it his head? Was it his heart? He was pulled through the rain, drops in his eyelashes, curtains of diamonds. Grey mist in his throat. The warm, musty smell of too many bodies in a small space, a fetid tang. The room dipped under him. He put his hand to his chest and dropped to his knees.

Dark figures stirred in the corner of the barn. A ring of stocky suspicious-eyed villagers: the women in black shawls and black dresses, some veiled, the men in black woollen caps and trousers with braces.

Light fell in pale lines through the cracks in the wooden roof onto the dried grass rushes on the floor. Two men held up lanterns on long poles. The flames trembled, sent shadows flickering across the faces, spectres creeping into crevices and across the metal rings of a thick chain which dangled from a hook in the roof. Twisted grey rags hung there, revolving slowly in broken creaks.

Rosita bent beside him, holding his elbow. A balding man with a large stomach pushing over his black trousers stared down at him.

'Papa, he's mine,' said Rosita.

Czeslaw shook his head, tried to speak.

The women pointed at his hair. One touched his head. A murmur went round the group: '*Bel ragazzo.*' '*Monete d'argento nell'acqua.*'

Sophia edged forward and put her hands on her hips. 'I saw him first. So he's mine.' A tall woman with bolts of grey in her black hair caught at the girl's hand, saying, 'Sophia!' but the girl jerked away, kneeled on the other side of Czeslaw.

'He'd much rather come with me.' She opened her eyes wide. 'Wouldn't you?'

Rosita moved closer to Czeslaw.

'Let him choose,' said Sophia. She leaned in, thrusting her chest at him.

'*Puttana!*' shouted Rosita and hit Sophia across the jaw. The girl was knocked to the ground; her hair fell – a veil the colour of clouds in a stagnant pond – over her face.

The balding man jerked Rosita away by the shoulder. Blood trickled from Sophia's nose. 'Mine by right,' she screamed. 'The look-out gets the biggest share.'

Shouts erupted; the grey-haired woman put her hand over Sophia's mouth and muttered, '*Scusi, Signor*' to the bald man. Two women grabbed Sophia by the arms and dragged her away. The black wall of bodies opened to let her through. When Czeslaw turned his head, Rosita had also vanished.

'I need to make my confession,' said Czeslaw. He must have spoken in Polish because the villagers shook their heads. 'A priest,' he said in Italian. The group stirred, murmured, 'Father Dante.' As he turned to look, a big man with a broken nose grabbed the satchel from his shoulder.

The contents scattered among the hay stalks and the big man crouched. Czeslaw saw red grooving the lines in the cracked dry hands. Grape juice, surely. The big man poked at the compass, the map, the thick wad of lira in the gold clasp, Czeslaw's Bible.

'No.' A thin stooped old man with blue eyes so faded they were nearly white stepped forward so that the other was forced to retreat, reluctantly, on his haunches.

The old man turned. Czeslaw saw the splintered wooden walking stick, the black robe, the knotted rope around the waist, the rough wooden cross hanging on the long metal chain.

Czeslaw reached under his shirt and pulled out the wooden crucifix. With a feeling of intense relief, he kneeled and kissed the hem of the black robe.

Father Dante put a gentle hand on his head and said softly, 'You are safe now.' The crowd murmured. The priest raised his voice and said, 'You have my word. Let him speak now who says God's word is not good enough.'

The Father helped him collect his belongings and led him from the barn. As he went, Czeslaw tried to see into the corner. He was taller than most of the crowd and, as he craned his neck to the revolving grey rags, what was hanging there made no sense to him.

The village rose on either side of the cobbled street in lines of plain, two-storey stone houses. The narrow windows were dark and unblinking against the grey sky. The buildings tilted, overhanging the street, the washing strung between the walls further reducing the light. No curtains twitched at the windows. He thought of eye sockets in an empty skull. The front doors were wood, some coated in faded red, most unpainted. There were designs cut into the doors: crosses and other, almost-familiar images. The cobbles had the dark green of moss on stone which never saw the sun. Czeslaw slipped and Dante helped him up, saying, 'The mules are always breaking their legs in this street.'

As Czeslaw straightened, he saw dogs lying in the narrow gaps between the houses. They gaped at him but didn't move, their coats as dark and oily as the package against his heart.

The bald man took Dante aside and spoke to him in Italian too fast for Czeslaw to understand. The priest shrugged him away, leaning heavily on his walking stick. When Czeslaw turned, he saw the bald man was holding back the crowd with his raised hand.

Dante and Czeslaw climbed alone.

The street rose, steeper and steeper. The village must have been cut into the side of the rock, the houses built along lines of softer earth. A low square building squatted at the top of the street, its stone tower rising three storeys, the cross on its roof piercing the grey clouds.

Dante led him through the main chapel, past the wooden pews. The altar was simple: a white table, a plain iron cross, a tray of metal cups. Czeslaw thought of the gold cups and orb, the embroidered wall hangings and Renaissance paintings in the private chapel at Koloshnovar. He felt the familiar sadness flood him; the burden of the ten thousand sufferings he had to pay penance for. He heard his father's voice, the bored drawl which even at this distance of miles and years filled Czeslaw with desolation. The words beat against his heart, they chafed his mouth with dust. *The crying of the cargo kept us awake all night.*

Dante led him through a side door into a narrow room. Benches flanked a lit fireplace, a low wooden table between. A stone basin was at one end of the room, a long wooden box covered with blankets at the other.

'Are you more fluent in French?' said Dante.

Czeslaw nodded and kneeled on the flagstones. He held out the leather bag and said, 'Father, I must confess.'

Dante put a hand on his shoulder, pulling at him to rise. 'Eat first.'

'I have come,' said Czeslaw, pulling the lira from his satchel, 'to give your village money.'

Dante stared at the notes. 'No-one in this village deserves your money.'

'But you will hear my confession?'

Dante went to the stone sink and began filling a kettle. 'I am not as worthy as I was,' said Dante, his back to him.

'You're a priest until you die, surely.'

'Yes,' said Dante. 'Until I die.'

He turned. The bones of his cheek had tightened so the skin fell from them as translucent as paper. 'You wouldn't want me to hear you.'

'I do.' Czeslaw said, believing it, 'It must be God's will.'

'God moves in very mysterious ways,' said Dante. He smiled at Czeslaw, who smiled back at him.

Czeslaw sat on the wooden bench by the lit fire. The warmth relaxed his shoulders, made him realise how tense he had been. He yawned into the glowing heart and said, 'Where am I?'

'You're in the hills behind Castelmontrano,' said Dante. 'You are in the Triangle of Hunger.'

Czeslaw was driving. Or was he walking? He was gliding through the village. The afternoon sun tinged the white walls with pink and found blood in the water in the barrels under the eaves. The dogs lying in the shadows watched him go past, their flanks rising and falling. Now he recognised the strange markings on the doors: wolves' heads on men's bodies. The heads were in profile, watching him. The village seemed empty. He had seen figures in the hayfields in previous days so he presumed most of the villagers were somewhere down the mountain, bringing in the hay, tending their vines or their goats. He glided slowly down the main street, the car springs squeaking over the cobblestones. Occasionally a curtain twitched. He told himself this was natural. Houses without people were like eye sockets in a skull. He reached a scattering of squat buildings and went to the nearest doorway.

It was dim inside. He stood, adjusting to the light.

In the corner, what looked like twisted grey rags hung over hay scattered on stone. The rags moved slightly as though someone had brushed past not so long ago.

He went forward. Not rags; a pelt draped over a large rusting hook hanging on a chain from the rafter. The chain turned, clinking and creaking. The pelt revolved slowly. Old, grey, dangling. Matted in places. A dark drop fell to the floor and trembled on the stone. The drop was dark water in this light. Or oil. It took him a moment to realise it was blood.

The pelt turned. It was matted with blood. Dripping blood. Black blood.

The pelt kept turning. It turned and turned and turned its face to him.

It was a wolf. The hook was caught under its throat.

It turned and turned.

He saw now. The hook was not caught under the beast's throat. The hook was through its throat.

The pelt turned. The wolf opened its eyes and looked at him.

Czeslaw woke on a cry, a feeling of being smothered, pressure on his chest, the beast's fur covering his face.

He was lying on the bench next to the fire. He sat up with a start and almost hit his head against Rosita, who was leaning over him. She jumped back and muttered an apology, then stared at him, mouth open.

Dante was nowhere to be seen.

'The Father has gone to get your dinner,' said Rosita. He saw himself reflected in narrow panes in her shiny black eyes; she never blinked that he could see.

Rosita gave him a quick smile and looked serious, frightened even. Czeslaw wondered if she would get into trouble for bringing him up to the village. This was the south, he reminded himself. Honour was more important than trade here, the villagers in Siracusa had said, hooking their thumbs at the ground. In southern villages, they said, spitting on the floor, power is more important than love. *'Chi gioca da solo, non perde mai*: He who plays alone never loses.'

He scrutinised Rosita: the stocky plump figure under the shapeless dress, the round jaw, the shadow across her upper lip, the black down on the side of the cheeks. An unattractive child. He supposed he should be grateful to her; she probably wasn't allowed to help a stranger.

He managed a smile and, dredging up his Italian, asked her how old she was.

'I'm sixteen,' she said, sliding down the bench. Her drab brown skirt had hitched up; he saw a plain tan petticoat in rough linen. Not linen, sacking. Potato sacking.

'Do you like?' she said and held out the brown material. On it were embroidered flowers in coarse red wool: roses, the lumpy red heads eating into the rough material like stains.

'*Bella*,' he said, gesturing a sewing motion. 'You are good at needlework.'

'I am,' she said, clapping her hands. 'And cooking and housework.' She dipped her head, pleating the skirt between her fingers. 'All the things to make a good wife.' She turned her head away, glancing across her cheek at him, a sideways look that reminded him of something. Maybe the deer in the mosaic.

He saw the faces of the young men in the barn: broad-faced, broken-nosed, mouths already set in classic lines of mistrust. The poor girl. She wouldn't have much to choose from.

He began to feel a lack, as though he was cold. 'I'm sure you deserve a good husband,' he said, absentmindedly. He felt for the bag at his chest. It wasn't there.

He swung his legs off the bench as Rosita said, 'You have a wife?'

'So far I haven't had the good fortune.' And never would, he thought as he bent over the side of the bench.

'You deserve a good wife,' said Rosita.

He shook his head, distracted, his hand inching across the paving stones, feeling the crevices packed with dried mud. Finally, his finger slipped on slimy coldness. He hooked the gold drawstring and sat up, clutching the bag.

Rosita was next to him. Again, that faint sour smell.

He was surprised to find her so close. He drew back.

'How old are you?' she said.

He wanted to move but he stayed still. 'Twenty-four.' He held up his hands and counted off the years. 'An old man to you.'

'Very good,' she said, stretching out a hand to touch his hair. He couldn't help himself: now he did move, abruptly, not caring if he was rude. But she had grasped his hair. His scalp twinged as he jerked his head.

'*Monete d'argento nell'acqua*,' she said.

'What?'

She was still staring at his hair. She said it again slowly and, after a struggle, he translated it as 'silver coins in water'. She didn't seem to notice that he was leaning away from her. 'Better than Sophia's hair,' she said. 'Sophia thinks she can have everything she wants.' Again that sideways look. 'She thinks you want her.'

'Who? That little girl?' he said.

Her black eyes were unblinking; maybe she didn't understand what he was saying.

She put a hand on his thigh.

He was shocked into inaction. She mustn't realise what she had done. But she met his gaze squarely and moved her hand slowly and deliberately up his leg, massaging the inner flesh with her thumb. He could see himself reflected in her black eyes. Her hand moved higher and higher, pressing in, unhesitating, the strokes longer, more languid. Her mouth was open, her lower lip was wet. She was moving closer to –

He stood, backed away to the fire. 'I won't be marrying.'

'Not soon, no,' she said.

'Never.' He didn't care how harsh he sounded.

'You have a wife?'

'No.'

She shrugged. 'Well, then.'

'But I am promised to someone.' He clasped his hands, as though he was shaking hands with himself. He felt ridiculous but he wanted to make sure she understood. 'A sacred promise.'

She laughed and pointed around the room. 'Your woman can't see you here.' Her confidence made him uneasy. It was almost as though she was refusing to understand him.

'Another kind of promise,' he said. He made the sign of the cross, looked upwards. Surely she would understand now.

She stood. 'I saved you,' she said.

'I didn't promise you anything.'

'You came to the top of the hill with me.' She put her hands on her hips. Her face was flushed. 'I do not think there is anyone else.'

'There is someone else.'

Red washed her face. 'Who?' she said loudly.

He gripped the leather bag with both hands. 'God.'

She snorted and spat on the stone floor. 'God does nothing for us.' Her voice swelled into a shout. 'God does not come near Santa Margherita.'

Her eyes were black marbles. When she clutched the collar of her blouse, he thought she was going to pretend he had strangled her. As she hooked her hands into the white cotton, he was already laughing in derision. She stared at him. He heard the wind howling outside, the small cracks and pops of the fire behind him. She ripped, tearing the material at the neck, exposing her throat. She ripped, the sound louder than the wind and the fire. She knuckled her fist, hit herself again and again. The skin below her collarbone mottled red.

'Stop it!' His voice was too loud. Maybe she was in some kind of shock.

He raised his hands, palms to her. 'Please,' he said. 'Let us talk, calmly.'

She shook her head, her black shiny hair swinging. 'When they know what you did to me,' she shouted, 'you'll have to marry me.'

'You don't understand,' he said. 'I must get to France. A matter of honour.'

'This is honour,' she shouted. 'I'll tell them what you did.'

She ripped again. Her throat and upper chest were a vivid throbbing red, with darker lines where she had scratched herself. In a moment, blood would begin welling up, like dark water, like oil.

'No-one else saw what you did,' she screamed.

'I saw,' said Father Dante, coming into the room.

The priest carried a wooden tray with bread and bowls of soup. He crossed the room in silence. Rosita was still panting, her eyes narrowed. Now she blinked, Czeslaw saw, fast and convulsively. Dante set the tray carefully on the table. A rich smell of bacon and garlic rose from the bowls and Czeslaw realised how hungry he was. He almost felt as though he would agree to anything just to be able to eat. He tried to catch Dante's eye.

The priest straightened, deliberately averting his gaze.

Czeslaw felt a moment of utter desolation. If the priest was against him, too . . .

'Father,' he said.

Dante raised his hand.

Czeslaw bowed his head. Was this God's work?

Father Dante said in Italian slow enough for Czeslaw to follow, 'Think carefully, Rosita. A man's honour is at issue. What happened here?'

'He attacked me,' she panted. 'See?' She pointed to her neck.

'He was trying to take advantage of you,' Dante said.

'Yes,' she said.

'He was trying to seduce you,' said Dante.

'Yes, yes.'

'You will swear on the Bible?'

She never hesitated. 'Yes.'

Czeslaw sat on the bench.

Father Dante advanced slowly. The light from the fire caught his white eyes and made them shine. He looked remorseless, thought Czeslaw.

The priest fumbled for the cross at his waist and lifted it on its long chain.

'This is very serious,' he said. 'I ask again. You swear on the Bible?'

'Yes. Yes.'

'Then,' said Father Dante, gripping his cross, 'Rosita, you are a liar and you will go to hell.'

Colour drained from her face.

'I could hear you all the way across the chapel.'

'No!'

'I wasn't the only one.'

Czeslaw held his breath.

Rosita stepped back. 'There was a witness?'.

Dante let go of his cross, raised both hands. 'Think what you are saying.'

She opened her mouth, looked at Czeslaw, who turned his head away.

She said, 'He promised me.'

'Did he?' said Dante.

Rosita peered from one to the other. Tears in her eyes made them glassier than ever. She clenched her hands.

Dante held up the cross. 'Are you prepared to swear this in public?'

'Don't say another word, Rosita,' said a voice at the doorway.

The man with the bulging stomach came into the room, carrying a tray with a bottle and two glasses. He dumped the tray on the table and faced Dante, arms folded.

'Our mayor,' said Dante to Czeslaw, who got unwillingly to his feet. 'Franco Rossetti. The man who rescued us during the war.'

'I did what needed to be done, Father,' said Franco sharply. 'People like you forget what we faced.'

'I never forget, Mayor,' said Dante.

'Then remember your part,' said Franco, shaking his finger. Dante bowed his head. Franco stared at the ripped cotton at Rosita's throat. 'Cover yourself.' She clasped the torn blouse, not meeting his eyes.

Franco looked Czeslaw up and down. 'This stranger did that to you?'

'Rosita misunderstood,' said Dante.

'Papa,' said Rosita.

'Be quiet.' Franco stepped closer to Czeslaw. His mouth worked silently. He said, 'You pay the consequences.'

'Papa – '

'Quiet. Consequences, stranger. Every man here will make sure you do.'

'Sir, I assure you – '

'Papa.'

'Mayor, Rosita misspoke – '

'Are you calling my daughter a liar, priest?'

'PAPA!'

Rosita's face was scarlet but she held her head high. 'Nothing happened, Papa. You'll have to let him go.'

'But, you said you wanted him,' said Franco.

Rosita stared at Czeslaw. The tears brimmed and ran down her cheeks.

Dante said gently, 'Kiss the cross and beg forgiveness, child.'

'Forgiveness,' shouted Franco, his face as red as his daughter's. 'She'd better ask forgiveness off the signori, priest. There is dishonour here. I smell it.'

Dante said, 'The only thing you smell – '

'Careful, priest.'

'God knows what honour is,' said Dante.

'When has your God ever helped us? We're alone on this mountain.' Franco pointed at Rosita. 'You know what the signori can do. If you want this stranger – '

'She's a child,' said Czeslaw.

'Stop it.' Rosita put her hands over her eyes. A log popped on the fire. She looked from Franco to Czeslaw, drew a ragged breath and howled, 'No!' and ran from the room.

'You had better wish that she changes her mind,' Franco said to Czeslaw.

'She won't,' said Dante. 'I told her there was a witness.'

'Witness?' Franco scanned the room.

'In the chapel.'

Franco snorted. 'A witness who contradicts the daughter of a signori?'

Dante said steadily, 'Yes.'

'The signori don't like dissenters,' said Franco. 'You know that.'

'The witness will speak in church,' said Dante.

'Be very careful, priest.'

Dante pressed his lips together.

Franco said, 'You should hope the signori don't find your precious witness first. Or your witness's relatives.' He gestured at the wine tray. 'The wind is coming up. It will be a cold night. I suggest you drink and reflect. Especially you, priest. Reflect on your life. And your relatives' lives.'

Dante sat heavily on the bench, looking at the floor.

Franco went out. A draft of cold wind sliced through the room and the chapel door slammed shut.

'Who are the signori?' said Czeslaw.

'The signori are the friends of friends,' said Dante. He was breathing quickly. 'They are everywhere.'

'Will they hurt you?'

Dante straightened. 'There is nothing they can do to me.'

'And the witness?'

Dante didn't reply.

'Whom do I thank?' said Czeslaw. He saw the priest's hand tremble on his knee.

Czeslaw waited for a moment then said, 'Was there a witness?'

Dante looked him in the eye. 'My son, there is always a witness in God.'

'So this is the map you were using,' said Dante in French. He pushed aside the bowls of soup, the platter with a few crumbs of bread. The bottle of wine sat, un-poured. Czeslaw supposed the old man didn't like wine with his soup.

He studied Dante's hands resting on the fibrous parchment. The skin was creased like tissue paper; the fingernails deeply grooved, their white moons tinged blue.

The priest traced a line along the Italian coast, south from Venice, pausing at the notations of money written beside the occasional village.

'I made good time along the coast,' said Czeslaw, 'until I got to Castelmontrano. Falling rocks blocked the road. I had to turn inland.'

He had got out of the car to feel the fury of the sea. The waves were tipped with luminous green as they dashed themselves against the black rocks. Foam was hurled against the cliffs, white-green rain fell on him as he stood, swaying in the wind. The horizon was lost in the black sky. Somewhere out there were Tunisia and Algeria. Just a boat ride away.

Dante pointed. 'Santa Margherita, you are here. Castelmontrano is on the other side of the hill.' He retraced Czeslaw's journey across white paper. 'But no Trepani, no Ferromignana.'

'It is a Dutch map,' said Czeslaw. 'They are meant to be the best.'

'Maybe,' said Dante. The light from the fire turned his eyes gold. 'But mapmakers are storytellers. They only include what they think is important. Sometimes the blank spaces tell you more.'

He carefully opened the map to its fullest. Europe and the Mediterranean lay spread across the low wooden table. The Jesus stared upwards, his hands pointing west and east, to China and the Americas, his feet planted in the beginnings of Africa.

'Mappaemundi,' said Dante reverentially. 'A map of the world. I have seen similar charts on the walls of the Galleria della Carte Geografiche in the Palazzo Vaticano.'

'Rome?' said Czeslaw with the familiar catch in his heart.

'Map-makers were once known as world describers,' said Dante. He ran his hand gently down the elaborately painted side panels, over the dragon with the human head rearing in the small ocean between Sicily and Tunisia. Along the creases the ink was scratched, the coloured paint flaking. But the blues and reds were still vivid.

'Magnificent,' said Dante softly. 'The blue: powdered lapis lazuli. Sulfide of arsenic for the desert.' His finger hovered above the gleaming palm leaf centred over Rome. 'Gold powder with ox bile?

No, real sheet gold.' He traced the edge of the continent. 'Wood cut then hand coloured. Sixteenth century. The great age of mapping.'

'My father's map,' said Czeslaw.

Dante examined the illustrated panels which made up the borders. 'See these tables in Latin? Lists of popes, Roman emperors. And these pictures: Noah and his ark, the Temple of Solomon, the Battle of Lepanto where the Christians defeated the Muslims. This is a history of civilisation. Sub specie religionis Christianae. A world within the world of the map.' He touched the gold palm leaf. 'Rome as the centre of religious belief, Italy as the centre of the world.'

Czeslaw said, 'My father told me it was a Dutch map. A copy.'

'It could well be,' said Dante. 'The Dutch were in love with maps. They hung them on their walls. They saw their charts almost as paintings.

'In his picture *Art Of Painting*, Vermeer paints an elaborate map of the Netherlands on the wall. Apparently, the map he painted did exist, it was a real map, a sixteenth-century map of the Netherlands as it should be, with all its traditional borders. Supposedly, the point of the picture is not the map: it is the artist in his black beret, maybe Vermeer himself, who is painting a portrait of a girl holding a thick book, a wreath in her hair. She is Clio, the muse of history. History is at issue here. So maybe the map is the point of the picture. At any rate, the map is so finely detailed that it has become one of only two copies of that real-life map. The original, the real map, has been lost. The picture has become a map itself.

'We in Sicily are obsessed with maps,' said Dante. 'Only our obsession with our honour is greater. Sicily has been at the mercy of maps for thousands of years. Kings we never heard of claimed our soil on the notion of territory defined by longitudes and latitudes. Men fighting and dying for ink lines on old parchment. For abstractions.'

'Not only soldiers,' said Czeslaw, his fingernails cutting into the soft leather of the bag in his lap.

'Treasure seekers?' said Dante. 'Yes, Sicily has been plagued by them. Sweeping down from the north, coming up from Africa. The coast is littered with the broken crockery of ships trying to land here.

We have never had a decade in which we have not been invaded. Everything has been taken except for the pagan sacrifice tables. Not for any superstition but because they are too heavy to lift.'

He sighed, took out a pouch and rolled himself a cigarette, gazing into the fire. 'I do not think this map is a copy.'

Czeslaw said, 'I am an accessory to theft.' He thought, To more theft.

Dante said, 'Only because you believed your father.'

Czeslaw stared at the bag sitting like a dark stain across his thighs. He threw it on the floor.

Dante looked at the bag and at the map. 'The notations of money you have made here and here and here,' he said. 'This is what you gave to each village you came through?'

'Yes,' said Czeslaw, making no move to pick up the bag. 'I confessed to the priest in each village.'

'Confessed your crimes?'

'The crime of being my father's son. And I gave them money not to do business with my father again.'

'And you think they will not do business?'

'The priests took the money.'

Dante closed his eyes. 'So this journey you are on,' he said, 'is not for pleasure.'

Czeslaw said, 'It is a penance.'

Dante smoked his cigarette in silence.

'I want to start again with a blank map,' said Czeslaw. 'That is why I am travelling.'

'There can be good memories,' said Dante. 'Good journeys in time.'

Czeslaw said, 'My good memories . . .' He hesitated. 'So few.' He felt gravel beneath his feet, heard the sound of horses whickering, saw a long row of half-doors, horses looking out at him, ears pricked. They knew he had sugar and apples for them. 'My only pleasant memories have nothing to do with earthly goods.'

Outside, the light began turning over into dusk. The fire burnt low and Dante slipped more logs onto the embers. A chorus of dogs howled for a few moments, stopping in mid-yelp.

The priest picked up the leather bag and placed it on the edge of the map. He touched the oily surface. 'I feel the sea.'

'Whale leather,' said Czeslaw. 'Specially cured, an old Polish recipe, so that the hide doesn't crack.' After a long moment, he said, 'What is inside is a terrible burden.'

Dante considered him, then he bent over the map again.

They gazed at the grid of latitudes and longitudes. Clumps of fine black inverted Vs covered the heart of Sicily, running through Santa Margherita, nearly down to the double black line of the sea.

'The hills are at their highest here, their most barren,' said Dante. 'From Santa Margherita, the ground flattens before the final cliffs overlooking the sea.'

'The forests are sparse,' said Czeslaw.

'We have been cursed since the war,' said Dante. 'The sea winds stripped the soil. Everything is stunted here now.' He tapped the map. 'There used to be a village at the cove called Castelmontrano. Before the war, the floods. We were fishermen then. Coast dwellers. Now we tend goats.'

'Why leave?'

Dante hesitated. 'The villagers were driven out.'

'And you?'

Dante rested his chin on his walking stick. 'That is my penance. To stay with them.'

It was the half-veiled hour between the end of dusk and the beginning of true night. The wind dropped and, briefly, the air was warmer. Czeslaw and Dante left the church and climbed through the shadow of the tower. They went up the broad stones set into the hillside until they reached a flat path with a broken wall on either side.

Dante raised his lantern and Czeslaw saw a mosaic set into the paving stone: a picture of a man, clad in white with a wreath on his head.

'Roman,' said Dante. 'We are standing on the wall of a Roman fort, before the lava came.'

'There are black faces,' said Czeslaw, pointing below the village, 'painted on the hillside.'

'Sicily has been invaded from the north and the south for three thousand years,' said Dante. 'The Greeks, the Phoenicians, Carthaginians, Romans, Saracens, the Germanic tribes, the Normans. You can find daggers and implements from all the different ages. Above Castelmontrano, there is the stone table where they sacrificed humans to Baal.'

They looked at the sprinkling of yellow lights below. The layout of the streets made no sense, running off at crazy angles, some so steep they were only reached by steps between the levels, the houses built so close together that there was no way in that Czeslaw could see.

'There are villages built on top of villages here,' said Dante. 'Ruins on ruins, from before the Romans. Lowland villagers often moved to hilltops to escape marauders.'

'Practical,' said Czeslaw.

'Isolated,' said Dante. 'Inward-looking. Festering.' He rubbed his chin on his stick. 'Once you are in a maze, unless you know the trick, you cannot leave.'

A lantern was lit suddenly beneath them, revealing a walled area of cleared earth criss-crossed with ropes at head height and pale squares that swung in the low light: lines of washing.

The wind swirled up the hillside. It blew through the lines so the sheets flapped back and forth in angry snaps, revealing a group of women. The women's hair escaped from their black scarves, lifting in tendrils to the sky. A moment later, the wind reached Dante and Czeslaw, making the priest's robes billow around him.

'It wasn't good for the children,' said Dante, 'when we moved.'

Czeslaw peered through the dusk but it was only when the group stood directly under the lantern that he saw Rosita, surrounded by three others. The grey-haired woman who had been in the barn raised her hand and slapped Rosita. The sheets dropped, obscuring his view.

'It's a village matter,' said Dante, behind him.

'If she is in trouble because of me . . .'

Dante caught Czeslaw's arm. 'You can't interfere. You are already . . .' He said, 'Rosita is the Mayor's daughter. She has protection.'

The sheets lifted again. Rosita was shouting, her words spiralling up to them. The grey-haired woman shouted back. The sheets dropped over them.

'What are they saying?' Czeslaw asked Dante. 'She's not telling them I seduced her?'

The lantern's light was trapped in the hollows under the priest's eyes. His eyes became black pools, his face a mask. 'You would have been better to take Rosita's offer,' he muttered.

Dante walked slowly along the parapet. Czeslaw hesitated. The last dusk light was gone, the lantern cloaked. The sheets were faint squares in the gloom. The wind lifted, the sheets rose. Czeslaw stared over the low wall. The sheets swooped down then lifted again. The wall seemed to sway against his thigh. The yard was empty. Rosita and the women were gone.

Czeslaw stood at the window in Dante's room. The shadow of the tower made it seem like night already.

'Even in the bright sun of the farmyard,' said Dante, 'there is the smear of blood on the hay stalk, the dog jumpy on the chain. Smoke from a shotgun. Shouts on the wind. Agonies.'

The firelight was low in the room, wavering over the tapestry on the wall and the rug on the floor. The smoke rose in black veins to the rafters. Dante sat, his chin on his stick, staring into the fire.

'Villages do not change much,' he said. 'The people look around and say everything in their village is the same: the drunkard is still drunk, the woman who secretly hated her children still secretly hates her children. The priest – '

' – is still saintly,' said Czeslaw.

Dante grimaced. He bent over the tray and poured two glasses of wine. The liquid was black, the light from the fire slicked the surface with orange.

'You should leave early tomorrow,' he said. 'I'll sit up with you tonight.' He took a sip and closed his eyes. 'That is all I can do.'

Czeslaw drank and put the glass down, held his head in his hands. He said, 'I can't confess to my past sins because I have forsaken my past life. I have no memory of it. I have given away my father's money to pay for his sin.'

Dante waited.

Czeslaw picked up the bag. 'I stole this from the man who stole it.'

He untied the gold string and smoothed back the leather. An oblong shape lay there, wrapped in ivory silk.

Inside was a book, the pages bound into a cover of black leather. Czeslaw used his fingernail to open the cover, turn the pages. The paper was nearly diaphanous, covered in bold sprawls of inked writing.

'Wax weave pressing,' said Dante. 'It looks almost new.'

Czeslaw turned the pages. The language was French: diary writings, scraps of poetry, sketches of landscape: the desert, mountains rising out of a flat plain under a crescent moon.

Dante read, '*We are made so that nothing contents us.*' He said, 'You stole this because it has value?'

'Its value is obligation. I am the son of the man who stole it.'

Dante thought. 'The writer values it?'

Czeslaw hesitated. 'The writer is – was – a traveller. I have his family's address in France. I will give them the book and a photograph I found of my father. Then – it is God's will. Once I have returned the book, I will go to Rome.'

'For absolution,' said Dante.

'To enter the seminary, yes.'

'To pay for someone else's crimes?'

'Yes.' Czeslaw clasped Dante's hands. 'The minute I saw you, I knew it was a sign that I was on the right path.'

Dante said, 'There is a terrible irony here, that you were sent to me.'

Czeslaw dreamed he was in the barn again. He saw the grey pelt hanging over the hay scattered on the stone floor. The chain creaked as it turned. Turning and turning and –

He woke to a drawn-out note of rage, the echo of it deepening and narrowing in his ears. Man or beast?

He was no longer in Dante's room but lying on a straw mattress beneath a vaulted ceiling. Moonlight fell through the small windows, enough to see the stone walls and floor in blacks and whites. Stalks jabbed into him; there were no sheets, no pillows. He wore a rough cotton shirt and trousers, not his. His feet were bare. They had taken his clothes and he was naked underneath. They would have seen the cuts on his back when they stripped him.

He sat up, awkwardly. His hands were bound. A thin piece of wire wound tightly around them, the ends twisted together. He slid off the bed, his legs heavy.

He went around the room: small windows in three walls, a thick door on black metal hinges in the fourth. The door handle was an iron wolf's head. He tried to turn it. Locked. He banged on it, shouting, the sound rushing into his ears like treetops being torn up for spite by the black wind.

No reply.

He walked around the room again, slowly, feeling in front of him with his feet, his clasped hands. Nothing but the bed and a heavy sideboard in dark unpolished wood. He kneeled on the cold floor and pulled at the hanging metal strips which made the handles. The sideboard doors didn't move. His fingers probed the small dark shadow beneath the right handle. A keyhole.

He went to the nearest window, unlatched it, hooked the window back on its metal arm. The frame was cold beneath his hands. He looked across the church's flat roof to the village.

He was in the stone tower.

He leaned out. The wind slapped at his cheek; far below, the trees were wrenched back and forth. He stared down the jagged side of the mountain: too high to jump.

He swallowed his rising panic and examined the wire around his wrists. The ends were separate. If he could part them further . . .

He bent his head and tried to get his teeth between the wire ends. The metal scraped his gums and blood flooded his mouth. But he

opened the gap enough to wedge one end under the metal window
arm. He twisted his hand and, before it slipped, the gap widened.
He bent his head again and jerked his jaw, only stopping to spit out
a mouthful of blood. The wires parted further.

His lip and chin were badly cut and he spat out two more mouth-
fuls of blood before he was able to catch one end and hold it with
his thumb and forefinger while he gripped the other with his teeth.

Moving his jaw in careful circles, he slowly unwound the wire.
It dropped to the floor and lay on the pale stone like a red ribbon.
When he used the shirt to wipe his face, the material stained pink.

It was only then that he realised he hadn't seen the leather bag.

It couldn't all be for nothing. The quarrel with his father, this trip.

He went to the door, shouted until the trembling in his throat
shook him to his knees. He pressed his face against the wood, the
metal hinge cold against his forehead. A line of light crept under his
closed eyelids and colder air brushed his mouth.

The wood was warped. There was a gap between the door and
the wall, as much as a finger's width in some places. He saw the
stone landing, the first steps, a lit lantern hanging on a bracket in
the wall. Below it, on a thin nail driven between two blocks of stone,
was a small key on a metal ring.

He stared at it for a long time. It was barely an arm's length away
but only his fingertips fitted through the gap. He looked at the wire
gleaming wetly in the moonlight and straightened it, fingers slipping.
He measured it against his outstretched arm.

He bent one end into a hook, held the other end firmly, and
pushed the wire through the gap.

The thin red line snaked along the wall towards the key.

Somewhere below him, a door banged, voices echoed up the stairs.
He stopped, rigid, the wood cutting into his cheekbone, splinters
separating his eyelashes. The lantern shuddered in a new eddy of
wind. He held his breath but no-one came.

Please God, he thought, be with me.

The hooked end of the wire was almost at the key. But he hadn't
reckoned on the thinness of the metal: it was beginning to bend

under its own weight. The further he pushed it, the more it bent. It was nearly at the key but diving down past it.

He stood on tiptoe, moved his fingers up in the gap so the wire was above the key now. But it was curving badly; he doubted if he could get the hook through the metal ring. He tried anyway, jerking wildly. The hook missed the ring completely the first time. He tried again, another miss, but closer. He took a deep breath, willed himself to slow. He brought his arm down and up again quickly, like flicking a whip. The hook rose, caught the edge of the metal ring, kept rising; the key was coming off the nail. He brought his hand down frantically, the hook dropped, the key fell, the hook caught the ring, it held there, swinging in the light, so close. The wire buckled.

The key fell to the ground.

He pulled the wire through the gap, threw himself down and looked under the door. The key lay, trembling in the lantern light. It was much nearer than before. The metal ring was slightly raised. He saw space between it and the uneven stone. If he could hook the wire under it . . .

He folded the wire back and twisted it to make it shorter but thicker. He also bent the other end to make the hook deeper and longer. Then, lying full length, he pushed the wire out, closer and closer to the key. Against the ground, the wire was easier to handle. It went straight towards the key and he felt a thrill of elation.

Yes, he thought. Then told himself, Don't get over-confident.

The wire was already at the key. He flipped it over so the hook was dragging against the ground and pushed. The sharp point ran up and over the key-ring. He dragged back, sharply, and the hook slid under the ring and caught it.

He willed himself not to rush, moving his hand back a few inches at a time. The key came easily across this piece of stone paving. There was barely half an arm's length between it and him.

But at the grouting around the next piece of stone, the key's teeth disappeared into the gap. The key stopped. It was caught. He pulled, sweating now despite the cold. The cuts on his chin had re-opened; red was pooling near the door. He pulled again, felt the resistance. He eased off then tugged, sharply. The key came free.

As he lay down and yanked the key the last few inches, a door slammed. More voices. Someone coming up the stairs.

He pulled the key under the door, ripped it off the hook and threw the wire to one side. The footsteps were closer. He shoved the key into the lock. It disappeared almost up to the ring. Unable to believe the evidence of his own eyes, he turned the key, willing the door to open.

He turned and turned. The key spun wildly, unable to catch the lock. He turned and turned the wolf's head knob but the door didn't move.

The key was far too small. He knew it even as the footsteps sounded on the landing outside.

He threw the key behind him and slumped against the door, gasping. Blood was running down his throat, falling on the wolf's head doorknob as though it were weeping red tears.

Why have You forsaken me? he thought and bowed his head.

The footsteps stopped on the landing. He heard breathing as ragged as his own.

Rosita's voice came through the gap. 'Signor Rimbaud.' She scratched at the door. 'Arthur.'

'That's not my name,' he said in Polish.

'Arthur?'

'You have the book,' he said in Italian.

'If I keep it safe for you?' She pressed her mouth against the gap; her warm breath touched his cheek. Their mouths were less than a hand's width apart. She said something that sounded like, 'We could almost kiss from here.'

'We'll never kiss,' he said loudly. 'I'll never marry.'

There was a long silence. Her breath stopped. She had turned her head away.

'I'll never pass on my father's blood. Do you understand?'

'Yes.'

'Will you let me out?'

'They'll kill me.' Her voice faltered into a sigh.

'Where is the priest?'

'He won't come,' she said. 'He's ashamed. He betrayed you.'

He had an image of his father laughing at him, sitting up to his waist in treasure, drinking red liquid from cups made of gold as bright as the sun.

Czeslaw said, 'It's all been for nothing.' He sat down and placed his hand in the red stain on the floor. The mark left there reminded him of the palm leaf on his map.

'Rome,' he said. 'I'll never see you now.'

'If you had said you would marry me,' said Rosita, 'they wouldn't have trusted you but they would have let you live. Why couldn't you just say it? Am I that ugly?'

'No,' he said. He rested his head against the door.

'Couldn't you have lied?' she said.

'That's what my father said. I'm sorry, Rosita. It was beyond my control. It was God's will.'

She gave a scornful laugh. 'Men always say that.' He heard her slap the door.

'I didn't want to be part of a lie anymore,' he said.

A long pause. She said, 'I know.' Her fingers reached through the gap. He stood slowly, like an old man, and touched her fingertips with his own. She pressed back and, with a choked sound, withdrew.

'Dante didn't betray you,' she said. 'He was drugged too.'

But her voice was already growing fainter. 'No-one ever gets away.' Her footsteps receded.

'Help me!' he shouted.

He listened. The door slammed. She was gone.

He didn't know how long he sat. He dozed and kicked out his leg so that it caught the key on the floor. The clinking metal woke him completely.

He looked from the key to the sideboard.

The small key.

He picked it up and squatted next to the sideboard. The moonlight was falling almost directly onto the wooden doors and he found the keyhole easily, slid the key in and turned.

The cupboard opened. He yanked the door back onto its hinges with such anger that he felt the metal buckle. The moonlight fell on the two shelves inside. On the top was his satchel. He ripped it open, but found only his compass.

The maps, the money, the leather bag were gone. And the Frenchman's diary.

He searched the bottom shelf. At the front were four folded sheets, large ones, made of thick coarse cotton. Stout cotton. He put them to one side, felt around the back of the shelf, in the darkness, and grasped a sack of clothes.

He sorted through the shirts and trousers and skirts and blouses, all different sizes. Good quality: he recognised the Viennese tailor on the label on one silk shirt. On another, he found rust-coloured stains; more stains on a fawn driving coat.

He was turning the Viennese shirt between his hands when he noticed writing on the inside seam. The ink had run but he recognised German: *Mein Liebling*, it read, *Ich bin ein verlassener Mann* —

A thread had pulled, the words blurred together in the low light. He shoved the shirt into the sack. He didn't want to read any more.

He used the compass's sharp edge to work a hole between the threads. Deliberately thinking of his father, he put all his strength into tearing the material.

When he had twisted and knotted the strips into a long thick rope, he dragged the sideboard over to the window, tied one end of the rope around the wooden legs and threw the other end away into the darkness. He checked the knot and climbed out.

For a moment he couldn't make himself let go of the window sill. The cold air between his toes made his soles flinch. He hung, fingernails digging into the sill, feeling flakes of old metal — was the window rusting? With a gasp, he grabbed the sheets and fell a body's length before he tightened his grip. He grazed his knuckles on the stone, which reassured him. He lowered himself, hand over hand, curling his soles around material already stiff with cold, feeling the wind at his back. He hoped it was a Polish wind.

The wind hauled at the sheets, making Czeslaw swing out from the wall. Returning, he hit the stone. He flattened his back, slowed and slid down the twisting rope, revolving in the black wind, his face going round and round. Two faces in the black wind.

Ripping sounded above him. He dropped half a body's length and kicked out, desperate for a toe-hold. He felt himself falling before he actually fell. The wind was cold against his temple. The ground was coming up to meet him. It would show him its harshest face. He twisted and landed on his back. Rocky teeth cut his shoulder blades, he jolted, flipped over, fell further through air then hit hard ground. He was flung onto his back again, still moving. He slammed into a tough bush, grabbed at the stunted trunk with both hands. His lungs felt flattened. All he could do was swallow at the air, like a fish.

A long howl sliced the night and he forced himself onto his knees. He breathed.

Lights flickered above him. The outline of the tower was misty against the night sky; a few smaller buildings huddled in grey smears beneath it, more leaning away into the slope, their square lit eyes watching him. He had missed the houses as he fell and landed on the mountainside.

He shivered. It was not as cold on the ground but he was going to be ill without warm clothes or shelter. And he didn't know what poison was in his system. He tried to stand, was too weak, and resorted to a half-scrabble, half-crouch. Rocks clattered nearby; he thought he heard breathing – panting – an animal sound. If he could find a cave or a hollow, he might stay there until first light. Hopefully they wouldn't realise he was gone until after dawn.

His fingers touched threads of silk. For some reason he thought of the picnic basket at the base of the mountain. He was visualising thimbles and rose petals when his hand felt cold flesh.

He saw the red hair, the reflection of the moon in dead eyes. The body of an unknown man. There was a pair of driving goggles wrapped around the man's wrist and nothing below the knees. The wolves or dogs had been at him, were probably nearby.

He sent up a prayer for the stranger and turned to go. Far above, a shout, and a rushing sound. He ducked, hands over his head. He thought a wolf was jumping at him.

A weight hit the ground nearby. Chips of rock cut his cheek, grit blinded him. He cleared his eyes, listened. The weight was not moving. Was it rubbish? Was this the village rubbish tip?

He slid gingerly over to the dark shape on the ground. He knew what he would find even before he turned the body over, before the moon caught the white in the old eyes, before he felt the wooden cross on the long metal chain. He knew even before the voices sounded nearby.

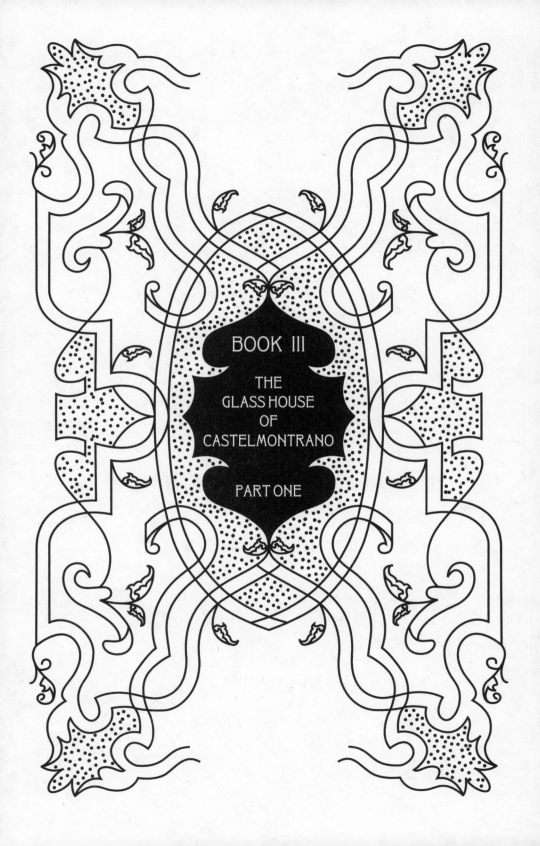

BOOK III

THE
GLASS HOUSE
OF
CASTELMONTRANO

PART ONE

SICILY, TEN MONTHS EARLIER

FRIDAY

I stand as close as I can to the edge of the cliff and look at the rapidly thinning line of light on the horizon. Swelling purple clouds fill the sky. Lightning pitch-forks into the black sea, funnels of black air revolve along the edge of the world. Black crows are stationary above me, battering the wind. Far out, towards Tunisia, the white crests of waves turn over like scrolls; a tanker is rolling, a whale at rest under the purple clouds. The rain comes down in flat sheets; the wind plucks my hair – my new blonde hair – and I close my eyes and lift my face to the hard cold needles.

A gust of wind tugs my skirt. Beside me, the man who calls himself Devlin curses. He stretches out a hand, drops it.

'Would you goddamn come away from the edge?' he says, pulling at the collar of his leather jacket. His hands are shaking, not with cold.

'Like this?' I say, stepping closer to the sea. He stares at me, not meeting my eyes. The blood ebbs under his tan.

'You agreed,' he shouts.

'What about this?' I say, stepping closer to the edge.

'I don't have time for your bullshit. We've only got two weeks.'

'Your schedule.' I turn my back on him.

'I'm not saving you,' he says. 'I'm not.'

I tilt my head, opening my mouth to let the black air in.

125

'It's a trick,' he shouts. 'You won't get your passport.'

A dull bang, and another. He is by the Mercedes, trying to open the driver's side door, but the wind snatches it out of his hands. It is slamming and reopening. He heaves the door back and slams it shut so brutally the car rocks.

He looks at me. There is maybe three coffins' lengths between us. 'Do it!' he shouts. 'I dare you.' He waits, hauls the door open and climbs inside. He bends over the wheel, opens his briefcase. There is a flash of silver at his lips.

I am alone but I know, now that I can't watch him, he is watching me. I raise my arms to the sky, enfolding the swollen clouds. The metal on my wrist flashes.

I shout, 'Rise up, you black mottled sea. Rise up, you roiling boiling waters. Rise up from your labyrinth of canyons and caverns. Rise up past the splintered mast.'

I am encircled by the malevolent metal band around my left wrist and the wind which grasps my ankles, jabs between my fingers, under my nails. Rain flattens my eyelashes, pricks my tongue, runs down my throat. The grassless ground beneath me turns to mud. Below the cliff edge, the roiling water swallows the jagged rocks, an endless mouth shifting and swallowing.

'Rise up,' I shout to the black sea. 'Rise up under the bloody sun. Play with your dice of bones. Play with the broken crockery on your shore. Roll out your deep black flint-backed bolts.'

My soaked skirt is heavy, weighing me down. But still a fierce gust sends me backwards, skidding on the slicked earth. I almost fall; the wind reverses direction, catches me across my spine. I am pushed forward, cold rings my neck. I raise my hands higher, see water drops flying from the silver bracelet. Beneath it, the bandage around my wrist is sodden and cold.

'Roar with your mouth as big as the ocean,' I shout. I am almost at the cliff edge. The wind hits the ground like a hammer. The white scrolls turn over and over, the black clouds wreathe my shoulders. There is black fog in my mouth. I can breathe clearly for the first time in months. I stretch my arms to the black mist. It looks solid enough to walk on. I think to myself, Why not?

I lean back into the wind, supported by it. The wind tugs at the bracelet on my wrist, trying to drag it off. Impossible, I think. I've tried.

Another dull bang. I smell salt, feel splinters of ice and rock; dirt hits my cheek. I take one last breath. I put out my left wrist. My stigma, my shame. A circle of pure anger.

'Rise up,' I shout, 'and swallow everything I have known.'

I step out onto the black air. For one magnificent second, I am flying. My heart is empty. The relief of not having to remember is enormous, pure euphoria. Better than every drug. This is what I have been searching for, I think. For three years.

Then – I am earth-heavy again. Maybe the silver shackle around my wrist won't let me go. Maybe it is the weight of my soul returning. Those twenty-one grams that should vanish from the body at the point of death. I fall through the black air. In a sour irony, the silver circle around my wrist is illuminated like a halo.

A hand grabs me by the throat, the other grips my arm. I am lifted and thrown, landing on my back, my skirt a lily pad around me. Devlin above me, his hand still at my throat. He puts one knee on my shoulder, grips my throat with both hands. I can barely see him through the rain. The set lines of his face are smudged, trembling. He could be crying but I know he is not.

He says, 'Look at what you've done to yourself.'

I put my hand on his hand, so that the bracelet on my wrist cuts into him. A green shadow seeps from the bracelet's inner rim. It turns the wet bandage green, it tints the grey air. I pull his hand into my throat. 'Do it,' I whisper. He can barely hear me but his grasp tightens. He knows what I am saying.

Banging sounds behind us. The car door slamming and bouncing. He turns his head. The rain lessens and I see his thin straight nose, the heavy jaw, the raindrops caught in the precisely cut sideburns, the thick cropped dark hair flecked with grey. Then he pushes back and stands.

'You've really hit rock bottom,' he says.

The rain is bending my lashes into my eyes. I see him through black lines across my vision. 'Oh,' I say, 'I think I can fall further if I try.'

He says, 'Your father was a criminal' and what sounds like, 'and so are you', but the words dissolve in the wind as he turns away.

I sit up. The metal bracelet slides down. It always looks like it is going to slide off. But every time, it catches on the bandage, on the top of my thumb-bone. I hold it against me, feel the tiny pulse inside the green illuminated panel.

My dead hair hangs like seaweed over my shoulders. He is walking away. I wonder what meeting him would have been like without the disguises. The double acts.

'I want to renegotiate,' I shout after him.

He goes to the rear of the car.

I scream, 'I don't want to know anymore.'

He hasn't heard me. He is taking something out of the boot. It is my small suitcase, the one with my books. My art books, my poetry books. My diary. He goes past me, to the edge of the cliff. I see webbed fingers of black mist wrap around the polished wood handle, stroke the gold monogram.

'Get in the car,' he says. 'Or . . . '

He dangles the case over the edge. It swings through the black mist leaving a vapour trail. He is black in the rain. I can't see the expression on his face.

'Make yourself presentable,' he says. He opens his hand, lets the suitcase slide an inch down his fingers.

I get up, unsteadily. He is watching my feet, waiting for me to move. But there is too much distance between us. Too much ground to cover.

'I'll go over the edge,' I shout. 'To spite you.'

'You're confusing me with someone who gives a shit.'

He opens his hand. The suitcase slides down to the tips of his fingers. He sways. The case arcs, back and forth, back and forth, higher and higher, wilder and wilder. His hand is shaking, his arm is growing tired.

I shout, 'You can't do the job without me.'

'And you'll do jail without me.' He opens his hand and throws up his arm and lets the suitcase go. I scream his name. His real name. The case rises in the air, parting the rain. It contains everything I have. It rises and rises, turning in slow motion, seems to hover for a moment in the air. A strange drowned kite. I can't see it, rain fills my eyes. The suitcase falls, turning in the mist, descending into the sea.

The suitcase is almost past Devlin when he reaches out, hooks his fingers through the handle, catches it and holds it above his head. He stands there, looking and not looking at me, the way he does.

'It's mine,' I scream.

He throws the bag at me with both hands. I duck and the case lands beside me.

'Go then,' he says. 'I dare you. It'll be a relief.'

He gets into the car, slams the door.

I grab the suitcase, hold it to me, look around.

The clearing we are parked in narrows to jagged hillocks of dark treeless earth. I think: Childe Rolande to the dark tower came. The wind is trumpets in my ears. Black knights are among the rocks; the lacing of light is the chain mail on their chests. I know they are only shadows, only tendrils of mist, but I want them to be magnificent harbingers of doom.

It would make the whole thing a little less sordid.

The rain has soaked through my coat. With a feeling of inevitability, I open the case. It is as I thought. My diary is gone. It is a punishment. There is only one person he's more furious at than me. Himself.

When I open the car door, he gets out without a word and stands under the umbrella while I change.

When I have finished, he gets back in. He looks at his watch – he doesn't look at me – and starts the engine. There is a taint of Scotch in the air.

The windscreen wipers struggle against the falling torrents, the heater blast is a miniature thermal wind. I bend my head to dry my long blonde hair, watching the dead strands rise in fine silver lines. I hold my hand in front of the vent, warming the wet bandage around my wrist. The green panel fogs.

'Oh for fuck's sake,' says Devlin. He reaches across me to open the glove box. His thick hair has been made completely black by the rain. It is close enough to touch. But I don't.

He sits back with the first-aid kit. 'Take the bandage off.'

'It's fine.'

'You've got five seconds,' he says, 'then I'll handcuff you and do it myself.'

We look at the burns smeared scarlet around my wrist, the cross-hatching of red lines made by the knife. He takes out a new bandage. 'You need to keep away from water.'

'That'll be hard,' I say.

We move through the rain. On my left, the cliff drops into nothingness. I imagine all of Sicily un-tethered from the earth's crust, sailing like a galleon through the black mist. The first Arab sailors landing here, struggling ashore, their ship more likely than not broken on the rocky teeth, watching the cold rain hit their brown skin in shattered blots, smelling the water: acrid, malevolent. Sulfurous.

We enter the tunnel. The engine mutes in the hollow; the sound of sea and rain is cut. Devlin switches on the headlights. The weight of the cliffs presses overhead. There are tiles on the tunnel walls, an exhausted cream crossed with black veins and shiny triangles of reflected water. Midway, a stone vase is bolted to the wall, a bunch of dried flowers inside; a fresh bunch is propped against the lower tiles. The car goes on. I hear his breathing.

I turn to him. I see the tight muscles at the corner of his mouth, the lines at the corner of his eye. The scar on his temple is raised in the light. He looks grim, haggard, worried. Not worried about me, worried because of me.

I say his name. His real name. His eyelids flicker but he won't turn his head.

I say, 'John – '

'You're not my only case,' he says. 'We're all on the clock here.'

A circle of light appears, the size of the bracelet on my wrist. If my wrist wasn't in it.

'This is all about time,' he says. 'Remember that, will you?'

I wonder what would happen if I reached out and put my hand on the shadows circling the base of his neck.

'And for God's sake,' he says, 'don't tell them you were in Venice celebrating your father's death.'

The storm seems worse on the other side of the tunnel. Whirled spouts of water rise high above us before dumping broken seaweed and crushed shells and fistfuls of gritty dark brown sand. I think hail is hammering the roof until I see hard black pebbles bouncing on the bonnet.

A huge rock the size of a mule smashes down. Chunks hit the windscreen, leaving spider-webs of cracks in the glass, more chunks breaking up on the road or cart-wheeling over the edge of the cliff. Devlin hauls at the wheel to avoid the biggest piece. We hit a water plane and skid sickeningly. As the car jerks to a stop and the engine dies, he flings out his right arm to pin me to my seat. I put my hand over his hand, feel the broad wrist, the long fingers. He is still for a moment, shocked maybe, and I find his pulse, press in. He twists his hand away.

'This bloody country,' he says.

He starts the car.

'I'd like to emphasise,' he barely opens his mouth, each syllable as compressed as stone, 'that I didn't mean – ' he almost shudders at what he is about to say – 'on the cliff. I do care about . . . '

Even for the sake of his work he can't bring himself to say 'you'.

He says, 'I do care about the job.' The Scotch taint is replaced by sharp mint. The same mouthwash my mother used, by the smell of it.

'If you care about the job,' I say, 'why can't I have a few days off?'

'You had a few days off,' he says. 'In Venice.'

He slows down to avoid a large white boulder lying in the middle of the road. The fog on the window softens the edges; it looks like someone in cream robes, kneeling in the road, praying to Mecca.

'This is our only window of opportunity,' he says in the voice carefully bleached of all emotion that he uses whenever he tries to reason with me. 'Pietr is putting his affairs in order. He's relocating – South America. Venezuela. You know the Americans have no extradition deals there. You agreed to do this now.'

I raise my wrist, jangle the tracking bracelet viciously.

He won't look at me. 'That wasn't my idea.'

'Why then?'

'If I told you it was as much to keep an eye on me as you . . . '

I cover the bracelet; the green light hums warmth beneath my fingers. Sending out its little calculations, its little messages. 'You can take it off.'

'You made the deal,' he says. 'It's this or jail for being your father's accessory.'

I turn my head to the glass. The cliffs tremble past in dark blurry shapes.

He says, and maybe his tone is softer, 'I thought you wanted to find out – '

'Don't say it.'

' – what happened to your brother.'

Everyone is so sad now, I think to myself as I draw twisted figures of eight on the fogged window. The cliffs move past in a dark parade. The windscreen wipers beat their faltering rhythm, straining under the heavier falls of water.

When the waves come up the cliff, we move through light dampened to an aquamarine glow. I am immensely relaxed, the way I am when I see a fine piece of art or read a poem from the soul. I feel as safe and secure as when I was a child. I am reminded of the games I played with my brother, draping old blankets over the sofa and chairs in the living room to make intricate tunnels and little rooms; our own tiny kingdom. There was one blanket we liked the best: an old green one. It had holes in it, enough to let the light in, enough to let us look out. Spy on everyone outside.

Everyone is so sad now. Where did I say that? The green curtain falls over the car and I remember. I remember saying it to my father at my brother's funeral, the funeral with the empty coffin.

I slump, exhausted. 'The cliffs are black glass. Imagine living in a land which constantly reflected black images of you.'

'Lava,' he says. 'Sicily is a volcanic land. There used to be more volcanoes, not just Etna.' He presses his lips together.

'Go on.'

He stares ahead. 'I'm not a tour guide.'

'You say that in exactly the same tone that women say, I'm not a secretary.'

'I rest my case.'

'I am interested, Dev,' I say, as meekly as I can.

'Stop talking to me as though you know me.'

I shouldn't let his disdain get to me — it is what I deserve after all — and I say to myself that I don't care what he thinks. But I can't help myself. I can't not say anything.

'I'm as interested now as I was the night we met,' I say slowly.

His face contorts then settles into its usual impassive lines and planes; his Embassy face. But I bet there's another face under there. Another face revolving in the black wind. I can always tell.

'Nothing happened that night,' he says. The emotion has gone again from his voice; he's forced out any tell-tale inflections. 'You don't know me.'

'No biblical knowings allowed in your schedule.'

His foot comes down hard on the accelerator. The car leaps forward. He can't remember, that's his problem. The only thing he can remember is how furious he is with me. All those timetables that he clings to, all those hi-tech gadgets in his briefcase — everything derailed by one too many Scotches.

I look over my shoulder at the briefcase — the new one — on the back seat. I wonder if he knows I picked the lock of his old briefcase the first time I met him. I think so. I never saw that case again. The one he has now is bigger, made of some light steel, with an electronic pad instead of locks. Fingerprint identification. I bet my diary is in there.

'Can you please check the map,' he says in that clipped monotone. He thinks I won't be able to rile him if he stamps everything down. But I am convinced I know what subjects get under his skin. Misguidedly convinced, as it will turn out.

'You know, we are alike,' I say. 'You have your maps, I have my poetry.'

He shakes his head.

'You don't like poetry,' I say, 'because it seems useless to you. But it is a magnificent uselessness. People die every day for the lack of it.'

'I don't like poetry,' he says, wiping hard at the misted windscreen, 'because it stirs up emotions. In feeble-minded people who should just get on with the job and stop thinking about their feelings all the time.'

'You mean me,' I say. 'The famous Miss K.'

'The infamous Miss K,' he says. 'It's not so attractive when you get older, the stories.'

I try to laugh but this is one of those times when the land disappears from under me and I have to scramble to get back.

I unfold the map, trace the red line of road. This section of the coast is sparsely populated, nothing but the inverted black Vs of the mountains running down to the sea, a village or small town here and there. 'Trepani,' I read out. 'Partanna. Santa Margherita. Great names.'

He grunts. 'Mafia villages. The satellite photos are on the back.'

The other side is covered with blue-grey images. I recognise a farm building and the jagged shadows of a dried-out river. These are aerial shots, taken far above. Up near the moon maybe.

The country in the map is draped with a fine black lattice which clings even to the steep cliffs along the coast road. The land is divided into grey squares; a small number lurks in the right-hand corner of each.

'These numbers look like scavengers,' I say. 'Alien invaders.'

He blows out air, exasperated. 'Work your way back from 37N 15E. There are no signs in this bloody place.'

'I know we passed a statue of Saint Agrippina a few kilometres back.' He looks blank.

'Near the first rock fall,' I say helpfully. I don't bother to say, Near the ruins of the Saracen temple, near the first real reminder that we are in Arabic territory. My father's old route.

I find the temple on the map: a hatch of pale bones. Even Agrippina's statue shows as a pale dome and an upraised arm. I trace my way forward, through what must be the tunnel; the road disappears for a while under the mountain's shroud.

I reach a black circle marking a road running sharply to the right, up the side of a hill. There is a house on the top, and the dark oval of a driveway. But the house is surrounded by what looks like flat panes of water, a ghostly shield where the building's inner walls, pale and distorted, seem to show through. They are smudged, like Devlin's face in the rain.

He takes a quick look at the map. 'Probably a misprint. These things are never as accurate as you want them to be.'

I stare at the fine squares, the land reduced to its essentials. I see Agrippina's pleading hand. The grey tree tops tremble in my lap as the car slides on the wet road. The map seems very accurate to me.

We go on. Twice we have to swerve sharply as boulders hit the road. The next time, a rock lands on the roof and makes a bulge in the metal over the back seat.

I touch the distortion. The vinyl has stretched but held.

'They'll need to fish-oil that quick smart,' I say, 'to keep the rust out.'

'Like you know anything about cars,' says Devlin. 'The party princess.'

'My brother loved cars. I helped him fix up his first one.' I have a sharp image of blue sky and jacaranda. My brother wiping his hands on an oily rag and saying, 'It's a long way to the shop if you want a sausage roll.'

I smell wattle and gum leaves. 'Aren't you ever homesick?' I say to Devlin.

He says, 'Don't even think of trying that one on me.'

The rain comes down, harder. The windscreen wipers are barely clearing the water when he says, 'There.'

The side road looks as though it rises almost vertically. But it is paved with large heavy stones wedged into the earth, enough surface for the tyres to grip. There are thick stone columns on either side; on top of each is a wolf's head, cast in steel. In the glowering light, the rain running down the twisted grey metal looks like tears.

The car climbs the steep hill, the motor whining. We lean forward in our seats to stay upright, feel the weight pulling at us, in our lower backs, in our stomachs, the pressure wanting us to slide back into the sea. The bracelet is heavy on my wrist. I wonder how high we will go. I wonder if the light on the bracelet will change.

Balls of mist roll slowly past the windows. The land is black wet scrub: stubby bushes cling to small pockets of soil between the scattered rocks. I wipe a circle in the smudged window and look into the side mirror. Behind us, the drifting sheets of rain have settled into steady, falling walls. There is no sign of the horizon, just a glimpse of clouds swelling like sails out of the sea. The road disappears into them.

The slope seems to ease; statues appear on either side: more wolves, a boar with long curving tusks, a bear on its hind legs, clawing up out of the grey mist. A garland of mist as thick as fairy floss is wrapped around its throat.

'Do they have bears here?'

'Probably some homage to the local Mafia leader,' Devlin says as the car crawls on.

Here are statues of women, saints presumably, bowed heads under lovingly carved cowls, their clasped hands protruding from the carefully draped robes. Their eyes are downcast, their faces long-suffering. Passive. Resigned. Ineffectuality as survival.

I have an image of black shawls, hidden faces. Imagine never feeling the sun on your head. I feel a moment's pity for them: living in this backwater, far from the world, cut off from all events.

I stare at the panel at the top of Devlin's map: a miniaturised outline of Sicily, set between Europe and Africa. There is barely a square's width between Sicily and Tunisia, just under three to where Iraq sits, an innocuous patch to the right.

I think of my father's business. For business, Sicily was the most strategic point in the world to him. And to Pietr's grandfather. Only Pietr's father escaped – what had they called it at the trial? 'A century of deliberately orchestrated looting and plundering.' Was there a better word than 'looting', something other than 'plundering', for what my father did? I didn't think so.

The road flattens; the land on my right falls away more gently. The strain on our lower backs is immediately relieved.

We are on a natural plateau. I rub at the window and see six broken columns reach from the ground like massive arms.

'Jesus,' says Devlin, but he is not looking at the ruins.

A mule comes into view, its head bowed beneath the rain. The black sacking it wears has holes to allow the long ears through. The mule tows a painted wooden cart, the vivid blues and reds dulled by the rain. A man sits hunched on the front seat, wearing a black plastic sheet as a poncho. The raindrops hit the plastic, forming small rivers that run down the shiny surface. The mule steps carefully; the sound of its hooves reaches us.

We sit in the road. The idling exhaust blows past us, broken up by the rain. The cart comes on, the man doesn't raise his head.

'Jesus,' says Devlin again, reversing the car in a tight left-hand curve off the road, across a shallow waterlogged ditch and onto soft ground which sucks at the tyres.

The cart goes past. The hooves fade into the distance.

The six columns shiver in the rain-soaked rear window. They are set into a raised stone floor around a huge statue, pale against the dark land. A stone face with almond eyes and a square beard looks at me, the cracks in the white marble show as veins on the white eyeballs. Rain runs down his face to his massive shoulders and planes off the arms bent along his legs, rain drips from the palms cupping the giant knees. In front of him is more white marble:

a heavy square block with a twisted crown of snakes – or are they thorns? – carved on the front. It must be shadows made by the rain which stain the tabletop.

I stop rubbing the window.

'What is it?' says Devlin.

'A ruined temple. A sacrifice table.'

'Really? Well, you're the expert.' He doesn't sound convinced.

'I was good at what I did.'

He is silent.

'I could have been good,' I say. 'If they'd let me.'

I wind down the window. New gravel encircles the temple; three shallow steps lead up to the dais and the table.

When I open the door, Devlin reaches across and yanks it shut. I push at it. He grabs my hand with his right hand and punches down the lock with his left.

'Do you have to see every goddamn thing?' he says. 'Do you have to touch it?'

He is leaning across me. I look up at him. His face changes.

This is the first time he has touched me directly since the night we met. Time enough for me to wonder if my information had been incorrect. Time enough to become irrevocably trapped in that inner circle of rage.

Even when he was arresting me the next morning, he was careful never to make contact with my skin; he snapped the handcuffs around my wrist with only his fingers on the metal, cuffing my hands in front. He held the chain between the cuffs as he led me out of the palazzo to the motorboat. At the time I thought it was to humiliate me, to show me off – the prize – in front of the paparazzi huddled along the Branintini Bridge. The Bridge of Sighs. Later he told me it was to get the front pages, to make the story plausible for Pietr.

Now I think there was another reason. I am so sure of it that I raise my free hand and place my thumb in the cleft of his lip. He lets go of the lock, grabs my hand as though to knock it away and – he doesn't move. Rain slices in through the open window, there is mist in the car, the grey light from outside clouds his eyes, rain hits my cheek. He holds my hand, not painfully, not like a jailer. I sway towards him, I can't believe it, after what he did to me, he can't believe it, he can do nothing but wait, not trusting me. I don't trust him either but I want him so badly I am turning to water.

His phone rings. He lets go, stares at the incoming number.

'Shit,' he says. 'Mitch.'

He takes three deep breaths and answers the call.

Even with the plastic tight against his ear, I sense the dark energy seeping out. I wind up the window. As the smeared glass rises, I see silhouettes in the low swollen grey clouds. They match the faint, malevolent echoes from the phone. I see rabid sky dogs, howling.

Devlin says, 'We're on track. Half an hour. Maybe less.' Without blinking, his eyes travel down my body. There is nothing sexual about it; maybe he is looking for weapons. He looks at me the way a vivisectionist examines the body on the slab. It happens every time he talks to Mitch.

'She said she was going to cut it but she dyed it blonde,' he says now. 'Yeah, as slutty as hers. Pietr is expecting a delicate grieving Audrey Hepburn lookalike and now he's getting – yeah, damaged goods.' He stares at me, unblinking. 'Yes, it is still on. Yes, Mitch, the panel is green. Well, the tech-heads must be screwing up at your end.' He lifts the receiver slightly away from his ear. More dogs howling. 'Yes, I've still got her passport.'

He listens then he shifts his gaze, staring out through the windscreen. He puts one hand to the glass as though to push it away and says, 'I don't think we can do that, Mitch.'

He drops his hand. 'Let me check my diary.' He covers the receiver and counts silently. 'That should be all right. I'll call you from Trepani. But you tell Accounts that the October expenses go in on the first of November. So they should get off their arses and input it.' He puts the phone away.

He looks at his watch and takes out his small notebook. He says, writing, 'If you can't get your act together, Mitch is coming down.'

I turn to stare, obviously, over his arm. He stiffens but keeps writing. The day's hours are listed down the left-hand side of the page; all the ones until now are crossed off. He has an odd way of crossing out: a broad horizontal stroke through the word then a quick nearly vertical slash. It marks the page with little crucifixes. I see *3 pm – Arrival. House.* He has crossed out the *3 pm* and written *3.30 pm.*

'You write like a soldier,' I say, trying to see what comes next. I hear his quick, furious intake of breath. He hates that I deliver these accurate judgements about him. It makes a mockery of his own files.

He puts his thumb over the writing below.

'Four o'clock appointment,' I say. 'Torture cheeky girls.'

'You think I'm bad,' he says. 'Mitch is a thousand times worse.' He closes the notebook.

'You're as bad as each other,' I say, without thinking.

Either he has taken another sharp breath or he has actually winced. He pushes his mouth into a smile and turns the key. 'Thanks,' he says, letting out the handbrake.

I want to say: I didn't mean it.

Instead I say as the car rolls forward, 'Buckle up.'

Ribbons of mist stream across the wet brown ground, the scrubby bushes, the black fingers of trees. But nothing is as thick as the strange mist which rings Pietr's house. 'It's too regular.' I touch the cluster of broken squares which spill down from the hill opposite and read the name beside the fragments. Santa Margherita. 'So Pietr sits in his house and looks straight across to this Santa Margherita. Through his own personal hedge of mist.'

'I told you,' says Devlin, 'it's a misprint.'

A gust of wind hits the car and a last fierce spatter of rain. I turn slowly in my seat. Devlin is staring at the road but I know he is watching me out of the corner of his eye, like the hunting scenes on the Assyrian stone tablets I saw in my father's warehouse. The scenes where the hounds are bringing down the desert leopard. But is it the leopard which looks back over its shoulder, the gleam of white in its eye, or is it the hounds?

The heating seems almost quiet now. Even though we are on nearly level ground, he has made no attempt to increase the speed.

I look at him. I see the ridge at the corner of his mouth, the older man ridge, the over-forty ridge, the ridge I see coming in my own face, the moment when the smooth planes begin to fall inwards, the shadows that don't leave even after a good night's sleep. The point of no return. Where years passing become years remaining.

I see the beginning of drinker's veins around his nose, the grey flecks in his sideburns, the dark stubble on his chin. All those schedules and watches and notebooks can't stop the inevitable. I think, We're in the same boat, Devlin. A huge longing swells through me. At first I think it is the old addiction: the lump in my throat, the dark hole growing out from under my heart into my stomach, my lungs, the itch under the skin you can never quite scratch, the constant barking of the black dogs in the sky, the whole world turning to black water. I have immense longing for the instant fix, desperation for the sweet rush of what I always thought was pleasure but which I learned – eventually – was infinite layers of something far more mundane. Or maybe something irreplaceable.

I lean in. My lips part. I lean further, closer. I almost feel the rough tips of the growing-in beard along his jaw when he says, his mouth barely moving, 'Don't.'

I say as soothingly as I can, 'I was just – '

'Don't.'

I sit back. 'Don't flatter yourself. I was trying to get my diary.'

He puts his foot down. The car surges forward. 'Exactly,' he says.

The road passes between two tall stone columns and the start of a stone wall which wraps around the peak. Full-size metal sculptures of wolves spring off the columns, their iron hind legs melded to the top.

The car rolls onto a paved oval dotted with black Mercedes cars. Ahead is an archway between long concrete boxes with clear views down the mountain and road. The flat buildings look like garages or storage places or –

'Guardhouses,' says Devlin.

A man stands in the archway; he waves at us.

'Trusting,' I say.

'They've probably been watching us all along the coast,' says Devlin.

As we creep through, Devlin winds down his window and says, 'Signor Devlin and Signorina – '

But the man does not want to hear. He puts up doughy hands and waves us on.

We drive through and stop before the shallow steps which rise through three stone terraces to the house on the summit. The sky presses down. Behind and below us, the sea chews at the rocky shore. Around us, the mountain falls sharply away. The paved courtyard ends in thin air, as though we are sitting in clouds.

The house. In the low light, the structure appears wrapped in gauze threaded with bars of silver. The rain slides down and catches colours reflected from far away, so the house seems to be moving slightly. Steel beams gleam through the gauze like the ribs of the cargo plane that brought me to the deserted airfield outside Palermo.

The wind buffets the car, the house sways over us.

'Jesus Christ,' says Devlin. 'It's made of glass.'

Steps rise through a terrace of manicured lawn, the hedges dark black now in the rain. The next terrace has a tennis court on one side, wrought-iron benches and tables on the other, with concrete cylinders where the summer umbrellas would be inserted.

Beyond are the steps to the last terrace: a massive block of white concrete – or is it marble? – on which sits the house.

I wind down my window.

The house is barely a structure to be recognised: a flying galleon made of beaten silver, grey metal and glass. There are windows and partitions and glass spines and soaring roofs at odd angles and even – I blink – some kind of tower.

The front left of the house begins as a conventional glass box defined by large glass windows set in steel frames, the whole cleanly and geometrically divided. But then the lines distorted, recklessly, crazily, with a supreme confidence I had only ever seen in the most headstrong art. I think, This is a house meant never to be sold.

Midway, the glass panels jut out at increasingly severe angles to become a series of huge parallel shelves slanting over like spines on some mystical animal's back. Gradually, the spines folded over to make the beginning of the right-hand section of the house: a giant two-storeys-high extension curved like a snail's shell and moulded in textured silver metal. The shell reflects the clouds, so that now, under the sullen sky, the whole section is a deep grey.

'Beaten titanium,' I say. 'They must have brought it in by helicopter.'

Devlin says, 'It's preposterous.'

I get out of the car, unaware of the cold.

'It's Frank Gehry,' I say. 'Or one of his disciples.'

I study the second floor. On the far left, the glass box is covered with a steel lattice: a purer, whiter steel than the silver which gathered across the front of the building until it met the tip of the silver shell on the right. There is a sense of sturdy white walls behind the lattice, of rooms which must look away from the sea, over the plain to Santa Margherita.

Caught between the silver lattice at its sharpest and the silver shell at its highest is a hexagonal glass tower, delicate and insubstantial until you saw the steel posts behind the broad panes. Its pointed roof is unexpectedly tiled black like a Bavarian castle's. A black steel staircase curved around the tower to meet a small walkway which ran along the back of the house. In the centre of the walkway is a flag, the material whipping back and forth in the wind.

Devlin gets out of the car. 'Polish flag. I pity the fool who has to go up there and change it.'

'What makes you think he wants to change it?'

Devlin grunts. 'Where's the bloody front door?'

I laugh. 'Between the glass spines?' I point at the broad white marble terrace which runs around the house. 'Maybe a door at the side?'

'Handy to have,' says Devlin, staring up at the walkway. 'Shoot your enemies as they flail around trying to get in.'

'It's aesthetic, Devlin. It's art. Beautiful things don't always have to have a function.'

'Like your precious poetry. No purpose.'

'Poetry's different. Poetry's a way of talking.' The silver shell changes colour again, pulsing whiteness, as the dark clouds part briefly and the sky lightens. 'Besides, I think there is a purpose to this.'

Devlin takes out his briefcase, slams the door and stands, staring up at the house.

I wonder whether he wants to open the case, to have a drink. I should know him well enough. But I have an uneasy feeling that I don't. Files don't constitute a person. Ashes from a photo can't resurrect the subject; water is the only substance that regenerates itself after use. I had thought the way he drank that night we met was due to me, to the tenseness of the situation, to the intolerable layers of disguise we were both floundering through. I wonder if the sight of me now makes him want a drink. I don't think so. Or, not me alone. He is almost convinced of who I am, of how I can be categorised and filed. He is – he was – confident enough not to care what I think if I catch him drinking. But he also doesn't want to be seen to be doing anything compromising. Anything recorded.

He looks at my hair. An expression almost of pain crosses his face.

'Go on,' I say. 'Have that drink. I won't tell.'

'Charming,' he says, but his hands tighten on the case.

'Can I get my diary back?'

'No.'

'Well, then.'

'Well, what?'

'Well then, you brought it on yourself.'

'Oh, for God's sake.' He's fumbling at the lock, so furious that he forgets to key in the combination. He is trying to open it with thumbprint identification only. I should look away. My watching makes it worse. But this wave of anger fascinates me – this heat that flares up from nowhere. It's so at odds with how he likes to see himself. Calculating. Cold. Unemotional.

I know you better than you know yourself, Devlin. I am betting on it.

'How did your hair become my fault?' he says, hitting the identification pad.

'I told you what would happen if you kept taunting me about my brother.'

He finally remembers the combination, jabs at the keys and wrenches the briefcase open.

On top of the files is my diary.

He says, 'You'll get that when you start behaving.'

I make a grab for the diary. He's faster – I've barely moved when he seizes my wrist, forces it down, pins it on top of the pale cover. The metal bracelet cuts into my hand, casts a mossy shadow over the marbled cream cardboard.

His hand is tightening, definitely a jailer's this time. His eyes are black, shiny, unreachable. He is waiting for me to retreat but instead I press myself against him. As he feels the full length of my body – as he takes a quick breath but doesn't move – I say, 'That's what you did when we met.'

He lets go immediately.

'You never fight fair,' he says and slowly closes the briefcase.

'Oh, you don't know the half of it,' I say and pull off the long blonde wig.

He is stilled by shock. Loathing rises off him like miasma in a drowned graveyard.

I throw my head back. The wind is cool against my shaved scalp. I feel raindrops hitting the bare skin like small hard blows. Every blow is sharp and stinging, a welcome pain. The rain runs down my forehead, into my eyes, down my cheeks. I am so relieved to be free of it, all that dead hair. To be rid of at least one disguise.

'Every time you box me in, I hurt myself,' I say. The rain runs into my mouth, down my throat, through my veins. It cools the burns on my wrist.

'That's fucking ridiculous,' he shouts. 'Like what, that'll teach me?'

The rain is in my eyes. He is behind black bars again. 'No,' I shout. 'Because I enjoy it. Because you've made me enjoy it.'

I open the car door, throw the wig onto the back seat. Devlin hasn't moved. He is rendered beyond stillness with the inability to move.

I slam the door. '*I descended black impassive rivers*,' I say, '*I sensed haulers were no longer guiding me.* That's what I said when you arrested me, Dev. *Screaming Redskins had taken them for their targets . . . nailed nude to coloured stakes . . . barbaric trees.* It fits. Doesn't it fit, Dev?'

'Yes,' he says.

The front door opens. A stocky man I don't recognise, dressed in black, comes out and stands on the terrace, in the rain. After a moment of watching us carefully, he puts up a big black umbrella, like a raven putting up its wings.

Devlin hunches his shoulders. 'What will Pietr say when he sees you?'

'That's your problem,' I shout. 'I'm your spy, not your play-doll.'

He has the set, miserable look of a man who loathes every moment of what he is doing. I know that look. My brother had that look.

'Why don't you go?' I say. 'I'll tell them I made you go.'

He shakes his head. He can't think of me as an ally. It's beyond him. And he can't walk away. My brother couldn't either.

'You're more trapped than I am,' I say, but he can't hear me.

'What?' he shouts.

At the first terrace, I stop next to a stone lion grimacing in the rain, heavy water drops hanging like icicles from its gaping mouth and its sharp teeth. Black dirt crusts its face.

Devlin hasn't moved. I walk on. The next terrace is speckled with small branches and seashells. The storm must have been worse up here.

The man with the umbrella comes forward to meet me. Behind him is a high narrow silver door set between the two widest glass spines. As I cross the main terrace, I see the jagged cracks which radiate like massive spider-webs across the huge panels of glass.

Devlin is coming up slowly behind me. The car is already wreathed in mist, the guardhouses blurring in the grey air.

Later, when I stare at the white pages of my diary, the vast plains to be crossed before I can extract some truth from it all, that is one of my clearest images of Devlin. I suppose I like it because, at the time, it symbolised what was happening between us. Of course I was completely wrong, the way that I read that image of Devlin coming up to me, walking away from the mist. But then I was wrong from the start, about Devlin.

As the stocky man holds the front door open for me, I say, 'Hello, how are you?'

He glances around to see who I am talking to, then grins.

'He doesn't understand you,' Devlin says in intense irritation.

'Give me a shove along,' I say. 'You're dying to.'

A tide of red goes up his throat. The man in black smirks.

'Yes, you,' I say to him. *'Buon giorno. Come sta?'*

He is tanned with thinning grey-white hair, no side teeth, laugh lines by his mouth. He is weather-fit, not weather-beaten, with the powerful shoulders and barrel chest of an ageing wrestler. He says in careful English, 'Very well, thank you. And how would yourself be?'

'Very well myself,' I say. 'And you're called – ?'

'Tarfuri, miss.'

'More of a madam,' mutters Devlin.

'Poor Mr Devlin has a hangover. Your first name?'

The man hesitates and says, 'Stefano, miss.'

'It's a pleasure to meet you, Stefano.' I step into the marbled hall. 'Do we wait here?'

'Please. I will fetch sir.'

The door closes behind us. We are in a marbled hall, the walls covered in heavy white wallpaper, embossed with silver. There are three doors on each side and a polished wooden staircase which rises in a gentle curve to join the first floor landing.

Stefano walks around the base of the staircase and disappears.

Devlin says, 'Try not to be so obvious.'

'I bet you would have taken a photo with your super-secret tie-pin camera and scanned the world database to check his name.'

'So?'

'Sometimes it's easier to just ask.'

He makes a noise in his throat.

'Oh, come on, Devlin. As though you don't already have files on everyone in the house.'

'They're incomplete,' he says. 'That's what you're here for.'

He plants his feet on the white floor. His eyelashes flicker. He is counting the doors off the hall.

'Oh, Christ,' I say and go to the nearest door and open it. We look into a vast living room with thick rugs laid on the marble. Beyond are glimpses of a valley lying in a trough of clouds.

I close the door, open the next which gives on to the same room. I move towards the third.

'For God's sake,' says Devlin.

I say, 'Devlin, whatever gave you the idea that you could control me?'

He puts his briefcase down with a snap on the marble floor. When he straightens I see an edge in his face. Something he has thought of gives him confidence.

He says, 'You came, didn't you?'

I turn my back on him and see the glass table against the wall. On it sits a vase, old and delicate, coloured the deep ocean blue of lapis lazuli with fine gold around its rim. Chinese, fifth century. In the vase are huge dark purple roses, so dark as to be almost black. Above the roses is the painting.

It glows in the late afternoon light, sailing through the cloudy air like a mosaic. It is huge, covering the left hand wall between the last two doors. It is a map of the world dominated by a bulbous purple-coloured Europe. This world has *Heaven* and *Hell* inscribed in gold leaf at the top and bottom. Black ink drawings of dragons rear out of aquamarine waters and, on the right, in the sea between Sicily and Africa, is a fine-etched compass topped by a lion's head.

I catch my breath. 'Mappaemundi,' I say.

Devlin comes over. 'That's bloody inaccurate. What's the point of that?'

'You mean, apart from it being five centuries old, a record of religious and philosophical attitudes, and an example of exquisite workmanship? Maybe you'd be impressed to know that its value is probably beyond price.'

'No need to sneer.'

I laugh. 'Admit it, Dev. We're just two foreigners in a strange, strange land.'

We look at each other. His eyes travel down my face, my throat. I am sure I sense a swaying towards me.

His gaze flicks up. He avoids my eyes.

He says, 'At least I don't look like a freak.'

There is an eddying in the air across my cheek. 'Sir asks you wait here,' says Stefano from behind us, holding open the door to the living room.

Devlin looks furious. Neither of us had heard Stefano return.

I see Devlin eyeing the shadows spilling out from behind the staircase. There must be a door in the alcove there.

Stefano ushers us through and I gasp. This side of the house is built out from the mountain like the stilt homes in Los Angeles. The wind hits the side and I swear I feel the floor tremble. Devlin stamps his feet.

'Marble on concrete slab,' he says. 'I hope.'

I go past the long silk sofas, the huge mirror in the carved frame, past the heavy polished wooden side tables – more delicate vases, more black roses – to the wall of windows.

Beyond the marble terrace, the tip of the next mountain pokes through a layer of clouds as white and thick as stones in fire. I do not understand where the storm clouds have gone. This mountain is veiled in solid matter, a pale blanket with skeins of clouds lifting off it, like Anna's wool rug, the one she had in hospital. Tendrils of white and grey filaments stroke the terrace. More clouds stream past: animal shapes. Monster shapes. They make me remember lying on the grassy ledge overlooking the bay, counting off faces in the clouds – with my brother and Anna, my best friend, my alter ego.

But there, the clouds were far away.

Devlin comes to stand next to me. 'Wild nature,' he says, without enthusiasm.

'It's . . . ' I can't find the words. 'Where did the storm go?'

Devlin points up.

The dark clouds are drawn aside like curtains, allowing columns of light to fall through. But even as we watch, the clouds smash together, the light is eaten away. Diamond chips fall against the glass and, a moment later, the sound of hard blows. Rain.

'November,' says Devlin, grimacing.

He touches a long crack running from ceiling to floor.

'Pietr must own the glass shop,' he says, peering at the ceiling. 'All that money,' he continues. 'To do nothing but – '

'Defy the elements?' I stare at the roiling clouds. *'Après moi, le déluge.'*

Devlin runs his hand along the steel joints. His fingers come away wet.

'Reportedly spoken with a fatalistic shrug by King Louis XV,' I say. 'After me, the deluge.' I draw a circle on the wet glass, a curved line. A smiley face. 'I can understand that.'

'French,' says Devlin. He takes out his notebook, writes, and points at the huge mirror with its elaborately carved wood frame of roses and vines. 'Antique?'

I look at the signature fleur-de-lis hidden within the roses. 'Eighteenth century,' I say. 'Finest quality; a master craftsman. Smuggled out from France.'

'To a little house in Sicily,' says Devlin.

'Some people like to admire their treasures in private.'

'Gloat over them, you mean.'

As he writes, I say, 'And you call me obvious.'

Devlin says, 'It doesn't matter if they're suspicious of me.'

I look down at the vase beneath the mirror, a twin to the vase out in the lobby. These purple roses are nearly as black.

'No family happy snaps,' says Devlin.

'We never had photos in our house either, after my father got rich. What about you?'

'No.' He frowns. 'You'll know him, won't you? Even after all this time?'

'You don't forget Pietr.' I touch a purple petal. 'The last time I saw him was at Anna's funeral. He was under indictment too but they hadn't served him. He came to Sydney for a few hours.'

Devlin stares at the painting.

'My father was under house arrest,' I say. 'As you well know. And my mother was still locked down at Kalangi.'

He keeps staring at the painting. 'It was a blazingly beautiful day for Anna's funeral,' I say. 'Just a plane's exhaust leaving chalk smears across the perfect sheet of blue. I hated that. I wanted it to be rainy, overcast. Thunderous.'

I open the French doors. A cold breeze gusts past me, rocking the vases on the glass tables, slamming the door into the lobby.

The marble in the terrace floor is veined with blue. In parts the creamy white is touched by darker shadows. The bruises that tired breaths make in old ice. I see a form in the marble, the way that Michelangelo must have dreamed of men in ice, imagined himself in a vast and snowy landscape, tracing his path through the cracks. Cutting and shaving and sculpting to reveal the man within. I imagine a vastness only broken by hanging curtains of white, an exhausted tree struggling in the cold wind. The anticipation – or terror? – of raising my chisel. Not knowing whether I will open fissures or treasures.

'Can you see the man within?' I say to Devlin.

That gaunt look re-appears. I wonder whether I've misread his worry. Under-estimated his fear.

'For God's sake,' he says desperately.

I step outside. The curtain of rain cools my cropped skull. I remember my bare feet digging into the frigid marble of the vast bathroom, and the horrified look on the hairdresser's face in the mirror. She hadn't brought her razors and when I told her I wanted my long dark hair shaved off like the women who had slept with Nazis during the war, she had dropped the new blonde wig. A faint broken light came into her eyes, like the reflection of sunlight on far-off water. She had looked at the door, as though she knew Devlin was waiting outside. She refused to shave me, instead had used her finest scissors to cut my hair to the roots. After she left, and with Devlin banging on the door, I tried my own razor. But my hand was shaking with rage, and I nicked myself almost immediately. Now, when I put my hand on my head, I feel water drops trapped in the uneven prickly field.

'It's all right, Devlin,' I say now. 'I have a mind for winter.'

I walk carefully across the marble terrace to the iron railing.

Lightning forks behind the clouds. A crow – no, a raven they call them here – falls sideways, head down, plummeting past me. There is a smell of sea and dirt and dank crumbling bodies in the wind. The rain beats on my bare head.

To my left, the marble runs around the corner of the house to meet the front terrace. To my right, the wet terrace slides into a dark mirror. As my hands seize the railing, the wind buffets my skirt; clouds twine around my ankles. The ground cracks, I see slivers of ice. The wind encircles me and I almost slip despite holding the rail.

Devlin's words spiral into the grey air. He shouts from the doorway, 'My responsibility.'

'Your custody, Devlin.'

He flinches but stands his ground. 'They're just words – '

'I've seen how you use words, Devlin.'

He turns his back on me.

Hail falls and warmth flares. I touch the back of my head; my fingers come away flecked with blood. On the railing, I draw another face with the smile turned upside down. Almost before I finish adding the rosy cheeks, the lines smear into pink and slip over the side.

I shout, 'They're not just words to me.'

I pull myself along the railing, closer to the dark mirror. Water slaps against the concrete wall and the wind whines up the side of the house, whistling as it crosses the terrace. The Polish flag flaps wildly, the silver buckles hitting the rattling pole. Now I am closer to the end of the terrace I see ripples spilling over the edge.

I go on.

Drops of water rise from the surface; the lightning freezes them in mid-air. When the flashes stop, there is nothing but blackness curdling overhead. My hand is a blur; my skirt so wet that even the wind can't lift it anymore.

I am near the dark mirror. It is moving back and forth – I wonder whether the building is shaking but the railing feels firm enough. Chips of ice jab into my face. I smell sulfur.

'I know you,' I shout.

I wonder what I will find when I look down. Who will I see? Myself? Anna? My brother? Someone else?

Rain runs down my spine. I am the coldest I have been since I was told my brother was missing. There are odd spots of warmth in the chill encasing me. I imagine it is the blood from my cut scalp. I welcome it. I want more.

I go on.

Now I see what the dark mirror is. It is an infinity pool, built to extend past the building, so it seems to topple into nothingness. The blackness is the water, reflecting the dark clouds overhead. Without a barrier to stop it, the wind rakes the surface, plucking up small waves into white peaks, hurling fine white spray, creating water structures which hang for long moments twisting in the grey air. The hard waves rock back and forth, higher and higher, spilling over the edge. The sulfurous smell is chlorine.

I lean over the dark shadows in the waves. I take a deep breath. I must go on, I think. I lean further.

A shout behind me. Not Devlin's voice. A tall man with silver platinum hair walks, fast and sure-footed, to me. He catches my wrist just as the wind knocks me into the pool. I see myself hovering over the dark water, reflected endlessly in the reflections in the eyes of the figure in the dark water.

The man pulls me back, against him.

He says, 'Not today, my little Ophelia.'

I rest my cheek on his sleeve and look to the shock on Devlin's face. I sympathise with him. Nothing in the photos prepared you for the colour of Pietr's hair.

Pietr helps me inside and tells Stefano to bring tea and blankets. The room is warm; piped water under all the floors, says Pietr. He sits beside me, holds my hand in both of his in a peculiarly European gesture and looks down at me without blinking. He is immaculately dressed, in dark suit and silk tie.

'I was so sorry,' he says in precise English, 'about your loss.'

It takes me a moment to realise that he is talking about my father.

'Thank you,' I say in a rush to make up for my pause.

'You look very well,' he says, still holding my hand. He has the measured neutral tone of the internationally educated, of someone who is thinking carefully about his words but only because he can choose from four languages.

'Better rested than the reports indicated,' he says. There is the slight, heavier emphasis on the last letter that would always mark him as Central European.

I wait for a comment about my hair but his gaze doesn't waver.

'The last time I saw you,' I say, 'was Anna's funeral.'

For a moment there is a sheen like glass over his face.

'I don't think she wanted to go on,' I say. 'After my brother.'

'No.' He presses my hand and stands.

I say, 'This is John Devlin.'

Devlin comes across the room.

There is a notable silence before Pietr puts out his hand. 'From the Embassy?'

'My fame precedes me,' says Devlin, shaking hands briefly.

'Italy is small, signor.' Pietr looks down at me. 'We all saw the photographs of your arrest. Naturally, even though we were sure the authorities would not be stupid for very long . . . ' He stares at Devlin. 'We were a little concerned.' That clipping of the final letter, almost a "t" in the final "d", makes him sound angry; even "little" has an ominous ring, the "t"s turned to compressed explosions. 'We saw you in those photographs, Mr Devlin.'

'I had passport difficulties,' I say. 'Mr Devlin was kind enough to help me with them.'

'Yeah,' says Devlin. 'Don't shoot me. I'm only the babysitter.'

They stare at each other.

'Who should I shoot, Mr Devlin?' says Pietr. 'To treat a woman this way. And so soon after the death of her father. If you wish to punish someone for the father's sins, Mr Devlin, you should punish me. I was his partner.'

'All I was told,' says Devlin, raising a palm, 'was that an Italian citizen offered to vouch for her while her passport problems were sorted out. My job is to sit tight and wait further instructions.'

Pietr presses his lips together.

I say, 'Pietr, it's okay, really. It's some bureaucratic bungle. If you can put me up for a few days . . . '

As I touch his arm, the bracelet shows beneath my cuff. His eyes narrow, he is about to speak when I whisper 'No'. He raises an eyebrow, his glance flicking up and down Devlin.

The door to the terrace springs back. As Devlin closes it, a fine grey spray drops like a curtain over the terrace. Cold shivers in.

'The snow is coming,' says Pietr, going to the drinks table.

Devlin raps his knuckles on the glass. 'You've got bad cracking here.' He bends. 'And mould.'

'Stefano will replace the panes,' says Pietr without turning his head. 'My mother thinks this is a folly.' He smiles at me. 'Like those imitation Greek villas on top of Californian cliffs. Swiss chalets in Argentine jungle. Green squares cut into land the colour of vultures.'

I smile back at him. 'I'm sure Mr Devlin would like a drink.'

'You're charitable,' says Pietr under his breath. He raises the decanter to Devlin.

'No,' says Devlin.

A gust of wind hits the house and the windows rattle.

I sip my tea. 'There are – irregularities with my father's business. I'm about to be subpoenaed again. So Mr Devlin says.'

'My lawyers got one, too,' says Pietr. 'Even though your father is dead.' *Deadt.* The word reverberates across the marble. He says to Devlin, 'Your government doesn't seem to be accepting that I severed all business relations with Australia.'

'Really?' says Devlin.

The lights go off. Dark seeps into the room like a tide. Outside, the clouds are backlit by lightning; their constantly convulsing outlines sidle past the wet balcony.

'The generator should come on in a minute,' says Pietr.

'You're quite self-sufficient,' says Devlin, staying by the door.

'We have to be,' says Pietr. 'In heavy weather, we're completely cut off.'

He turns to me. 'Of course you can stay as long as you need. You were Anna's best friend. I'll never forget that.'

'Your mother?'

His hair is an aura in the gloom. 'She would welcome you too.'

The lights come on slowly, the bulbs seeming to grow into radiance. Devlin has a file in his hand. 'You'll want details – '

'No,' Pietr says, not looking at him. 'Leave the paperwork with Stefano.'

'I'm a criminal, Pietr,' I say.

'Don't say anything in front of . . . ' Devlin's name hangs in the air. Pietr sits and again holds my hand gently between his.

'There are things,' I whisper, 'I could have done . . . '

His thumb presses into my wrist so I feel his pulse beating against mine.

'You were your father's daughter so there was nothing you could say,' he tells me. 'It is impossible to speak out against a parent.'

I shudder against his arm. 'My brother.'

'I was your father's partner,' says Pietr. 'I chose my relationship with him. Just as Mr Devlin chose his job. You could not choose.' He touches my shoulder. 'You have to forgive yourself. Otherwise, every day your heart is a graveyard.'

There is the clink of glass. Devlin has a drink in his hand.

'Forgiveness.' I bite my lip.

As he puts his arm around me, Pietr says, casually, 'I don't think we need you, Mr Devlin.'

An hour later, I am in a sea of books. The rain is beating in all the corners of the day and I am swimming in books in Pietr's library in the glass tower. Books rise to the ceiling on three sides. The fourth wall is given over to a wide window which faces the sea. The mist drifts past in sheets. A small triangular buoy is rocking on the purple sea. Beyond, tankers are at rest, a grey plane nosing the hard horizon. I think I see the red outline of a country, like a woman lying on her side, under the far-falling curtain of iron sky.

'Tunisia,' says Pietr. 'Africa.'

A faint sweet sound reaches the tower. 'I hear bells.'

'It's the buoy,' he says, pointing. 'Just a platform with struts for a light. But my grandfather added an old brass bell. For the sailors to swim to, to ring for help.'

'Your grandfather sounds like a community-minded man.'

'Some would say so.'

The library is on the second level in the glass tower. The third level is taken up by the darkroom where, he explains, he develops his photographs. 'Another hobby,' he says, 'I don't have enough time for.'

His bedroom is on the first level. It is accessed by the external spiral stairs which also join the walkway running past the back bedrooms. The walls here are broad: thick frosted-glass bricks slotted into steel frames. He opens the steel door to show me a big plain room dominated by a four-poster bed with velvet drapes; an alcove of shelves makes a dressing room. The light struggles against the thick glass. Beyond the steel walkway are dark, bent lines; the outside world as a blur.

'It's like being inside an ice cube,' I say to Pietr. The ceiling is made of glass, too, except for a circle of small lights set around a large steel fitting which bulges from the pale centre.

We climb the stairs to the library. This door is locked and Pietr uses a small steel key. We go in, skirting the large globe of the world which sits on a big round dais in the middle of the room. It is an odd ugly feature, the kind of thing the pre-war Fascists would have loved but which I find incongruous in Pietr's home.

The floor is warm beneath my feet.

I drift along the shelves, past the rows of books rising to the ceiling: novels, anthologies, bound volumes of magazines, encyclopaedias, biographies – many of them military – all arranged alphabetically, categorised by subject. The poetry alone takes up an entire wall. I run my hands gently over the red spines, the cracked gold lettering. The bracelet chafes me; Pietr stares at it but he stays silent. I walk along the bookshelves. I almost see the words glittering like crystals, taking flight.

'I sensed haulers were no longer guiding me,' I say.

'Rimbaud,' says Pietr.

I stop at R. I search the shelves. 'No Rimbaud?'

He hesitates. 'No.'

I say, 'My father told me your family had a special connection with Rimbaud. That your mother said her father-in-law, your grandfather, met Rimbaud in the Moroccan desert. You don't know how transfixed I was, imagining that meeting.'

'My mother knows nothing about poetry,' he says easily. *Nothingk.* The Polish returning, despite the years away. 'Families always exaggerate their famous connections.'

He reaches over me to a row of tall thin books with pale cardboard covers tied with red ribbon.

'Maps,' he says. 'The family accounts from my grandfather's estate at Koloshnovar.'

I stare at the dates. I see years stretching back to the end of the 1970s, then a big gap for that entire decade, then more years going back through the 1950s, with the years 1953 and 1954 missing, then books all the way to the 1920s, a gap for the war years, then more, the years sporadic now, back to the turn of the century, into the previous century.

I point to the books marked through the 1890s.

'My grandfather's journals,' says Pietr. 'He went to Africa to make his fortune, barely an adult. Koloshnovar, his family estate, was failing. He needed money.'

'No personal diaries?' I say.

'My family doesn't believe in reflection.'

I say, 'I call my diary my little book of subversions. The secret map of my life.'

Pietr nods. 'A diary contains all the clues to decode the country of the self, the inner landscape. The problem is that if you don't know how to read the map, the symbols are useless.'

I say, 'Beyond here lie dragons.'

'Imagine maps with the face of God inscribed over the capital city of your country,' says Pietr. 'What does that do to the sense of the self?'

'We have the upside-down map,' I say, 'with Australia at the centre of the world.'

'I have no sense of you Australians,' he says. 'You look so easy-going, so simplistic, but there's a ferocity there.'

'The colonials went mad when they first saw the landscape,' I say, 'and we've never recovered.'

He takes down a book with pages so thin they could be seen through. Pages shaded and drawn in spidery ink. 'The maps of the French explorers,' he says. 'From before the First War.'

He unbuttons his cuff and rolls back his sleeve, turning the pages carefully, revealing charts of desolation: endless pages of desert with a name here and there inscribed in the wilderness. No roads, no train lines, no airports.

'Every clue is useable in a map,' says Pietr. 'Even absence is a clue. Look at the maps of Poland during World War II: whole towns disappeared, whole communities vanished, new unnamed enclaves of gas ovens. Look at America's map of the world now. No mention of the secret prisons, the hastily made airports for the rendition flights. No mention of villages razed to the ground, the mass graves of civilians killed in the cross-fire. Nuclear sites are never mentioned on the map. You'll never find the nuclear mines and American bases labelled on your tourist maps of Australia.'

'You sound angry.'

'It is something I have begun to think about.' He draws a deep breath. 'You make me think of it more.' He puts the book back and stares at the top shelf. 'I have another book you might like, a journal by a French explorer.'

He stretches up; his sleeve shifts and I see the beginnings of a tattoo. But this is nothing like the pain etched into Devlin's body. These blocks of black look smoother, with odd white lines running through them.

'Is that a stencil?' I say.

Slowly, he rolls back the sleeve. The inner arm, I think, always the easiest place to etch your pain. Like the stomach, the chest, over the heart: all those accessible places in that early time when you don't want to be caught. When you are hesitating about moving to more secretive areas: the inner thighs, between the toes, behind the eyeballs.

Just below his elbow is a black and white image of – at first I'm not sure what I am looking at. The world tilts for a moment. It is a face but not a tattoo. It is – I bend closer to make sure – a photograph on the smooth skin of his inner arm. I see an image of dark hair, a carefree expression. I even know when it was taken. At a picnic, years ago. I flinch in the moment when I think it is me.

'Anna,' I say.

'My daughter might be dead,' he says, 'but I've got her under my skin.'

There is a gleam of water through his light eyelashes.

'Can I touch her?' I ask. He nods. Faint blue-black smears my fingertip.

'The skin doesn't hold the image for long,' says Pietr steadily, 'unless you overload it with fixer. Then the area burns and flakes.'

'Easier than a tattoo.'

He says, 'Avedon did it. And the Paris artists in the last century, using plates from the old Brownie box cameras to develop directly onto the skin. You have to get the amount of emulsion and developer just right. You place the plate over the skin area for about three times the usual exposure time and coat it quickly with fixer. That seems to set the image for a few days. The developer works best on areas of the body that contain more water near the surface.'

'So women would be good carriers,' I say. 'We retain more water.'

'Women are always better carriers for memories,' says Pietr.

'When my brother found out about women retaining more water, if we ever fought he teased me that I needed to be drained.'

'How often did he tell you that?'

'Once that I can remember.' *Everyone is so sad now.* 'Maybe twice.'

160

Anna stares up at me, unblinking, tearless.

I say, 'You should patent the process. Sell it to people who don't want to carry photographs of their loved ones and can't stand tattoo needles. Soldiers going to war, office workers having secret affairs.'

'Explorers could print their maps directly on their body. They wouldn't ever worry about being lost.'

'As long as they didn't get sunburnt,' I say.

We have dinner in the narrow room opposite the living room. Spotlights along the roof illuminate the sheets of mist floating through the dark air outside and turn the raindrops into fireflies.

'It is the best floor show a man ever had,' says Pietr, lighting the candles flanking the orchids on the dining table. He turns off the ceiling lights, leaving one tall lamp in the corner which throws haloes over the courtyard and guardhouses, over the dark tongue of road snaking down the hill to the ruined temple. Dusk like dark blue water soaks up the coarse sheets of cloud and mist and rain and sky. I imagine the slow descent down the slope, the wet branches slapping against the black ground, the masks of clay under the beating palms of earth.

The vase on the table in the corner is filled with the same purple-black roses as in the lobby.

'Emperor's roses,' says Pietr. 'They grow wild around Koloshnovar. The soil is rich enough so the cold doesn't kill them. Rich from the blood of dead Polish cavalry, so the locals say. We try to grow them here but they attract frost and die.'

I bend to sniff the flower. There is no perfume. I say, testing him, 'I didn't think you still owned Koloshnovar. I thought it was abandoned.'

'The house is empty but we lease out the land,' says Pietr. 'It's like Santa Margherita. Too many memories. We can't sell it.'

Devlin comes up behind me. 'What did you talk about while I kicked my heels in here?'

The words hang in the air like snowflakes. 'Nothing,' I say, moving along the window. In our reflection, his dark shape looms over me. Even in the glass, I see the shadows under his eyes, in his cheeks. Over by the drinks table, Pietr turns to watch us.

'You're lying,' Devlin says, stalking my reflection. He grabs my elbow.

'Darling, I didn't know you cared.' I bat my eyelashes.

He stares at me as though he hated me. 'Tell me,' he says and his words form their usual clouds. But now I see ice glittering in the air, some aura hardening. I shove him, so he steps back.

'We're on the same side, Devlin.'

'Are we?'

'I told him exactly what you told me to say.'

He catches his breath, opens his mouth. But as usual he doesn't have the words.

In the reflection, Pietr stands, a tall glass in his hand. He says, 'Mr Devlin, I know you'll have one.'

'My mother has been delayed,' says Pietr as we sit. 'She sends her regrets.'

The tablecloth is heavy white linen: damask, with an embossed design half hidden by the plates and silverware and the white orchids floating in the glass bowls, their red stamens spider-like in the clear water.

'I'm surprised you get mobile coverage here,' says Devlin, raising his glass of red wine.

'It's erratic like everything else in Sicily,' says Pietr. 'We don't have land lines in bad weather. We have the old smugglers' way. Lit lanterns on the hill-top of the Roman ruins at Santa Margherita, which is the village opposite – '

'I know where it is,' says Devlin, drinking.

Pietr says to me, 'If you climb to the remains of the battlements – the place where they used to pour boiling oil on their enemies – you see clear across to Castelmontrano. I can stand on the walkway and use Morse code if I need to reach my mother.'

'So your mother lives in Santa Margherita?' I say, frowning at Devlin who is reaching for the bottle.

'The village is deserted,' says Pietr as a girl in a black skirt brings in the soup. 'But my mother's family lived there. So she likes to visit.'

'Alone?'

'Yes,' says Pietr, picking up his spoon. 'Start, please. It's a local specialty. After importing three star Michelins from Paris I finally realised the best cooks were the grandmothers in Trepani.' He sips a mouthful. 'Which is where you stay, I believe, Mr Devlin? Most travellers prefer somewhere bigger, like Palermo.'

'He's in Trepani to keep an eye on me,' I say. Devlin presses his lips together.

Pietr delicately touches the side of his bowl with his spoon. 'You'll find the locals hard to talk to unless you've got contacts.'

Devlin takes a large mouthful of wine. 'There's always Mr Lincoln on the greenbacks.'

'Possibly,' says Pietr.

'Or we can make a few calls to certain Yank federal prisons,' says Devlin, flicking his finger at the delicate stem of his glass. 'Didn't that work after World War II?'

'The Americans brought Lucky Luciano out of prison,' Pietr says to me, 'to help them get up the east coast of Sicily faster, to fight the Fascists on the mainland. Yes, I agree, Mr Devlin. The locals were happy to help strangers then.'

'Only after they'd already helped the Nazis go through three years earlier,' says Devlin. 'Nothing like a deutschmark or greenback to make quick mates in convenient places.' He finishes his wine.

'I'm sure you're right,' says Pietr.

'And I'm sure you'll be the first to know,' says Devlin.

By the second course, Devlin is drunk enough to start asking about Anna. He had picked his way through the stuffed mushrooms and now, after pushing the seafood gnocchi around his plate for several minutes, he takes another deep mouthful of wine and says to Pietr, 'About your daughter Anna – '

'I'm flying on a jet plane,' I say loudly. I am still thinking that Devlin is merely tactless. I don't comprehend how thoroughly he has thrown himself into treacherous waters. 'Anna used to like any song about travelling: hello, goodbye – miss you, kiss you.'

The glass is half falling from Devlin's slack fingers. 'She lived here?' he says to Pietr.

Pietr shakes his head. 'Her mother and I married very young. It was arranged; that was still done in Europe in the 1970s. Even now – strategic alliances, for the good of the family.' His mouth twists. 'Later, the marriage failed. Anna's mother went to Australia, with my blessing. We remained friends; I visited as often as I could. That was how I met your father,' he tells me.

'Anna was fun at school,' I say. 'Always breathlessly waiting for the next party. She liked to make her own clothes. A happy child.' The words are cold ice in my mouth.

'You both were,' says Pietr.

'Were we?' I say. 'I can't remember.'

Some memory turns over in the dark water behind his light blue eyes. 'You look so alike,' he says. 'You could have changed places.'

'Maybe if I had,' I say, 'Anna would be alive now.'

The wind is rising. Ivy has been allowed to grow up against the windows on this side of the house and when the light flickers, the bony branches look like clawing skeleton hands.

The third course has been brought in. Devlin is still not eating. He mutters under his breath and holds his glass up. The red liquid sloshes back and forth in miniature waves.

'The last time I saw my father,' I say to Pietr, 'he had the look of someone who can't believe where he is.'

'How much did he tell you?' Pietr asks.

Devlin stops tilting his glass.

'Fragments,' I say. 'Things which made no sense.'

'You would have to know the – how do you say? – the big picture,' says Pietr.

'I think Mr Devlin knows. But he won't tell me.' I lay down my fork. I open my eyes wide. 'No matter how much I try to persuade him.'

Devlin's hand tightens around the stem. 'You give me too much credit.'

'Oh, we all know your function, Mr Devlin,' says Pietr. 'But this is Sicily. The wolf revolving on the rope has two faces. There is no reason why we can't all get what we want.' He puts his hand over mine. 'What I want is for my – friend to get what she wants,' he says. 'You were good to Anna,' he says to me. 'Everyone else failed her. There was no other woman to help her.'

'Your mother?' I say.

He slowly spears a small piece of veal, presses it against the china until it flattens. 'Once my mother adopts a position she doesn't alter,' says Pietr. 'She murders her memories.'

Murder. I wonder whether the word is deliberate.

'I want to find my brother,' I say. 'I hoped he would contact me after my father died. I always assumed he would come out of hiding then.' I look at Devlin. 'That's all I want.'

'To find him?' says Pietr. 'Or find out what happened to him?'

The ground is black water beneath me. 'Either.'

'Mr Devlin promised to help you?'

'Yes.'

Devlin's eyes are unreadable in the low light.

Pietr picks up his glass. 'Then, whoever supplies that answer will be – most fortunate.'

'And you think you're the guy?' says Devlin.

Pietr raises his glass. 'To the victor go the spoils.'

The girl brings in dessert, a chocolate and cream confection with wafers. 'I can never imagine you with my father,' I say to Pietr. 'You, the cultured European.'

'Your father appreciated culture.'

'Did he? I wonder.'

Devlin pulls out a wafer and begins snapping it into little pieces, dropping them on the tablecloth.

'The papers were full of the trial,' I say.

Pietr says, 'You get used to it.'

'The notoriety?'

'Yes.'

We look at each other.

There is the sound of glass against metal. Devlin has knocked over his wine. He puts his hand in the spreading pool of red, levers himself up.

'You won't make Trepani tonight,' says Pietr.

We look through the window. Mist drifts past in distinct sheets.

'It's clearing,' says Devlin.

At the door, he says to me, fast, 'You talked about something.'

I say, 'If I tell you again that it's nothing, you won't believe me will you?'

'No.'

'We swapped good times,' I say. 'You know, when I was eighteen and super-wild and he was thirty-five and we did drugs and orgies together.'

Devlin is still.

'Joke, Devlin,' I say. 'I rarely met him. He was mostly in Europe.'

I put my hand against the light spilling onto the front terrace.

'We talked about Anna,' I say. 'He showed me the house.' My hand makes strange shadows on the passing sheets of mist. 'He read to me in French. Are you satisfied?'

He says, 'That's worse.'

SATURDAY

My bedroom is on the first floor, tucked behind the silver lattice. It is above the living room, looking away from the coast and facing the plain and Santa Margherita. This room has a low ceiling and white concrete walls with recesses for lighting and bookshelves; a warm wooden floor with a few scattered rugs – Moroccan, probably, from the weave – and a small wrought-iron balcony which steps up to join the rear walkway.

The bedroom sits under a small section of the same black tiles which matches the roof of the glass tower rearing over me. Pietr's mother's room is next to mine and then the spare room he had offered Devlin. Under the eaves are two video cameras enclosed in metal hoods. I see more cameras on the curve of the silver shell and fixed to the walkway railing.

I step onto the balcony. Rain falls in light strands on my face as I look down to the plain.

The peak the house is built on falls steeply for about a hundred feet with only tough scrubby bushes clinging in pockets to the stony hillside. Some of the land has the sullen, unforgiving baldness of forcible clearing. There is a gravel path, its steps made by holding the earth back with the split trunks of pines. Glass lamps sit on stocky black metal poles at regular intervals down the path.

It would be hard to approach without being noticed, I think. Even at night. Almost impossible if the lights were on and the cameras cover every angle.

Beyond the denuded land the peak falls into ridges which gradually flatten to the plain. Where the ridges begin, so does the forest proper: a thickly wooded swathe of trees gripping the hillside, many slanted, some growing out at extreme angles, knotted wood arms chafing the sky. Peaks and furrows, light and shadows, step off into the distance. Directly below are pockets of dark green firs, pines, oaks. I think I see the glint of water through the trees, a flat dark strip that might be a road.

A sound above me: Pietr is standing on the walkway. He points to the glass tower. 'Do you want to come up and see me, as your famous Mae West says?'

'We're not Americans yet, Pietr.'

'True. And nice girls don't visit men's bedrooms.'

'Oh, we all know nice girls finish last these days. Nice men, too, I'm sure.'

'The police would say I wouldn't know about that.'

'The police.' I slap the railing. Water drops rise slowly in the pale air and fall, weighted, onto my hand. 'You're the only one who doesn't make me feel like a criminal.'

'What about Mr Devlin?'

'He always makes me feel like a criminal.'

'Really?' He points down. 'Meet me.'

The lobby is deserted, the dining room empty. I walk around the staircase. The doors leading to the kitchen and staff room are both closed. A murmur of voices rises and falls between the cycle of a dishwater.

In the softer light in the alcove behind the staircase, I see a door set into the wall. I try the metal handle; it won't turn.

Pietr is waiting on the terrace outside the back sitting room. He leads me down the path into the woods. The sun is trying to break free of the grey clouds and it isn't more than chilly.

As the clouds separate and the light increases, the house's silver shell blazes into white; light reflects endlessly back and forth in the metal and glass panels.

Pietr is watching me. 'Why a glass house, do you think?'

'Because you can see what everyone is doing?'

He narrows his eyes as the sun judders forth and the house flares. 'Maybe,' he says.

The temperature drops once we are under the cover of trees. With short half-hearted gasps, the wind tugs at the treetops although it hardly reaches us on the ground.

We cross onto a narrow road which looks new.

'My mother has it redone every other year,' says Pietr. 'It's the back road that runs parallel with the coast road, but on the other side of the hill. We use it to get down to the plain or along to Trepani.'

On the opposite side, white posts with reflectors are set, tightly spaced, along the curve. I rub at a plastic diamond, making the red cat's eye wink.

'Is it a dangerous corner?' I ask.

'It's above the lake,' he says.

We walk down the slope, through colder air. The soil looks darker here, the leaves blacker. The cold bites the inside of my nose and the back of my throat. A branch cracks nearby.

'There it is,' says Pietr. Through the black spears of trees, I see a dark blue oval patched with silver, its surface adorned with shadows and fissures and crusted ice glittering in the sun. The lake.

Pietr picks up a branch and moves forward slowly, probing the muddy patches. Every now and again, the branch disappears into ground that looks solid. When it comes back, it is dripping wet black earth.

'We won't go all the way,' he says, but he continues walking. Several times he hesitates but each time, he goes on.

No sound except for the wind breathing across the dark wet earth and the occasional creak of branches. The leaves are rough with glitter. There are no birds here. The tree nearest me looks as though it is covered in water. My finger slips; the trunk is sheathed in ice.

Pietr stops on the steep bank. Around the lake's rim, jagged brown rocks poke through the dirty brown slush – half ice, half mud – along the waterline. The slush grows darker and thicker until at the lake's centre, it forms patches of ice on the surface. I hold Pietr's arm and lean over carefully.

'It's always the coldest place,' says Pietr. 'It always tells us when snow is coming.'

Through the fissures in the surface glitter, the water moves richly in the winter light: not blue, not black, but a turquoise veined with orange and red.

'Did you know,' Pietr says, not taking his eyes off the surface, 'in medieval times, in Dante's time, they believed the sky was made of crystals. That the light from the sun passed through crystals to illuminate our world. If the crystals were withdrawn it would be a time of blackness – the crystals were directly linked to the age of learning. The alternative was a world falling in on itself, into blackness.'

'Before that, they believed the world was made of water.'

He points across to our left and a shifting of light, water running over the larger rocks on the opposite bank.

'The water runs off the mountains into the lake,' he says. He points to his right. 'When it spills over the north end, it runs back into the ground where it joins a network of underground rivers which feeds this whole region. Fresh water is worth more than gold here.

'That is why it was so devastating after the war when the factories at Palermo and Modelphi dumped their chemicals in the lake: heavy metals, plastics, poisons. Noxious gases still erupt like volcanoes from the bottom of the lake, spuming upwards, toxic, deadly. Rising to the surface, lying like wreaths of sighs, thick as toffee, turning the water blood-red in places. The chemicals make strange patterns in the surface: faces, animals. Butterflies. No wonder the locals think this place is cursed.'

He stares at the water. 'Eventually, the plastics and poisons seep back into the ground, through the network of subterranean waters, into the deep caverns. The labyrinth of dark places and wet walls.

'Everything that's important,' says Pietr, stamping his feet, 'happens underground.'

'That's the same everywhere isn't it?'

'More so,' he says, 'in the Triangle of Hunger.'

The cold presses into me. I pull my jacket hood over my head, put my gloved hands on my cheeks. Pietr throws a pebble into the lake. It sits on the surface for long moments; finally, it sinks, leaving a sullen bubble which slowly subsides.

Pietr says, 'Italians returning from the concentration camps – from Auschwitz and others – told how the prisoner children would spontaneously start drawing butterflies on the wet walls. Even those returning from different camps told the same story. Some said it happened on the same day. Others said it was only children with certain numbers tattooed on their wrists. Anything with the figure eight. A misshapen butterfly lying on the skin.

'Now,' he says, 'the locals won't come near the lake. My mother's road is rarely used. Castelmontrano is isolated.'

He picks up another pebble, throws it into the water. It sinks as slowly as the first.

'A few minutes' exposure is all it takes,' says Pietr. 'Just as you become aware of the smell of rotten eggs from the sulfur, the brain ceases to be able to absorb oxygen. You lose control of your arms and legs, find it hard to think.' He stares without blinking. 'Just as you recognise you must leave, you lose the strength to drag yourself away. So you lie on the edge of the lake as your brain gradually dies.'

He says, 'You should know; someone will surely mention it. There's bad blood between the coast people and anyone from Santa Margherita.' He stabs at the crusty slush along the waterline. 'I wouldn't want you to get the wrong idea.

'It was an overcast day,' he says, 'a day drenched with winter light, which means little light at all. My mother says they got out of the crashed car quite easily. It was resting on the bank near the most stagnant water. She dragged my father out, he was unconscious, and covered him carefully. He was alive when she went for help. But when they came back, his body was gone. There was nothing there except his jacket and shoes. He had broken the shoelaces.

'They found his body hours later, floating face down in the reeds on the far side of the lake.'

Pietr says, 'Sicily in the 1950s – you can imagine what they thought.'

'Poison,' I say.

'She was suspected – the peasant girl, the beast. How did she snare the shining Polish aristocrat? She would have suffered more but she was pregnant with me. When they discovered that, the Polish family – my grandfather – decided not to pursue the matter. And then I was born, a son.

'It took years before the talk died down. She had to hire a geologist from America, a famous man attached to the government, to probe the lake bed and issue a report. He assured the locals the eruptions are sporadic but they are too scared to breathe the air. We have to pay the staff triple the usual wage. Most of them are relatives of Stefano's wife.'

As we walk to the road, Pietr stops next to a tree and puts his hand on the trunk. '*Lass dich nicht in die dunklen Wälder locken von den trügerischen Stimmen. Die Wälder sind wunderschön, doch sie sind wild*,' he says. 'Do not be lured into the black forests by the deceptive voices. The forests are most lovely but they are wild.'

'You prefer German,' I say. 'Not Polish?'

'I used Polish,' he says, 'when I was a child and we lived at Koloshnovar. As I got older, I grew . . . ambivalent.' He pats the trunk. 'Isn't English the international language for success?'

'Don't tell that to the French,' I say. 'Or the Chinese. Or the Arabs.'

The sky is lightening as we climb the slope to the house. The dull silver skeleton shimmers under the shifting clouds.

'When the sun hits it,' I say, 'you must be able to see it for miles around.'

He says, 'Everyone knows where to find me.'

We reach the back terrace steps, high enough to look across the plain to Santa Margherita.

I say, 'You would have a great view from there to here.'

'I never go there.'

'Oh.' I stare across to the pale ruins. 'But your mother goes?'

'Yes,' he says, kicking at ice rimming the step. 'But she knows her way around. The ruins are dangerous for visitors.'

'Point taken,' I say. But I continue to stare at the village.

We go up the steps and around the back sitting room to the infinity pool. 'Look,' he says, pointing across the guardhouses, the garage, the descending road. The sea falls out in all its shifting white-humped glory, moving slowly under the lowering sky, darker ripples running through the light green below the rocky cliffs to merge with the blue-black of the deeper water.

'Forget Santa Margherita,' says Pietr. 'I'll take you out in the boat on the first good day. That's the better view.'

I look at the green waves which sawed against the dark brown rocks. 'Where do you launch boats?'

'There's one spot,' he says. 'Only the locals know.'

As I watch the horizon wavering under the rolling clouds, rolling steel grates behind me. Pietr stands by the infinity pool, his hand on a switch in the wall. Steel rods holding metal panels slowly extrude from the flat roof. They grind out across the pool, darkening the water. When the panels stop above the edge of the terrace, Pietr touches a bolt, one of several on the inside of the railing. He kneels by the pool, feels the water. 'It's designed to be enclosed in winter.' He shrugs. 'I haven't bothered since Anna stopped coming.' *Comingk*. That hard finality again, maybe a reflection of the struggle to control his own stress.

He says, 'I can put up the wall panels. I can heat it.'

'To swim,' I say slowly.

He looks up at me. 'To forget,' he says.

My image is a dark shroud in the water. 'Swimming is forgetting for me. And poetry.'

Pietr frowns down at whatever he sees there. 'You would like the book I mentioned. Poetry as redemption by an unknown French explorer.'

'I would like anything that was not my father's lootings.'

Pietr stands up, carefully. 'It was not looted by your father,' he says. 'But maybe another day. Too many ghosts today.'

'You'll have to be wary of these people,' says Devlin after lunch. 'You don't know what they're capable of.'

We are in the forest between the road and the house. The rain is still falling but not hard; an umbrella and a raincoat over my jacket and jeans are enough. The forest has a damp smell, laced with heat. The leaves are soggy on the ground, curled with the year's knowings. I press my foot down. Frail little vessels, scrolls of the past and the future. The rain falls on my umbrella, vibrating the wooden handle.

I say, 'I know what they're capable of.'

It is quiet between the beats of rain: only an occasional rustle; the drip of water on the sodden leaves. I stare at the twisted roots, the rotting bark, the mould in radiant patches on the broken trunks and fallen logs, the centipede moving like a caravan of tiny, hunched, black-robed refugees.

Devlin sits on a fallen log, an umbrella propped over his shoulder, his notebook on his knee. He says, 'How do you know?'

I walk away, skidding on a muddy patch. A small clump of white star-shaped blossoms pokes up between black roots. When I touch a petal, fine silver specks coat my finger. I taste salt.

'How?' says Devlin.

'Because you keep telling me.'

I look back. The house rises not like a building but a silver moment. A preposterous attempt to defeat the landscape. I see the cracks in the glass. A stagnant hour.

'Pietr's mother is right about it being a folly,' says Devlin. 'I saw it in Borneo. Assault by renovation – it never worked. If you missed even a few days of pruning, the jungle came. You could close the doors but the nightmares crept in, the sense of not belonging.' He raises his eyebrows, as though his eloquence has surprised him. He says firmly, 'The reality.'

The house glitters through the black trees. 'It's an ice palace,' I say.

Devlin says, 'All I want to know is, where's the reflector rod for lightning strikes.

'So,' he says, taking off his gloves and flexing his fingers. 'How are they treating you?'

'You mean Pietr?'

He scribbles a thicket of black lines on his page. 'Any of them. Yes, Pietr.'

'He's – kind,' I say.

Devlin makes a noise under his breath.

'He set up the swimming pool for me.'

'Yeah, well,' says Devlin. 'Easy for the rich ones.'

'He doesn't treat me like a criminal.'

'Criminals never do. How's the old woman?'

'She's away,' I say. 'Doing business or something.'

'Oh, well, don't waste too much time on her,' says Devlin. 'Mitch says she's not important.' He presses his pen down into the page. I see the point disappear into the white. 'So – no visitors, no odd packages?'

'Pietr says the locals steer clear of the place. Because of the toxic lake.'

'That sounds like total superstitious bullshit.' He bends over the page. 'You'd better start snooping around. There's got to be an office somewhere, documents. They won't be on their guard. They think you're one of them.'

I lower the umbrella. My hood falls back. Usually I enjoy rain on my head but now the coldness is an irritation.

'It would help if I knew – ' I say.

'Need to know only,' says Devlin. 'Just note anything unusual. Anything valuable.'

'Pietr wants to show me a book of poetry by a French explorer.'

'Oh, not poetry,' says Devlin, waving a hand. 'No-one cares about poetry. Think what would impress Mitch and the Americans.'

'Money,' I say. 'Antiques.'

'You didn't hear it from me.' He makes more marks in his book. A trio of frozen water drops falls from the bare branch behind him.

I say slowly, 'But Mitch has started looking for my brother?'

'Sure,' says Devlin. He meets my gaze without blinking. 'It takes time to check every old building, every deserted farm.'

I think of the peak I can see from my room, the ruined village across the plain.

I say, 'You think that's where he could be?'

'Sicily – land of kidnappings. Some of these villages made their living that way for decades. The Mafia would snatch rich kids in Rome or Bologna and fly them down here. Still do. You can land a plane any number of places inland.'

I think of the plain in summer: flat, dry, dusty, the road running almost straight to Santa Margherita. I imagine flares lit on the ground, the plane coming in at night, low, under the radar, the dark shadows against a moon chosen precisely because it was three-quarters eaten. The steps being let down, a blindfolded figure being dragged to the waiting car.

'Or boat,' says Devlin casually. 'You could bring them ashore if you knew the right place to land. But our guys say this part of the coast is impassable.'

He reaches across and pushes my jacket sleeve up. I had taken the bandage off. The burns and cuts flare red beneath the silver circle.

'The steel will chafe,' says Devlin. 'You need to pad it.'

I move until I am directly in front of him. 'Dev, you will tell me if you hear anything about my brother?'

He drops my sleeve but I am sure I see sympathy in his eyes. He had this way of looking at me as though there was something else – some memory, some image – superimposed over me, the way that if a living being walked into the frame of an image which was already being photographed, the human would be made misty by the shorter exposure. The human would become a ghost in the photo, the real background showing through harsh and clear. I wonder if it is images of when we met that he sees when he looks at me. I don't think so. Nothing he has shown me – even that night – makes me think he can't completely shut down that side of himself. Of course, I realise later, that had always been my mistake with him. Misjudging the limits of his control.

He blinks and goes back to making the marks in his book. 'I can't do anything if Mitch doesn't okay the funds. None of these guys have long attention spans. So you'd better find something in the next week.'

'I can't find something in nothing,' I say.

'That never stopped the Americans,' says Devlin.

THURSDAY

I am dreaming of swimming in the only land where I can be myself. In a past-less land. I roll over in the patient liquid, talking to someone I can't see, explaining myself, my obsession. *Don't you understand? It is a democratic country. There are no boundaries, no surfaces between skin and water. Language is useless here, entire conversations conducted with fingers as gentle as anemones.* I wave my hand and clear bubbles rise like fireflies lighting dark gardens. *Don't you see? Look around us. The anxious, the unsteady, the regretful, they are all buoyant again.* Ripples of blue light play beautiful patterns across the dimpled flesh moving slowly past me. I am swimming through liquid chrome. I see the shiny coin of an elbow, the unblinking eyes of the lap swimmers. *Don't you see*, I say to the person who is with me. The unknown person. The one.

Water flows into you in infinitesimal particles.

Like tears. Like pulses.

I am dreaming in water. The reflection from the pool plays across the metal roof in waves of light. I turn over and over like a seal. This is one of only two places where the absence inside is filled.

Where I don't want to shoot up heroin. I dive down to the bottom of the pool, touch the gritted concrete with my knuckle and swim up.

Through the liquid veil, I see Pietr. He waits with a towel as I climb the ladder.

'You're fast,' he says in a tone of surprise.

'I swam a lot when I was under house arrest.' I see him looking at the marks on my arms. I wonder if he can see past the word written across each inner elbow. I think so. He can imagine the small pinpricks, the old purple scars, the clotted red holes, the twisted veins. The red holes are hard to see under the tattooed words but he knows they are there. He would have searched for them on Anna's arms. In the morgue.

He looks away.

'It was a long time ago, Pietr. And you know what they say about rich junkies.' I can't halt the self-disgust. 'They can afford much better gear.' I look down at my arms, past the faint purple of the word, the trembling Rs and Es, to the tiny trails of holes. Little marks on some other page. Refugees from another country.

'Now, I don't even know why I did it,' I say slowly. 'One year it was fun, it was something you did. And then – the next year it wasn't. After Anna. My brother.'

'Anna told me you were the only one who visited her in hospital,' he says. Then, in wonderment, 'All those parties, all those friends. And no-one came.' The hard explosion on the last word. I see it in the air, with the same initial letter as my last name. *Kame.*

I wrap the towel around my shoulders. 'It was another time. Sleep until early afternoon, get dressed, go shopping. Dinner. Party till dawn. I remember the bouncer at Zone saying to me, You've got a very 1980s attitude.'

'It helped Anna, you being there,' says Pietr.

'Did it?' I shake my head. 'She would sit for hours in the same position, sifting dirt through her hands. She said she was holding a millennia of bones.'

'She had photos of you,' he says. 'And your brother.'

'I know those photos.' I am silent a moment. 'If you take me out of the fine clothes you hardly recognise the girl. I couldn't recognise her at all in the news photos. A small, worried-looking girl. A stupid girl.'

He touches my arm. 'You must have been strong not to go under,' he says. 'After the rest of your family.'

'No-one knows,' I say sharply, 'what happened to my brother.'

'Not even Mr Devlin?'

'He says not.'

'Do you believe him?'

'I have to.'

The shifting light from the water reflects on his face. Outside, rain streams down the glass panels which are bolted now to the railing and the metal roof. The heat from the pool mists the panels but every now and then, the cold air eddying between the steel rods hits the glass and there is a glimpse of the day outside. I imagine the deserted ruins of Santa Margherita. Beckoning.

Later, when we are standing on the back terrace, Pietr says, 'I planted the forest here. I wanted a reminder of Koloshnovar – my grandfather's estate – before it was spoiled.'

The sky is a flat grey. Rain falls in fitful bursts, the wind slaps at the treetops. There is a faint scream: an eagle rises slowly on the current, drifting, beginning to turn, wings scything the air lazily, rolling over to look back along its shoulder, turning tighter and tighter, corkscrewing down through the hazy air, almost a straight line, faster and faster until it seemed to dive into the trees. A pause and then the bird reappears. It climbs steadily into the leached sky, a crumpled body in its beak.

'Rabbit,' says Pietr, turning to follow the bird, and I think he shivers.

'You always refer to Koloshnovar as your grandfather's estate,' I say. 'But wasn't it also your father's?'

'My father wanted to get away from it,' says Pietr. 'When I was a boy I asked the staff about him. They say he wanted to become a monk.' He lets out a short disbelieving laugh. 'And he married my mother.'

The storm rolls in again, the clouds close over. I say, 'I think Devlin knows more than he is telling me.'

Pietr takes my hand in his and examines the bracelet, becoming still when he finds the illuminated green panel.

He says, 'You can get those for alcoholics. There is an alarm inside, to make noise if you drink too much.'

'It's not for drinking, Pietr.'

'Pity,' he says. 'I would suggest giving one to Mr Devlin.' He reaches into his pocket and takes out a set of finely curved steel hooks hanging from a small ring. 'Jeweller's hooks,' he says as he tries to insert the smallest into the hairline join in the metal. The point slips but he nods. 'I can get that off.'

'They would know you were helping.'

He pushes my sleeve further. He reads the word tattooed along my inner elbow. *Remember.*

He says, 'Remembering.' *Rememberingk.* 'Who has the luxury to forget?' He pauses; I try not to feel it is deliberate. 'When I see you,' he says, 'I think of Anna.'

I look at his hand on my arm. I think about time passing and Devlin taking my diary. I say to Pietr, 'This is what I will tell Devlin: this is what happened. This is the truth.'

FRIDAY

After lunch, I go to meet Devlin. The cold creeps in under my hood, it chills my skull. The burned skin on my wrist itches. The ice seems thicker on the trees today, hanging in crystal slivers which chime and tinkle in the wind. A bird calls over and over.

Below me is the tongue of road; beyond, the glinting lake. I am drifting down, half annoyed that Devlin hasn't showed when a branch cracks nearby.

I turn to see a shadow move behind a tree.

'Devlin?'

Silence, just the wind tugging at the leaves. The sun is watery, like a golden lake in the centre of a land of air, with clouds for peaks and strips of mist for fields.

My boots sink into black mud up to my ankles. Glitters of ice crown the odd blade of grass, coating fallen twigs, shearing off in minute plates from the grey stubby rocks and boulders. I struggle across to look behind the tree, convinced I see a figure.

There is no-one.

'You bastard.'

My words splinter in the cold air. I try to read the letters in the thin black lines of the stripped branches. They are messages spelled out along the horizon, struggling through the cold air, past the uncaring trees, to the no-one who is there.

SATURDAY

Pietr and I are in the darkroom on the top floor of the glass tower. He has run black curtains on rails all around the hexagonal room. 'But the light still gets in,' he says. 'Winter is easier and often I work at night, so the photos don't get exposed.'

The dark is a pulsing cloak around us; the red light bulb casts a warm glow over the liquid rocking in the tray he is holding. The photo begins to grow through the chemicals. He hasn't used a tele-photo lens but has left the graininess of distance so that the woman moving across the bare landscape blurs into the dark trees. The glitter of frozen water hanging from the branches shows as white absences; the earth is as dark as opened arteries between the fallen mounds of grey leaves.

The woman is walking purposefully down the slope, putting out a hand to grasp the next tree trunk. I see the dark oval on the bottom left hand corner and I understand why he hadn't gone further: the lake was between him and the woman.

I look at the picture. It is a season between seasons, a waiting world. Even the walking woman is waiting. I know, I recognise myself despite the lapping tides in the developing tray.

I wonder which day it was. Where Devlin was. I trace my path. Above the woman – me – is a dark shape merged with the trees;

185

someone is watching and waiting for his moment to come out. If you didn't know another person was there you wouldn't pick the shape as human. It is a hunched and hooded blackness. I wondered if Pietr realises. I wonder how much longer Devlin had waited.

There are photos hanging clipped to a line in the corner.

'Can I see?' I say.

Pietr hesitates.

'I understand not wanting to show.'

'Go ahead,' he says.

The first I choose is a close-up of me, walking through the woods. I have an absent-minded expression.

'You can really see the freckles across my nose,' I say.

'You look like your brother.'

The word hangs in the room. 'It's not how I remember him.'

Pietr says, 'Maybe it is – was – how he was over here.'

When I think back on this conversation, I wonder whether I left things out. Was there more that he said? Did he give me clues about my brother? He must have known all along – and I must have known that he knew. Should have known. He was my father's business partner after all.

'I can't remember my brother,' I say. 'He's already a dark outline, like one of those cloaks, those shrouds the women wear in the Middle East.'

'Burqas,' says Pietr.

'It happened,' I say, 'when he started going to Koloshnovar.'

'As though you were already saying goodbye to him.'

I touch the photograph with my finger. Even here he was misty. I put my fingers to my eyes but my eyes are dry. I'm not crying. I never cry.

I try to think of a concrete memory. 'The day he bought his first car,' I say. 'The old bomb. We were rich by then but my father didn't believe in giving us anything. So my brother saved up, odd jobs. He liked working in the open air. He would have been happy being a labourer. But he felt forced to go into the business.'

I remember he had parked the car down the street near the small park overlooking the bay. Where my father couldn't see it. There was salt in the air, the sky was a perfect sheet of blue.

'You could see the rust on the back panels a mile away,' I say. 'But he was so proud. I remember saying to him, *It's a beauty*.' I saw the car, the white gull wheeling overhead, the scalloped sails of the Opera House across the water.

I say, 'Now, when I remember, I hear his voice but there is no-one real beside me. Just lines and borders, a displacement of light.'

Pietr closes his eyes for a moment. 'I see Anna all the time. It seems to be getting worse.'

I say, 'At least you don't have the guilt of forgetting.'

'You always have the guilt,' he says.

I run my finger along the bracelet. I am becoming used to it. Whole hours go by when I forget I have it on, the way I forget my hair is cut short, until one of the housemaids gives me a startled look or Stefano carefully averts his eyes. Whole hours go by when I am not enraged. Or frightened.

In my memory, in the memory I am writing down now in my diary, I say to Pietr, 'What do you think happened to my brother?'

'I think your brother was looking and found more than he wanted.'

My heart climbed into my throat then, hammering like the first bad rush after racking up, that gut-chilled instinct that the stuff was no good, it had been cut with cleaning powder, or worse.

'Do you think my father was involved?' I say, barely above a whisper.

He looks at me. *No coward soul is mine*, I thought then, seeing Emily Brontë's words hanging in silver above me. No trembler in the world's storm-troubled sphere.

'I don't want to tell you,' says Pietr. 'And I don't want to lie to you.'

Pietr takes me out to photograph the forest. We follow the path through the woods, across the road, past the guard rail. I have a hollow feeling, remembering Devlin here. But we swing further east. I guess that Pietr wants to avoid the lake but a fallen tree blocks our way. Its branches are tipped with frozen water drops which catch the light, as though the tree is a giant chandelier on its side.

We are forced to double back to the ridge above the lake. He climbs, eyes down. I follow him, my boots sinking into soft ground. There is a blur of russet: a squirrel half-hops half-leaps past us. It spreads its arms and legs like a sail to catch the breeze. When it lands in a pile of smeared wet leaves, it sinks until nothing shows but the glossy red pelt along the spine.

Sloped grey through the trees: the slate tiled roof of a hut, with a stone chimney set over stone walls and small windows with wooden frames.

'Abandoned,' says Pietr. 'Because of the lake. We keep it stocked: blankets, old clothes, wood. Snowstorms come quickly sometimes. Hikers still get caught by them. '

The door has a big round black metal handle with a wolf's head hanging over the keyhole.

'To keep the wolves from the door?' I say.

Pietr turns down his mouth. 'My mother's logo, for the catalogue and the website. The marketing people say it helps sell the wines.'

He moves past it. He doesn't offer to show me inside.

That night, like every night I stand on the balcony and stare at where the forest shadows were deepest, where the wild things were. Where Devlin could be standing. I feel the house sliding into blackness and I look out and wonder, If you can't see me am I invisible?

I sleep heavily for the first time since I arrived. I have barely climbed into bed when I am dragged down to a dark blue-green world. I swim along the sandy floor, ripples of light imprinted behind my eyes. Swimming is my abstraction, my salvation, I tell the other who is the only one who can ease my burden. Swimming is my desire, my occupation. My drug.

I wake, climbing through black waves, past the lost wrecks of ships, past sailors' drifting hearts, swimming in time to a regular but un-nameable sound. It is only in the morning that I place it: bells.

I am waiting for Devlin. I swear I will only wait half an hour this time. My fur-lined parka hood is up but my head is still chilled; the bracelet is ice around my wrist.

The house's profile is unreadable in the cold air.

A muttered curse. Devlin is behind me. He puts his back to the nearest tree. There are ice sheets on the trunk.

'You'll get wet,' I say. Already his weight is making the sheets crack.

'Yes, Mum.' He pulls out his flask, holding it awkwardly with his gloved hands.

'If you're going to be like that – ' I turn away.

'Wait a minute.' His voice is peculiarly dead. Later, I understand it is the effort of holding in his temper.

'Mitch is coming down,' he says. 'He's in Paris now. Then he goes on to Rome.'

'No wonder you're drinking,' I say half-joking, still not realising. 'You've had two weeks. What have you got?'

'What have you got for me?'

'I need information before I give you any.'

'You're a pimp, Devlin. You never do it because it's the right thing.'

I got to him. Not my words but my tone. The pause is too long before he says, 'You're not doing anything you don't want to do.'

'So you and Mitch are keeping your side of the bargain,' I say. 'You're looking for my brother.'

'I told you we were.' He takes off his gloves, uncaps the flask, offers it to me.

I shake my head. I want to ask him straight out but the hammer is back in my throat. But I am not crying. I never cry. Water never leaves me.

He says, 'Oh, right. Needles are your thing.'

'I never used needles to inflict pain.'

He curses under his breath. He is trying to put the cap back on but his hands must be cold. He can't get the thread to catch. It is only now that I wonder whether he has already been drinking.

'I've seen your scars, Devlin.'

'Nothing happened that night,' he says quickly. He grips the flask with both hands. I see past the defiance in his eyes to the worry behind. The uncertainty. He can't remember, that's the problem. For him. For us.

'So why did you come to my room?' I say.

He waves a hand irritably. 'Travel arrangements. Your passport. What the fuck difference does it make?'

'You woke up in my bed.'

'That doesn't prove anything!' he shouts. 'You're not getting me like that. You're nothing more than the job.'

'Disposable,' I say. I raise my voice. 'Unnecessary.'

'Yes.

'The enemy,' I shout at him.

'Yes.'

'Someone who doesn't need to know anything?'

'Yes.'

'Then why did you tell me your real name?'

When I come downstairs for lunch the dining room is deserted. I look around the empty lobby and peer into the alcove behind the staircase. The door is ajar. Inside are spiralling concrete steps

191

descending beneath the neon lights which are set like Morse dashes in the low ceiling.

I slip through the door, closing it behind me and go down. I think I hear voices and hold my breath. The neon light fizzes. I go down more slowly, one hand against the wall. I reach the bottom step. A door is set on each side of the landing. The door on the right is closed, a murmur inside.

I open the left door. The light falls on all fours into a room which seems as long as the house. Rows of wine racks disappear into the gloom. I don't switch the light on. Instead, I pull the door to, leaving a strip of light, enough to see the nearest wine bottles.

The racks stand in six rows, shoulder height. I kneel and ease out the nearest dark brown bottle. It is coated in patches of something thicker than dust. I hold the label to the narrow oblong of light. *Santa Margherita Lambrusco Di Sicilia*. There is a year stamp: 1984.

I am staring at the black grit smeared across the label when I hear a faint click. It seems to me the oblong is growing brighter. The other door has opened, is spilling more light into the room.

Voices. Fragments of sentences. '. . . be notorious,' someone says. A woman. 'Notorious.'

The words hang like lanterns lighting dark gardens. Lighting me. 'No,' Pietr says loudly, almost in the room. I feel as though the ground is shaking. But it is my heart shaking me.

Silence falls. The light recedes. Minute black chips glitter on my finger. The smears where I had touched the bottle are clearly visible. I wipe the bottle over using the hem of my shirt and, squatting by the bottom shelf, take out the first bottle there and move it to the space left in the middle shelf. Then I put my cleaned bottle on the bottom rack. A shadow presses against the glass. Something heavier than wine is inside. I raise the bottle and study the base. A small square package rocks in the dark liquid. I look at the gap on the shelf. I put the bottle back.

The landing is empty and so are the stairs. The door opposite is still closed. I step towards it, stretch out a hand. The door opens: a woman, head turned, is talking to someone behind her. I throw myself back into the cellar. She moves past me, saying, 'Exactly what I expected.'

Pietr comes out. He is looking at the map in his hand. Behind him is an office with computer screens on a desk, steel filing cabinets and what looks like a large microscope. He closes the door and they go up the stairs. In the silence, I count off two long minutes. Then I come out onto the landing and try the door. It is locked.

I look up the curving stairs. Impossible to know whether anyone is waiting on the steps above. I creep up, keeping as close as I can to the wall. There is a roaring in my ears, like the sea turning over. I round the corner, too fast, anxious, stubbing my toe on the top step. I look down, knowing I will see a graze, a scuff mark there that would eat into the concrete. Some human stain. But there is nothing on the stone, nobody around the corner. The landing at the top of the stairs is empty. As I try to turn the handle, the lights go out.

I press my ear against the door. I have the image of severed ears in sacks lying on the floor, like peach halves. Listening to me breathing as I press against the ground. I hear the earth breathe. Somewhere the earth is saying, *Enough*.

I am rigid against the wall. I remember Devlin saying to me as the police boat churned waves down the Grand Canal and the water turned a malevolent brown, 'I can't even begin to tell you how wrong I think you are for this.'

If it wasn't true then, I think, it soon will be.

The door opens. Someone is coming in. I move down the steps. There is a murmur; the door begins to close. I run up, catch the door as it touches the jamb, count to ten and slip through.

The staccato beat of rain on the silver shell is loud enough to cover the door closing behind me. I peer from the alcove. Pietr is crossing the lobby. When he turns to look, I am at the base of the stairs. He holds out his arm. 'Come to lunch with us.'

A woman stands at the head of the dining table, her back to the main window. She doesn't look up as I come forward but lifts the cover of an earthenware dish.

'Eggplant from Morocco – good,' she says. Her English is buffeted by the rolling Italian cadences and some darker, guttural edge but she has obviously been well-taught.

'Friends send it over,' she explains, spooning slices into a shallow dish. 'You try it.'

She is a stocky grey-haired woman in her early seventies, small but expensively dressed in a black tailored pantsuit. She wears thick black eyeliner. The mist outside the window streams past her and makes her look as though she is trailing scarves of smoke. My father had always been non-committal about her, barely mentioned her. I had expected some backwoods peasant, a quavering pensioner, not this war-eyed woman.

A piece of eggplant slips from the spoon. She says, '*Ofanculu*. Bastard thing' and throws the eggplant on the floor. She comes around the table, still against the light, and says, 'What do you think of my son's folly?'

'My mother,' says Pietr. 'Rosita.'

'Rosza,' she says. 'I took the Polish after my husband.'

She folds her arms, studies me. She wears only one ring on her hands, not on her wedding ring finger but on her little finger: a signet ring with a wolf's head crest.

'In Italy after the war, some women had shaven heads,' she says. 'They had it done to them. Did you deserve it too?'

Pietr frowned. 'Mother – '

She holds up her hand. 'She can answer.'

'Not without sounding rude,' I say. 'Or contrary.'

'I like the contrary, yes,' she says. She takes a flat cigarette case from her trouser pocket and lights a small square cigarette in dark paper. A pungent tobacco smell floats through the room. A cigarillo.

I say, 'I did it to annoy the man who brought me here.'

Rosza exhales a dark plane of smoke which hangs like a veil in front of her face.

I say to Pietr, 'I don't think Devlin is just some Embassy guy assigned to help the Americans on terrorism. I think he's been investigating my father.'

'To spy on us,' says Rosza.

'Not you,' I say. 'Me.'

Rosza exhales another dark veil. I think her eyes dart down to the bracelet but when the smoke shifts, she is staring at me steadily. 'So you led this Devlin to our house.'

'I'm sorry,' I say. 'I had nowhere else to go.'

She throws her cigarette on the floor and grinds it out with her foot. Then she rubs her hands briskly together.

'What we thought,' she says to Pietr.

I say, 'I am making . . . difficulties.'

'People always called me difficult,' says Rosza. 'There's nothing difficult about being straightforward.' She raises her arms. I think she is going to strike me. Instead, she embraces me. 'You must let us take care of you.'

She smells of honey and jasmine.

'Don't give me any sympathy,' I say. 'I might cry.'

She pats my back. She says, 'I never had time for sympathy.' She holds me by the shoulders. Her eyes are all black pupil. She says, 'Don't worry about those government pigs. Stay here and rest.'

I nod, but as she moves away, I see Anna in the window's reflection: Anna in the hospital with her pale face, the shadows under her eyes, the strands from her blanket twisting in the antiseptic air.

Pietr pours a pale red wine into my glass. The bottle dips towards me and the wolf's head crest gleams gold on the label.

Rosza says, 'From Santa Margherita. Our vineyard.'

Pietr says, 'Technically, we harvest on the other side of Trepani.' He sits opposite me, unfolds his napkin. 'Margherita is a wreck. But you can find it on the map. So, to impress the overseas buyers . . .'

The rain increases, as loud as hail. Rosza spits a pine nut into the bowl on her left.

'My mother follows Sicilian customs at table,' says Pietr. 'Plain speaking. And plain eating.' *Eatingk*.

'You sound like your father when you say that,' says Rosza.

'I would hardly know, would I?' says Pietr.

Rosza makes a noise between a grunt and cough and watches me, unblinking, over her clasped hands. The water running down the glass softens the dead black of her eyes. In the rippled light, they seem dark grey.

She nods at me. 'You have good manners.'

I say, 'They were thrashed into us.'

'Thrashings,' says Rosza. 'You had no love for your father.'

'I was brought up to be dutiful,' I say. 'Sometimes when all that is expected of you is duty – '

'Yes,' she says. 'There is no room for love.' She picks up her fork. 'And children feel – '

'Everything,' I say.

'Yes,' she says. There is a spark of recognition in her eyes. 'Pietr, we should have a party. A Christmas Eve gathering to introduce your friend. Just whoever has not run away from the weather.'

'My mother likes you,' says Pietr. 'She only entertains for people she likes.' He raises his glass. 'We'll have to invite your lover.'

I have an image of Devlin lying on the bed. His breathing fills the room as I bend over him and unbutton his shirt and look down at what is on his body.

'It was a joke,' says Pietr. 'But what a long silence. You had to think through all the names.'

Out of the corner of my eye, I see Rosza frown. 'You'll make her blush.'

'Yes, I'm sorry,' says Pietr. 'Mr Devlin called.' The small deadly dislike coils through the formal address. 'He has to prepare a report for his boss who will be arriving soon. He said he would call back.'

After lunch, Rosza takes me into the living room for coffee. We sit on the long sofa while she knits and talks. I am tired – I think of Anna growing paler – and I slouch on the huge soft cushions and watch the light flash off the points of Rosza's steel knitting needles. She says, 'Pietr tells me you were a friend of Anna's.'

'We were at school together. And then on the nightclub scene. She dated my brother before he went away. Before she – got sick.'

'So many of these girls,' says Rosza, 'are butterflies on lounges. All they want is excitement.'

I think of Anna's small sad face.

'At first the clubs were fun,' I say. 'We knew everyone, we had plenty of money. But after a few years there was a nasty pushing quality to the dance floor. Girls getting drunk too easily, getting sick. Girls waking up in the back of crashed cars the next morning, clothing disarranged, far from home. It was predatory.'

'Wolves,' says Rosza. 'Wolves are everywhere.'

'The men got older,' I say, 'and the girls got younger.' I remember the teenage girl in the bathroom. A cotton smock dress, plastic princess clips in her hair. Talking about her mother and six sisters and brothers in the country. Smelling of lavender talcum powder. I saw her on the dance floor only briefly after that. The bodyguard of one of the old men came and got her and she went to the back room with him and I never saw her again.

'Anna should have known better,' says Rosza.

'No-one knows,' I say, 'that they'll have horse steroids slipped in their drink, and get raped, and become sterile.'

'Well,' says Rosza. She takes out one of her small dark cigarettes and lights it, blows a perfect smoke ring and watches it break up into small dark sails.

She puts her head on one side. 'You survived,' she says.

'I was always bloody-minded. And I had my poetry.'

'Poetry . . . ' She blows another smoke ring. 'I never understood the value. My husband was obsessed with books. Living according to the good book. Carrying his book of scraps. Out of touch with the real world.'

I run my hand over the silky pillow on my lap. It is threaded satin with tassels and brightly coloured embroidered birds: peacocks, parrots. An exotic flavour, African. I rub my finger against the shiny material. It comes away with the same black specks I had seen in the cellar.

'Volcano ash,' says Rosza. 'No matter what you do, it creeps in. Like the mould on the glass. The salt under the doors. Fine black powder everywhere. Soot. It is like being back in the village.'

'I didn't know there were any active volcanoes left in Sicily.'

'Don't let the water fool you,' says Rosza. 'This is a dry island, an island of fire. No-one can tell when Etna will erupt. The maids think the soot flies around and around and settles on houses which are cursed.' She snorts, smokes her cigarette. 'These old *ofanculu* superstitions. Wearing fear like a medal pinned to the chest. Pinned so the rusted point goes in. Thank God I got away from it.' She stubs out her cigarette. 'My mother used to say that I was born with a map of calamity in my hand. As though it was my fault. For years I would turn my hand over, to see where the map was.' She sits back, her black eyes glassy. 'One day, she grabbed my wrist and bent it backwards and said, *In there, you stupid girl,* and drove her long wooden washing peg into my palm.'

She lights another cigarette, her eyes hooded. 'My father told me I would twist my own head off to get what I wanted,' she says. 'As though that was a bad thing. As though he hadn't done exactly the same.' She plants her feet on the Moroccan rug, pushes against the sofa. I feel the heavy frame slide. She is stronger than she looks. 'Pietr tells me you didn't stay when your father was arrested.'

'He wanted me out of the country.'

She is still for a moment then she nods. 'Sensible enough.' Her eyelids droop. 'I always rest after lunch.'

I glance at the slicked wet terrace. The rain is falling in flat sheets from the beaten grey sky. 'I might go for a walk.'

'Oh, no, my dear,' says Rosza. 'It's too wet for that. Mudslides are common. You will rest in your room.' She stands up. 'Build up your strength for your Mr Devlin.'

She is watching me. There is nothing I can do but nod.

In my room, I open the balcony doors. Pools of black standing water are cupped irregularly down the slope. The trees bow under the weight of water, the clouds make knotted fists of shadows across the plain to Santa Margherita. I think of the crest on the bottle of wine in the cellar. I think of wolves.

Under the dark reaching arms of the trees on the edge of the forest, a silhouette watches me. Devlin. I raise my hand. He stands. The trees shift in the wind, the shadows move and he is gone.

After dinner that night, we sit in the living room looking at photo albums from Koloshnovar. The photos are of her husband's Polish family, Rosza says. She turns over pages of women in corseted dresses, men with stiff white bibs and precisely creased trousers, some with slim elegant dogs, their noses raised, sniffing the wind. Here and there is a dried flower so colourless, it is hard to even tell what is pressed between the pages. One page has an embroidered handkerchief pinned to the stiff cardboard.

'I always wonder what happens either side of the photo,' says Pietr, stooping over the back of the sofa, swirling brandy in a large glass. The light illuminates the liquid's inner fire. 'There.' He taps the page. 'That's the perfect moment. But the perfect moment is always backed by messiness and sweat.'

'Like the plain brown paper behind the silver mirror,' I say.

'Exactly.'

I smell the delicate aftershave he used. He has changed for maybe the third time today. There are cufflinks at his wrist. I look to see whether they have the wolf's crest. But they are plain mother-of-pearl.

'Poor Georg.' He points at a photo of a thin worried-looking man hovering at the edge of a tennis party. 'In his suit and tie, trying so hard to fit in. Always so anxious at weddings, luncheons.'

'A failure,' says Rosza. 'Expecting pity.'

'Vulnerable,' says Pietr. 'He would hold onto my pocket and say, What shape is yellow?'

'Synaesthesia,' I say. 'The ability to blend two senses. It's a mark of creative people. Some ability to leap between left brain, right brain.

All the great poets have it.' I feel the brandy slide down my throat. 'Rimbaud was famous for it.'

'Georg was a failure,' says Rosza. 'I never expected anyone in this world to give me anything before I proved myself. No-one deserves respect unless they contribute.'

Behind me, Pietr says, under his breath, 'Unless they win at any cost.'

'But you have the right to expect respect as a human,' I say.

'No.' She raises her eyebrows. 'Why?'

The rain beats down. The terrace spotlights fall away into the black air. Through the dark, a drawn-out sound crosses the plain. Not so much a sound as a ghost falling through two dimensions.

'Wolves,' says Pietr. 'At Margherita.'

Rosza turns over the pages of the album.

'Who took these early ones?' asks Pietr.

'Your grandfather,' says Rosza. 'My husband's father,' she says to me. She taps a photo of a fierce-looking man with very black hair and a handlebar moustache who stands in a garden filled with black roses. By his side is a dark-skinned youth, bare-chested with loose flowing trousers and a curved dagger in the sash around his waist.

'It's another world, isn't it?' says Pietr.

'That's the servant he brought back from Morocco,' says Rosza.

'Slave, I would more believe,' says Pietr.

Rosza stares down at the photo. 'Your grandfather didn't like me at first. Natural, I suppose. The foreigner. The peasant girl.'

'You said it was guilt,' says Pietr.

'He was crazed by the death of his son,' says Rosza. 'He blamed himself for Czeslaw leaving.' She puts her thumb over the face in the photo. 'He felt something in his own past had driven away his son.'

Pietr reaches down. After a small hesitation, Rosza lifts up her hand. Pietr turns the next few pages and says, 'Here we are.' Tall, perfectly matched and spaced poplars run beside a long straight road to the white chateau in the distance. The house itself is only glimpsed through the trees but I know what it looks like: the huge bay windows along the broad stone terrace, the narrow balconies jutting out from the second storey, the tall pointed turrets. But when I saw it, the windows were broken and gaping, the roof was missing its tiles, the poplars were snow-blighted.

'Poland,' I say. 'Koloshnovar.'

'Yes,' says Pietr as though I had asked a question. 'I remember my grandfather's voice echoing down the long halls. You couldn't get away from him. And the incredibly heavy red curtains. Red velvet wallpaper. All the colour of blood. Oh, and horses' heads looking over the half doors in the stables.'

'That was a story of your father's,' says Rosza. 'I told you.'

'Yes,' says Pietr. 'Because he couldn't.'

He turns another page. 'There should be a view of the stables. Here.'

This was a photograph taken in a cobbled courtyard of a glossy black horse – a thoroughbred – being brushed down by a boy in shirt and braces. Nearby, a gate opened onto a field, bushes in the distance, a light hovering sky, the darker hump of low windowless buildings.

'Those fields are famous,' says Rosza.

'Infamous,' says Pietr. He says to me, 'The Polish cavalry rode out to meet the German tanks there in World War II. All the men in silver and tassels. Swords. Of course it was total carnage. My grandfather gave them horses but refused to go himself. He said it was madness. He wouldn't let my father go either.'

'He saw it though,' says Rosza. 'He watched it all from a ditch. It made a terrible impression on him.'

'You never told me this,' says Pietr.

'Oh yes,' says Rosza. 'I am sure that is why he wanted to become a monk.'

'Until he met you,' says Pietr.

Rosza nods.

'You had so much in common,' says Pietr.

'We did,' says Rosza, meeting his glance squarely. 'I was more mature than most girls my age. You don't know what it is like to go through a war. The things you see.'

'I think all my father wanted,' says Pietr, 'was to be pure.'

'That is impossible in this world,' says Rosza. 'The best you can hope to be is changed.'

The beat on the roof slows, the rain easing. Pietr touches the photo. 'There should be a memorial there.'

In the voice of one who has argued the point before, Rosza says, 'We had to put the landing strip in. The business was in trouble. We needed to make use of every acre.'

'Leasing out is not making use,' says Pietr.

'We survived, didn't we? You enjoy the comforts of it now, don't you?'

He looks out the window. The sound of the sea is clear from this side of the house.

I turn the page. There are more shots of the house and the flat fields which stretched to the horizon under a sky of threaded blue fringed with clouds. Next came the moustached man flanked by two unsmiling black-haired young men; the one on the left had a duelling scar on each cheek.

'The sons from his first marriage,' says Pietr.

Rosza mutters under her breath, 'Bastards.'

Pietr frowns. He says to me, 'Literally, bastards. My grandfather disinherited them for me. They were very bitter. One shot himself, the other drank himself to death.' He turns over the page. In the next photos, his grandfather had grey in his moustache; he stood beside a small woman with very light eyes and hair a shade deeper than Pietr's platinum. Next to her was a little girl, with almost the same colour hair.

'My mother-in-law,' says Rosza. 'The Count's second wife. That's her daughter Agnieska. A pigheaded girl.'

'My father's younger sister,' Pietr says to me. 'She was the only person my mother could never bend to her will.'

'She was too much like her brother,' says Rosza.

Pietr says slowly, 'A solitary.'

I touch Agnieska's white hair. 'Striking.'

'Her hair darkened when she got older,' says Pietr. 'I wonder if Father – if his would have darkened, later.'

In the silence, I open another album. More shots of the family and servants at work in the garden. There were hedges, a fishpond, a maze, views of a lawn sweeping down to a tennis court, a bench with an elderly woman sitting under a huge spreading oak tree; servants carrying trays which glinted sunlight in silver out to a long table under a marquee.

A baby started to appear, a child with gleaming hair who gradually became a slender boy with a wistful expression, a youth with the same expression, a young man in boating clothes, overalls, riding outfits. He seemed happiest next to one of the glinting cars which gradually shrank over the years to become a sleek, bullet-shaped convertible. But the colour of his hair didn't change. It was an impossible shade of silver – the colour of light reflected off the small statuette of the winged woman on the bonnets of the cars behind him.

'My father,' says Pietr.

'Czeslaw,' says Rosza. 'My husband.'

She looks at her watch. 'You should show her.'

Pietr beckons me to the window. The rain has cleared the air. He points. At first I see nothing but the dark trembling carpet of sea.

A light beams across the water. It winks three times and stops. A long pause, it winks again.

'The buoy,' says Pietr. 'The rocks are deadly if you don't know the coast.'

'Something to swim to if a boat goes down,' says Rosza, bringing me a small cup of coffee. I thank her but say, 'Not at night.'

She nods. 'Hot milk, that is best for you.'

I look out to the flat, shifting darkness. I imagine my boat breaking up, the sound of creaking timber, cracking ice, the slow descent to the bottom through dark green water and clinging seaweed.

'I'm surprised you don't have a lighthouse here,' I say.

'There's been talk for years,' says Pietr. 'But with so little traffic it's not worth the expense.'

'It's mostly local fishermen,' says Rosza, 'trying for extra on the table.'

We look at the light sending its long wavering beam across the black water. The sea rolls over and over in a steady rhythm. The wind has dropped.

'Another quiet day tomorrow,' says Pietr.

It rains again the next day; hail coming down irregularly. We stay in the warm living room. Rosza spreads her accounts on the corner table, the smoke curling up from her cigarette. Pietr and I sit on the floor and play card games. I surprise myself that I can laugh so much.

When I come down for lunch, they are nowhere to be seen but the door behind the staircase is open and I guess they are downstairs.

A sixth sense warns me not to go down. I go into the living room and kneel on the sofa and stare at the clouds drifting past.

When they come in, Pietr is holding a map. He drops it next to me as he goes to mix a drink.

I expect them to say something about Devlin but over lunch they discuss the flooding in the next village, a shipwreck off Trepani. After the first course, Pietr unfolds the map. 'Have you seen one of these?'

'It looks like a satellite map.' I search for the misty outline of the house on Devlin's map. I find it, a speck next to a vast mass of blurred shadows and peaks. Something which looks like the desert but is not.

'Not land?' I say.

Pietr nods. 'The sea. Another country entirely.'

I trace a path through the dark valleys and troughs, the ripples sweeping across from Africa.

'The old philosophers believed that reflections double the world,' I say. 'Water creates another world in the sky, a world peopled with shadows and thoughts.'

Rosza looks at me curiously. The water streams down the windows. I feel the house swimming through its oceans of water and wind. I think, Water is the greatest kingdom; it absorbs everything without killing it like fire. Water is my substance.

'It is as important to us as any estate,' says Pietr.

'You talk like a fisherman,' says Rosza.

'You never like coming down off the mountain,' says Pietr.

'I always thought water was an invitation to be consumed,' I say.

'I always thought if you gazed too deeply at dark water it was like a dark mirror. It revealed what was inside you,' says Rosza.

We look at each other in strange sympathy.

'I pity you both,' says Pietr, 'if you ever find yourselves in the desert.'

Rosza taps the map. There is a signature I know in the bottom corner.

'Your father's map,' says Rosza.

'My father was no fisherman,' I say. 'His interests were – '

Rosza moves her hand across the deep blue to where a lighter mass shows on the far side of the sheet.

'Africa,' she says.

WEDNESDAY

 I tell Devlin that on the days when I don't see him, I take long walks by myself. It is partly true. Often after lunch, I follow the back path through the woods. Usually I won't go far, sometimes only to the road or down to the pool. Sometimes Pietr comes with me. More so, after he gives me the camera.

On that afternoon, when Rosza has dozed off over her knitting, I go to my room and find something wrapped in black velvet on the bed. I pick it up – it is heavy, a hard skeleton of metal. Under the velvet is an old Hasselblad camera, the kind that you open with both hands, like opening an accordion, so that the heavy metal lens pushes forward like the flowering heart of a silver rose.

Pietr is in the garage, bent over the engine of a vintage car, under a bonnet that folds up and back. He says, 'My father meant to take the camera with him on the last trip to Paris. But he left it and my grandfather gave it to me.'

I grip the leather case.

'You can use my darkroom,' says Pietr. 'Whenever you want.'

'Thank you.' I feel the deep, warm cracks made by harsh sun and mountain rain.

Pietr says, 'Photos on these old cameras have an entirely different feel.'

'They capture ghosts,' I say. 'That's what my art teacher used to tell us.'

He stands for a moment, a spanner in his hands. Outside, the rain falls in sheets. 'Another bleak December,' he says, 'another morning marooned in rain.'

I look across the courtyard to the drop over the valley. The clouds rush past, blown upwards, rising at an angle, colliding and merging and dissolving.

'It seems odd to see you with a spanner,' I say.

He stares at the tool as though he has forgotten what it is for, turning it over in his long delicate hands.

'I like the focus on detail,' he says. 'Having a hobby is a form of unconsciousness. I would have liked to have been a mechanic.' He shrugs.

'Devlin needs a hobby.'

'He needs an outlet,' says Pietr. 'For his disillusionments.'

'That supposes he had illusions to begin with.'

'There is nothing as dangerous as an idealistic man in the process of becoming a cynic,' says Pietr. 'The rage overwhelms him.'

'So it is better to . . . ?' I say.

'Be disillusioned young,' says Pietr. 'It becomes part of you, like dragon scales.' He bends over the car again. 'Sometimes I think I only took this up,' he says, 'because I thought it brought me closer to my father.' He wrenches at something under the bonnet. 'Stupid,' he says.

I say, 'The last time I saw my father was in the courtroom. With all the public gawkers.'

Through the doorway, the trees slap against the hillside, the winter light struggles through the rain. The air is the colour of grey water.

I make a decision. 'You know this is all a public relations exercise.'

Pietr stays bent over the engine.

'The Americans need scapegoats,' I say, 'for the missing art from the Baghdad Museum, for all the other – ' as always I find it hard to say the words – 'the lootings.'

'That is what my mother thinks.'

'You don't seem worried.'

'We've got insurance,' he says. 'It's just a matter of letting the right people know.' He straightens and says, 'Does Devlin know about Poland?'

'I don't know about Poland,' I say. 'What is Poland?'

Pietr says, 'The insurance.'

He takes me back to the house. I automatically turn to the living room but he crosses the lobby to the rear of the staircase and I realise that he is going to show me the rooms below.

He unlocks the door with a small silver key and we go down. As he unlocks the right hand door, he catches me looking at the door on the left.

'Is this the – ?' I can't remember whether I have been told about the cellar or not.

'The cellar,' he says. 'Not very interesting.'

'Yes,' I say after a pause. 'Stefano mentioned it.'

He motions me in. The light falls on his hair; the fine cheekbones make luminous shadows. So unlike Devlin's ravaged darkness.

I move past him into a small, windowless room with grey concrete walls. There is another desk, one I hadn't seen through the doorway, and a felt board on which were pinned maps of the local coast, and computer print-outs of what look like weather maps and shipping lanes to Africa. The third wall has floor-to-ceiling shelving. A very wide steel box, the height of a man, lines the last wall. It makes the room look like a bunker.

Pietr pulls out a narrow drawer in the steel box. The interior is lined with red velvet raised in small ridges like tiny red waves. In the padded troughs are rows of crusted rocks, some small, some the size of marbles. 'Uncut sapphires,' he says. 'Ilakaka roughs. Not so pretty to look at.' He pulls out the drawer above. On the velvet are cut squares of dull gleaming blue, like sea water in a bottle. They catch the light in uneven patterns so the colours seem to shift in a minute universe of swirls and clouds.

'Cut sapphires,' says Pietr. 'The business runs on these. You would think it would be diamonds. But no. These are the workhorses of the industry.'

He closes the drawer and opens the next. Dull green glitters. Emeralds.

'Madagascar, old earth, new gem rush,' he says. 'Basaltic sapphires formed in the volcanoes to the north. Emeralds in the east were hurled up when superheated water broke through the earth's crust and the mountains rose. And in the centre of the region, pegmatites: long rich veins of hardened magma studded with aquamarines. Left totally undisturbed for a millennium. Imagine the animals that must have roamed there: elephant-birds ten feet tall, gorilla-sized lemurs. Even now, war, poverty, bandits keep it isolated.'

He says, 'We lease open-cut mines and try to convince the locals that when they dig holes thirty feet deep into soft clay earth they need to put in retaining walls.'

He says, 'You mightn't believe me but we're better than most bosses.'

He takes a lumpy stone from the scattered mix in the next drawer. Tawny red flares through crevices in the stone's crust. 'Garnets,' he says. He picks up another and holds it to the light. It glows a deep scarlet.

'Cheap but popular.' He closes that drawer and pulls out a lower one. The padded velvet here is a royal blue with small mounds of cut stones in each section. He picks up a blue stone which is perfectly clear.

'You want me to say this is the best?' I say.

He nods.

'It is too perfect. Too cold.'

He smiles. 'You've got an eye. It's synthetic, heat treated. You can tell it apart from the real thing because it is flawless. No cracks, no discoloration. No personality.'

He picked up a deeply glowing brown stone with traces of toffee yellow.

'The locals call this beerite,' he says. 'It's cut from a locally made and cast beer bottle. The cooling method gives it that unusual colour. They sell sack-loads to the tourists.'

'You wanted to know about my business,' he says as we climb the stairs.

'I didn't mean to pry.'

'You need to know,' he says, 'why the Americans are still taking an interest.'

'You're using the same route my father used.'

'Not to move anything else. I've told my mother that. Just stones from now on.' He stops abruptly. 'Yes, we're not declaring, avoiding the tax. But we're also not – '

'Looting,' I say. 'Plundering.'

'Yes.'

I face him. 'You know all I want is to find out what happened to my brother?'

He nods. 'Anything else is . . . irrelevant.'

FRIDAY

 I go down to the lake to wait for Devlin. The sun sidles behind dark clouds in the lowering sky. There is thick grey mist in the air but the rain has stopped. The branches are hung with frozen tear-drops. Inside one, a small beetle looks at me with pleading eyes. A tiny being trapped in ice. I try not to see the obvious symbolism. I go past the beetle. The ground is hardening: it is growing another layer the way animals grow a layer of fur. An ice beast.

After three steps, I go back and crack the ice on the branch with my fingernail. The beetle drops, groggy, to the ground and crawls away, leaving a silver trail of water in its wake.

I wait an hour for Devlin.

Every few minutes, I get up, stamp my feet. This must be what old age feels like: the legs that refuse to work, the coldness in my knuckles, the ache inside my chest.

He had told me that it would all be all right. I knew he was lying to me. Yet I had desperately wanted to believe him. It was too intoxicating, the feeling of finally being able to rely on someone else. Of not being alone.

But now, when I want to conjure up Devlin telling me it would be all right, instead I see a world where fish beat their heads against glass, where the sky is black, the grass is white. I try to find a positive image to counter the rising panic. I make an image of myself reading a book and the book says, *I carry your heart. I carry it in my heart.*

It's going to be all right, I say to myself fiercely. It's going to be all right.

To keep warm, I walk around the lake, photographing the light trapped in the crusted surface. Still no Devlin. I climb through the mud and leaves and mouldering branches to the gleam of slate through the trees. I think about climbing the ridge, seeing whether the hut door will open. Peering through the windows.

A branch snaps behind me. I turn, saying, 'I thought you stood me up – '

But it isn't Devlin. A red fox, its back darkened by mud and water – or maybe it is blood – runs in front of me. Its nose quivers and it almost stops in mid-stride. I see the wildness of remorseless nature in its eyes, the chilling stare of implacable survival. Then the fox goes on, driven by urges it cannot control. I laugh. I put my hand over my mouth, to stop the brittle sound.

I wonder what Devlin would say. Too much poetry, he would say.

I watch Devlin as he walks along the road to the guard rail. He is wearing sunglasses. He hesitates. A few steps more and he could have gone around. But instead he grips the metal between his gloves and awkwardly swings his legs over. The rail is only low but he stumbles when he lets go. He comes down the slope.

He gets quite close before he seems to register my presence. He takes off his sunglasses and rubs his eyes.

'Too much partying, Dev?'

'Yeah,' he says in a flat tone. 'Party, party in Trepani.'

His shoulders are hunched. He avoids my eyes; there's a grey tinge to his skin.

He sits heavily on the fallen tree trunk and takes out his flask. 'Mitch is really on my back.'

'Dev – '

'Don't call me that,' he says irritably. He unscrews the cap. 'It's a job,' he says to himself. 'Just a job.'

I sit on the other end of the log.

The surface ice on the lake has thickened although it is still not fully set; there is constant expansion and sounds of cracking and splintering. More cracking as an animal moves through the stiff bushes nearby.

The distance vibrates into a deep rumble. Devlin puts his face up to the weak sun.

'Car?' I say.

He moves his head drowsily. 'Bigger. Lorry.' He closes his eyes.

I climb the slope and stand behind a tree near the road. The rumbling grows louder. An unmarked grey van comes around the corner. It drops down through the gears and shudders past me. The ice on the guard rail falls off in small glassy plates.

I go back.

Devlin is swaying on the log, his eyes closed.

'Shouldn't you write that down?' I say.

He mutters under his breath.

I say, deliberately, 'For Mitch.'

He opens his eyes. 'Mitch wants hard news. On your friend Pietr.'

'There's nothing there, Dev. He showed me the office. Maps, files, computers.'

'You'll have to check it out after hours,' says Devlin.

'It would help if I knew what I was looking for.'

'Transportation documents. Anything passing through Sicily to Africa.' He thinks for a minute. 'And maybe the other way.'

'How big?'

'Could be small.'

'Is it jewellery?'

'Jewellery?' He stares as though he can't comprehend the word.

'Gemstones. Garnets.'

'Garnets? For God's sake, the Americans wouldn't spend millions on garnets.'

'Well,' I spread my hands. 'There's nothing. They lead quiet lives.'

'You need to snoop around.' He bends to brush black slush off his boot, missing most of it. 'What do you do all day anyway?'

'Swim, walk around the estate, read. It's very peaceful. I sleep a lot. I haven't slept this well in years. Pietr's teaching me photography.'

'Cosy.' He stamps his feet, to jolt the ice free.

'It's not like that,' I say. 'He's like an uncle to me.'

'Except he's not.'

A bird's cry climbs the morning air like scales, climbing and falling, over and over. It is sweet and ineffectual and forlorn all at once. Maybe it is looking for its mate.

The notes rise and fall. Plaintive as crystal across the quiet landscape.

'Oh for fuck's sake,' shouts Devlin. 'Shut that bloody bird up.'

I place my hand on the rough bark between us. 'Did I ever tell you about waiting on the street for a cab, after an all-nighter? An old man, just a collection of rags and dirty fingernails and a leather tan, was going through the garbage bin next to me.

'I hear these sweet notes, clear as bells. I see a bird on a shop roof, across the intersection. I can't believe I can hear so far. Yet the bird seems to be singing to me.'

Devlin has rested his hand on the log. I don't have the courage to touch him.

I go on. 'Then I realise it's the man next to me. He's making this pure sound totally in tune with nature. I tell him, I thought you were a bird. He grins at me – he's missing his front teeth – and he puts his lips together and the light beautiful notes come out. Whenever he wants, he can make that sound, to please himself.'

I stare up through the trees, trying to find the bird. 'I'm always glad I told him. Beautiful.'

'I don't have stories like that,' says Devlin. 'I don't see the way you do.'

'What do you see now?'

'Don't fucking psycho-analyse me.' He raises the flask.

I wait. And wait.

'For God's sake,' he says. 'All I see are snow and cold and tall black trees that look like spears. Satisfied?'

'That's the way I see.'

'We're nothing alike,' he says. 'Nothing.'

He's far away on the other side of the plain. Rolande at the dark tower. I can't reach him.

He shakes the flask, I hear the liquid slapping the side. For the first time, it occurs to me that he wants to fail. I have an image of him in a minefield, walking out deliberately, arms stretched wide.

'Pietr says you know more about this case than you're telling,' I say.

'And you're going to trust him?'

He tugs at the collar of his leather jacket. He's wearing a tie. I wonder if a tie is a dead giveaway in a small village. Sicily is a formal country – maybe he doesn't stand out.

Still, it's as though he wants to be caught.

His shirt collar has parted. The skin at the base of his throat is almost revealed, the skin he is always so careful to keep covered, the marks he never wants anyone to see. It's impossible to know what is there unless you have seen them, uncovered. The marks he made on himself in Borneo, in the heat.

He's slumped now but I can tell by the tightening in his arm, the slight jerk of his head, that he's processed where my gaze is. He rubs the back of his neck, yawns too casually and closes his collar. He turns the flask over in his hands. 'I have to look like I'm getting the job done.'

'And are you?'

'What?'

'Getting the job done.'

'None of your business.'

I laugh. There is little humour in it. 'Whose business is it then?'

He stands. 'I have to go. I left the car in a lorry run-off.'

'You're throwing me to the wolves.'

'You know the rules. I can't help you.'

'How can I give them information if there's no information to give?' I shout.

He puts the flask away, stares at the steel sky.

I hold up my arm. The bracelet glints dully above the pink peeling marks. 'How do think this makes me feel? You say, look what I did to myself. Look what you did to me.'

He glances at me and turns away.

I say, pressing my back teeth together to stop from screaming, 'You told me you would get me proof the Americans have my brother.'

'Had him,' says Devlin.

I think, as I write now, that his face shimmered in the light. I thought then that I had something in my eye or there had been a tremor; I held the log, waiting for the earth to steady.

'What's the matter?' He takes a small step towards me. 'What is it? You're – silent.'

'I can be silent when I want.' I think for a moment. 'Occasionally.'

He grins. It is exactly the way he'd looked at me the night we met. In that brief period of euphoria.

'Dev,' I say, 'aren't you stressed? Doesn't this make you stressed?'

I think he was going to come closer but instead he looks at his watch. It is a rote gesture, something he does to fill the time, to put the person he is with in their place. In their place in his schedule.

He turns to walk up the slope, away from me. He says, over his shoulder, 'It's just a job. It won't kill you.'

I shout after him, 'Won't it?'

He keeps walking, leaning into the slope, his shoulders hunched. 'You've got three days, four at the most, before Mitch gets here.'

THURSDAY

The mountain looms above me, black against the light. It is not as tall as it looks from the other side of the plain but it is steep. The wind is harsher here. The metal at my wrist is a ring of cold; I can't feel the burns at all. I pull my jumper down over them, the jacket over that, tighten my scarf. The wind still creeps in, around my wrist, into my marrow.

I climb. The ground is patched with mud which skids off the steeper sections like brown paste. But there are enough rocks and small stone chips for traction. Besides, I can see the path she had made.

The cold air is pricked with seaweed, smoke and other dead, acrid fumes. Gusts of wind hit the back of my jacket with grit and gravel. When I turn, for the first time I see the tip of the tower of the glass house at Castelmontrano, rising above the hunched green of the forest.

With a soft sucking sound, the ground gives way. I slide, grab the nearest branches, feel wood cutting my hands. My boots find harder earth and dig in. I see a smear of colour.

I kick with my boot; mud lifts off in a shovel-shaped chunk, revealing stones forming a mouth, the side of a face, a cheek, a slash that could be a beard. A mosaic. The fine edging of black makes it third-century Roman. Or maybe fourth. I think to myself, Third. I never used to lack confidence about this. I always knew instinctively and I was usually right. Always right, I say to myself now. Don't lose your nerve.

The panel pulses its malevolent green. The cuts and burns on my wrist creep out. Unstoppable but dead at the heart. Like the look on Devlin's face when he saw me pouring boiling water over the metal. After I had tried the knife.

I force my hand into the ground and wonder whether the mud would erode the wires inside the bracelet, make the electrodes short and spark, the moisture spreading like a small lake across the chips and electrodes. Reduce the solid to mush. Re-make.

The bushes have been trimmed back and I can walk, bent over but still quite fast. It is warmer, the wind fractured against the trees; only the occasional needled gust hints at the cold air outside the canopy. I look for her footsteps, the sharp indents of her stick. Nothing. Either she hasn't come up this way or she knows the way so well that she didn't leave any traces.

Below the summit are the remains of a stone path leading between two narrow boulders. Beyond are steps made of flagstones forced into the hillside and a cobbled path which soon broadens. I come out onto the main road of the devastated village just as the rain starts to fall.

Santa Margherita is like nothing I have ever seen before. I guess that it was once a village covering the entire last third of the hill. Further up I see outlines of houses in the broken rubble but here, no buildings were higher than my waist.

I am shocked. I had imagined Rosza's home to be a small villa, or a picturesque cottage, not this blasted and devastated place. The cobbles are black green in the disappearing light, the wind keens down the street. A shutter bangs close by, half off its hinges. Shadows wash past like waves, turning the buildings into the silhouettes of broken animals kneeling in the dusk. I close my eyes, imagine violence being done in the village at the top of the mountain. Dogs would bark, maybe windows would open briefly, but no help would come, no voices would shout out. Only the sound of the wind jostling oranges, plucking at the laundry forgotten on the line.

I try not to hear misery in the sound of the wind, try to imagine it instead as being something playful: rippling the surface of the lake, sending leaves skittering across the cobblestones in the piazza in Trepani, dancing down the narrow alleys to Devlin's room.

A building more intact than the rest lies at the end of the street. I walk towards it, my boots striking the wet cobbles like drums. Black flutters at the corner of my eye – something slips between the houses.

These buildings have a looted look: no shutters, no window boxes, crumbling mounds of tiles where roofs had been, wrought-iron balconies hanging drunkenly. Through the gaps between the houses I see the rusted metal ladders and the crumbling stone steps which once connected the higher streets. A black door is set in the dark earth at the end of one alley. The sign on it reads *Scalini Che Conducono Al Cimitero*. Steps To The Graveyard.

The black wraith flutters again. It reminds me of the months after the news came about my brother's disappearance in Poland: how I would be convinced I saw him on the edge of my vision, the curve of his back disappearing around an invisible corner. I never caught him, no matter how fast I turned.

My breath is clouds of pale mist. I rub my watering eyes and Rosza is ahead of me, moving purposefully up the street. Her head turns slowly from side to side but only at certain points along the rise. She is looking but knowing where to look. Where the blackened stumps of burnt beams reach up from the crumbling bricks.

The bracelet light flickers. Maybe it is out of range here. I put it against my ear. No ticking, no whirring. The sound of death is silence, I think. I strain to hear; the wind turns over in my ears. I look at the bracelet. I am sure the green on the panel is darker.

I rub my finger on a shell of burnt stone; it comes away black, even after all these years. I wonder whether it would be cool inside the stone: in a fire would it be protected or would it become the hottest part, like the hottest part of the sun? What would it be like to crawl inside?

To be a person encased in stone. I wonder if that is how Devlin feels. I have always imagined him looking up through layers of water – the remote world making unstable patterns. But now I realise that is me. Devlin would be the bluest heart of the hottest flame.

There is a broader gap between this shell and the next. In the centre are the burnt and splintered remains of a wooden shelter collapsed over a hole in the ground. An eye looking up to the sky. I move closer. A drowned eye: a well. Choppy black water with a hint of green lifts in small silver-tipped waves, as though someone has recently dragged a hand across the surface.

The street is empty. The only place Rosza could have gone is further up the mountain. Unless she has taken a side street and doubled back past me. My neck tenses. She could be anywhere behind me. She knows every corner, every alley.

I tell myself not to be ridiculous. There has been no sign that Rosza is hostile.

The building at the top of the street is actually two buildings: a low white-washed box with a crucifix nailed to the front mantel. Behind it is a tall thin tower.

I open the church door to find plain wooden pews before an unadorned font. The water had dried out long ago, leaving nothing but a milky tide line. At the far end, a wooden cross is nailed to the white wall. On it, a plaster Jesus: the painted head bent, tears trickling down the shiny pink cheeks, eyes closed, hands in supplication. His feet are bound in heavy chains: real chains, I see. Long rusted iron nails have been driven through his feet, the punctures surrounded by red. There is none of the ornate-ness of the Sicilian churches in my art books, where even the smallest church had an altar dipped in gold, a luminous Renaissance painting, priests' robes with precious jewels sewn into the tunic. I wonder if the building was stripped on the Church's orders or by looters.

The door opposite opens onto a narrow room with a hearth on one side, a wooden box bed on the other and a stone sink under the window. Two wooden benches are drawn up next to the fire. Two dusty wine glasses lie between the benches; a black robe – tattered and stiff – hangs on the wall.

I shiver. This room seems colder than the village outside.

The door at the base of the tower is ajar, so I stop and call Roza's name. Inside, stone stairs wind up into the gloom. I can't bring myself to step into the darkness until I see the light edging through the window slits. I put my hand on the cold cracked wall. My sleeve slides back, the panel on the bracelet glows. My wrist is the colour of seaweed in the gloom.

I climb, glimpsing the countryside through the slits. The tiger-striped light falls across the steps which are coated in black dirt but lighter in the middle as though someone has scraped their feet back and forth. There are cobwebs in the corners with old clumps of dust hanging like teardrops from the misshapen circles.

Rosza has moved more quickly than I would have imagined and the silence is oppressive. At least outside there had been the sound of the wind, the creak of wood, the far-off birds, a sense of living no matter how cold and remote. At least I could look back at the glass house. I just stop myself from thinking of it as home.

I round the next corner and come up the last steps and am, suddenly, there. A door opens onto a small room, bare except for a stripped bed and a wooden cabinet.

Rosza is standing at the window opposite. Without turning her head, she says, 'Come to see the view.'

Below us the village descends to the plain in dark grey folds of hunched and brittle trees which flinch in the wind. Landscape as body of the twitching beast.

'I keep expecting it to snow,' I say.

'The bastard weather is too changeable now,' she says. 'I often think it would be better to live in a hot climate. One knows where one is in an *ofanculu* jungle.'

A peculiar sighing comes up through the trees, a rushing of expelled air. Blow, blow west wind, I say to myself. Blow your soul beyond the firmament of the dead.

From here, the glass house is easy to see. The light glints off the silver shell in veins of blue and green which snake into the air. The tower of Pietr's bedroom is almost level with this tower; it rises straight, sheer and high above the rest of the house. It is out of proportion, I see that now. I am reminded of something but can't think what.

'We're above the mist,' says Rosza.

I say, 'I prefer the water not the clouds.'

'Clouds are water,' says Rosza. 'These mountains are known as the mountains of tears. They cry over the Triangle of Hunger but never long enough to make a difference.' She slaps the window sill. 'Everything is water in the end. Everything is tears.'

'Do you come here to mourn?'

She lights a cigarillo. 'So bastard unfashionable now, to smoke. Who would have thought that smoking would be taboo in Italy? When I was a girl . . . ' She seems lost in thought. 'The doctors in white coats said on the television, smoking was good for you. That was the first time I went out of Europe, to Poland. I had never seen anything like it. I was shocked.' She exhales slowly. The smoke is snatched away by the wind. 'Television,' she says.

She leans out the window. I make an instinctive grab for her arm but she smiles and says, 'I won't fall.'

'I used to come up here and burn the diary pages I had written,' she says. 'Pages that would have seen me called a witch. About the stupid girls who teased me.'

'I burned my diary pages,' I say. 'I would eat the ashes.'

'Yes.' She is pleased. 'It was a way of overcoming your weaknesses.'

She says, 'Did you hide the car between the boulders at the bottom?'

I nod.

'Pietr gave it to you?'

'Yes.'

She smokes her thin black cigarette with her hand barely moving from her mouth. Her fingers are swollen around her rings. Fleshy folds at the little wrists. Round knuckles. An elderly pensioner living in a remote part of an ineffectual country.

'I wasn't following you,' I say. 'I just wanted to see what happens if I go high.' I push back my sleeve. The metal rings my wrist like cold mist, the green panel shining. My arm feels dragged down by its own weather.

Rosza flicks the dried mud off with her nail. She runs her finger over the panel, pausing when she feels the hairline crack. She touches the burn marks, more gently than I would have thought.

'Maybe there's nothing inside,' I say. 'Just a battery for the light. It's a psychological trick to keep me in one place.'

Rosza asks, 'What did they say when they put it on you?'

I rub the bracelet, trying to warm it up. I remember how Devlin had rolled over in the bed when I unlatched the shutters. I had felt the splinters beneath my fingers, smelled the fumes of oil and fish rising off the inky water. The dawn light was pink and blue tinted. I remember how I could have looked over my shoulder at Devlin but I didn't. I stood there and watched the sun come up, holding the coffee cup which felt cool in my hands, as cool as the inside of the early morning, feeling Devlin behind me. I remember how he had never touched me but I had relaxed against him and turned my head so that my lips were in that hollow where the shoulder muscle meets the chest, just below the collarbone, the coolest place, the colour of blue vein and pearl.

I had just closed my eyes when I heard the click of metal around my wrist.

After that the heat from the coffee cup burned and burned and burned up my fingers, my neck, the back of my head, behind my ears. But where it burned the most was under my eyes. Since then I've never stopped burning. And I hate the heat.

'It was just a technician,' I say now, 'who put the bracelet on me.'

She stares at me, unblinking. 'It would be interesting to know how far they will let you go.' She throws her cigarette out the window, watching the sparks break up in showers of tiny orange flares in the wind.

'Your Mr Devlin has become a lone wolf,' she says. 'What do the Americans say? He has gone off the reservation.'

The wind swells, battering itself against the tower. The stones seem to shudder. Rosza looks at the bracelet and says, 'We will go up.'

We take the last set of stone steps to the ruins of the Roman battlements. Past the crumbling parapets and the faint road is the graveyard. At first I think there is no order to the graves but then I see the stones lying in uneven rows around the peak's bony hillocks. Most of the headstones are plain but here and there is a magnificently carved angel or engraved crucifix. Set well back is a small flat-roofed stone building with a new brass padlock on its wrought-iron gate.

'You wanted to know why I come here,' says Rosza, pointing. 'My husband's vault.'

I peer through the gate past the high stone table to the five shadowed alcoves.

Rosza looks at the ledge over the gate. 'There should be a key there.'

I am barely taller than she but I stand on tiptoe.

'A little more,' says Rosza.

The green light on the bracelet turns red. A shrill sound cracks the grey air. I can't understand what it is at first. A city sound. An alarm. The note breaks into regular beeps. I jiggle the bracelet. The beeping goes on.

Rosza holds my wrist, examines the bracelet with care. She lights a cigarillo and exhales, staring down the mountain. 'Now we see how important you are,' she says.

The wind comes up the hill: a wind with the smell of decayed moss in it, a wind carrying the colour of death in it. I look at the sombre greys of the stones around me, imagine women with dead hair walking slowly up the path, looking down on the living. On those that killed them.

The beeping hammers through my head. I am finding it hard to think.

'You young people have no conception of what it is like to be poor,' says Rosza. 'To not be able to afford a doctor, not to avoid pain.' She scratches her stick across a mossy stone, leaving a pale wet trail in the glowing green. 'Pietr never comes to the vault.'

I think of Pietr by the lake. 'Maybe he cares too much.' I stare at the stone table. 'How did you meet Czeslaw?'

She studies the broken village falling down the mountainside. 'He was passing through.' Nothing stirs but the wind. Rozsa's breath is heavy in the cold air. 'All these women that criticise me,' she says. 'Fat Rosza, insignificant Rosza. I outlasted them all.' She beats her stick on the ground, in time with the shrill beeping. 'I would hear them whispering,' she says, 'huddled behind the long line of sheets in the drying yard. They thought the wind blew their words away. But it blew them straight to me. I wrote them in my diary then I burned the pages and I ate them.'

The beeping goes on and on. 'Eating the book of words,' I say. 'Yes.'

She grasps my wrist and swings it against the wall. I feel the shock in my arm as the panel meets hard stone. The beeping goes on. Rosza swears.

'Of course we made enquiries,' she says loudly. 'Did you think we would not? Your Mr Devlin is a drunk. He is a man collapsing into failure, of no good to anyone, embarrassment after embarrassment from Sydney to Borneo.'

At that past moment in the moonlight, Devlin opens his eyes and smiles at me. I press my knuckles against the cold vault wall.

'Then why is he here?' I say. 'If he is a drunk.'

Rosza slashes at a strand of wet moss with her stick. 'I suppose it is their idea of fairness. He has been on the case the longest.'

The beeping noise burrows into my spine, along my jaw line. Go to the dead and love them. Where were those words from? I saw them carved in stone by women with pale dead hair. *Go to the dead and love them.*

'Longest?' I say.

'I was sure he would have told you. Mr Devlin is the one who arrested your father.'

The beeping stops. The silence fills the cold air.

I look at the panel. It is still red.

In Venice, I didn't talk to him the whole time he bandaged the burns and cuts on my arms and hustled me out to the boat and down the blue green canal to the airport. He walked me in a careful arc away from the gleaming passenger planes to the sandbagged concrete sheds beyond the last runway. I wondered whether any tourists saw me, what they thought, whether they could see the handcuffs. Maybe they were briefly disturbed, the way that I had been as a child when we crossed into Morocco, driving past the wire cages and turnstiles and dogs twisting on leashes and the Africans sitting on the ground – their own ground – while surly police tossed their clothing into the dust. Inside the air-conditioned limousine, my father's business associates passed around the figs they had brought across from Spain.

It was as Devlin was leading me up the ramp into the rear of the cargo plane that I quoted the Rimbaud. I didn't even know if he could hear me: the propellers had just started turning and the wind was rushing in my ears. Wild bad tortured Rimbaud, giving up poetry, the thing he loved most, because he couldn't achieve the perfection he wanted. Poetry couldn't make him immortal. *I descended black impassive rivers. I sensed haulers were no longer guiding me. Screaming Redskins had taken them for their targets.* When I had finished, I spat on the floor – spat the devil out of my mouth – and said to the man who had handcuffed me, 'I'll never forgive you.'

Rosza was looking along the horizon. 'Nothing,' she says. 'Maybe you are right. Maybe you don't mean enough to them. It is all a trick.'

'You can't take that risk.'

She waves a hand. 'A few *fotutto* bureaucrats. Imagine a whole village against you.' She drags her stick across the moss. 'If you tell them you see nothing maybe they will leave us alone.'

I see the jewels winking in their velvet gullies. 'It's just trade?'

'That's all it's ever been. Trade and territories. Just maps. Nobody killed. Nobody disappearing like your brother.'

The wind swells again on the far side of the mountain. We hear a distant hammer striking wood, an approaching beat. A black shape rises above the summit; light flares off the metal body, the dark rounded windows, the turning metal blades. It hovers like a bird on the wind before falling sideways and disappearing from view. The beat fades down the mountain. For the first time Rosza looks as though she isn't sure what to do. The beat grows louder. The helicopter is coming back up, over the village.

She looks at the bracelet. 'It might switch off if you go lower.'

As I turn into the brittle wind, she raises her hand with an air of finality. Then she flicks her fingers, dismissing me.

I walk down through the silent village, hearing nothing but the creak of the dead wood and the old leaves raking their fine-veined husks along the cold cobblestones. I try not to think of shadows slipping between houses, black wraiths climbing out of the silver-tipped water in the well. The hunched trees close over me all the way down the mountain. *No coward soul is mine.* I find the mosaic path and look across to the glass house turning dull silver in the late afternoon. There is nothing in the grey sky – nothing on the plain. The panel is a steady red. I put the bracelet to my ear. Nothing.

I continue downhill, slipping in the mud. Trying to see the car from where I am. The noise of my boots against the falling stones almost obscures the approaching beat. The black shape moves over me. The branches vibrate, dried mud lifts from the ground, wet stones and smaller rocks fly upwards. The earth is joining the kingdom of water in the sky. Chips of stone hit my neck. I put up my hands to block out the sound, the wild air, and it is then that I see the red light on the bracelet has gone out. I lose my balance and land on my back, sliding and sliding until I crash into a bush.

I lie on the trembling ground, looking up through the branches which whip back and forth against the flat sky as the black body swings restlessly overhead. The metal runners reach forward like grasping metal hands, glints of light slice off the dark windscreen, the wind booms between the blades.

The helicopter tilts. I see a man peer out: black shirt, black sunglasses. Not Devlin.

I crawl further under the bush and watch as the helicopter finishes its arc and beats its way up the mountain.

I count to fifty then slide, using my hands to push me faster down the muddy slope. Too slow. I force myself to my feet and run.

The branches catch my jeans, I am constantly slipping on the mud and wetted mosaics. I see shadows waiting behind the bushes and when I reach the stonier ground, see more shadows between the boulders. A rock falls somewhere, stone chipping on stone, like a drop of liquid chrome. The helicopter is a faint thudding in the distance, a speck disappearing over the summit, falling upwards into the crown of mist.

I reach flatter ground, see the car between the boulders, am running towards it when a black wraith moves at the corner of my eye. I swing around and am grabbed by both arms.

'What the fuck do you think you're playing at?' shouts Devlin.

'Devlin.' I am so relieved to see him I try to lean against him. But his immediate tensing reminds me and I push myself away.

'I wanted to see,' I jangle the bracelet, 'how far I could go.'

The light seems brighter here, the scars on my wrist more noticeable. A shadow passes over his face. I smell Scotch and mouthwash, more Scotch than mouthwash.

'It's broken anyway,' I say. 'It went red then it went out.'

'I turned it off,' says Devlin. He looks up the mountain. 'That's why the chopper can't find you.'

'Dev – '

'When I switch the tracker back on, they'll think it was a malfunction. Hopefully.'

'Dev – '

'You need to go now.'

I see the shadows around his mouth, the grey skin under his eyes. He is drinking himself into illness.

I say, 'Pietr offered to help me get the bracelet off.'

'He won't be able to,' says Devlin.

'At least he offered.'

'That's his job.'

'Is it?'

'You can't play both sides,' says Devlin. 'You'll have to choose.'

After a moment, I say, 'Pietr wouldn't put shackles on me.'

He turns away. 'Go home then.'

·FRIDAY

I must have caught a cold because I wake sneezing the next morning. I am still sneezing at breakfast when Rosza gives me what she says is a lemon drink but which has a sour smell of spices. A shiver of nausea runs through me with the first mouthful but after that, it seems to taste better.

'It's the mountain air,' says Rosza, 'and everything else.' She watches me finish the drink. 'Did you have troubles getting home?'

I shake my head.

She picks up my wrist. The panel on the bracelet glows green.

'It came back on halfway across the plain,' I say.

'And the *ofanculu* helicopter?'

'It flew over me. Maybe it was a coincidence.'

'Maybe.' She doesn't sound convinced.

The clouds hold back the sky, filtering in another day of low light. I go to find Pietr. Crossing the courtyard to the guards' quarters, there are more reflections in the slicked wet ground than profiles in the sky. The secret world above revealed only in reflections.

Pietr is standing by the workbench in the garage. A large stainless steel box is in front of him; straw packing trailing from it. I think

230

I see the metal-grey outline of a gun beneath the straw but I am distracted by what is in his hands.

He turns when he hears me and puts down the object with just the right degree of casualness. If I hadn't been looking I wouldn't have seen the way his fingers linger on the gold base as though he can't bear to let it go.

'The days are darkening.' He moves so he is between me and the object. But I see it reflected in the steel side of the box: a rectangular bird, about a foot high. The great image of the Arabian desert. A falcon.

'My mother said you weren't feeling well,' he says.

'She gave me a drink which tasted horrible but it did the trick.'

'That is my mother's way. Unpleasant action which always works.'

He turns. I look at the statuette. I had done a paper at university on the classic Sumerian falcon, from the Gilgamesh era. This object has the cracked and shabby aura of the well-travelled artefact. I tell myself it must be a copy. I try not to think of my father.

Pietr is swivelling. 'You're admiring my bird?' he says, picking it up. My nails dig into my palms as I fight not to snatch it from him.

'Tell me,' he says, holding it out. 'Have I been swindled?'

'Oh, it was always more of a hobby. I scraped through my PhD. Daddy pulled strings, you know.'

I take the bird as casually as I can. It is so heavy it almost plunges through my hands. I imagine it buried in sand, carried secretly in the robes of monks and holy men, passed from father to son, for four thousand years. But even all the erosion and mishandling through the ages can't blur the deep eye rolling back to look at me.

'Is it Sicilian?' I say. 'Something local?'

'That's right,' he says, watching me carefully. 'Gold plate of course.'

I automatically heft the bird up and down, weighing it. 'A lead shell?'

He nods. 'To make the tourists think it is the real thing.' *Thingk.*

The bird is growing warm in my hand. It has absorbed heat from somewhere – from me – and it is burning. Fire and ice.

Pietr says, 'They make them here in the winter months. Write stories of a magical falcon to sell on carefully faded bits of paper. You know the sort of thing: two lovers cursed by an evil magician, he turned into a wolf, she a falcon. He doomed to the icy ground, she to the desert air.'

'Why is the woman never the wolf?' I can't resist running my thumb over the curved beak, the hunched shoulder, the graceful lines etched into the wings. I have an image of a grey-haired woman standing in a long hall, the shattered and empty glass cases around her. I think, This is the first time that Pietr has lied to me. That I know of.

'Men prefer to think of women in feathers, not fur,' says Pietr. 'Cleaner somehow.'

'Radiant women, on pedestals.' The grey woman is screaming as black-masked figures run from the hall. 'Yet we're not like that at all.' I see myself watching the woman on television, see myself with tears in my eyes. Maybe I am imagining the tears.

'I never felt quite clean as a teenager,' I say. 'I felt messy, untucked. I wasn't radiant.'

'A baby wolf.'

'Yes.' I put my hand over the golden eyes.

He takes the bird from me. 'It's worse living with real wolves.'

I watch him pack it away. 'It's a good copy. The weight makes it real. Most souvenirs are too light.'

'It's not especially dignified,' he says. 'But I keep telling myself that it's better than doing . . . other things.' He fits the lid onto the box.

'What other things?' My hands feel cold.

His lips press tightly together, the cords in his neck are rigid. I think of the grey-haired curator screaming at the looters running from the museum in Baghdad.

'You told me I wasn't responsible for what my father did,' I say. 'That was good advice. For everyone.'

His hands rest on the box as though he can't bear to let it go. Outside, the sky has a purple tinge. It reminds me of the days after my brother disappeared. Days like blue cylinders.

'I never wanted to lie to you.' He slides the box across.

His fingers are still resting on it. I think of the images of the looting of the Baghdad Museum, two days after the American invasion of Iraq. The dark hooded figures running down the shattered hall, the anguished cries of the curator. Systematic looting, the news reports called it. Looting. Always such an ugly word. Whole cultures appropriated. Systematic looting: not random but planned and organised. The vultures already there, helped into the city by the advancing army. Old connections, old friendships. A century of deliberately orchestrated plunder, the prosecution had said at my father's trial. Illegal smuggling, beginning in Africa one hundred and twenty years ago with the most heinous of trafficking. The connection to Poland particularly lucrative for all involved.

I touch the steel box. His grasp tightens.

'Maybe,' he says, 'it is enough that you know I have it.'

I walk with him across the courtyard. The sky has an unsteady look, as though it is rising and falling in a bowl of dark ice. The trembling is reflected in the wet cobblestones and in the droplets of mist drifting through the archway. Reflections endlessly escaping into the distance. The clouds clasp and unclasp, birds fall down the mountain, the trees quiver. A whole other world on the other side of the dark bowl. The world endlessly repeated.

Stefano is bent over one of the Mercedes, polishing a side panel. He glances at us and keeps working in tight, rhythmical circles.

'I could have left years ago,' says Pietr, 'but I wanted to find out what happened to my father.'

'Stefano doesn't know?'

'Stefano is totally loyal to my mother. He would never do anything to hurt her.'

'Would that be hurting her – to find out about your father?'

'I always feel Stefano is looking for something in me,' says Pietr, 'that he can't find.'

'You're the only blond for five hundred miles, Pietr. It's probably follicular jealousy.'

He smiles.

I say, 'Your father was the good man.'

'Maybe goodness is the delusion. A man who constantly wants to save the world either has no problems or has problems he is not facing.'

I stare at Stefano. I could swear he was watching us over his shoulder as he worked. I think, He must be around the same age as Rosza.

I say idly, 'You could look up the autopsy reports.'

Pietr frowns. 'The originals were lost. They only had typed copies.'

'Then the ambulance report,' I say. 'The driver must have had to file something. Some of the drivers might still be alive. Talk to them.' I touch the box. 'You could give them a souvenir.'

I tell Pietr I am going for a walk and go and stand by the lake. It is so quiet I hear a train going past, the long note of the horn barrelling into cold morning air. The lake has lost its blue purple. It is the colour of ashes reflecting the sky now. I taste frost on my tongue.

I drift towards the dark, squat outline of the hut. Nothing stirs, just the shifting trees, the splintering ice.

No sound behind me but I know before I turn that Devlin is there. He nods and awkwardly climbs down the muddy slope. He has the hip flask out before he reaches me.

'Happy hour's started, I see,' I say.

'What's happy about it?' he says, looking around for somewhere to sit before wedging himself against a tree. He looks greyer than yesterday.

I say, 'We're not scheduled to meet.'

'I wanted to see whether you were okay after your little jaunt.'

'No thanks to you.'

'All thanks to me. I convinced them it was a malfunction.' He grimaces. 'But Mitch is coming down from Rome – to put me off the case. What a stupid expression. I'm not just put off. I'm fucking put out.' He takes a drink. 'Anyway, now is your chance to bargain.'

'Will I find out what happened to my brother?'

He takes a step away from me; another towards me. I watch him. He is never this aimless. Finally, without looking at me, he says, 'Whatever you suspect is bad enough.'

'So you're not with me, Dev.'

'Stop calling me that. I know you think it's cute. It's not.'

I am tired suddenly. 'No, it's not.'

He caps the flask, puts it away and says, low, 'I'm offering to help.'

'You're against me.'

'For God's sake,' he shouts. 'I'm giving you a pass out of here.'

'Why should I trust the guy who put this — ' I jerk the bracelet up and down my burned wrist — 'on me?'

Under the ashen sky the marks are livid flames. Devlin reaches out and holds my wrist in both hands. I am so taken aback that he has touched me that I am still. His fingers are cold as ice. His face seems to fall in on itself. He drops my hand. The disappointment is a bitter tide dragging beneath my heart.

'I thought if we knew where you were, we could protect you.' He sounds uncertain.

'You could have asked me.'

He shrugs. 'It was above my pay grade.'

It is the casual dismissal which does it. And what I say next. Later I think, That is when it all started to go wrong. The ground began cracking under our feet, we began building to the words which would hang like black birds in grey air, never to be unsaid. I should have stopped. But of course I didn't. It was always my fault as much as his. Maybe more.

I say, 'And you wonder why I prefer to stay here with Pietr.'

He uncaps the flask again but he doesn't drink. He stands there, swinging the bottle from side to side. He says, 'I'll tell Mitch you're refusing to work unless you find out about your brother. He half expects it anyway. Maybe he'll pack you off home, blame it on me, clean house. Mitch likes cleaning house.'

'I won't go.' I start climbing the slope.

'If I say you go, you'll go,' shouts Devlin.

I stop next to a clump of slender pine trees shuddering in the cold. Tears are burning behind my eyes but I keep my voice steady as I say, 'You tell Mitch I know it's about Iraq. Those old smuggling routes Pietr's grandfather set up. It's all about the Americans.'

The colour seems to be back under his skin. Now he knows I am staying.

'I like it here, Dev,' I say. 'I like the cold. I can breathe, after years.'

'You like being here with Pietr.' From the way his eyes narrow, I know he regrets his words the way I do mine.

'Think what you like,' I say, trying to match his earlier dismissal. Trying to hurt him as much. 'You know, it's ironic. Everyone is always so busy telling me that they never ask me.'

'Ask what?' he shouts.

I start climbing.

'Ask you what?'

I don't stop until I have almost reached the ridge.

'About Koloshnovar,' I shout down. He moves restlessly at the name. 'No-one ever asked what I saw at Koloshnovar.'

SUNDAY

Both Pietr and Devlin think I have forgotten about my brother. But often at night I stand in the corner of my bedroom where the shadows are deepest. The lights lining the walkway send beams through the clouds of mist. I see faces there: at first it was only Devlin's because I was always looking to see whether he was watching me in the forest. Sometimes I see my mother; not very often, my father. Lately, it has been my brother. Never clearly, always out of the corner of my eye. Always leaving me. As the clouds twist and turn like wringing hands, I slide into the deepest shadows. I want to ask someone, If you can't see me does that mean I am invisible?

I wander the house at night. Rosza's hot milk isn't always enough to send me to sleep. I go into the small sitting room next to the back terrace to look at the bare ground running down to the forest. This is Rosza's favourite room, she says. It is quite different from the rest of the house. Three whitewashed walls with a feeling of stone, not steel, behind them; tapestry rugs on the polished wooden floor, two broad well-sprung sofas facing the bay windows. Crocheted cushions, a knitted rug over the back of the sofa, assorted boots and raincoats in the wicker basket by the terrace door. Photographs on the walls; some are duplicates of the ones in the album: the happy couples, gleaming cars, tennis players prancing on velvet lawns.

I still haven't seen any photos of Rosza's family. All these are from Czeslaw's home. Koloshnovar.

The room has the warm smell of Rosza's black cigarettes. Sometimes I find her sitting, looking without blinking at a roll of pages elaborately inscribed in ink, their parchment edges curling. The title deeds to Koloshnovar, she tells me. She likes to hold them. 'If you've ever known real poverty where you eat anything you can – rabbits, dogs, wolves – then nothing matches the triumph of owning your own land.'

There are things left absent-mindedly – discarded balls of wool, half-finished knitting – and others left maybe not so absent-mindedly: loose papers, notebooks, a pile of Rosza's accounts. I never touch those, I never even try to look at them. In the first days, it was because I suspected a trap: special powder to stain my fingers, a hidden camera to film me. Later, it was because I was ambivalent about my role in the house. Now it is because I don't care enough to look.

I sit on the padded seat next to the window, hug my knees to my chest. Ice-crusted rain has been falling all afternoon and the ground is patched in grey slush. Every now and then, a snowflake finds another in the swirls of mist. They make a join-the-dots shape, a tiny grey figure moving through the air.

Stefano tells me the house has a ghost that arrives with no warning and goes through and wrecks the place: tosses books off the shelves, cushions off sofas, leaves doors ajar. An angry spirit. Stefano says it only happens when Rosza is away.

I wonder.

I hear the wind punching the steel shell above me. It scatters the grey slush like wet, shredded newspaper. A brief rain of pebbles clatters onto the terrace, a smell of salt and sulfur creeps in through the cracks in the glass. The mist scatters. There is a moon after all, lighting the grey patches on the ground.

I wonder what it would be like to sleep under snow. Animals do it. It must be warm enough, under the mulch, the dead leaves, the flaking logs with their little heaters of mould.

A figure moves where the bare ground falls into the darker pool of the forest. Somehow he can see into the darkness in the room. He raises his hand, beckoning.

This can't be Devlin. Devlin is off the case, fed up with me, sick of the whole thing. Maybe he has already left.

I pull on a pair of boots from the wicker basket, put the shawl around me, a raincoat. I ease the door open. Too late I wonder about an alarm. I have never asked. But it seems obvious, in the Triangle of Hunger. I freeze but all I hear are the trees, sighing like the sea, shaking their fringes of leaves. Maybe nobody dares to rob Rosza. Not with the lake nearby. Not with her history.

I go across the back terrace, feel my way down the stairs and the path, clinging to the lamp-posts. The moon is dodging behind streamers of mist and cloud. There is enough light to see outlines but not details. No faces. The man moves slowly out from the trees and stops, watching me approach. The moonlight hits his hair. It is pale, much paler than Devlin's, but not as blond as Pietr's.

There is only one other person I know who has that colour hair. Had that colour.

The path has steepened or maybe the slush is thicker. My legs are growing tired, there is pain in my jaw. Please let it be him, I say to myself. The man hasn't moved. He is the right height, almost exactly the same as Devlin. That was the first thing I did – compare Devlin's height to my brother's. As a way of choosing whether to trust. Stupid when I think of it now. Just an excuse, I suppose. There was only ever one thing uniting us. Guilt.

I slip and almost fall, stop, start again. The man approaches. The moon is emerging from its shield of clouds. The light is streaming down brighter than I would have thought possible.

The man has almost reached me. I still can't see his face. *Please, please*. The moon swings out, triumphant. He steps towards me. Now the light hits his face. A voice says, 'You have to come. They want the book. You have to come.'

I see his face and I scream and scream and scream.

THREE YEARS EARLIER

'So this is the diary entry,' I say to the psychiatrist, 'for August the tenth: *I am standing in a field with ninety bodies. Incredibly, the sun is still shining. The grass is very green and the nectar from the honeysuckle almost covers the smell from the corpses.*

'*The Corporal says, These are the lucky ones.*

'*I shake my head. Yes, lucky, he says. He holds his bayonet tight to him, knuckles white in red, leaning on it. Lucky to have a doctor. His eyes are white pebbles. Lucky to have you. There is a fly crawling on my boot. Its wings are dipped in blood. Tiny, red, stained-glass windows moving on my boot. Soon it will fly away and I will be left behind. In a field with ninety dead bodies. I will be left. I will – '*

'Yes, yes,' says the psychiatrist, snapping his fingers, exuding busyness, control. 'You see? Key dream words: behind, fly away, left.'

'But the bodies – '

He waves a hand. The bodies are just window-dressing. Signifiers to what really matters.

I think ninety bodies matter. I want to tell him that this is not a quick pan over artfully arranged dummies. I see every face. I smell the honeysuckle, I am in the field. Back in the field. I do not want to tell him that I see all this when I am awake.

I smile cautiously. Big smiles are not good signifiers – I've learned that the hard way.

He smiles at me. Would I like to read something else?

I pretend to consider. There is no fine line between disclosure and appropriation in a psychiatrist's office. If I don't read, he will take.

In the early days, I read my own poetry. But that is a long time ago now.

'You know the arrangement,' he says, moderating his tone, proportional to the huge fees we are paying him. They are paying him.

I untie the long red ribbon around my diary, flick through it, my left hand gripping the cover, fingers digging in. In such a rubbery spongy world, sometimes only the pale marbled cover feels real.

'Here is a little something I wrote when I was sad.' More sad, I almost say.

I read a poem about the beauty of a rose garden, a piece I have constructed using key phrases from Eliot with a few clouds from Wordsworth and some Swinburne to soup it up. My need is greater than yours, TS.

I am halfway through when the psychiatrist begins tapping his gold-plated pen.

'It *is* a bit twee,' I say.

'I think you should start writing more realistic pieces. Daily doings. How you feel.'

'My family is really not going to like that.'

I see the concerns scurrying under his skin: back and forth, to and fro, money, duty, money, duty. His face settles.

'I'm in charge here,' he says.

I rise, slowly, from the red couch they brought in specially for me after I complained about the black one. Absence is a doorway, like caves, like mouths to hell, I had shouted, while the receptionist giggled. But I heard that she had shouted too, when she was fired.

The silky cover of the couch, as lush as moss, is brushed against the nap. The shadow I leave looks like a butterfly. But butterflies only live for a day. Maybe I should not say that. I don't care enough not to say it.

'Butterfly.' He looks pleased. 'Chrysalis. Emerging. Maybe it is a sign that you are mending.'

Not for the first time, I wonder whether he is qualified.

As I go out, I see the framed photo of his wife. The heavy silver square is angled conspicuously on the desk to reassure his unruly female patients, like me. I met her once in the waiting room. She had a short skirt which rode up as she uncrossed her legs. I saw the cuts on her inner thigh. Cuts I recognised. Her shiny brown eye rolls up at me.

'So I said to him that I feel like a plucked flower on red moss,' I say to my best friend Anna. She is sitting in a plastic chair in the corner of the hospital terrace. The light breeze lifts the hairs in the wispy rug over her knee, making the long strands of wool rise and vibrate like exhaust smoke from idling cars. The rug seems amazingly thin.

Anna is shading with black biro under the eyes of faces in a fashion magazine. Occasionally, her own eyes fill with tears, they run down her face. I yearn to comfort her but big sentences confuse her. She seems to prefer sounds. Or small words.

She shades eye sockets intently.

'Actually, I said to him, I feel like a fucked plougher on a bed of snots. That's Freudian, what do you think of that? Seeds and furrows and whatnot.'

She nods, her lips move. Almost a smile.

She is more doped up than usual, because of the last incident. I am tired, too. Winter grinds me down. It is time for my afternoon nap but I have agreed to keep Anna company while they search her room.

Everything sharp must go, the nurse says.

That seems to be my doctor's motto too, I say. But the nurse won't comment. They never will criticise the doctors.

The breeze lifts the fine hair on Anna's blue-veined forehead. For a moment I see her, all those years ago: the foreign girl, my new friend, daughter of my father's new partner, lying beside me counting dragon shapes in the clouds.

'Anna, you know I am – '

She nods.
'If there is anything – '
She shakes her head. The tears run down her face.
She takes a drink of water from the plastic cup.
The sadness is shit in my mouth.

It is August 15 and I am writing in my diary, like I have been told
to, like a good girl.
This is what I write:

AUGUST 15: *Here is a real thing to write down, doc. My parents
disappeared for several days. The chauffeur, the new one, tells me
they went to the island casino off WA. To get away from it all. At
first I think that means me but it turns out the nurses found a picture
of my brother hidden under Anna's mattress. It's a photo my mother
hadn't seen before and it set her off. So now I am alone in the Manse.*

*The one thing my brother left me, the one intact thing, was a bonsai
tree. At first I barely looked at it, certainly did not water it. Then I
realised it was still alive, despite me. It was an entire little world: a
minute pond with a Japanese-styled bridge in shiny bamboo and a
tree. Under the branches, the ground was dark in its own shadow.
The tiny veined leaves curled like living scrolls and around the trunk
was neon-green needle-grass which I trimmed with nail scissors. One
day, I discover a small black beetle has taken up residence under the
bridge. When I pour water over the tree, the drops catch in the little
parallel branches, teeter on the needle tips, making a jewelled casket.
The beetle comes out and stands in the shower. His? her? its? feelers
wave gently. The water trembles in the angles of the jointed legs:
onetwothree fourfivesix. The beetle holds the droplets like a water
carrier, retreating carefully. The black shiny round body becomes a
hood. I peer into the little darkness. Maybe there is a face in there.*

AUGUST 19: *The hospital entrance looks like a hotel foyer, all softly
rounded couches and very, very large pastel prints. Sizes are always*

extreme in rich places. Can Anna get something woollier than that thin rug? I say to the nurse behind the three silver computer screens.

The nurse looks at me with an odd crumpled expression. 'It's pashmina,' she says. It is contempt scrunching her face.

I give up on asking her about the pills the shrink makes me take. If wrong questions get you contempt, what does hanging yourself or slicing your inner thigh with the bread knife get?

The chauffeur takes me home to the Manse. The mansion. Or as my brother called it, the Mausoleum. Neither of us liked it. It didn't like us: if you tried to rest on the big stone blocks of the high estate wall or the low wall on the terrace, the cold ate into you, pushed at you, made you move away. My mother said the black wrought-iron draped around the house was black lace. But my brother called it iron spider webs. They cast odd shadows, not just on the verandas but right through the house, smudging the white marble floors and making the white walls look as though water was running down them. It didn't matter how much art my mother bought, the paintings never looked as good as in the showroom: the rooms were overcast, the colours dimmed, the vitality leached out.

When we first moved there, when my father became suddenly rich, I was too young to understand why we couldn't play castles with cardboard boxes in the living room or drape blankets over the furniture the way I used to with my brother. The marble floors struck back at us, just like the walls. When we tried to play chasing games, we slipped and fell. We weren't held and cushioned like we had been with our old scuffed and curling linoleum. We bruised right from the start.

AUGUST 21: *Usually I make allowances for my mother, for all she has been through, for duty's sake, for the sake that I really don't care. But today is different. I overhear the nurse saying, We found the blood in Anna's room.*

I come home for my afternoon nap. My mother is in the hallway. She has a tan and new blonde hair. The hair is literally new: it is someone else's, sewn in to lengthen hers, to give it body. Someone else's body.

'No lipstick,' she says, looking me up and down. She never calls me by my name any more. 'I expect you to come in and be social.'

I go in. A pall of boredom has made the room almost warm. I say hello to a circle of shiny nodding foreheads. Shiny chins go up and down. Someone says, accidentally too loudly, That must be her real nose.

'Now that you've had a little rest, what are you thinking of doing, dear?' someone else asks kindly.

'I'd like to buy a lamp so I can walk through Sydney looking for an honest person,' I say.

Silence soaks up the goodwill like blotting paper on a cat's mess.

My mother laughs, grips me above the elbow, saying over her shoulder, 'She's still a little stressed.'

Outside, she digs to the bone and hisses, 'Do you want people to think you are mad?'

I know she is suffering. Misery is making her sag, despite all the plastic surgery. Everything sharp must go. Even my shapelessness pierces her. But I can't help myself.

Won't two of us missing be hard to explain, at tennis?

I'm sick of you kids, she says.

Kid, I say. There's only one of us left now.

For my brother and me, our favourite spot was a grass-covered ledge which jutted over the bay. We loved to lie there, our feet dangling over nothingness, the warm earth hard all along the spine until the sudden drop off and the silky feel of bare air between the toes. The welcoming sky was laid out, a cloak of blue with a lion's face clasp. My brother, who had just started going to Europe for my father's business, would tell me that in Poland, the clouds were so low you could reach up and touch them. Not like the far-off gauzy smears here. The clouds were the best things about Koloshnovar, he said.

From our ledge, we looked across to the bridge webbed against the sky. At dusk, the cars pass in wet clay-coloured streaks, only their headlights distinct. You can't see the people inside clearly, our house is not that close, but you can see the lights as the cars go forward. It *looks as though the darkness is devouring them from behind.* Winning, says my brother.

Back at the Manse, the car stops exactly parallel to the wide steps. I thank the new chauffeur and tell him not to get out. He smiles shyly at me, his face pale in the gloom.

My father is crossing the marble hall. I hadn't realised he was home. I would be glad to see him, if he was glad to see me. The chill from the floor makes my soles curl. I wish summer would come.

My father looks at me warily. He has the same shadows under his eyes as Anna's magazine models.

'Dad.' I go to hug him but he catches me by the elbows.

'For God's sake, you're too old to call me Daddy. And the doctor says you've been faking your diary entries again.'

He opens the study door. Sometimes I think you're sending me bad waves to make my business go wrong, he says, and slams the carved oak door.

The last few times my brother was home he didn't come to the ledge even when he said he would. Finally I figured out that he had gone back to his old high school, the first one, the one he liked. I find him sitting near the statue by the football field. It is chilly. The stadium lights throw halos in the winter night. The wind wrestles the branches, sending shadows across the statue so the roughened stone seems to breathe. The statue is a man, wearing a loincloth and holding a dagger. He stares straight ahead, his right arm clamped by his side. His left is folded, pinned across his chest – this is a figure of right angles and straight lines – and across the throat of the small leopard writhing there. The leopard is almost finished, the feline body hanging limply, the tail kinking down his hip. Man and leopard, caught in an instant of time, frozen in a moment of extreme anguish.

I stare at my brother. Why strangle a leopard in the moonlight, opposite a football field where even now the swelling shouts of the players, creased by the light wind, graze the grey stone?

AUGUST 28: *I know you want reality, doc, but how accurate is it going to be if I am doped up on pills? Already I feel only what I see, and I*

246

am seeing almost in black and white. I have a new dream: children in black caves are drawing butterflies on the wet walls. I go closer: white wings, white heads, white eyes. But I know when I turn my head, the wings will be red.

SEPTEMBER 5: *Another week: nap, hospital, nap, a nightclub filled with starbursts of white light. The beetle seems to be building a nest under the little bridge. I watch it with interest. I ask the shrink to let me off the tablets but he says no. Dinners are long silences and the void of the empty plate which my father insists on setting. My mother does not eat. Of course, the anniversary is coming up.*

SEPTEMBER 10: *Anna gets thinner, if that is possible. She has tried to kill herself again, stealing another patient's tablets and crawling behind the boiler in the basement. She had a vial of blood, like the one they found in her room. Anna says the blood is my brother's. But I know that cannot be true.*

I read in the back of the car about a homeless man who was living in a tree on a riverbank outside a large country town. A large town, not some rural enclave. The tree had been set alight by five teenage boys. The tree burned and the man died.

He was Polish, says the chauffeur, whose name is Tadeusz. He is Polish, too, and he heard about the case from his chauffeur friends who know all the gossip because they drive judges and police chiefs. The boys had been from rich families. I stare at the newspaper. The story is twelve lines long. No photo. The man was sixty years old. He had a name. He was younger than my father.

But why? I say, helpless.

Tadeusz shrugs. 'For kicks maybe. To feel.'

No comfort, not even in a big tree.

When I arrive home, the police are there and an ambulance, and two of my mother's friends in tennis dresses, cheeping. She has smashed up the place again, all the mirrors are broken and she has scrawled obscenities all over my brother's room. The words are in red paint, which looks black in the late afternoon light. My father has taken her away and the maids are already washing down the walls. The room was painted in white gloss after the last time so it is easy to clean off.

Why wasn't it you? one of my mother's friends says when she thinks I am out of earshot. I go upstairs. I know as soon as I open my bedroom door that I should have hidden the bonsai. It is lying dismembered in splots of earth, little flesh sculptures, the roots already drying out. The beetle of course had been stamped flat.

I sit in the dark for a long time. When I look down at the dirt spilled on the thick white carpet, there are little black dots. Ants have come from nowhere to clean up my beetle, take it away. The spilled dirt makes crevasses in the squares of moonlight. The ivy in the wooden lattice on the wall outside scratches at the breeze.

Far away, a phone begins to ring.

I go downstairs slowly, certain it will stop by the time I get there, or someone else will answer it. But the maids have finished and gone. No-one answers and the phone keeps ringing. I go into the dark study. I have never felt so tired. The curtains are half parted, the room is awash with black milk, I am swimming through it, moving backwards. I sit down behind the desk. I pick up the phone.

'Come now,' says a voice with an accent. 'We are waiting for you in Koloshnovar.'

'No – what? It is too cold.' I reach out, fumbling for the switch on the desk lamp.

Static flares at a great distance. There is a click.

A new voice, faint but unbearably recognisable. 'You have to come. They want the book.' His voice is cracked by static, or pain. He says, 'Bring the book. You have to come now.' It is my brother.

Another click. The line goes dead.

Light blazes on. On the desk are two identical bottles. One has my prescription on the label, the other has a name – a woman's name – I don't recognise. The pills inside the bottles are almost exactly the same size and colour. My father leans against the door.

She didn't know what she was doing, he says.

I know.

After a minute, he asks who the phone call was for.

It was for me, I say. He straightens but the shadows stay, under his eyes and around his mouth. The next day I booked a plane to Poland.

'The next day I booked a plane to Poland,' I say.

'Stop it,' says Devlin. He grasps my shoulders. The dark presses in around us.

'What did you say?' I shout at him. There is water, wet and cold, on my cheeks, there is salt in my mouth. It can't be tears.

He says, confused, 'I brought your diary.'

'I thought you were my brother.' I twist. He doesn't let me go. The trees scratch the dark bowl of sky.

There is just the two of us. I know I'll never see my brother again, probably never even find his body.

The cold eats into my spine. I shiver and put my hands over my eyes. Devlin's grip on my arms tightens. I sense he wants to – what? push me away? pull me to him? There is that familiar smell – the Scotch and mouthwash.

He is a dark shape in front of me, boxing me in, unable to help. I feel dark ice growing around us. I say, 'You can't comfort me. You can't even help someone in distress because you're so damaged yourself.'

His face is a dark country of valleys and shadows. I visualise him putting the handcuffs on me. I want to hurt him. 'You're an indecent man. You could have helped.'

'You?' There is a note in his voice I read as contempt. I bunch my fist and hit him across the cheekbone. The blow knocks his head to one side. He doesn't turn back immediately. His profile cuts into the lighter patches of snow on the trees.

I think, I never reached you. You compartmentalised me, like everything else.

I say, 'I'm sorry.' But when I see the snow in his eyes, I know that apologising isn't enough this time. Why, in my deepest core, do I still think that I can control him? Nothing has ever hinted that I am right.

He says, 'How do you want me to comfort you?' He jerks me to him, rubbing my back ferociously. 'Like this?'

'Stop it.' I wrench my arms free but he grabs my hands between his hands. 'This?' he says, unsteadily. He gathers me hard against him, rocking back and forth maniacally, so I feel the strain on my lower back.

I get my hand up, around his neck.

'Dev.' I put my forehead against his chest. Then – I can't help myself – my whole body relaxes into him, I close my eyes.

His arms falls away but I don't move and after a moment he puts one arm around my shoulders, the other around my head, shutting out the moonlight. I am held, in warm dark.

'All I ever wanted was safe harbour,' I say, 'just for a few minutes.'

He bends his head. His lips are against my neck.

Now, he lets me put my arms around him. The coldness is going out of him – I can feel it. Warmth is seeping in. He feels it too; he tenses. He is wondering whether to pull away. But he doesn't.

I lift my head. He doesn't move. I am this close – I know it – I am this close – I put my mouth against his mouth. I kiss him and, for one moment, he leans in.

I feel his hands on my wrists. I am scalded, as I was once before. I open my mouth and hear the click. Like before.

He steps back into shadow. Only his hands are visible, glittering with cold steel in the moonlight.

I look at my wrists. The bracelet is gone.

'How ironic,' he says. 'At the mountain – you looked at me with such gratitude. I felt I had made up to you, for before. Then I realised that nothing will.'

'Dev – ' I step forward but he withdraws even further, the bracelet a dark ring in his hands now.

'I prefer to be alone,' he says. 'It's a relief. Don't you understand? This was impossible for me right from the start.'

'I was impossible for you.'

'This trip was meant to be punishment,' he says. 'It wasn't meant to be – '

I catch his arm. 'No more punishing yourself. Please.'

He puts his hand over mine. 'Don't write everything in your diary. Even if you're making it up. Don't tell anyone. Not Mitch. Not Pietr. I'm not saying that because I'm jealous. Don't trust anyone. Not even me. Well, I know you never trusted me.'

'Dev – '

He takes a book with a pale cover from his pocket, a blue booklet on top of it. I see the long red ribbon tied around the book. My diary, my passport.

'I won't take them,' I say.

He opens his hand. The books make small square shadows on the ground. Little doorways.

I say, 'When are you going?'

'Tomorrow.'

'After all this,' I say, 'you're just leaving me?'

'Yes,' he says, retreating into the shadows and he is gone.

MONDAY

 The next morning I wake knowing that Devlin is leaving. I go to find Stefano. He is standing on the back terrace, arms folded, staring down into the forest. It is only when I am closer that I see he is watching Pietr, who is walking slowly down the back path.

I ask Stefano to take me into Trepani. I haven't quite worked out my reason, I mutter something to do with supplies for the party. He looks at me as if he knows that I am going to see Devlin. It doesn't seem to matter to him. When he looks again into the forest, I guess what is on his mind: anything that keeps me away from Pietr is fine by Stefano.

It is a clear day as we drive along the coast. The white crests are being eaten by seagulls, the buoy rides the rolling waves.

'If you were on the south Spanish coast, you would see Morocco,' says Stefano. 'Africa.'

I look at the long line of cloud lying on the horizon. The buoy tips and the bell jangles. I wonder, again, about the darkness of Stefano's skin. Where does he feel at home?

We drive past a clearing which looks like where I stopped with Devlin. I touch my hair before I remember that it is gone. There is only dark stubble.

I say, 'My life would have been easier if I was a blonde.'

Stefano says, 'My sister Sophia's life wasn't easy.'

'Pietr's life seems – ' I stop.

Stefano shakes his head. 'Not easy.'

I look over the cliff to the water below. 'I'll need a wig for the Christmas party. Or they'll think I'm a – '

'Collaborator.'

Stefano doesn't hover, he doesn't crowd, but there is something dark and hunched about him. He looks the archetypal old stocky Sicilian: gap-toothed smile, brown face, but there is something dead in his eyes. He's never there, completely. I don't feel he means me any harm but he's watching for something. Maybe he is just sizing me up. My father's business connection doesn't make me untrustworthy. Or trustworthy. The only thing I don't doubt is that he is totally loyal to Rosza and Pietr. How far he will go is another thing entirely.

Devlin thinks I should be on my guard against everyone in the house. I think that I should worry outside the house. But I don't want to leave. This is the first place in years where I feel at home. Am I deceiving myself?

We are passing in and out of tunnels: one, two, three. When we come out of the next, I see a huge ripple running across the waves, trailing shadows. The buoy bows and rolls. The bell sounds, louder.

The car slows. 'See the darker water?' says Stefano. 'Trepani's Teeth, a line of rocks which the fishermen believe moves with the weather. They are never in the same place.'

Trepani. I think of Devlin in his room, with his black marks. And his alcohol. I can't bear the pain he is going through. I can't bear it.

Spits of rain hit the windscreen. 'A ferry used to run past here from Palermo to Calafu,' say Stefano. 'It went down one night in heavy winds. Only men survived – that should tell you something about this part of the coast.'

'There were only men on board?'

'Survival of the fittest,' says Stefano. He half closes his eyes so they are slits of black across his weathered face. I can't tell whether he is grieving – or remembering.

I am confused. 'So there were women on board?'

'And children. The women stayed with their children or were dragged down by their skirts. It was every man for himself. Only the strong survive in Sicily. It wasn't so long ago that they stopped putting weak babies out on the hillside.'

We are right on the coast. The sea shudders under its white crests, a school of darker objects – fish – move like birds through the blue water. Matted clumps of seaweed drift like crowds of people through the dark blue air of this other world. I see reflections of the clouds where the water flattens between the waves and think, The world is doubled.

'You didn't ever want to move away?' I say curiously.

The car is definitely slowing. 'Nobody likes strangers, especially Sicilians.' He stretches his mouth into a silent laugh. 'Even in Sicily.'

'But there are other places – America . . . '

'It's hard if you don't trust anyone.'

'You have Rosza here,' I say, looking to the horizon. 'You've known her a long time.'

'Since we were children,' he says. The car turns down a narrow gravel road. '*I cuccioli più piccoli e deboli di una figliata.* The runts of the litter stick together. We knew what it was like to fight for attention. Everyone followed my sister Sophia; they all thought Rosza was the quiet one. But she showed them.'

'She seems very far-sighted,' I say cautiously.

Stefano says, 'She heard voices on the wind. She knew the calamity, he was coming.'

'And was she right?'

'They all died,' says Stefano. 'The well was poisoned and they all drank from it.'

'But Rosza survived?'

'She wasn't there,' says Stefano. 'She had gone to Poland. I put her on the ferry myself.'

The road drops sharply. The smell of the sea oozes through the closed windows.

I say, 'Rosza showed me Czeslaw's grave in Santa Margherita. She still seems in love with him.'

Stefano says, 'It's not love.' The car slows to a walking pace. 'The Pole is nothing to do with us now.'

'Pietr has his hair.'

'That colour, it is not so unusual in Sicily. Sophia's was almost silver.'

'Still, like father like son . . . ' I say.

'He died before Pietr was born. He was never meant to be a father.'

'But Rosza must have cared once?'

'Maybe,' says Stefano. 'Yes, probably. She couldn't bear the lake being there. Every year she drained it. But it seeped back. Then they spilled poisons outside Piscia and it showed in the lake water. That was how her story was believed. She had spent years being blamed by the Polish family. They thought after what happened at Castelmontrano – the poisoning in the village – she was connected, but now . . . '

'The water proved her innocence.'

The road flattens, the pitted shadow of a small grey beach comes into view, capped by a restless sea. I think, Water absorbs all the suffering in the world. But it can never erase the blood. Blood clouds the surface of the clearest water; it makes running water slow down, become heavy.

The road finishes at a pile of rocks in front of the cliff face. Stefano turns off the engine.

'You should know what she suffered,' says Stefano. 'Before you judge. When she went to the Polish place the old Count, Pietr's grandfather, he wouldn't see her. The sons from the first marriage took her down to the catacombs and left her there. They wanted to frighten her away. But we have catacombs all through Sicily: when a country is poor, even the dead must do without coffins. Since medieval times, the bodies are buried upright in the walls.

'Still, they left her there in caves stretching into infinity – a labyrinth, she said. She wandered for hours in the dark until she felt cold air on her cheek and then she shouted words that the old

Count – Pietr's grandfather – couldn't bear to hear. So they brought her up to the surface.'

I say, 'She told them she was pregnant.'

'Maybe.' He flexes his thick fingers.

'She inherited Koloshnovar. Did you ever go there?'

'No,' he says. 'I never saw Pietr until he was ten years old.'

We get out of the car. The beach is grey and damp and pebbly. This water is not silent like the lake with its brooding meditation on death. This sea is constantly diving within itself, like divers excavating shipwrecks.

'She outlasted them all at Koloshnovar,' says Stefano. 'Later, when the Americans wanted to use the place, they thought they could browbeat her: the little Sicilian peasant. They learned.'

'How did she get on with my father?'

'He respected her,' says Stefano. 'They were the same.' He picks up a pebble, skims it across the water, between the waves. 'Mutual exploitation, she called it. That only goes so well when one side doesn't feel more exploited than the other. It is difficult to keep these things in balance.'

This is the closest I have been to the sea in Sicily and the water is quite unlike the thick syrup of the Castelmontrano lake or the oily greenness of the Venetian canals. The dark grey sea slides back and forth across the pebbled beach, trailed by tainted foam as dank as wet blonde hair. It has depth to it even on the shore and it carries fish hooks and plastic bottles, rotted carpets and broken shells. Stefano picks up a small square piece of wood, probes it with his thumb. He takes out his knife and begins to carve. The wood turns this way and that in his hands; the serrated blade with its wicked hook flashes light. Shavings fall between his fingers onto the dark beach.

He says, 'I used to make toys for Pietr when he was a boy. I sent them to him in Poland. He liked animals.'

'I would have thought he liked cars.'

'He only liked cars when he found out his father liked them.' He blows on the wood. 'Before that, it was hawks and dogs and wolves.' Dust motes spin in the salty air.

Gulls hover overhead, a tanker edges along the thin horizon. The waves break sluggishly on the rocks nearby. I pick up a small sea-shell. It is greyish pink, cracked along the spine. It feels powdery and old. I throw it away. I yearn for the sun on my face, wattle on the breeze. Home.

Stefano says, 'You should tell the Australian he doesn't belong here.'

'He's leaving. He never found what he wanted.'

'He made a nuisance of himself. Asking questions, searching houses.'

I stare at his bent head. He is a collection of heavy cheekbones, big fingers, broad wrists, blackness in the tan. There is no sense of light to him.

I say, 'I didn't think Devlin was doing anything.'

Stefano blows on the wood again. He seems to be carving two spheres, one higher and smooth, the other lower and warped. He says, without looking up, 'The only reason he didn't end up off the cliffs – ' he hooks a thumb at the rocky wall above us – 'was Rosza said it was a family matter.'

'About her family?'

'Your family. Your brother.'

He blows the last wisps from the carved wood and puts it in my hand.

The carving is a seated woman bent over a baby. She has the calm face of a Madonna but the baby is misshapen, twisted, in her lap.

The first thing I see when Stefano drops me off in the town square at Trepani is a broom against the cobbled wall. But not a broom with horsehair and a wooden handle. This handle is a bobbled branch with dried twigs bound at the bottom by rusted wire hammered into the wood.

In summer, this would be a pretty square, with its small church at one end. A fountain spills out of the wall, with the inevitable wolf's head. Beyond are six brass tethering rings for mules and livestock and a row of shops with metal frames for the summer awnings bolted into the pavement.

But in December, there is only one awning up, only one old man sitting on the bench outside the church, watching me with uncurious eyes.

The fountain is not running; a pool of brackish water broods under the dry-mouthed wolf. The church door is closed. There are no shadows on the ground; the flat, pastel-grey sky is streaked with yellow. The row of shops hides the view of the sea but the smell of salt is strong on the wind that blows across the square. A dried leaf, etched with black veins, skitters past me.

Café Flora is sewn above the scalloped edge of the lone awning. Chairs are stacked along the front wall under the broad windows but the door is open. I step down into a low-roofed room with booths on the right. A woman with grey-blonde hair and a lived-in face is polishing the long wooden bar.

I ask her if she knows an Australian staying in the village.

She stares. I am wondering if she understands English when she jerks her thumb upwards.

I turn to the front windows. Maybe he is staying in some kind of farmhouse in the woods running up to the ridge.

But she points to the corner. 'Up,' she says. I peer and see steep, curved wooden steps.

I look at the row of bottles behind the bar, the glasses gleaming in the low light. Of course Devlin would live here.

I go up the stairs, every board creaking. His room is at the end of a long narrow corridor. The door is unlocked. I don't knock, I don't hesitate. I go in.

The room is bare: a single bed, a washbasin with a shelf and plain mirror, wooden floor, a small desk in front of a tiny window which looks over a back alley. Grey sky and hills are smeared beyond the roof tiles and the lines of washing strung from the balcony railings.

I don't want to look at the sleeping figure on the bed so I go to the desk. His laptop is there, his files in a neat pile. There are three pens: two black and one red, all exactly parallel. The red pen lies inside the other two.

His breathing fills the room. He is out cold. The screen glows as I lift the laptop lid. I type in the password I got from him that night in Venice. Files come up. I see my name, Pietr's name. I find my brother's name. *Enter.* I read the blunt subheadings, the brutal sentences typed into the official boxes.

There are photos, three years old – I hadn't expected that. But I know these photos. I recognise the lattice light, the wet sheen on the stone floor, the marks of despair gouged into the walls.

I stare at one particular photo for a long time. When I saw these cells at Koloshnovar they were bare, deserted. But this photo – I can see the figures slicked with liquid pressed up against the wall, merging with the damp. Flinching in the darkness.

I close the laptop and turn. He is lying, face down, one arm thrown over the side. There is something falling from his fingers. It looks like blood. It looks like he has cut his wrist.

I can't believe it. I stand, stone inside my spine, then I step stiff-legged to kneel by the bed. I cup my hands beneath his fingers to catch the blood, the ribbon of red. Then I see it really is a ribbon. Silky and narrow. Not long: fringed at one end, cut sharply across at the other.

It is a section of the ribbon which is tied around my diary.

My knee nudges something on the floor. An empty glass, the faint shimmer of brown in the bottom, the smell of Scotch. There must be a bottle somewhere. I reach under the bed to the clink of glass against glass. I don't want to look. There are six bottles, all empty. Neatly lined up. Something about that neatness catches my heart. As though he had done it just before he passed out.

He stirs and I sit beside him. His shirt must be unbuttoned at the front because it is twisted, revealing almost all his lower back. All his marks. I place my hand into the black lines, feel the raised ridges. It must have been excruciating, the way he had it done. I remember the look in his eyes when he found my old scars beneath the words on my inner arms. And that was done for pleasure, I had said. Not to hurt, not to punish myself.

Was it? he said and I thought his eyes filled with dark water.

I want nothing more in the world than to kiss him. I know what will happen. But I can't help myself. I kiss the blackest mark, the pool of night below his shoulder blade. The worst one, I always thought. I kiss him and I am right. He wakes and rolls over and looks at me as though he hates me. I can't bear it. I go to the small window, put my hand aimlessly on the cold glass. The world outside is blurring. But I'm not crying. I refuse to cry.

His voice crosses my ocean of water. 'What day is it?'

'Monday.'

He says, 'I thought it was Friday.'

I am sitting with Devlin in the back booth of Café Flora. Outside, the rain falls: steady hard streams with diamond chips.

I say, 'It's about to snow, they say.'

'They always say that.' His hands are shaking on the wooden tabletop. He puts them under the table.

'It'll be a white Christmas.'

The woman at the bar brings us our drinks: coffee for me, two glasses for Devlin: Scotch, neat. He calls her Julietta, thanks her. I see the look on her face. It is not even eleven.

'Bottoms up,' says Devlin and throws back his first drink. Colour floods in under the grey shadows in his cheeks. He closes his eyes for a minute and rests his hands on the table. They lie still.

There is no other way to say it so I say it, straight out. 'What if I tell Mitch I don't want another case officer?'

'It won't make any difference.' He takes a sip, slowly, from the second glass. 'Mitch doesn't rate my skills that highly.'

'Tell him I've been sick.'

There is an expression on his face which I would like to think is concern. He's hesitating. But I know before he does that he's made his decision about whether to trust me.

'Mitch won't accept dog-ate-my-homework excuses.'

'Even if it's the truth?'

'Especially then.'

The coffee goes down, unpleasantly hot against my throat. 'Nice to know that the government doesn't worry about the health of its property.'

Devlin says, 'But you're not sick.'

'That's not the point.'

He tries to stop himself but I see it, the small smile.

I stretch out my hand, almost touch his arm. 'Dev . . .'

But it's too much for him. The way out is too easy, somehow. He can't head towards the light. He's unable. Dis-abled.

He moves his arm out of reach. 'I don't think you understand,' he says in that familiar locked-jaw voice. 'I've got other cases. I need to move on.'

He stares into his glass and whatever reflection is there reinforces his image of himself; the black marks are doubled. He is back behind black bars. I speak, knowing it's not the right time, knowing I am making a mistake but unable to help myself.

Dis-abled from help, I say, 'I don't want you to go.'

He wants to make some smart crack – it's the only fun to be had these days, for both of us – but even with the Scotch, he senses that some turning point is being reached. He's like a fisherman in a boat on a calm surface, suddenly feeling the tremors beneath, seeing the dark shapes moving below, the small churn of white water, the boat rising . . .

'You want someone to taunt,' he says.

'Stay a bit longer.'

'No.'

'What if I tell Mitch he'll get what he wants after the party?'

He forces himself to look directly at me, both hands clenching the glass. There is no light, no reflection in his eyes. Pretty soon the niceties will be well and truly over. I wonder – again – if he remembers anything. I can't believe that he doesn't. But if he does, and he won't admit it, then there is some darker sea inside him than I ever imagined.

I look at him and I know it's hopeless. Somehow I deluded myself because of that night. Maybe it was just an excuse. Maybe the way I mark myself isn't so different from the way he marks himself. Maybe I never cared either.

Now I think, I've swallowed all I can of thorn smoke.

He finishes his drink, holding the glass over his mouth so the very last drop runs in. The light through the window turns over in the brown trail running down into his mouth. The light disappears into the marks I know are there at the base of his throat. It is all I can do to stop myself reaching out to touch him.

But he hates me touching him now.

He says, too loudly, 'Quitting drinking. It was one of the conditions to coming here. All I have to do to be off the case is tell them I'm drinking. They'll find out anyway. They'll ask around.'

He's assembling his defences, stacking them up like walls of black logs. 'You'd better start worrying about yourself.' I wonder where the man of last night has gone, the one who unlocked the electronic bracelet. Obviously, he's thought better of it.

'Mitch won't believe you've been sitting around party-planning,' he says.

I push the coffee cup away. Here it comes.

He says, 'What do you do all day, with Pietr?'

I wonder if this is a standard move in the manual – accuse the informant of being a slut – or whether he really wants to know. Knowing my luck, it's the former.

'I don't see much of him.' I try to make my tone as neutral as possible. 'He's got his work.' Outside, the rain is thickening. 'I'm on my own a lot, taking photos. He lets me use his darkroom.'

Devlin has relaxed. His attention wanders back to his empty glass. He looks to Julietta behind the bar and raises a finger. He's almost forgotten what we're talking about. I stand and pick up my bag, my coat, my gloves. Devlin is turning, his face tightening, he senses what's coming. I stoop to him. We are so close that our mouths are almost touching. I breathe his breath. There are white lines around his nostrils, his mouth. But he doesn't pull back.

'And we read poetry together,' I say.

Devlin stares at me. Now I see reflections in his eye: myself reflected in his eye reflected in my eye reflected in his eye. Endless reflections into infinity. The world doubled, tripled, quadrupled. We are both very small in the pools of black.

He has stopped breathing. He won't open his mouth. He won't give me anything.

I walk past him, step outside. The grey has lengthened, become solid. The world is changing. It is snowing.

On the outskirts of the village, the air is white. The outlines of the small hunched stone cottages blur. I put up my hand and an ice crystal – hexagonal with a rainbow of colours caught in every face – turns slowly on my fingertip. It vanishes into a mirrored scale of water which glides slowly to the ground. The sky is a flat grey lake with yellow shiverings in the surface. The sun is a faint silver-white circle trembling behind currents of yellow-silver mist.

Although there is a mild ache in the joints of my hands I don't feel the cold. I have a mind for winter, I say to myself. I notice I am walking more slowly than usual but I see no reason why I can't walk back to Castelmontrano.

Once past the last cottages, I am right above the sea. The water is a gun-metal grey now, almost flat, with paler, crusted slabs – trapped water turned into ice sludge – washing back and forth off the coast.

There is a dark pebbly beach below me; wooden boats are drawn up in neat rows of faded blues and reds. A man-made promontory of dumped rocks and concrete runs like an exclamation mark into the sea; a tall dark figure faces the horizon. I see the graceful raised hand, the long hair beneath the draped cloak: the Virgin Mary blessing the departing sailors. On the shore, the bronze figure of one-eyed Trident glares at the village, his pitchfork raised. Like the sea, he is dark, scarred, implacable.

A curtain drops over the sea, a veil over the figures. The road before me retreats under the grey veil, there is a slow rumble and crack behind me – I think of a block of ice moving slowly over stars made of steel. I want to turn but my legs are ice. My hands are blurring, disappearing. I am about to enter another country, one I think has been here all along. *If you can't see me does that mean I am invisible?*

A car stops; the passenger-side window rolls down. The beat of the windscreen wipers drowns out the engine. The wheels are draped in glinting spider webs: steel chains.

Devlin leans across. 'Get in,' he says.

I can't move my arms. All I can do is hold my hands out, palms up. I am expecting a snide comment but he gets out without a word and picks me up and puts me in the passenger seat. Inside, he turns the heater up and spends the next ten minutes chafing my hands. He won't look at me but I stare at the dark hair meeting his forehead and I think, We are a long way from the no-touching rule now.

Just out of Trepani, we cross a rickety bridge. The snow falls more thickly, reducing the landscape to black and white. We take the side road, turn away from the coast. I look back. The sea has dissolved into mist. You can no longer tell where the land is or the ocean or the sky. All the worlds have merged together. No more reflections. No more doubling. Just one big world. Nowhere to hide.

The landscape streams past: wet fence posts poking out from the white page, dark patches on the road. The trees imprinting the sky with their black hieroglyphics. I lean against the car door. When I lift my head, my cheek leaves a round clear spot where the frost has melted on the glass. Devlin sits, one arm along the window sill, apparently relaxed. But his hands grip the steering wheel and when he coughs, a thin wraith of Scotch drifts through the car.

'I have a mind for winter,' I whisper to myself.

Devlin says, 'Why the hell can't you speak English?' He jerks at the steering wheel and the back of the car slides on the slicked road. The dark patches on the road aren't water. They are ice.

Another bend is coming up, and a smear of dark blue. The lake. We are closer to Castelmontrano than I had realised.

'I thought you were lying,' I say. 'Pretending to look for my brother.'

'I never lied about that. I only lied about knowing whether he was alive or not.'

Frozen rain rattles on the roof. The road narrows; the cliffs on the right give way to scrubby trees climbing the ridge.

Devlin says, 'Even if you know the answer, you have to ask.'

'Like you asked?' I say. 'In Borneo?' I regret the words instantly. 'I didn't mean that. I take it back.'

'You can't take back words,' he says. 'They stick to your skin.' He grimaces.

'You're starting to sound poetic.'

'Thank God I'm leaving then.'

I put my hand on the fogged glass of the window. The heat warms the mist away then my hand chills and the mist comes back.

'Yes,' I say. 'Thank God.' I see myself standing in the palazzo bedroom, listening to the ticking clock and his breathing.

I say, 'That moment just before you woke up in Venice. That was the happiest I had been in years. The happiest ever.'

He turns to look at me and the car hits ice and slides sideways. A sickening feeling of complete weightlessness as the tyres leave the road. We hit the first tree. The right-hand side of the bonnet crumples up and pushes back towards us: a metal sea, an incoming tide. Unbalanced, we jolt sideways, sliding down the bank. We hit another tree, the car spins around. I see the lake: a thin layer of glittering crystals, bigger than the sun. Devlin shouts as we hurtle through scrubby bush, shattered ice falling over us like tinsel. I just have time to wonder why the snow isn't slowing us when the car is airborne again. We twist – the weight of the engine pulling us nose-down – and plummet over the bank. We hit the glittering surface. Ice rears up on either side in crystal shards. The red-veined black water falls over us and we sink.

There is water in my skin, under my fingernails, caught in bubbles under my eyelashes. There is water in my eyes. Water presses against my mouth, my ears, my clothes are filled with water, spreading out behind me like galleon sails, expanding, lifting. I am being dragged out of the car.

I see Devlin behind the wheel. He is stunned, shaking his head from side to side, water escaping in small silver bubbles from his mouth, his eyes closed. He doesn't realise where he is. The usual hard line of his mouth is relaxed – the only time that happens is when he is sleeping. He is sleeping in the water and his mouth is beginning to open.

Above me, the waterlogged sun glows behind the world; the reeds murmur by the riverbank. The water plucks me away from Devlin who is trapped behind glass, pearls drifting from his mouth.

The car falls slowly through the dark water, the open passenger door making it turn slightly, as though it were pivoting on a wing. Pressure builds in my throat, my ears, behind my eyes. In my lungs. My eyes feel dry from not blinking. All this water and my eyes feel dry.

I catch the door, haul myself into the car. He is slumped over the steering wheel. I pull at the seatbelt – it doesn't give and I am suddenly conscious of how much my chest hurts. I feel bubbles spasm in my heart, I am shaking. I wrench at the seatbelt. In another moment I will have to go to the surface. I can't leave him. The spasms run up my throat, I convulse. I have to open my mouth. I look into the back seat. There is another shadow there, a presence, a man with pale hair. He puts his hand into the shadow of my hand, puts his hand on the shadow of my shoulder and urges me on. I jab frantically at the belt release panel. The car is growing darker. I put my hand over my mouth to stop myself from gasping.

I pull at the seatbelt. It comes free. I grab Devlin, kicking back-wards. I put my feet on the outside panel, hauling him. He hangs, too heavy – I will never be able to pull him to the surface – then his mouth opens – air and water rush out in a silver stream. He kicks hard and comes free. I place my right hand in his hand like a shadow and we rise.

In the shallow water, he half pushes me, half throws me up the bank. I feel him fall away and when I turn, he is on his knees. He is so still I think the water is already hardening around him, holding him upright. I push my way through, cracking sounds all around me, grab him. I open my mouth but no sound comes out.

He hunches next to me, eyes closed, chips of ice trapped in his lashes. I pull at his jacket, my hands shaking so much I can barely grasp the leather. I put my hands around his throat, try to find a pulse. 'Are you alive?' I shout. My voice emerges as a faint breeze. 'Are you alive?'

His lips never move but from somewhere I am sure he says, 'No.'

He is shaking but not as much as me. My body literally sways from side to side. I can't feel my hands or feet and it is an effort – it is like pushing a mechanical toy – to even breathe. To even be able to help your own body. I hit my leg with my hand. The blow is feeble because my hand is trembling but I sense contact. And now, a rank smell. Something chemical in the water.

Even as I watch, streams of snow fall, beginning to cover us. We are disappearing into the landscape.

'We need shelter.' His voice sounds a long way off. 'Fire.'

I look towards the frozen horizon: nothing but the disappearing trees. No sound but water roaring in my ears. I search for any glimpse of tiles or wood lying against the grain of the forest.

He has closed his eyes. My hands slip into his black marks. 'I see it,' I shout, my voice a whisper. 'A hut. Come on.'

We climb the white-patched bank. When the snow hits our skin, it is soft and damp. 'It's warm,' I say to Devlin. 'It's a beautiful day.' We are half crouching, half supporting each other. Our feet won't grip the ground and we keep falling.

We climb through the trees.

You never forget those moments when the odds change, when you know you will live. In one moment, across the black plain, a child with short dark hair is saying her mantra: No coward soul is mine. In the next, I think I see the hut. Then I do see it: the lapping of slate in the patch-worked ground. He sees it too and we change course, skirting a mouldy pile of logs, slipping on the wet ground, smelling the damp corroded leaves, the hollow cavities of dead animals. I am just thinking that it definitely feels warmer when skeins of mist begin rising from fissures in the ground, in long languid strands which part and re-join, almost stroking the air. A broken voice rattles next to me. Devlin forces out words through teeth clenched to stop them chattering. It sounds like 'oil' but he gives up, defeated.

In the hut, wrapped in old blankets while our clothes dry over the chairs next to the fire, he says to me, 'I hate it that you saved me. Hate it.' He wouldn't look at me as we changed, sits as far as he could from me in front of the flames.

He fumbles through his jacket. He takes out the hip flask and gives it to me with an odd expression. All I taste is bracken water, then faint warmth. I hold the flask out to him.

He looks nauseous. 'No,' he says. 'I've had enough.'

He leans on his knee, gazing into the fire, playing with the slender metal hook he had used to pick the lock on the door. 'The fissures, they remind me . . . I flew over Iraq when the oil wells were alight. After the first war, when Saddam was retreating and he lit the Kuwait wells. Huge streams of fire shooting up into the sky, black smoke spuming out of the ground.' He puts the hook back on his keychain. 'We had to keep climbing to avoid the flames. At fifteen thousand feet we were barely above it. We were in an army cargo plane and the noise was so loud you couldn't hear what anyone was saying over the vibrations. But I heard a hissing sound.'

'The earth was disgusted,' I say.

'Yes.'

'Apocalyptio.'

'Yes.'

He sits away from me. He has a blanket around his waist and another around his shoulders, covering all his marks. I remember how in Venice he didn't want me to look at him, wouldn't let me take off his shirt. At first.

The fire is building. Black smoke is drawn away on a slow slipstream. The smell of wood resin fills the hut, clears my head. The shadows of the flames move across the wall. The sky is the colour of old milk, feeble and hue-less. I keep thinking it is nearly night-time, that they would be looking for me, but it is still the middle of the day. The light seems to be receding. Time is slowing down.

The light undulates across the old logs. Snowlight, thunderlight. It isn't warming me. I am shaking so much the blanket keeps slipping.

I hug my knees to my chest.

'Now we know what happened to Pietr's father,' says Devlin.

'Yes.' My teeth are chattering.

'The cold alone would get you. Never mind toxic water.'

'Yes.' I am rubbing my hands together under the blanket, trying to restore circulation, the way he had done. But my skin is cold. I think of him leaving. I am colder still.

The logs crack and pop, the shadows writhe across the wall, long silences running between them. Through the window, snow falls from the frozen sky. I put my head on my knees. My forehead is chilled, the cold spreading through my head. My fingers are numb. The blanket loosens and slips, I sway.

'Wait a minute.' He takes the blanket from his shoulders and wraps it around me, sitting cross-legged behind me, putting his arms around me, rubbing my arms and forearms and legs with the same impersonal chafing he had done earlier.

'I'm cold, Dev.'

'For God's sake.'

My mouth quivers and I turn away but he pulls me so that I am lying against him. He rubs my arms again. But he has lost the previous rigid touch. He is rubbing into the skin now, not across it. His hands are slowing, lingering.

'Don't,' he says, 'call me that stupid name.'

I feel the warmth of his chest through the back of my neck. I turn my head slowly, expecting him to move. He is still. My lips touch the base of his throat, the blackest marks. I feel the ridge where the needle made of bone had jabbed in, time and time again, under his skin. Where the mixture of ashes and coal had been forced in.

I imagine it all done by firelight, under a cold blue moon, the jungle nearby, waiting.

He still hasn't moved. I turn my face, disappear into his black rivers, let my lower lip travel over the terrible absences. He shudders.

'I'm cold,' I say.

I slip a hand around his neck and wait. I think of the night we met. I will him to think it too.

He breathes out, slowly, and lowers his head. This time, I think, this time.

His lips against mine. As I turn fully against him, I feel the warmth finally at my hip. His arms are around me. The heat runs up my spine. I am triumphant. I press myself against him, open my mouth. I want all of his black marks inside me. Like before.

I must have said it out loud because he goes rigid and says, 'Venice?'

'I knew,' I say drowsily. 'The first time I saw you.'

But he is already withdrawing, contracting. It is as if he is programmed to lash out at any tenderness. 'Knew you could make a patsy of me?'

For a moment I see him standing under a huge dark wave, but not running from it or raising his fist like Trident on the shore. 'You want to torture yourself,' I say. 'You want to suffer.'

'Isn't that what you like about me?' he says. 'I'm – '

'Damaged.'

'Careless. Like you.' He wraps the blanket around his rigid shoulders. 'I don't get involved,' he says. 'Not after Borneo.' But I see a faint line of sweat on his upper lip and I think, I haven't lost you yet.

'It was a mistake,' he says. 'It could have cost me my job.'

Dark water begins falling around him. I am furious suddenly, if only to summon up the courage not to retreat.

'Oh, come on, Dev. I bet you're the only one in that pack of wolves who doesn't fuck for his country.'

His eyes are completely black in this light. 'That's what Mitch said. He never understood why I didn't take – advantage – in Borneo.'

'It's because you're not like them. You're not, no matter what you tell yourself.'

'I'm not like you,' he says sharply.

'I don't want you to be. You don't have to pretend with me.'

He stares at me. There is some indefinable change around him as though an indistinct lightning has snaked through the air.

'It's all words with you,' he says. 'It's never doing.'

'It's a different way of doing. It's a prelude to doing – ' I stand – 'this.' The blanket drops to the ground. He looks, then he deliberately raises his head, his eyes not leaving my face.

He says, 'I'm not being trapped again.'

'Is that how you remember – ' I couldn't say it. 'You read my diary. Do you think it was planned?'

He hunches his shoulders.

I kneel beside him, slowly, carefully. The thunderlight glints in the burning logs, giving the scars at his neck a red tinge. Even through my coldness I feel the heat from his body. He has warmed up.

'I knew all about you,' he says. 'Before Venice.'

I put my hand on his forearm. His skin flinches through the blanket.

'I had files,' he says.

'I know.'

'Don't you understand?' he says loudly. 'We were spying on you.'

'I know.'

He looks disbelieving.

'My father had more money than God towards the end,' I say. 'What do you think he was spending it on?'

'So you slept with me to find out more information?'

'No.' I debate what to tell him, how much he would believe. 'I slept with you because there was nothing I needed to tell you.'

'But – ' he was floundering through dark water – 'how did you know I wasn't using you to get information?'

I shift so my thigh rests against his leg. 'I knew you wouldn't.'

'That's bullshit,' he says but something writhes below the dark water. In a moment he will figure it out; I have no idea how he will react.

'There isn't anything else to know,' I say. 'I didn't know anything more.'

'You knew I wouldn't,' he says slowly. He is putting it together: he is remembering the pages out of order on his desk, the faint clicks on his phone. The things I know about him.

'I would have thought you would be happy.' I shift closer, against him. 'I'm not assuming men are dogs, that you'd sleep with anything.'

He is distracted: thinking, thinking.

'I know you don't want to sleep with me,' I say. He blinks – in shock? acceptance? – but he is rendered immobile, still struggling between past and present. I slip my left leg slowly across so I am sitting on his thighs, facing him. His hands come up automatically to hold my waist. His hands barely rest on my skin but I feel the tension in his fingers. If the conversation goes the wrong way . . .

'I know you don't want me,' I say.

'No.'

I extend my hand until I am a pulse-beat from the jagged black teeth etched across his chest. He tenses. I don't touch him, I let my hand stay there, feeling the heat from his body.

'It's not going to be like it was,' I say.

His hands tighten around my waist. 'I was drunk.'

Now I put my hand flat on his skin, below the collarbone, above the heart, in the deepest shadow.

'I made you start drinking again,' I say.

He hesitates. 'Yes.'

'Why?'

'I don't know.' He sounds genuinely puzzled.

'Because then you'd have an excuse. To deny it later.'

'But that means – '

'You knew what you were going to do, Dev. You can't call me premeditated and not know that about yourself.' I start easing myself off him.

'Wait . . . ' he says. His hands grip me, holding me still.

'Don't you think I understand?' I say. 'There's not so much differ- ence between these – ' I touch his chest ' – and these'. I turn my forearm so the firelight plays over the old pinpricks, the lonely words.

'You think we're so different,' I say. 'We're not. The only difference is you found drinking to fill the hole.'

'I read your files,' he says. 'I knew you weren't who they thought you were. It was obvious once you discounted the rumours.'

Here it comes. He is working his way there, he knows the answer, he just doesn't want to see it yet.

I try to move away from him, but he gives me a little shake. The black tide is rising again.

'The files,' he says.

There is nothing I can do to stop it. I wonder how bad it will be. It is unknowable, how deep his pain is.

We look at each other. We both remember how he channelled his pain before. At the thought of it, a shiver runs up my body, under his hands. I force myself to stay still.

'You think you have no control when you lose control,' I say. 'Don't you see losing control controls everything?'

Deliberately, carefully, he rests his head against my heart. I feel his lips against my skin and I can't help myself, I throw my head back. He opens his mouth, presses his teeth into my skin. I grip his head, run my fingers through his hair. I feel every strand, longer than my own. He pulls me down to him, so I am lying across him, looking up at him as he kisses me. I feel his tongue at the base of my throat. I am swimming in molten water. I cry out, a low humiliating sound. 'Yes,' I say. Then, 'Yes.'

He kisses me again, his hand running slowly down my back. He says, his fingers digging into my shoulders, 'How much did you know about me?'

I know I can't lie. He would feel it. I am being dragged back into the cold. I resign myself. 'Everything,' I say.

His face is as rigid as when he put the electronic bracelet on me. There is nothing to stop it. 'Before Borneo.'

'No,' he says. 'No, no.'

He shoves me away.

I say, 'Why is me knowing about you worse than you knowing about me?'

'Because I didn't know you knew.' He pushes me off his legs and stands, wrapping the blanket around his waist, staring into the fire.

I am cold without him. I am sitting in a pool of darkness; dark water in my bones. The light trembles across the outline of his lower ribs, the hollow of his spine. He is cold too but not as cold as me. Anger always keeps him warm somehow.

An ember falls onto the stone and he kneels to flick it back in. The firelight makes his body a frightening place of jagged cliffs and shadows. I pull the blanket around me and say, 'I thought the one across your shoulders meant *Forgive me.*'

He stiffens. 'You got that out of me.'

'That's right, Dev. To blackmail you. Or talk you out of arresting me. Except that – gee, I forgot to do any of those things.'

'If you knew from the start, then – ' He can't see the whole picture. It is beyond him. All he can do is fall back on what he knows, on what Mitch and his goons believe. I feel like saying to him, How much do you know about your own people?

He's shaking his head. 'All this,' he says slowly, 'must be some kind of elaborate revenge.'

The warmth he has given me is extinguished. But I refuse to pursue him. I sit back, against the wall. I give up, I think. Maybe this is how it is meant to end. It was always meant to be a punishment.

'From the first moment,' he says, 'you knew it was me.'

'The first moment I saw you,' I say as evenly as I can through my shaking jaw, 'I thought you had the blackest eyes of any blue-eyed man I had ever met.'

I close my eyes. I see the garden, the light from the palazzo's ballroom spilling onto the tiled terrace, the images of the great works of art projected on the high stone wall, the moonlight caught in falling stars in the fountain, the boats rocking in the black water at the jetty. The bells tolling in San Marco square, the vaporettos growling in the lagoon.

Tremors run up my spine. I say, 'I remember you sitting on the bench across from me. In the darkness past the fountain. You weren't drinking. You were watching me.'

'You knew why I was watching you,' he says, his voice coming from a long way off.

I shake my head, stiffly. 'Not at first. The lawyers only gave me one photo of the man on the case. It wasn't very clear.'

I am sliding down into chilled water.

'I thought you had lost too much weight for your build,' I say drowsily. 'Like my brother – eaten away by shadows. I thought you were ill under your tan. So a time spent in illness maybe. You should have been heavier. Cuddlier.'

'I was never cuddly.'

'Everyone's cuddly, Dev.'

'Don't call me that.'

I slide into ice. I try to remember his hands on me but the ache and throb of it are a long way away now. It isn't going to happen again, I accept that.

There is a long silence. I want to see whether he is looking at me but it is too much effort to raise my head. I feel like a clock running down.

The water is in my chest now. In my heart. How odd, I think, I never had any thought of giving up in the lake.

I force my lips apart. 'Everyone's lovable, Dev. No matter what you think.'

The waters close over my head. I see the moon moving away from me through the dark water. I want it back – I want something. What did I want?

'Ash,' I say. 'Ash.'

I am back in the garden under the swollen yellow moon. It is late. The jetty is nearly deserted – just a few security guards minding the motorboats; all the other guests are inside. Voices escape in scraps through the tall windows of the marbled ballroom. Occasionally the spray from the five-tiered fountain floats on the breeze, falling across me like a cold veil. I raise my glass and imagine the two hundred guests seated at their tables, the tall red candles in silver holders, the waiters changing the crystal glasses between each of the nine courses. The smokers would be lingering on the upper balcony, admiring the view across the lagoon, pointing at the moonlight touching the wings of the golden lions lining San Marco square.

Everyone is inside except for me and the man who sits across from me.

I close the book in my lap and look at him. Did I know then? I think so. I recognised something. A way out of misery, perhaps. that was all it was.

He gets up and comes towards me. He is more sinewy up close. Gaunter, older.

'Your guests are a rude lot,' he says. 'Eating while the party-giver goes without.'

'I thought maybe you were welded to that chair.'

'I heard your accent earlier.'

'Really.' I pick up the champagne bottle next to me. 'Drink?'

He smiles tightly and sits. 'I'm at a stage where it doesn't agree with me.'

'I'm not hanging out with you then.'

His mouth twists in what is supposed to be a smile but is more of a grimace. He raises his arm. 'Waiter!'

'Go on.' I hold out the glass. He looks at it, with a look I had seen on my brother's face. I am ashamed. I put the glass down.

'I can get you a mineral water,' I say. 'Or orange juice. There's caviar too. Russian purple. And smoked salmon thingies.'

'Don't try to be a hostess,' he says. 'It's obvious your heart's not in it.'

'And I thought I was putting up a good pretence.'

'I'm an expert,' he says apologetically.

'At hostesses?'

'At pretences.' He half turns away, as though the crack has been surprised out of him, as though he has surprised himself.

I look up at the blue mist threaded across the yellow moon.

'Maybe this should have been a masked ball,' I say. 'You can tell a lot about someone by the masks they wear.'

He turns towards me on the bench, his face serious. 'What mask would you wear?'

'What mask would you?'

'You first.'

'No,' I say. 'All right – together. Three, two, one – '

'A happy face,' I say just as he says, 'Something happy.'

'Well,' he says. His fists are clenched on his knees. I am a little disconcerted myself.

'It's the goal of adult life,' I say. 'Pretending to be whole. Learning to get through life with the cracks. That's what everyone does.'

'That's insane.'

'I know.' And we look at each other and laugh.

Above us, Edward Steichen's painting *The Pond-Moonlight* is projected on the high wall. A picture of darkness and light, the trees doubled by their reflection in the quiet water, the light breaking through radiantly in the centre, like the flare of a new day, like the flare of birth. Doubling the hope.

I refill my glass, lift the champagne bottle at him. He turns his head.

'Right, I forgot,' I say. I run my fingers through my hair. A long dark clump comes away in my hand. 'Stupid extensions,' I say, throwing it away. It lies like a black snake in the flowerbed behind us. 'That'll give the gardeners a thrill,' I say.

'Another front page story.'

The champagne sourly slicks my throat. 'So you've come to have a look at the infamous Miss K?'

He shifts back into the darkness. 'I'm an Embassy drone,' he says, trying to sound meek but not succeeding. 'You sent us an invitation. I was dispatched to – '

'Spy?'

'Find out why you invited us.'

'What's your verdict?'

'I thought at first it was vanity,' he says. 'Now . . . '

I take another sip.

'Perversity,' he says.

'I'd call it a malicious sense of humour,' I say.

'Aren't they the same?'

'Only to someone who has no sense of humour.'

'That's pretty much everyone at the Embassy then.'

'Hard for you,' I say.

'Not really,' he says. 'I don't have much of a sense of humour either.'

I take another drink and face him, gathering the hem of my silk dress so I can curl up on the bench. I have the feeling he wants to move further away but he stays still. Holds his ground.

'I suppose surveillance guys don't need humour,' I say.

'I'm not spying on you,' he says, sharply.

'But you are a man on a mission?'

He hesitates.

I raise the glass to the moonlight. The liquid, coiled and gold and oily, rolls back and forth. The bubbles are gone already.

'You want to know about the stories,' I say.

He shrugs. 'That's not what the Embassy is interested in.'

I laugh. 'Really?' I hold the glass out, under his nose. 'Just one little drink,' I say. 'You'll feel better.'

He looks at me. The moonlight catches the edge of his eye, the sliver of deep blue, like the sea where it meets the horizon on an overcast day. But then he moves his head back and all I see is black.

'Which stories?' he says, mildly. 'The drug stories? The loony bin stories? The men stories?'

I drain the glass, reach for the bottle. 'All you file-collecting Embassy types want to know the men stories.'

'But if we're efficient Embassy types, we already know the men stories.'

'Never as interesting second-hand.' I raise the bottle. 'One teensy drink?'

'You can't taunt me into drinking.' He closes his mouth, hard.

'Is that what I'm doing – taunting you?'

'Forget it,' he says. 'That is too . . . personal.'

'What's wrong with personal?'

'Well . . . ' He says slowly, as though he is feeling his way through the words. Cutting away dangerous jungle. 'I don't expect you to tell me anything . . . intimate. I'm a stranger. I might use it against you.'

'What if I want you to use it against me?'

He stares at me. I half fill the glass. The bottle is empty. I throw it onto the gravelled path where it breaks in two with a loud crack which makes the security guards at the jetty rush forward. I drain the glass and raise it. A guard waves and speaks into his walkie-talkie.

I throw the glass onto the path and turn to the man on the bench. 'Here's the thing, John Devlin,' I say. He draws a breath. 'I just got back from Poland where I was arrested for trespassing and deported, as if you didn't know. Nothing my lawyers couldn't handle, of course, because even though my father is a convicted looter who was busted smuggling art from Baghdad to Casablanca, and who had his assets frozen in three countries, everyone still thinks I have billions – ' I hiccup and put my hand over my mouth. 'Excuse me.' I wait to see if I am going to hiccup again. I'm not. I take my hand away. 'Where was I?'

'Everyone thinks you have billions.'

I stand, unsteadily. There is a crunching on the gravel: a waiter carrying a silver tray with a bottle of champagne, two glasses and a large pot of caviar.

'Thanks, Italo,' I say. 'Just give it to Mr Devlin here.'

Devlin is still. He takes the tray.

'You'd better bring another bottle,' I say to Italo as he retreats.

Devlin puts his hand on the cork.

'Can you open that?' I say.

'Yes,' he says.

A breeze smelling of salt cools my cheek. I raise my hands against the sky, to enclose the moon and the stars. 'Look,' I say. 'My hands are full of stars.

'I have to be by the water,' I say, walking towards the jetty, still conducting to the stars. 'My idea of hell would be a dry place. A hot place. Not to smell the sea. There are no boundaries when you swim. No expectations. No dark cities. It is a democratic country. You forget the shipwrecks inside yourself.'

I reach the stone wall above the jetty. Across the canal the palazzi sit eyeless and darkened, water lapping against the old stone. Over the doors, gargoyles' heads glower, turned black-green by their mossy growths. Some of the lower levels are boarded up, uninhabitable as the water rises.

'One benefit of being rich,' he says, behind me. 'You can choose where you live.'

'Only for those with no memory.' I wonder how close he is.

'That's a little self-indulgent isn't it?' he says.

I prop myself on the wall. The guards are at the far end of the jetty, their backs discreetly turned. The sparks from their cigarettes float into the darkness like tiny lanterns, up into the slipstream. 'Goodbye, lucky voyagers,' I whisper as I always do.

I hear liquid falling and imagine stars in a waterfall. I look over my shoulder. He is pouring champagne into a glass. 'What exactly are you celebrating?' he says.

I turn back. 'Death.'

There is silence behind me. I look to the mouth of the canal, where the lights from the lamps in the piazza trail like tresses on the water, the pale oranges and silvers breaking up in uncertain lines.

'To water,' I say. 'Everything is absorbed by water.' There is the clink of glass on stone. I stretch out a hand. 'Whole cities. Silence.' The trailing lights are sinking, the harbour is blackening. 'Even darkness itself,' I say. The guards have turned, curious. I stretch out to grasp the light falling through the black water. 'Water is the material of despair.'

Devlin yanks me back. He holds me a moment. His hands drop.

'Do you want them to think you are mad?' His voice is steady but there is trembling somewhere.

I was sure I could feel it. I was sure then. Later, of course –

'What's wrong with you?' he says.

He takes the bottle and glass and goes up the path.

When I reach him, he is flicking through the book but not really looking at it.

I sit beside him. 'I'm not drinking alone while I tell my story,' I say, extending a hand.

He looks at the bottle. 'It makes me careless.'

'Do it for your country.'

He says, 'You won't like the results' but he fills the second glass and raises it to his lips. It seems as if barely any liquid goes down his throat but his mouth tightens. He rests the glass on the bench, moving the stem so the liquid swirls slowly in a miniature whirlpool.

He says, 'Quid pro quo.'

I say, 'My story is the usual sad tale of a poor little misunderstood rich girl. The end. As of tomorrow.'

'Tomorrow – why?'

'I've done nothing but sit and read poetry for three years.' Pain twists through my stomach. 'I was meant to go to Poland three years ago. But I lost my nerve. Now I think I should do something.'

'You'll never get out of Italy,' he says. 'You can't use your father's money.'

'I've got some of my own,' I say. 'But you couldn't know that, could you?'

He meets my gaze without blinking. 'No.'

'I bought my first painting when I was seventeen,' I say. 'An Aboriginal artist. A landscape depicting Australia as a great lake. I liked the hidden shapes in the water. ' I put my hand up against the sky. 'Radiant with hope and despair.'

'Paintings,' he says.

'A Jasper Johns sold last month for eighty million. Private sale. No commission.'

'Jesus fucking Christ.'

'You said it, bub.' The moon outlines my fingers in silver. 'I always had a good eye for the authentic. Not so good with people.'

'They'll take all your assets, once they find them,' he says. 'Now your father's dead, they'll come after you. They've got nothing, they're furious.'

'Then I'll write. I've been doing articles and appraisals.' He picks up the glass. 'I write under another name: Emily Dickinson. In case you didn't know. Do you want me to spell it?'

He stares at the liquid inside the glass. 'I told you, I'm not a policeman.'

'So I'm free to leave tomorrow?'

He looks at me over the rim of the glass. 'Absolutely.' He takes a small sip, then another. He raises the half-empty glass, throws his head back to drain it. There is a shadow at the base of his throat I can't make out. In this light, it could be burns.

He says, 'The Embassy has resources. They can help find your brother. Get Interpol and everyone else off your back.'

I fill my glass. After a moment he holds out his. I see black stars in the liquid as it falls.

'If I collaborate,' I say.

'Co-operate,' he says. 'Avoid jail.' He drains the glass, pulls at his black tie. The collar comes undone. I see darkness move like snakes at the base of his throat.

'No-one's talked to me about jail,' I say.

He sighs, runs his fingers through his hair.

'I shouldn't tell you this,' he says. He avoids my eyes, flips open the book beside him.

But you're going to, I think. 'I don't want to get you into trouble,' I say.

'No, well . . . ' He looks at me. 'You should know – wherever you go, you're on a plane, you go to the bathroom, you're at dinner, you put your bag on the floor, you leave your coat at the cloakroom – wherever you go, whatever foreign country you are in, sooner or later, someone is going to find heroin in your bag.'

I look up at the image on the wall. It is Catherine Todd's *Three Girls On A Hilltop Facing The Sun*. More radiant colours, more hope. The very colours of Australia. Why am I always turning towards the light? I should know better. I should know it is water I need.

'I'm sorry.' He sounds sincere. 'Obviously, I don't agree with it.'

'No-one thought to appeal to my patriotism?' I say. 'My love of art? No-one ever thought to just ask me?'

He stares at me. 'No.'

'I don't think we'd make very good collaborators.' I stand, put out my hand. 'My book please.' The moon trembles above me, the stars shift. I put my glass down carefully, almost missing the bench.

He turns the book over. 'You mustn't think much of your own party if you're out here reading.' He sees the gold lettering on the spine. 'Collected poems,' he says. 'Oh, poetry.'

'You say it like it's a disease.'

'I don't get poetry.' He sits back, with the book. 'You should explain it.'

The breeze blows the skirt of my dress around me. 'You must think me simple to fall for that trick.'

'I told you I wasn't very good at this job.'

'I think you're very good at it.' I sway a moment on the wind.

'If you think you must go . . . ' He holds out the book.

As I take it, my hand touches his. He sits back, flexing his fingers. 'What's it good for?' he says. 'All those emotions. Interfering with getting things done.'

'You prefer men of action,' I say.

'Yes.'

'It's a way of communicating.' The back of my hand is burning where he had touched me. 'Part of the dance. A way of talking about emotions too private to be spoken. Like music.' I sit, slowly. 'It's a release.'

He picks up my glass, takes a mouthful. 'Persuade me.'

The moon is yellow and satiated above us. 'Say the two of us are sitting here . . . '

'As we are.'

'And I wanted to let you know how I feel but not too directly because I don't know who you are . . . '

'As you don't.'

'Then I might look up at the moon and I might quote poetry, a few meaningless words, in the moonlight, to see how you would react.'

He gives a short laugh. 'But it's just words. It's not doing.'

'It's a way of doing,' I say. 'It's a prelude to doing.'

He shrugs. 'Well, what are these mystical words?'

'It won't work if you scoff.'

'I'm not. Seriously.'

'Seriously, you are. But maybe . . . ' I consider him. 'Maybe that makes it better.'

'What better?'

'Your surrender.'

'Oh, bullshit.'

'Can't mistake that,' I say. 'Two Australians far from home.'

He leans forward. 'What about your precious words?' For a moment, I think he is about to put a hand on my knee. He is supremely confident – in some knowledge he thinks he has over me.

I put my hand around his hand so the pulse of my wrist is at his wrist. I put my other hand around his neck, below his ear. The moon is warm overhead. He is still. I move until I am a breath away from his mouth and I say, 'I carry your heart. I carry it in my heart.'

I sit back, slowly.

His eyelids flicker. 'That's cheating.'

'Why?'

'Because of the touching.' He takes his glass, bends to pick up the champagne bottle.

'What about if I touched you like this . . . ' I put a hand on his inner thigh. He lets out a short shocked breath. 'And what if while I'm doing that, I say, *Gee you look familiar?* Do you think that has the same effect?'

'You broke the mood.'

'Maybe. But you didn't answer my question.' I reach for his glass. He takes a long sip.

'You do look familiar,' I say.

He gives me the glass. 'Us office drones are all alike.'

A large gondola floats past. The black-backed water sidles restlessly in the canal, like silk dragged back and forth, so the moonlight glimmers in the puckered material. Revellers wearing party hats shout at the security guards on the jetty. I raise my hand too, wave, miss the air.

He pours me another drink, to the brim. His own glass is half full. My hand trembles as I pick up my glass. 'I hope to do the same to you one day.'

'I'm sure you will.' He reaches out to touch the book in my lap. His fingers graze my leg through the silk. The satin underskirt slides like the sea over my skin.

There is a muted riff of ferry horns; orange lights swing back and forth restlessly across the mouth. A long blast and the lights settle, heading north. The bigger ferry to the Lido has won the right of way.

He nods at the water. 'I keep forgetting the lagoon is a working harbour.'

'In our old house – '

'The mansion,' he says.

'No, our first house. In the western suburbs. There was a creek, just a little one, which ran past the back yard. Bits of scrub but it was packed with birds and possums and lizards. It was a whole universe. Or it seemed to me then. The animals never spoke but the water talked to me the whole time.'

'I see why you read poetry,' he says. 'It's the only thing that translates you.'

The image on the wall changes again: Brueghel's *The Temptation Of St Antony*. I stare at the small figure looking up to the grey sky, the winged monsters approaching. A speck of humanity in a monstrous landscape of cruelly jagged rocks and stony peaks.

'What are you celebrating?' he says.

'My father's death of course.' A wave of fine black mist passes in front of my eyes. I say, 'What's the one thing you remember about your father?'

He holds the glass up to the light. 'For my first driving test he bribed the marker.'

'To make sure you'd succeed?'

'So I'd fail. He thought it would be character building.' He lowers the glass. 'Shit. I've never told anyone that. Shit.'

'How did you celebrate his death?' I say.

He stares at me. 'You can't say that to people.'

'I'm not saying it to people. I'm saying it to you.'

'You can't let people know things like that about you. They'll make . . . assumptions.'

'Not if they're the right people.' I wonder how drunk he is. He seems a long way from sober but from what I know of him, he has a bottomless capacity for alcohol. For poison.

'But how do you know if they're the right people?' he says.

I reach across and pull his collar aside. His hand grips my wrist, tightens, until I hear the bones grate. 'No,' he says and I appreciate how angry he is. The reference to his father had been a mistake. The pain washes through me, a familiar tide, it is like the first plunge as the needle goes in. I wait for the rush of sweet feeling but there is only him, watching me, his eyes black in the light.

And now we come to the moment. I look at the patterns of hooks and knives curved across his upper chest, like a hangman's noose lying loose below his neck. He wants me to cry out, to say anything, so he can release me. But I am silent. I force a small smile, I gaze without blinking. He draws a harsh breath and lets go, shaking his head. He gets up awkwardly, as though his legs are stiff.

'I'm the wrong man for this,' he says.

'I think you're the perfect man for this.' I stand near him, so that when I sway, I brush his shirt front.

He puts his hand on my wrist again, this time pulls me to him. He bends his head. Our mouths are almost touching. I feel the heat blazing off me but he seems perfectly cool, cold even.

He steps back. 'Sorry. That was – ' he pauses '– out of character.'

The black mist drops over my eyes. I sway again.

His voice comes closer now. 'How do you know if they're the right people – to tell things to?'

I look down at the book in my hand. Under the moonlight, the words break up and re-form themselves like waves at early light. I reach and find his black marks like rocks in a slowly warming sea. I rest my hand there. This time he lets me. I wondered about that later. I always wanted to ask him. But I never did. Maybe I already knew I would be afraid of the answer.

As the heat floods into me, I say, 'Because they are as guilty as you.'

The light scatters. I close my eyes as he puts an arm around me and says, 'Where's your room?'

As I write this now, I write knowing that he may read it – will read it – and I wonder how much I am censoring myself. I don't think I am. I am writing everything I feel – everything I felt – at the moment. I am sure of it. I am not looking back, colouring it in for effect, trying to make us nicer people. The words will lose their power then. They won't have any effect if they are burned and eaten. They won't enrage. They won't destroy.

I wake in the hut, next to the fire. The flames play across my eyes, there is warmth all down my spine. I am at peace. It takes me a moment to realise he is lying behind me. His right arm curves across me, cupping my left shoulder. His breathing is steady in my hair.

I wonder whether he is asleep. I know I should savour the moment. But I have to see his face. I start to turn, very slowly, trying to shrink myself in his grasp.

'Don't,' he says.

'I just – '

'Goddamn don't move.'

'That's an invitation to rebel.'

'For you.'

'Always,' I say. His arm tenses, pulling away.

I catch his hand, hold it between both of mine. 'I'm cold.'

'Five minutes,' he says. 'Then we should go.'

'Five minutes.'

His arm relaxes. 'I need to know why there's nothing in your diary about – you know . . . Did you rip those pages out?'

'No.'

I can almost feel him thinking. He's wondering if there are other pages, what they say. He's wondering whether I'm lying. Worse, he's wondering whether I'm telling the truth. That is what really puzzles him.

'I couldn't write it,' I say. 'I didn't have the words.'

The afternoon is a white blanket against the small grimy window. He has pulled me tighter against him or maybe I have rolled closer. I turn my head. I see the hooked tips of the tattoos on his upper chest, his jaw, the lines on his neck, another scar I never noticed in Venice, near his sideburns. A scar I never had the time to find.

He looks down at me, grips my shoulder. 'You cannot tell Mitch what you saw at Koloshnovar. If you do, Mitch and his goons will fuck you every way they know. And I mean, every way.'

'I'll trade them,' I say. 'For what happened to my brother.'

'You wouldn't even last to the airport.' He looks at his hand on my skin, he processes how close we are and he lets go. He rubs his eyes.

'Have you been there?' I say. 'To Koloshnovar?'

'No.'

'But you know what's going on?'

He doesn't answer. I think about what I saw on his laptop and I wonder how much he is lying to me.

'You know you're going to do something,' I say. 'You know it's burning you up.'

'I thought that was you.'

I lift my hand so it makes shadows against the roof beams. The firelight on my fingers is edged with black. Always the shadows pressing in. I say, 'It's ironic how much depends on a piece of paper.'

He raises himself on one elbow. I feel it is the first time he has really looked at me. He says, 'I didn't realise you cared so much. About your brother.'

'Would it have made a difference?'

'I would have understood the guilt.'

His mouth is just above mine. I can't hear his breath above my own.

'I need to know,' he says, 'if it was revenge . . . that night in Venice.'

'Maybe I just wanted to save someone.'

'Your brother.'

'I think I already knew,' I say, 'my brother was beyond saving.'

'Well, then . . . ' He wants to ask but he doesn't want the answer. It's too much for him. I wonder whether he believes he can walk away. I am afraid that he thinks he can.

'Don't worry, Dev. I'm not the clinging type.'

I curl onto my side, away from him. 'It doesn't matter. You're leaving tomorrow.'

'Wait a minute,' he says, slipping a hand under my neck, raising me to him. I put my hands to his chest to push him away but he shakes his head and pushes back.

'I need to know,' he says, 'that you're not angry with me.'

'Frightened of a little female rage?'

'You bloody bet. I'm not stupid.'

We look at each other and laugh. He says, 'There's nothing like a love song for a good laugh.'

'That's right.' I smile at him.

His arm tightens, he brings me closer. Heat spirals against my stomach. 'Don't flatter yourself,' he says. 'It's not personal.'

I spread my fingers on his chest, rubbing my thumbs against the black marks. He doesn't move but his eyes narrow.

I say, 'You'll show any girl your marks.'

'No. It's been years.'

I place my hand against his cheek. The snowlight falls through the window, the thunderlight moves on the logs.

I brush his lips with my finger. 'You know I understand,' I say. 'You read my file.'

Finally – finally – I feel the heat running up his body. 'Bloody words,' he says. He throws the blanket away, puts a hand under my back, lifts me to him, grips my hip. He bends his head, his mouth touches mine. His tongue slowly traces the inside of my bottom lip. The heat runs up him, up me, there are pinpoints of water on his upper lip, sweat running down my back. I put my arm around his neck, press myself closer to him. His leg tightens around me. I am shaking. He grips me, he comes closer.

'Anything you want,' I say against his mouth.

He pauses. No, no, no, I think.

'Anything.' I am frantic.

I see his eyes, black as thunderlight. 'I want – ' He stops.

I brush my lips against his mouth but he is far away. He has climbed back inside his marks, he is leaving. The coldness serrates my skin. It is too much to bear. It is impossible to rescue him.

I start to turn away, to give up, when he puts his mouth against mine and says, 'I want Venice back.'

I hold my breath. He stares at me, frowning. Then his face relaxes and he smiles and says, 'I carry your heart. I carry it in my heart.'

And he kisses me.

The next morning, Pietr looks up over his croissant and says, 'Your Mr Devlin has been leading an exciting life.'

'He'll never be my Mr Devlin.' I help myself to sausages and eggs on the sideboard, not turning around. I wonder whether Stefano had told him I had gone into Trepani the day before.

'His car went into the lake,' says Pietr. 'Black ice – it is a problem this time of year.'

My knuckles are white on the tongs. 'I hope he's okay.'

Pietr laughs. 'You should sound more concerned. He's a fellow Australian.'

I look at the washed-out sky. 'That hasn't helped me so far.'

'No,' says Pietr. 'I suppose not.' He stares down at his plate.

'I'm sorry,' I say. 'Anything about the lake must bring back bad memories for you.'

'It's time I exorcised them,' he says. 'Like a grown-up.'

'Exorcise what?' says Rosza, as she enters.

'Old ghosts,' says Pietr. 'Maybe at the party,' he says to me. 'A dance with you would do it.'

'No point looking backwards,' says Rosza firmly.

Pietr gestures at me. 'Our guest is a woman after your own heart. She doesn't seem too concerned if Devlin went down with his car yesterday.'

'Why should she?' says Rosza. 'He's made her life a misery so far.'

'You are both bloodthirsty women,' says Pietr, picking up his coffee cup. 'Heaven help the men who cross you.'

'Don't defy me today,' says Rosza. 'I need you to go to Palermo for the party.'

Pietr looks at me. 'Do you want a drive?'

Streaks of light slant away to the horizon. 'I might take photos here,' I say.

'Some time soon,' says Rosza, at the sideboard, 'we'll have to see your photos.'

'Of course.'

'You'll need boots with spikes,' says Pietr. 'It's dangerous out there.'

The snow has fallen all night and now the forest is covered in a thick layer which looks like sculpted cream until you are close enough to see the hard glitter of ice crystals.

I descend through the trees. The blackened branches droop towards the ground and click their leaves of ice, a constant chime of splintering. Every few moments, snow falls to the ground in a slow stream of crystals.

The air chills my lungs; I keep my scarf around my face, stopping occasionally to see if Devlin is waiting for me, hoping he is behind the next tree or slouching against the guard rail. I walk back and forth along the road, to see if he has hired another car, parked it around the next bend. But there is nothing: no tyre tracks, no idling engine, no warm interior.

I hoist the camera bag over my shoulder, skirt the guard rail and follow the ridge above the lake. The surface is frozen. There is no trace of the car, where we had lain in the mud. Our footprints have gone and there are no new prints that I can see. I wonder whether they will leave the car there until summer, whether it will sink slowly into the lake's muddy floor, become encrusted with algae and moss until the remains of my breath on the window harden into inexplicable patterns.

From the ridge the hut is dark and desolate. No smoke shows in the chimney. I walk down slowly. Here and there, the snow gives way to water set into a clear frame, like a dark mirror. I see black smears, the suggestion of tired green far below, my face imprinted on the ground: frozen, trapped. Yearning.

As I turn the heavy handle, I look over my shoulder. No-one is waiting, or watching. I let the handle drop with a bang against the wood. The door swings back.

I go in.

The floorboards creak under me, the gloom grows out from the corners. A small square of light falls across the fireplace but fails to pierce the murkiness. There is a faint smell of the burnt wood from yesterday. I can just make out the old blankets folded on the chair by the table. The other chair seems to be missing.

I stand by the fireplace, staring down at the blackened embers, the dashes of silver in the carbon. I put my boot against the fireplace grille, close my eyes, remember certain scenes from the previous afternoon. My fingers dig into the mantel.

Wood creaks behind me, the blackness stirs. A man is getting up out of the chair in the corner. With his bulky coat and thick trousers, for a moment I think it is Stefano. Wishing me ill.

Devlin says, 'You shouldn't come into Trepani anymore. It's getting too crowded.'

I am having trouble breathing. I force my voice out. 'People arriving for the party, I suppose.'

He nods and shifts his weight as though he is about to step forward. But he stays where he is, a vast distance away.

'They didn't ask you,' he says, 'about yesterday?'

'Everyone was out when I got back,' I say. 'Stefano doesn't seem to have mentioned it. They know about your accident though.'

He frowns. 'Very good bush telegraph.'

I am dizzy. I feel my way along the mantel to the wall, put my hands behind me to support myself.

'So,' he says, 'we shouldn't meet again.'

I nod.

'Did you hear me?'

'You're leaving.' It isn't a question.

'No.' His words are cut by a cold anger like far-off lightning flashes on a dark horizon. 'They won't let me. They say I can de-tox here.' He puts up a hand. It is steady. 'Funny – I haven't wanted a drink since the crash.'

'But you want to go.' The wall is trembling behind me.

'Of course I bloody want to go.'

I rub my temples.

'So,' he says, 'you agree – it's not a good idea for us to meet again.' His tone is light, throwaway, but I sense he is watching me closely. Then he says, and his voice is different somehow, 'Privately.'

'Yes,' I say. 'Pietr could get suspicious.'

'Pietr . . . ' Now he moves. He is in front of me. 'Has he said anything?'

'They're distracted. He's planning something for the party, I think.'

'The party,' says Devlin, as though he has just considered it. 'You'd better get me an invite.'

I raise my palm. '*Sieg Heil.*'

'Look,' he says, 'yesterday was – '

'I get it, okay?' I shout. I am exhausted. My arm shudders.

He stares down at me. 'You're not well.' He puts a hand on my arm. I try to shake it off. 'I'm sure Pietr will take care of me.'

His fingers tighten. 'Don't play that card with me.'

'Why not?' I shout. 'You don't care.'

He pushes me back, against the wall, puts his hands on the cold stone on either side of me. He is about to say something but as I look up at him his expression changes. He puts a hand behind my neck, his thumb against the pulse in my throat.

We are both perfectly still, then he looks down. 'You're wearing a skirt,' he says.

'Easier access.'

He stares at me. Without dropping his gaze, he runs his hand down, pulling at my skirt, moving his hand under and up, slowly, trying to rip through my stockings, his nails scratching me through the wool, digging in, trying to climb in under my skin. I hold my breath, press against him. He moves his hand, very slightly. I cry out, put my hands on his hips. I can feel the jut of bone and muscle. I begin to slide down, hard against him.

He catches my hand, pins it against the wall. 'No.' He watches me without blinking.

'But I want – ' I can barely think – 'to make you feel too – '

'No.' He pulls me closer to him, so close I can't slide my hands in. He holds me from behind, his fingers spread so that wherever I move there is exquisite pain. His other hand pulls at my jacket. He begins to run his mouth up and down my throat. There is a rhythm to it, a fixed robotic quality, that I find unbearably exciting. His concentration is ferocious. He is unstoppable.

He pulls my shirt aside. I grip his head, my fingers deep in his thick hair as his mouth moves down my cold skin. I feel drugged. It is what I spent years trying to capture in a needle, trying to force this sensation, this supreme drowsiness, in under my skin. Total forgetfulness.

His mouth moves lower. I try to free myself to touch him but he traps my wrists against the wall. His breathing is perfectly even but there is some force building – some anger, some need.

I try to shift position, to lead his mouth to where I want it but he won't change direction. He isn't going to let me do anything that he doesn't choose – we both know it – until that one perfect moment. When I break his control.

'Kiss me,' I say.

He bites my skin. I can barely see his face, just a sliver of light down his jaw-line. The scar on his cheekbone is a miniature raised ridge, the lines at his eyes tiny rivers. The muscles shift, the shadows deepen.

'You're a haunted man,' I say.

'I'm a nothing man.' He shakes his head. 'For Christ's sake.'

He rests his cheek against mine as though he is suddenly weary. As though I have drained him.

'We're going to be really screwed if you start talking like me,' I say.

He grins. 'No chance of that.'

It is the thing I like most about him: his quicksilver moods. I want to say to him, It makes me think I can reach you. *Control you.* But I don't. I pull my hands free and throw them around his neck, burying my face in the comforting warmth of his jacket. He is still for a moment then he grasps my shoulders and holds me away from him. He says slowly, 'I could get obsessive about this. It wouldn't be healthy.'

'Who for?'

He won't meet my eyes.

'All right,' I say.

'All right?' His hands relax. He pulls me closer. I put my mouth over his mouth, run my hand down his body.

I say, 'Will you meet me tomorrow?'

He kisses me, probing the roof of my mouth with his tongue, delicately at first, then insistent, harsher. Tremors are running up his body. Or maybe it is me. I move my hips a little. His breath breaks up, becomes uneven, finally.

'Think of this as anaesthetic,' I say.

He stares at me, his eyes as dark as water in the well once the moon has left.

I move my hand. He shudders and says, 'Now.'

SUNDAY

I meet him every day that week. At first we are both circumspect, conscious of time, the need for secrecy, barely spending more than an hour together. But then he begins stopping me as I try to leave – or am I the one refusing to go? I begin staying until lunchtime, through lunchtime. I don't care about food – I can barely eat breakfast, my stomach would be twisting in anticipation, the pulse climbing my throat, waiting, waiting until I could leave. Pietr looks at me curiously over the breakfast table and once he asks me if I have a fever again, but he says nothing until the day he tells me he has something he wants to give me before the party. I smile and thank him but I am miles away, across the ice, next to the fire.

Devlin begins bringing food so he can stay longer. He says his appetite has come back with a vengeance, he is eating everything in sight. He refuses to talk about Mitch, implies the case has been put on hold, nothing is going to happen, nobody is coming down from Rome. I want to believe him so I don't ask.

He loses the dark shadows under his eyes. It seems to me his face is filling out, there is more weight on his chest when he presses down on me. He says that he has stopped drinking. I take him at his word.

298

Sometimes, as I come through the door, he will hold me and not let go.

'I'm ravenous,' he says.

When I look through my diary for that week, for those days before the party, before it all changed, there is almost nothing written. Is that because I was too busy living life or because it was impossible to describe?

There are phrases: faint, scribbled, unfinished. At the beginning of the week, they are tinged with disbelief, a falling away of the pen under the dark mist that swirled around me in those first few days when he would often push me from him, tell me to go, not to come back. He only stopped doing that when he understood that he would always come after me.

Finally, there was the afternoon when his mouth traced intricate patterns on my back and he said, reluctantly, as though he had dived deep into some well and found the words lying there, rusted and fragile from being hidden, that the only thing he wanted to do was spend the whole night with me, to see my shoulder naked in the moonlight.

After this, there were days of nothingness in the diary, of white pages, of only one word over and over again.

Ravenous.

From then until the end there is only the photo. He never wanted me to take his picture; he said it was dangerous for me and for him. A close-up could give too much away: they can tell by the light, the shadows, he said, exactly where we are, when we are.

I say, 'They can tell what we are.'

One day, when he is asleep, I can't resist. I take a photo of him, of his face. He is lying on his back, in the light from the window. His chest rises and falls. I have spent the last half hour watching him. I know I should go soon, go and help with the party, the party I have no interest in, despite Pietr's hints about a special celebration.

'Ash,' I say as he wakes, kissing him below his shoulder bone, the deep ridge, as he holds me to him, his scars moving like tiger stripes in the low light.

'You can imagine having a name like Ashley in the army twenty years ago,' he says. 'Now, of course, they're so desperate, they'll take anyone. But then . . . once I sorted a few of them out, it was fine. Actually,' he laughs without humour, 'it was good. I was able to thrash all the guys I'd wanted to in high school.'

He says, 'It was my mother's choice of name.'

'What did your father call you?' I say.

'My middle name. John.' He closes his eyes. 'You little bastard John. You little devil John.'

I put my hand over his eyes. 'Despite all the files, I don't think I know you at all.'

He takes my hand away. He says, holding me close, 'How much do you know about my father?' His thumbnail scratches my thumbnail, pressing in at the cuticle. I want him, immediately, which is maybe what he intended. I wonder whether it is all an act: if deep down, he is laughing at me. I wonder whether once he saw my weakness in Venice, whether that became the plan. A bit of fun on the side to break up the job monotony.

He rubs my fingernail. I want to say it, to show I don't care. But I know with the dead weight of an anchor pulling me down, that I shouldn't tell him everything.

I say, 'I know enough to know you didn't do anything wrong.'

He is silent, waiting.

I say, 'I know there was a break-in.'

'It was my fault,' he says. 'I had finally decided to chuck the army, do what I always wanted to do. I was celebrating.'

'What did you always want to do?'

'A childish dream,' he says. 'It went, later that night. I don't want to talk about it.' He is climbing back into his marks.

'Ash,' I say.

He holds my hand in both of his. 'Forget that name. If you get used to using it, you'll blurt it out. We'll both be in danger.'

I say, 'I have a tendency to say what I think.'

'I never say what I think,' he says.

MONDAY

I am queasy the next morning. I oversleep and come down late to breakfast. The sky is the colour of white rum. I see blue veins under the skin on the back of my hand. My fingers tremble as I pick up my knife and fork.

Pietr looks at me with concern.

I smile at him, or try to, and he says, 'If there is anything I can do . . .'

'I'm relying on it,' I say.

'Maybe your present will cheer you up,' he says. I smile and nod, but I am sorry for him, thinking, You can't give me what I need.

Devlin isn't at the hut. I wait. Staring through the window, tracing patterns in the sky. Seeing his name spelled out in the black spears climbing towards the horizon. Maybe he is furious, I think, that I used his name. He can't trust me not to do it again.

I wait until lunchtime. He doesn't come. I go outside. A raven is sitting on a skeletal branch – a black rose on the hook. It turns its head, its black eye reflecting the world.

I set off for Trepani.

302

I come into Café Flora, shaking off the snow dusting my coat. The café is nearly empty, a couple of locals, a small fair man hunched over coffee. I go upstairs.

I knock on Devlin's door. Outside, the rain lands in beats on the tiled roof. The tired morning light edges through the smeared window over the landing so the creases in the wallpaper shiver.

I press against the door. No sound inside. I put my hand on the cold round door knob, rest my finger in the keyhole beneath. There is a draught on my skin as though a window is open inside. I turn the handle. The door is locked.

Voices on the stairs below. The sound travelling up in spirals so that the words almost seem to make sense but turn in on themselves at the last moment, unintelligible.

The rain spatters the window overlooking the small back alley. A black Mercedes with tinted windows is drawn across the end.

A voice which strikes a chord. I look over the banister. Devlin is coming up slowly, his shoulder scraping the wall. The sickly light is a slash along his cheekbone. It makes him look grey. I wonder if he has started drinking again.

He turns his head, his fingers feeling their way over the creases in the rough paper, the water stains. Like a blind man moving through fog.

He says, 'I didn't agree to this.'

There is another man behind him, still in the shadow of the turn in the stairs. I can't see his face, just his arm: the cuff of his white shirt, the edge of his suit-sleeve, his hand. He is holding a mobile phone, reading the text on the screen. I see a cuff-link, square gold around a dark stone. He is about to take that last step into the light.

Devlin rests his head against the wall. 'I don't think she's the woman we thought she was.'

The man snaps his phone shut and says loudly, 'They never are.'

The words come up to me, deadly little clouds. The man goes down the steps. Just as he disappears, the mobile rings.

Devlin climbs the stairs like an old man. He is right beneath me when he looks up. The light from the little window can't flush out the shadows under his cheeks.

'Who was that?' I say as he puts the key in the door.

'No-one,' he says without looking at me. 'Just someone from the Embassy.'

Inside the room, I put my arms around him, partly because I want to kiss him, partly to smell his breath. I kiss him but his mouth is stiff and cold under mine. He smells of mouthwash. Maybe there is a tang of something underneath, maybe not. When I look up his eyes are open, watching me.

'I haven't been drinking,' he says.

'I know.'

'You shouldn't have come. It's dangerous.'

I press myself against him, run my hands up and down his body, try to force my tongue into his mouth. 'I came for you.'

'Oh, don't bullshit,' he shouts. He grabs me under my arms, moves across the room, not so much carrying me as sweeping me before him. Just as I slam into the wall, he slips an arm around my back but my head still hits the hard plaster. A gun-shot cracks between my ears. The sound rolls around the small room. Everything else dies away: the faint sounds of a car on the cliff road, the far-off relentless turning over of the sea.

'You bastard.' I put my hand to my head, feel the lump already rising, see the blood on my fingers.

'I always knew you'd end up beating me.' I am only half joking but he has a stricken look in his eyes. His hands freeze.

I want to hurt him. 'You drunk. You never cared.'

'That's right,' he says.

'Bastard.'

'Yes.' He puts his hands on my arms.

'Devil.'

'Let me see,' he says softly, starting to turn me.

I pull away. There is a faint moisture in my eyes. I blink. 'It doesn't matter.'

He won't let me go.

'You've overstepped the line,' I say.

He meets my gaze, nods.

I wait and raise my bunched fist. He doesn't move. I draw closer. He watches me. I press myself against him, run my mouth up his neck, bite him, not hard. I turn my face to the wall.

I feel his fingers, gentle on my bristled hair, my skin. He probes around the lump. I wince.

'Sorry,' he says. 'And – sorry.'

'It doesn't matter.'

'Doesn't it?' He leaves me. I feel his absence before I hear the clink of glass.

I lean my forehead against the wall. 'I don't think Scotch fixes this problem.'

'Neither do I.' He is right behind me. There is the sharp tang of disinfectant, something wet and cold against my head.

We stand for a moment then he puts his mouth against the back of my neck. I feel his tongue on my skin, at the top of my spine. I shiver. Something plummets past me. A small square of cotton wool lies on the floor, a smear of blood at the matted centre.

'You should take a picture of that,' he says. 'As evidence. Tell them later I coerced you.'

'Later?'

'Forget it.' He is leaving. I draw his arms around me, push back against him. I take his left hand between mine, begin massaging between his knuckles, pulling on his square fingers, the fingers of an artist, I think.

'That feels good,' he says, kissing me up and down my neck.

'You hold too much tension in your fingers.' I turn. 'It's too much, Dev.'

He takes my head in his hands and kisses me, hard, again and again – like the first time but with a new emotion. Not anger, I think. Desperation.

'It's just the job,' he says as he starts unbuttoning my jacket.

'Aren't I the job?' I say.

He slips his fingers in under my collar. The cotton rips.
'Not in here.'

When I come downstairs, a landscape made of snow is growing up
from the ground outside, turning the blanketed houses into square
white boulders. The only movement is the thin tendrils of grey smoke
which lifts from the chimneys, past the white-patched tree trunks
and the leaves tipped in cream.

Julietta stands next to me. 'Stefano is coming back,' she says. 'He
can give you a lift – ' she pauses – 'home.'

I nod. 'Thanks.'

She shakes out her tea towel. 'So you walked all the way here
to see your man.'

'Stupid,' I say.

She smiles. 'Oh, I would do the same for Stefano.'

'Stefano?'

'My husband.'

She goes back to the bar. I sit in the front booth and take photos
through the window to have something to show Pietr if he asks.
The roll is soon finished. I rewind the film, carefully ease out the
canister. It has Devlin's picture on it. I put the canister in my satchel,
zip the inner compartment.

A shadow moves across my eye. Someone slides into the seat
opposite. A man. For a millisecond, with the light behind him, I
think it is Devlin. Then I register that this man is smaller, finer built.

'So you prefer the old things,' he says as he sits down.

It is the fair-haired man I had seen on my way in. He wears a
puffy parka with a fake fur collar. I think I see a black tie underneath.
He puts his hands under the table.

'You don't mind do you?' He has the almost completely neutral
American accent of the eastern seaboard. Of the very rich.

He says, 'I'm desperate to talk English after all this Mafia jabber.'

He looks at me directly, unblinking. He has a boyish face, a
certain pallor, a smattering of freckles across his nose. He could be

any age between twenty-one and thirty-one. But I think, looking at the lock of pale hair falling artfully over his forehead, that is all part of the misdirection. I try to place the translucent shade of his skin. After a while it comes to me: the colour of bone.

He smiles, showing small even teeth.

'Pretty much everyone speaks English in Italy,' I say. 'Don't they?'

'When they want to,' he says, still smiling. 'But I'm the big bad American. Never mind that we're spending a fortune in this hick town. But, what can you do?' He puts his hands flat on the table. He has narrow hands, with milky blue nails cut sharply across. There is a gold signet ring on the small finger of his left hand. I recognise the raised eyeless curves, the slender crossed lines. Skull and bones. A rim of white cuff protrudes from the parka sleeve.

'So,' he says. 'What about you? You seem to have fitted in pretty well.'

'Everyone has been – pleasant,' I say cautiously.

'I'll bet. Still, party times can't last forever.' He reaches beneath the table and brings up a thin metal briefcase similar to Devlin's. It has a small pale screen between the two locks. He presses his thumb on the screen. The locks pop open. He takes out a manila folder, turns the pages inside. The black stones in his gold cufflinks wink in the light.

'We've been pretty impressed by how you inserted yourself into Pietr Walenzska's house,' he says. 'But I think we all agree you have to step up the pace. If you want to avoid jail.'

'My lawyers told me jail wasn't a serious – ' I am about to say "threat" but I change it to, 'option.'

He is still turning pages. I see shiny skin between the strands of his pale fine hair.

Now he looks up. 'Not for you. For Devlin.'

My hands clench. 'But he works for you.'

'That's debatable. He's just admitted he's still drinking.'

'Really?'

'That can't be too rewarding for you.' He puts out his hand, touches mine briefly. As he withdraws it, he makes a small sharp movement. The edge of his nail scratches the back of my hand. I can't believe it is accidental. Only the thought of Devlin stops me reaching across the table and hooking my nails into his eyes.

He says, 'Unrewarding in all areas.'

A red welt is growing on my skin. 'Devlin's taken care of me.'

He watches me, unblinking. His eyes are a very dark brown. That must have hurt him career-wise, I think, not having blue eyes. Or he would have thought it did.

'You think Devlin cares,' he says. 'But really, how high are your standards? He's an incompetent. A drunk who's done little but lose valuable merchandise.'

I should have known what was coming next. He reaches out, grabs my wrist and pushes up my sleeve.

'It fell off,' I say.

'It fell off. Yes, that's what Devlin told us. Where exactly?'

I hesitate.

'The two of you should get your stories straight,' he says, sitting back.

'I don't want to get him into trouble.'

'Touching. But I can't play footsies with you all fucking day. I've already had to spend extra money – money I don't have – to retrieve the fucking thing from the bottom of that fucking lake. At least the fucking car was covered by insurance.'

'The lake,' I say.

'Next to the hut,' he says. 'That's a cosy set-up. We've all enjoyed the photos on Devlin's camera. I sure hope you'll take me there some time.'

'Aren't I bit old for you?'

'I'll keep my eyes closed.'

We look at each other.

'You're lying,' I say.

He reaches into the file and throws a half-dozen photos at me. They fan out across the table: shadows and absences, heat and light, sweating skin blurring into black. I want to look to see which day they were taken, which hour, which minute. But I won't give him the satisfaction.

'My lawyers – ' I say.

'Don't get paid until the funds are unfrozen. And we know you returned all the paintings. Fucking crazy.' He smiles. 'You're in a foreign country. With no friends.'

'Devlin – '

'Devlin isn't your friend,' he says. 'This whole time in the hut – do you understand? It's all recorded.'

'You won't play those recordings,' I say. 'Not the ones where we discuss how you used to read *Soldier Of Fortune* magazine in the staffroom. When you were the mail boy.'

His eyelids twitch. 'Promoted over Devlin,' he says, 'the disgruntled employee.'

'An Australian court will make mincemeat of this,' I say.

'You won't be tried in an Australian court. It'll be US military, closed.'

'Who's the star witness? Devlin?'

He leans forward. I have to stop myself from thinking that I see a ring of yellow around his pupil, like a dog's. 'John Devlin cares so little about you,' he says, 'that he agrees you'll say yes when Pietr asks you to marry him.'

I stare at him. 'Pietr won't – '

'He's been shopping for a ring,' he says. 'What he doesn't tell his mistress he'll tell his wife.'

I look behind me, to the stairs.

'Devlin can't help you,' he says. 'Those tapes damn him more than you. He'll do years. You know he won't make it.'

'Actually,' I say, 'I think prison will be a relief to him.'

'You two.' He shakes his head. 'They said there was something weird going on with you two.'

'We're locked together,' I say. 'Like magnets in blood.'

He studies me. 'We were told you weren't using.'

I think for a moment. 'I wouldn't be much use to you then, would I?'

'Maybe you just need more information.' He pushes across the manila folder. 'Devlin's personal file. His own words. Pick any page. See if you know the man in there.'

It is the typed transcript of an interview with Devlin. I feel black ice growing in my spine when I see the word in bold at the top of the page.

Borneo.

I begin to read.

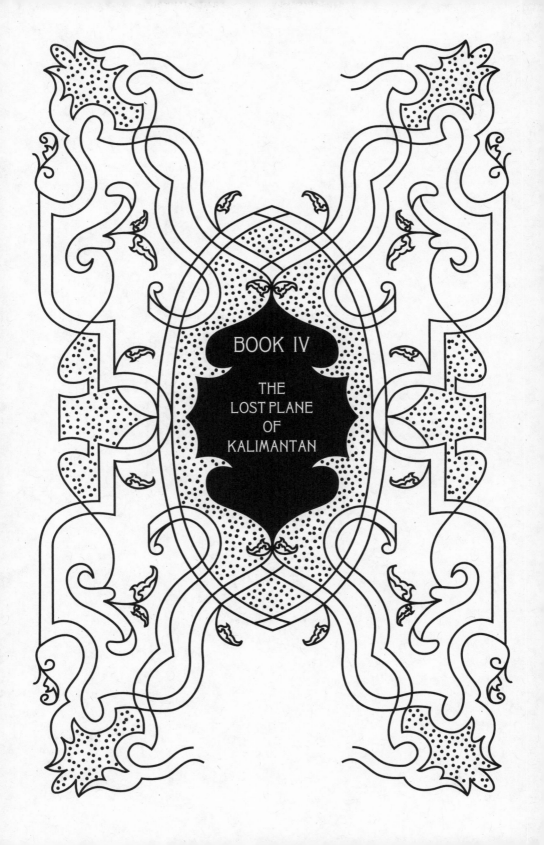

BOOK IV

THE
LOST PLANE
OF
KALIMANTAN

BORNEO, 2004

Devlin woke to lapping water and a drumming and clicking in his ears. The sky had the soft blue blackness of pre-dawn, the stars already withdrawing. The frogs' castanets were deafening in the last calls of the night.

Something tapped his finger. He thought it was Kenje trying to wake him after a lapse. Lapse. What a quaint word. He swatted, his knuckles grazed cold serrated skin. The ridged ground rocked beneath him; the smudged and shaking world was dissected by bars.

His hands went down to grip the ground and he felt bamboo poles, smooth but for the occasional knot, spaced six inches apart. If he sat still, the rocking settled.

He probed carefully: poles above him, thick rope lashing them together. A bamboo cage then, big enough to sit in but not to stand. He ticked off what he was left with: work boots, watch, shirt, shorts. What day was it? Was it the day after Friday? It was too dark to read the watch face. He peered, rubbed at the glass. A useless instrument for twenty years of service.

Hello, he shouted. Hello. Some of the cries and clicks paused but most of the frogs clapped on. I'm just an engineer, he shouted. *You've got the wrong man.* He waited. The frogs snapped on. What day was it?

Devlin dreamed it was Friday afternoon. He was in his office. He was laying out his pens – the red one inside the two black ones – his laptop, the satellite phone, the diary turned to next Monday's page, the clean trousers, the blue tie, the socks, the boots, the two ironed shirts, two pairs of underpants, the four packets of dried biscuits, the dozen litres of bottled water. The towels. The buckets.

He must have fallen asleep again. When he woke, the frogs had stopped, silenced by the usual inexplicable shower. The light was soaking in cautiously. He was curled on his side, his clothes damp but not cold, the occasional gritty flick of water hitting him.

He saw that the cage was lashed to chunky wooden poles driven into the bed of a river. The river? He was assuming he was still within distance of the mine site. He peered down. A long ridge of gun-metal grey humps moved slowly beneath him. He sat up too sharply and the cage dipped to one side, swayed back, dipped again – it felt even lower – swayed, dipped, swayed, trembled to a stop. Foam swirled below a knot on the nearest pole.

Hello? he shouted. Is anyone there?

He looked at his watch. It was five in the morning of the twenty-fifth.

The cage was almost exactly in the middle of the river, thirty feet each way to the nearest bank. The trees and scrub went right to the edge; the gnarled roots of the mangroves poking like irritable fingers at the muddy water. A kingfisher hooted its familiar jokes in the treetops and he saw small hunched figures moving along the upper branches. Ironic – the mine site was the only place where the monkeys weren't hunted for food. He'd enforced the ban – it would help when Jakarta produced a fake environmental impact study in another grab for bribes. The miners had snickered and rolled their eyes when they thought he wasn't looking. The next day there were two monkey heads nailed up in the gym. The men took the ban seriously once he sacked four of them.

He wondered now if the cage was payback for the ban. But he thought not. He had inspired plenty of other reasons for revenge.

He peered down. The water seemed to be swirling less vigorously around the knot. He didn't know how many crocodiles were in this section of the river. Until recently he had only left the mine site to take the chopper to Belipatan for the plane flight to Jakarta. When he had to see Mitch.

He stared up at the criss-crossed blue. There was a grinding pain behind his temple and when he felt the back of his head he found a lump; dried blood flecked his fingers.

He tried to remember. He saw the office: the old fan clicking overhead, stirring the diesel fumes which drifted in from the generator. He heard the raucous shouts from the gym: a four-hour work-out session in progress, lines of speed on the window sill, the bets getting bigger and more dangerous as the weights were piled on.

Behind him: the wind-up radio with a Singapore pop singer cracking the high notes. Devlin could remember saying to Kenje, 'There's nothing like a love song for a good laugh.' He saw sunlight falling through the window onto the files arranged in precisely spaced rows, Kenje's thin brown arms as he put the mail in the trays on the desk. He saw his own neat writing on the labels on the trays – every letter the same width and height – *Site*, *Jakarta*, *Canberra*, *Washington*. He looked around the room, searching for the cardboard box. He couldn't see it. So it was not Friday afternoon.

Kenje was placing an envelope in front of him. The Embassy's crest crouched over the brown paper like a scorpion.

'This needs now,' said Kenje. 'Not this afternoon.'

'Have you read it?'

'I only read Monday mail.'

The reference to the weekends silenced them both.

'You such a lazy bastard,' said Kenje quickly. 'Another lazy whitey sitting around doing nothing.' He hesitated and took a small orange-painted wooden fish from his pocket. He placed it on Devlin's desk. 'Come to here,' said Kenje, fast. 'Take our land.'

'Blame Jakarta,' said Devlin. 'They do the leases.' The coloured wooden fish gazed up at him. It had thick wavering black lines drawn on its body, thinner lines on the fins.

'Is this a piranha?' said Devlin.

'Right,' said Kenje. 'A whitey bastard eating piranha.'

Devlin picked up the fish. There were yellow triangles stamped in odd spots, to represent scales. *Love Borneo* was written along the belly in uneven capitals. The wood felt cool and smooth to his touch.

'No wonder they don't want Dyaks as foremen,' said Devlin. 'You'll have my head on a stick soon.'

'Too right,' said Kenje. 'Where all whiteys should be.' He took the fish from Devlin, tore off sticky tape from the dispenser and taped the fish to the edge of the desk.

'So you can see it,' said Kenje. 'On Saturday.'

The cage began to rock. Foamy water slapped around the wooden poles. A ridge of grey humps passed beneath him, and another, and another. The hooded eyes rolled back at him. But the humps swam on and he saw why: a small monkey, a baby, its fine russet hair lifting in the early light, had come down from the trees. It was sitting at the water's edge, drinking. As the crocodiles closed in, a chorus of shrieks broke out from the canopy. The monkey froze, its hand raised halfway to its mouth. The crocodiles sank from view. The monkey turned to look behind it. The brown-grey water lifted and the crocodiles came out, fast, one from the right, one from the left, one directly in front. Working as a team.

In his first month on site, he had done little but sort papers and eat the greasy chow. He slept in his office. After the inquest that was all he wanted to do. If he couldn't break his Friday afternoon ritual, he would do nothing but work in between.

He processed the pay, collated the findings in the new tunnel and mopped up the bad bookkeeping of the previous manager, a Jakarta drunkard – another one, thought Devlin. The manager had propositioned a Dyak girl and fled from the site at news that two hundred of her relatives, armed with machetes, were coming down from the mountains.

'They get really worked up about things like that,' said the company representative who was showing him around. The rep was British with spindly white legs and a big belly rolling over his shorts. His half-undone zipper was being pushed lower by the weight above it. Whenever he talked to any of the Dyaks on site, he raised his voice and spoke very slowly, as though they were deaf.

Now he said, thumping his fist on Kenje's slender shoulder, 'When the mine started, the locals all thought the lights were the lights of heaven.'

Devlin glanced at Kenje, who stared into the distance, unblinking. 'Really?' said Devlin. 'Well, they wouldn't think that now, would they?'

The Brit laughed as though it was a compliment, but after he had gone, Devlin said to Kenje, 'I bet the locals didn't dream up that lights of heaven bullshit.'

'No, boss,' said Kenje, staring at his feet.

'Should I tell him his fly's undone?' said Devlin.

Kenje raised his head and smiled. 'No, boss.'

Two months into the job Devlin sat, head shaking, hands shaking, the usual Monday morning tremors rocking his stomach. He had washed out his mouth but the memory of vomit was acid on his tongue.

He stared through the window of the prefab office, across the tamped-down dirt, past the other boxy buildings. There was no greenery here, the mine was a cleared circle of dirt and pebbles, like the blast radius of a rocket. It stepped away from the jungle, its tiers of scraped earth and dead dirt descending into the dark holes which, all day and all night, regurgitated men and trucks.

There were no trees or flowers or pot plants on the site but somehow, on this Monday, he was back twenty years, gawking out the window of the squad room as the sergeant demonstrated weapon dismantling.

The naming of parts was the lesson that day. He saw himself, the fleshy young recruit, so in love with history and military manoeuvres, his carefully painted Napoleonic tin soldiers banished – but not forgotten – to the garage of his father's house. The house he now couldn't bear to return to.

The sergeant was droning on; he had a blocked nose and breathed heavily through his mouth at the end of every sentence.

Outside, practically touching the glass, was an apple tree. Its blossoms were white tipped with pink spilling into red; a bee was hovering languorously over the pollen, its wings a blur as it plunged and the blossoms shuddered and the pink deepened. Devlin could almost smell the perfume trembling through the room. He almost asked, Can anyone smell that? Can I go outside to smell that? But the sergeant snapped at him and he stopped looking.

Kenje was in the doorway, telling him he had to call Jakarta, but outside the gym Devlin saw someone – a miner, judging by the overalls and boots – carrying a shotgun and heading for the jungle. Going off-site. Another monkey-hunting fucker. Without thinking he pushed past Kenje, ignored the metal steps, and jumped down, landing heavily in the dirt. The jarring in his temple enraged him. He set off into the jungle.

The D road was a roughly cleared track which ran parallel to the river. He unlocked the padlock on the gate, pulling it shut with such force that the steel clanged and a bird overhead – was it a heron? a magpie? – let loose its liquid notes so they rose like rainbow-coloured balloons in the misty air.

Even a few steps down the track, the shouts and smells of the mine were fading. He thought about what he was going to do to the miner if he found him hunting. Flouting authority. There would be no excuses, Devlin said to himself, and it was his father's voice. Sympathy is a sign of weakness in my business.

The track stretched on. Already the jungle was growing back over the side, twigs and leaves drifting in, blurring the edges. Devlin didn't know the names of the trees or the plants. To him the jungle was a mass of green. Vines, there were lots of vines, and some muddier green things which might not be vines. But those on the edge were vines, vines with green tips much brighter than the sections behind; they stretched out into the churned earth. They were growing as he watched but not enough to cover the prints of bare feet.

A hunched figure walked away from the corner of his eye: tallish, in the shapeless brown miner's suit, dusted with red, mud maybe. Devlin left the track, aimed for what appeared to be sparser jungle, but immediately found himself caught on thorny bushes. He heaved back, felt another bush behind him and, reduced to a crouch, had to move forward with his hands outstretched, trying to push the branches away. The light grew dimmer, the branches closed overhead, he was almost on his knees. He saw splashes of colour, a centipede moving like a stilt-walker over the slender points of the brilliant red mould on a rotting log.

The tough cloth of his shirt caught and, after a particularly savage wrench, he thought he heard it tear. He was furious: at himself, at the miner, at the monkeys stupid enough to stray too close. He was swearing under his breath, the words billowing up, silencing the jungle. He put a foot on a log which collapsed in a cloud of dried splinters and sodden mould-eaten patches. He toppled to one side – for a sickening instant there was the black pressing down and he was lying on the path outside his father's house, sweating alcohol, raising his head to look at the jimmied door, hearing the shouts inside, the breaking glass.

He lay on his back. The light was low, the ground damp and cool. The flat-nosed face of a small, white stone statue stared at him in lidless fury from under a bush. It was very quiet, an occasional creak from somewhere behind him; the wind must have been coming up through the trees. Through the fringed branches he saw a figure in white. Maybe the miner had taken off his suit, was so determined on a kill that he had climbed the trees. There was a rhythmic slapping, something rapping – softer than metal – against nearby bark.

Ants were crawling over Devlin's leg, into the cuts. He forced himself up, took a fix on the position of the white man, and pushed through the bushes, trying to follow in the general direction. The figure disappeared, reappeared, it almost seemed to be swinging from the branches. A man gone ape. An ape man.

Then he saw the real thing: a procession of brown shapes on the upper branches. He saw the hairy red-brown bodies, the long arms, the smaller shapes embracing the shoulders of the larger. A family of orang-utans. The biggest male stopped, his black bubble eyes fixed and unblinking. His leathery red-grey breast-plate was twice Devlin's width. Devlin lay very still. A call from up front and the male climbed on, flexing his long arms, peering over his shoulder as though to memorise the location, as though he would come back later.

Devlin couldn't place the slapping sound. He forgot about following the hunter and walked towards the noise. He had a sense that the river was behind him, on his right. But when he turned and searched for the path, it was as though the jungle had already grown back.

He wasn't worried. There would be a shift change in a few hours, the siren should be loud enough to hear. He still thought the mine owned the jungle. He didn't like to think of lost explorers, deluded white men, failures.

He was so focused on the sound that was not the usual rustlings and creaks of the jungle that it was a shock to find himself in the latticed thicket.

All other sounds curled away from him. He was alone, finally.

He looked up and it was as though light was kindled in the gloom of the jungle.

The pilot or what remained of him hung in his webbing, surrounded by the billowing folds of his cream parachute. He was a suit filled with air or earth or water or fire: hands or the remnants of hands inside thick gloves, a head covered in goggles and the hood of his jump-suit. When he knew he was going to crash, he must have pulled it up, as meagre protection. Now, he turned slowly as though someone recently passed by and pushed him – Devlin had an image of the monkeys patting him, as a totem – and there was enough movement to suggest breathing.

When Devlin drew closer, he saw the flare of ivory, light on bone.

The pilot hung from an oddly shaped tree, caught the way the branches had tried to catch Devlin. The tree had become a giant cross, overgrown with creepers and patched with moss; shredded brown bark plugging the hole torn along the metal trunk. A World War II bi-plane crashed in the jungle, its pilot – maybe his neck broken – unable to escape the ties that bound him. The canopy was a vaulted roof around him.

A scream; the birds scattered. The site siren tunnelled straight through the jungle at him. Devlin looked at the pilot hanging in his pale cloud in his jungle cathedral: sacrificed on the altar of his job. Unable to escape his work.

'You and your lame duck causes,' said Mitch. Devlin heard ice cubes rattling over the static on the line, imagined the whirr of Mitch's tape recorder, the breathing of some Kopassus thug listening in.

'I'm not a kind man,' said Devlin. He pushed the open envelope away from him. 'This isn't kindness. The locals won't stand for you wiping out villages.'

'Natives,' said Mitch. 'Headhunters. Primitives.'

'That's bullshit. My foreman is a Dyak.'

'Yeah, and Jakarta is pissed about that.'

'So I can't promote the best man for the job,' said Devlin. 'Doesn't that kind of blow my cover?'

'You can't promote locals without Jakarta approval. You know that.'

Devlin reached forward, put his hand over the wooden fish, covering its eye.

'We're surprised,' said Mitch, 'you're taking such an interest. After the inquest, we thought you'd want a bit of quiet.'

'As Jakarta's lapdog,' said Devlin.

'All you have to do is unlock the D gate on the twenty-fifth. That's it.'

'So the Kopassus jeeps can get in closer to do their dirty work.'

'The army wants to go in, clean out some villages, the mine is en route. Do the math.'

'I'll be an accessory to genocide.'

'It's Asian business, not ours. No-one's asking you to shoot anyone. You unlock the gate, you're doing nothing. Kick back, have another Scotch.'

Devlin opened his hand. The fin had imprinted red lines on his palm. Like scales.

'Don't go crazy on me now,' said Mitch. 'I sorted your mess.'

'I didn't ask you to.'

'You still owe me.' A pause, more rattling, a spurt of static not quite disguising a sigh in the distance. 'And you need to stop wandering around the jungle.'

'Rainforest.'

'Whatever.'

'The miners have been hunting monkeys. It'll make us look bad.'

'Who gives a fuck? Jakarta's grabbing the land anyway.'

'If I open the gate.'

'Don't even think about not doing it. You get caught, you'll be shot or dumped in one of their little river cages. Either way, we'll deny we ever knew you. Hear me?'

'Yes.'

'Watch your back.' He slammed down the phone.

Watch your back, Devlin thought. Always such a stupid phrase. And impossible.

He took to going out at sunset. At first he went to contemplate cutting down the dead pilot. He took crampons and a small axe and got halfway up the tree supporting the plane's tail. But the metal above him quivered, the black web vibrated and slipped. As he retreated, he caught the gleam of silver a stone's throw away. He searched, thinking it might be debris from the plane, or more of the small stone statues and the shrunken faces of gouged bone and tufted hair wedged onto sticks which lay, precisely placed, in this part of the jungle.

That was when he found the rock pool.

The water was clear to the bottom, not veined like the muddy grey river with the chemicals dumped in from the sites up north. He plunged his hand through a coolness which coated him, entered his bones, put out whatever smouldered there. He took off his boots and socks and shirt and waded in. He floated on his back for hours gazing up to where the light fell in ribbons through the canopy.

He thought, It is a cathedral for the unreligious.

The jungle folded around him like roses. Night fell within seconds, into a blackness alive with rustles and clicks and long moaning cries building around him, and the moon leaving traces of silver in the rock pool that lay a few paces from the dead airman, the water matching the gleam of the liquid eyes of the creatures hidden in their secret places, watching him.

He felt he could walk blindfolded through this green land. He could sleepwalk through it, as though in a dream. He learned how to move with the forest: by touching, by travelling on the sound of his weight on the fine twigs and fallen bark. He learned how to sit still, to breathe deeply for the first time in years. He slept better, ate better. 'Not so much drunken white bastard now,' said Kenje approvingly as he stacked the Friday afternoon boxes in the storeroom.

One sunset, as Devlin watched a baby fern slowly uncurl to the fading heat of the day, he became convinced that the rainforest could erase memories. And excavate them.

At night, staring up at the pilot sleeping above him, Devlin closed his eyes and smelled wattle. He saw swaying silhouettes against dark blue sky and heard the frogs' claps and bellows. Ahead of him was the creek bank with its myriad tiny white lights ringed by blue haloes. He was back in one of the few pleasant memories of his childhood.

The air was cold on the creek bed. The tiny lights were steady.

Glow worms, said his mother, lighting another cigarette.

They're like – he stopped, remembering the talk his father had given him, his big-knuckled hand gripping Devlin's arm. Occasionally he would dig in on a key phrase like, *Get it out of your head.*

Go on, said his mother. She coughed a little. She was already coughing then. She blew on the lit end of her cigarette, making it smoulder.

She said, There's no-one else here.

They're like . . . tiny people.

Go on, she said. She touched his cheek briefly. He let himself stretch out and stroke the soft moss. His hand sank into the warmth of the earth.

He said, Tiny people living in tiny homes between the roots of the gum trees.

Exactly, said his mother.

Don't turn into another old white bastard with shaking hands, Mitch had said on his next call. Don't get jungle madness. You're a good organiser, no-one better at keeping lists. Do your job and the slate gets wiped clean. Retirement, relocation – not a dishonourable discharge. Everyone's impressed by how you've juggled all three sides. You leave the gate open, who's to know? Jakarta wants this, the army wants it, Canberra, Washington. No-one minds if you have a few drinks but just remember: the back of Borneo is ours. Not the locals'.

That day he almost missed the village. He had wandered farther in than he realised, following what looked like a track. When it meandered into a vine patch, he stepped off to stare at the family of monkeys in the branches above. The rain came down, suddenly, fiercely, large splots of water making the ferns shake. The old grey-chested male glared at him, too stubborn to move.

The rain stopped. Devlin leaned against the damp bark, breathed the warm mouldy smell. He liked the heat. Already Mitch was talking about the next job – 'No ambiguities, nothing to trouble your conscience over: a looter, an art thief. You should read what he did to his son.' Trust you, thought Devlin, to pick up on that theme. Trust you to find the wound. Devlin saw Mitch as a little boy, poking at an ant's nest with a stick. Mitch had taken his silence for hesitation and said, 'And perks, dude. There's a wack-job daughter, an easy fuck for sure.'

Devlin rubbed his head irritably against the bark and felt a knot. He peered up: vines were twisted into ladders against the tall trunk. Then he saw the huts: bark and wood and palm leaves blending into the landscape. The land had been partly cleared but working around the trees, not against them.

He slowed his breathing, the way he did at night when he moved through the forest. A twig cracked on his left and he saw the silhouette of a man, haloed by the sunlight, next to a tree. He saw other faces merging with the brown jungle shadows. He thought he saw Kenje, dappled with light and bruises, retreating into the dimness. He saw a baby asleep on a flat rock under a fern, a dog watching him in a square of light, its muzzle held by a thin little girl with bottomless eyes. He saw a stream of smoke idling up through the branches. He thought for a moment. He said, 'I'll never tell,' and kneeled on the steaming earth.

The cage rocked again but there were no crocodiles beneath him; they were all on the bank. Instead, there was a rush of water, tinged with green and malevolent yellow. He smelled rotten eggs. Some site flushing out their sewage and tailings, up river? Dumping their acidic water. The crocs were lucky to be out of it.

He stared at the bank. The crocodiles had been ripping and tearing. Now each backed away, bloodied flesh in their teeth. A crumpled heap of bones and pink fur lay stamped into the mud. The pungent smell of hot blood drifted across the water, overpowering the chemicals. The forest was silent. Devlin saw eyes watching him from between the roots at the water's edge. He blinked, the water shifted and the eyes vanished.

Where had he gone wrong? Was it on that first day, twenty years ago? He saw himself sitting in the squad room: the new recruit, holding his breath, upright on the metal chair, the cold from the concrete floor creeping through his new boots up his legs, into his marrow.

'Today we have naming of parts,' said the sergeant, a freckled-faced square of a man with thinning orange hair and white arms under his red-brown markings. They had seen him in the pub the night before, standing for hours on a bench, wedged against the wall, singing quavering bush ballads about farm foreclosures and disappearing women.

The sergeant said, 'Tomorrow you'll have daily cleaning and then maybe if you're lucky and don't cock it up, you'll have what to do after firing. And then if you don't cock it up again, then you might even have firing. But we'll have to see about that.'

The hut was at the back of the base, an after-thought, a reminder of their lowly status. But its windows faced the fence of one of the base houses – maybe the colonel's – and there was an apple tree growing over it. The blossoms were just opening and Devlin could see – as clearly as if he saw it now, as if he was inches away instead of staring across dead ground and graveyards of bones – the bee crawling from the blossom, dusted and drugged in pink and white and rose-red pollen.

'And this is the lower sling swivel,' the sergeant was saying, 'and this is the upper sling swivel. You'll see what that is for when you get your slings. And this is the piling swivel, which you haven't got yet.'

The sky was very blue. He had never seen a painting that captured that peculiar blue, a blue so intense that even though you knew it was millions of miles away, it was as though it was there, pulsing, forcing colour under your skin . . . .

'The safety catch is always released with your thumb,' said the sergeant. 'DO NOT LET ME SEE YOU USING YOUR FINGER. Even you little tossers should have enough strength in your thumb. God help us if you don't.'

Devlin remembered thinking, If I was painting that sky, I would use the broadest brush I could find and the thickest paint, paint so thick you could only fall into it.

But he didn't paint it. He went to the pub with the others and sat in the corner, with nothing to say for himself, and he drank. And he kept on drinking – he felt dizzy now when he tried to visualise the endless rounds of beers, the endless pubs, the box of half a dozen bottles of Scotch delivered every Friday afternoon. He felt that all he had done in twenty years in the army was drink. It had been nothing but drinking until the Monday morning when he squinted up from the bucket and realised that Kenje was gone.

'You bastard,' Devlin said when he saw Mitch. He was shaving his four-day beard in the marble bathroom of the office in Anurandpura Street. The smoked-black walls and floor reminded him of the goggles on the pilot in the trees. He moved the mirror to get a better view of the office.

Mitch was at the desk, feet propped on the polished mahogany, raising a crystal glass.

'Quid pro quo,' said Mitch.

Devlin glanced at his reflection in the mirror. His skin was grey, his eyes were bloodshot. He thought, I hate you.

He said, 'He's got kids, Mitch.' Ten years younger than me, thought Devlin, and four kids.

He heard the creak in the chair as Mitch sat up. 'You haven't gone native have you?'

In this light the wet facecloth looked like the cream silk of the parachute filled with rain. Mitch's chair creaked again. He was getting up. Devlin thought of the vines tightening around the pale cloud in the trees.

He said, 'I need Kenje back.'

'Everything we do is for your own good, Devlin,' said Mitch, from behind him. 'Just remember, today's the fifteenth.'

Devlin knew if he looked up, he would see Mitch in the mirror. He turned on the taps, began to wash his hands. He said, 'You don't need to worry about me.'

He came out onto the cluttered street. The air had a nasty yellow haze to it; the traffic cops were wearing surgical masks again. He stepped back to dodge a scooter which had mounted the pavement to avoid the small tuk-tuk colliding with a car and a bicycle. The air shuddered under the weight of shouts and whistles.

In the city, in any crowd of people now, he had the feeling of being blindfolded and handcuffed, of fingers trying to entwine themselves around him. He always wanted to get away. Am I a solitary? he thought. The only place he wanted to be was in the rainforest.

He looked at the address Mitch had given him. Too late, he thought, for reverie.

There were other things in the glare of the city, tucked away, behind the squat stone police headquarters. He slipped on damp steps curving down through the dank air to cells as old as the stone figureheads scattered through the jungle. It was hard to see; fifteen watt bulbs were strung along the ceiling. Even the doors were iron. Medieval. Remorseless.

He looked through the grille in the first door. A clot of thin brown bodies was squatting or sitting on the floor. A smell of sweat and shit and fear and some other pungent odour.

'How long can you hold them?' he asked the bored guard by his side.

The guard raised his nearly hairless eyebrows.

'How long can you hold them before the families make a stink?'

The guard shrugged, lovingly smoothed the creases in the banknotes in his hand. He smiled; he was missing most of his bottom teeth. He put the notes away.

'I need to see more,' said Devlin.

'You terrorist,' said the guard. 'You American spy.'

'Oh, fuck off,' said Devlin. 'You don't know what you're talking about.'

The guard made a pistol with his forefinger and thumb and pointed it at Devlin's head. 'You go bye-bye soon.'

'Just piss off, will you?'

The guard showed his black holes.

Devlin walked down the hall, looking in the cells. No sign of Kenje.

'Nothing there,' shouted the guard.

'You've been paid,' said Devlin, not bothering to turn. 'Take it and shut up.'

The bulbs were strung more sparsely here. The walls seemed darker, rougher, the doors smaller, wider, the pungent smell stronger. Animals. They were keeping some kind of animal down here.

The light was a dim mustard glow. Devlin pulled out his pencil torch, played the light in a wide arc. The beam caught the wet walls, the jagged surfaces. The cells were built into caves.

'Nothing for you,' shouted the guard through the gloom. Devlin ignored him, put his torch up to the next grille, caught the slinking turn of a low black shape, a rumble cut with breaking glass. Golden eyes glared at him, the teeth a curved white blur in the dark.

There were birds of paradise in cages in the next cell and a heap of matted fur in the corner. He was walking towards the next door when the guard shouted, 'All right.'

Later when he bandaged Kenje's fingers and got him drunk on the first Scotch he had ever tasted – it had taken five shots: four for Devlin and one for Kenje – he had helped him carve *ALWABSADNIB* – Another Lazy White Australian Bastard Sitting Around Doing Nothing In Borneo – into the leg of the desk.

Devlin told him that he was worth his weight in panther pelts and paradise feathers. Kenje smiled carefully, holding his broken ribs, and that was all they ever said about it.

The crocodiles on the bank had finished tearing at the monkey, at each other. They had eaten but they were not satisfied. As he watched, another rush of green water hit two of the wooden poles. The cage rocked, Devlin was thrown to one side, his weight making it worse, he sensed buckling just as the pole was forced out of place. He leaned away from the tottering support but it was too late. The cage bucked and swayed and sagged, sharply.

The movement attracted the crocodiles on the bank. Their heads swivelled, they turned on their short fat legs, put their great jaws in the air, sniffing the wind. They set off at a run for the water, heading straight for him.

The lead crocodile had almost reached him. Its ridged snout came up out of the water in a rotting fog of snapping jaws and yellow teeth. But its feet were off the bottom, it had no leverage and it could only lunge and fall back, lunge and fall. The second crocodile tried to clamber up over the first which twisted, mouth open, trying to bite. They disappeared in the violently churning water. When a tail hit the already-teetering pole, Devlin knew it would only be a matter of moments. The third crocodile had hung back to watch but as the cage dipped even lower – water was soaking the vines in the corner – it put its shoulder to the sinking cage and pushed, experimentally. The cage tilted further, water was over Devlin's feet. He heard monkeys hooting in the trees. He gripped the roof bars, shaking them wildly, not caring if the cage rocked now, trying to break off a section of bamboo, anything that he could defend himself with. The crocodile's snout poked through the brown water and bit down with a crack. A splinter must have pierced it; it shook its head violently, mouth open, bamboo shards falling from between bloody teeth. It swerved away, became part of the threshing grey bodies. The cage dipped. Devlin thought, I have wasted my life.

As he fell, a blur of slicked grey aluminium came alongside him, seemingly out of the water. He heard rain falling on a tin roof, a ripping and snarling as the crocodiles were wrenched away by their tails, more rain, only later did he realise it was rifle shots, and then a bandaged hand pulling him up, past the outboard motor, into the dinghy.

They blindfolded him and walked him through the jungle. He stumbled frequently, more when he smelt the smoke. He was jerked to a stop. The blindfold was taken off. When he finished blinking in the light falling through the hole in the jungle, he saw that he was alone in a charred clearing. It was worse than he thought. The forest looked as though it had exploded from inside: debris from the huts lay scattered on the smouldering ground. Here and there were broken crockery and smashed plates but almost everything else – clothes, tools, people, dogs, pigs, chickens – had vanished. He saw a trickle of dark liquid glinting across the splintered wooden planks and dismembered vines, leading away from the embers through a path made by branches forced back by something barrelling through the bush. He followed the blood and was not surprised when he came out on the riverbank to the dozen crocodiles lying in the mud. They gazed at him incuriously, resting on their swollen bellies.

He knew he should look in the water for any remains of the villagers. He promised himself he would collect evidence. But for now, he had to sit in the mud and the broken leaves and the blood, and bow his head. He felt as though a giant bowl of desolation was above him, descending slowly. As though he would forever be on a bender, forever waking with acid in his mouth.

He went back to the smoking ash and picked up a smouldering stick and blew on it. The stick dropped an ember on his flesh. He watched it curl like a leaf, singeing the hair on his arm. He blew on the point and deliberately pressed it into the skin of his upper chest. He picked out several glowing sticks and went back to the riverbank. He sat down, close enough so that the nearest crocodile, a grey and brown speckled male the length of a horse, smelt the smoke and retreated in uneasy arcs to the tide-line.

Devlin blew on the stick and pressed it under his skin.

He had cut a jagged line under his collarbone when a branch snapped behind him. He didn't turn, he waited for whatever was coming. An arrow went past, so close he felt the feathered tail stroke the air near his cheek. It struck the crocodile on the tide-line; the animal snarled and squirmed backwards into deeper water.

Kenje sat down next to him. He was carrying a machete but no bow. So there were others, nearby.

'I'm sorry, Kenje,' said Devlin. 'This is a story about bastards.'

Kenje said, 'This is a story about work.'

'I didn't do it for the money. Well . . . ' He struggled to be honest. 'Yes, I suppose.'

'We all have to work,' said Kenje. 'Make choices.' He shrugged. 'Maybe those choices – ' he slapped his hands together – 'sometimes.'

The words were jammed in Devlin's throat. 'How – many?'

'You want to know the consequences of your actions?'

A hiss sounded in the dappled light behind them. Devlin felt the heat of bodies pressed into the shade. He could already imagine the blade at the base of the neck, the arrow in the back.

'Do it,' he said. 'It would be a relief.'

Kenje raised the machete. Devlin saw his father, his face red, throwing a beer bottle at him, shouting, 'You'll leave the army over my dead body.'

The blade was cold against his throat. Devlin closed his eyes, felt the blade turn to scorching steel. The naming of the parts: this is my cowardly neck, this is my betraying mouth, this is my black heart.

Kenje took the blade away. 'If they were really dead,' he said, 'we would have left you in the cage. The crocodiles had Jakarta takeaway dinner, not Dyak.'

Devlin opened his eyes.

'You told me to read your mail, John Devlin,' said Kenje. 'And so it was only logical to bug your office. Geigerstadt 1000, accurate to five miles. We bought it off the internet.' He admired his reflection in the metal. 'It was in the wooden fish.'

'Fuck,' said Devlin. He put his head in his hands.

Kenje rested the wooden handle on the back of Devlin's neck. 'We don't cut today,' he said. 'But my relatives still think you unlocked the gate. They are not happy.'

He took the machete away.

Devlin said, not raising his head, 'I can't remember.' The shame was fire in his mouth.

'Maybe,' said Kenje, 'a lazy white bastard went to sleep by a rock pool and was clubbed unconscious.'

Devlin looked at him. 'I don't know, Kenje.'

'You have to go,' said Kenje. 'That's your punishment, for doing nothing. You have to leave this sleeping place.'

'I'll never find it again,' said Devlin. The dark bowl pressed down. He said, accepting it, 'I'll never find it.'

'Maybe you'll find it in a person,' said Kenje. 'The garden you want, where you can dream.'

It was the morning of the twenty-sixth. Devlin stood in the doorway of the office, stared at the opened boxes, the overturned chair, the soiled towels, the buckets filled with coils of oily black and brown. He moved his foot and the empty Scotch bottles clinked.

The clock ticked over. He went down to the gym. A small wind was blowing up the cleared hill and the smell from the tailings dam stung his nostrils.

There were two digger drivers inside, doing reps and lines of speed in front of the scratched and grimy mirror. They loaded up the weights and offered him a line.

'I'm cleaning up,' said Devlin. 'I'm off the booze.'

They laughed, not unkindly. 'This time for sure,' one of them said. 'That's right,' he said. 'This time.'

He started bench pressing, saw himself in the mirror. *I hate you.*

He had lost weight. Where did the stocky recruit go? That fleshy young guy. He'd been stripped away years ago.

'We hear you're the man to get things,' one of the drivers said. 'Yeah.'

The driver said something about an electric grill, how they were sick of the cook's greasy breakfasts. Devlin couldn't be bothered with the details.

He said, 'Leave a list on my desk.'

He got up. He couldn't bear to look at himself anymore.

He checked his watch. He visualised being at the rock pool, swimming through the blue-black coolness, the latticed light lifting off the water in scales of silver. The image got darker and darker and finally disappeared. All he had was the job. Again.

A tinny sound broke the silence. The phone ringing and ringing. It stopped and someone shouted, 'It's the Embassy.'

BOOK V

THE
GLASS HOUSE
OF
CASTELMONTRANO

PART TWO

SICILY, EIGHT MONTHS EARLIER

MONDAY

 The front door of Café Flora bangs open, bringing in a flurry of winter air. Two men with parkas over their dark suits nod at the small fair man opposite me. They sit at the end of the bar, near the stairs.

I touch the typed pages of Devlin's file. 'Is this faked?'

'No,' says the American. 'But don't worry, he comes to his senses soon.'

'What a shame.'

A car stops outside the café, its exhaust smoke scattered by the wind.

I say, 'So Devlin disobeyed orders in Borneo?'

'Don't sound so admiring,' says the American, turning his signet ring. 'He never made it. He passed out by the river. The villagers were removed.'

'He tried.'

'He failed. You don't seem to be getting the real picture.' He reaches, flips over the pages. He leaves his hand lying next to mine.

I look at the photo in front of me. It is a copy of the picture I had seen on Devlin's laptop.

I say, 'What's this?'

'Don't play coy. We know you went through his briefcase.'

'I couldn't crack the password.'

'We assumed Devlin gave it to you. When he was drunk.'

'No.'

'You can see what it is though,' he says. 'There's the tunnels, there's the cages. There's the people.'

'Where's the American flag?'

'Ha, ha.'

'And this is where?'

He gives me a disgusted look. 'It's Koloshnovar – where you were picked up trespassing. Like sister, like brother.'

He moves his hand closer. I feel the heat from his fingers.

'Devlin knows all about it,' he says. 'So don't go thinking he's some kind of hero. I'm surprised you're not furious. And ashamed.'

'Why should I be ashamed?'

He blinks. 'What you did in the hut. How you – gave everything away.'

I lean forward. 'Say it: how intense it was. How it blew your mind.'

He withdraws his hand. 'We had a good laugh about it. We were surprised the old man could – well, you know. After all that booze.'

'You're jealous,' I say. 'You don't think you could ever get a woman to feel that.'

The first faint colour washes under his skin.

I say, 'You're the one who gets his jollies perving on other people. But is it me or Devlin you liked to watch?'

The red flush highlights the texture of his skin. It isn't as smooth as I thought. It is dry in places, scaly.

'By the end of all this,' he says, 'you'll be begging me. On your knees. Bent over.'

'I'm sure that's your preferred position.'

'It is for whores.'

'Trust men like you to have a whole vocabulary of disgust for other human beings. It's projecting the disgust you feel inside.'

'Skanks,' he says. 'Sluts. Cunts like you.'

'I know why you bend them over,' I say. 'So you never have to see their faces. Their looks of revulsion.'

The colour dies away. He smiles but I think it is an effort.

'You've already lost,' he says. 'You just don't know how badly.'

The door bangs again. Stefano is standing there. I rise. The man opposite pulls a page out of the file and tosses it at me. 'Devlin's report. That'll put you straight.'

I focus on the white square lying on the table.

He says, 'You won't be seeing Devlin again.'

'So I'm done? I'm out?'

He laughs. 'You're in for as long as we say. You'll do what you're told. Beginning with reporting to me.'

'I don't know your name.'

'Sure you do,' he says. 'You know my code name. Mitch.'

Stefano starts the engine without comment as I get into the car. We pull away and something rolls out from beneath the seat. It is a familiar shape: a thin leather roll tied around the middle. I imagine the needle inside, the small plastic bag of dirty cream powder. The spoon; the tourniquet. Later, I wondered whether Stefano was deliberately trying to ruin me, make me fall. But I don't think so. I think he was too distracted by Pietr's distress. Stefano had returned to his former dabblings; like me, he is already plummeting.

I let the leather rest against my foot as I read the page from the file. I see my father's name, my brother's. *Koloshnovar.* My heart starts climbing into my throat. *Extraordinary rendition. Torture. Non-American soil.*

I read it twice before I look at the name typed on the bottom.

'I'm going to be sick,' I say to Stefano.

He turns the car off the road. I half-fall through the door and throw up in the snow, retching even after my stomach is empty.

Above me, the sky is an empty bowl. I think of how convinced I had been when Devlin told me all he wanted to do was kiss my shoulder in the moonlight.

I retch again, so violently I fall to my knees.

The wet ground is eating through my jeans when Stefano gives me water to wash out my mouth. On the hard glittering earth, a slowly inching snail is leaving melting snow in its wake.

I spit out the last water and stand. 'I need something,' I say. I stare at the snail's slow trail of passion, at the abandoned drops of water which hold the light in milky pearls. The snail continues on. There is a dusting of snow on its grey shell.

'I need to feel – ' I say.

'Better,' says Stefano.

TUESDAY

'You don't have to tell me,' says Pietr. 'But I would like to know what's making you look so white.'

I think of yesterday: the rain against the windows, the beating of the windscreen wipers, the car rocking in the wind, Stefano with his hand braced against the roof, lying back in his seat, his eyes closed.

I remember the exhilarating rush when the needle went in: that warm blossoming inside, that familiar feeling that was always on the edge of being the greatest feeling there ever was but which never became it, that always teetered but never delivered, always promised to be the most sexual experience of all, but never was.

'It's poison,' I had said to Stefano.

'They can never prove it,' he said. He didn't open his eyes, his voice was slurred. He said, *Sophia*. I knew where he was: falling backwards on a rush of something that is always heavier than water, warmer than air. A rush of blood.

But this time, I remember thinking even before the black stars flared that I had made a horrible mistake. It wasn't Devlin inside me.

'It won't happen again,' I say to Pietr.

WEDNESDAY

The next day in the sitting room he says, 'You're ill.'

I try to say as lightly as I can, 'It's punishment.'

'Don't say that,' he says. 'That's how I felt about Anna for years.'

'Pietr, you don't have to feel responsible.'

His face is grey in the cloudlight. 'If I hadn't met your father in Morocco . . .'

I wonder whether it was on the trip we had taken when we first got rich. I had been eight, still furious at being removed from my old public school, already fighting with the girls at my posh new school. All I remember of Morocco is the zebra light in the narrow passageways of the old medina, the smell of spices, the incense, the faint music behind closed shutters, the cats' piss in the gutters. The antelopes' heads nodding in a line on the hot stone in the souq.

'It was hot,' I say. 'I didn't like it.' I study his fine cheekbones, the silver hair. 'I can't remember you.'

'I remember you,' he says. 'I thought even then you were going to be hard to control. And your father wasn't a family man.'

'My father needed his children the way an axe needs the turkey. He's beyond forgiveness. I don't forgive him.' I look at Pietr. 'My wild colonial ways offend your European sensibilities.'

He says, 'Sometimes, extremes leave the truest marks.'

342

The blur of pain lifts and with it the shroud of regret which fell over me every time I thought of Devlin. 'God, it's such a relief to have a conversation which doesn't consist of shouting.'

'Is that what you have with Devlin?'

'That's the non-cursing version.'

He gets up and stands at the window. The light picks out the blue ice of his eyes.

'I thought you might be homesick. You might need another Australian here.' He says, very evenly, 'I could get Devlin for you.'

I wrap my shawl tighter around me. 'He gives me no comfort.'

Pietr sits next to me. A spasm curls through my stomach. He says, 'I'll tell you anything you want to know.'

I think of the typed report with Devlin's name down the bottom. A wave of nausea runs up me, I hunch.

He says, 'You need a doctor – '

'It's not – it's withdrawal. I lapsed.'

There is a moment's silence. His face is drawn, shadowed.

'I know you don't believe me but it won't happen again.'

'If you tell me,' he says, 'I believe you.'

'Devlin would believe the worst.'

'Well, I won't say the obvious,' he says. 'But tell me if it doesn't go away. You might be having a reaction to the water. Some of the springs travel over volcanic rock. The carbon in the water can disagree with visitors.' He plays with the fringe on my shawl. 'You could tell Devlin's people about the jewels downstairs. It might be enough to distract them.'

'I can't give you up to save myself.'

'It would be a relief,' says Pietr.

I stare at him. 'You men. You all want to be caught. You want to go to prison.'

'I wish,' he says quickly then he laughs. 'Don't paint me a martyr. They'll never punish me publicly. I know too much.'

'About Koloshnovar?'

He says, 'Koloshnovar is just a way station. My grandfather used it to smuggle exotic animals up from Africa and through Sicily to private zoos in Germany and Austria. He had special quarters built.' His head is bent over the fringe on my shawl. I think of the cages I had seen in the underground tunnels. Cages tall enough for a man to stand upright. Pietr says, 'We leased the land and outhouses to the Americans for a while. They were moving suspected terrorists through Europe. They wanted the airfield to refuel.' He glances up. 'They said it was legal but I took precautions. Hidden cameras.' He straightens and says, 'Do you want to know about your brother?'

I am overcome by panic. 'I think the worst,' I whisper. 'I have nightmares.'

Pietr holds my hand. 'Unfortunately, in this life, the ugliest answer is often the truth.'

A cramp grips me. 'Sometimes I think that my brother discovered . . . obscenities . . . at Koloshnovar.'

Pietr says, 'But that's not your question.'

'I think he was killed for it.'

Pietr is silent, waiting. I say, 'Did my father know?'

After a long while, Pietr nods.

Another spasm coils through me. I am afraid of what is inside me. Everyone is so sad now. I don't want to know anymore. But I have to go on.

'Maybe it was an accident,' I say. 'Maybe it wasn't for business. For money.'

Pietr is silent.

'Was it on my father's orders?'

Pietr looks out the window. The clouds have made the sky fleshy, pulsating. His hair is dimmed in the low light.

Finally, he says, 'Yes.'

Spasms of revulsion run up my throat.

'The money was a curse right from the start.' I hold my hand over my mouth. When I am sure I can speak I say, 'Did he do it himself?'

Pietr shakes his head but I know it isn't a denial. It is an attempt to clear the shroud of black air which swirls around us. *Everyone is so sad now.* He says, 'I don't want to be the one you'll remember forever saying the words.'

'I won't hold it against you,' I say. 'Do you know how guilty I feel? I could have tried to find out years ago. I told everyone I was going to find out. I wrote it in my diary. But in reality, I did nothing. I let myself believe what I was being told. I got to Paris and I kept on partying.' I draw a breath. 'Now I need to know.'

Pietr turns my hand over and bends and kisses my wrist. Then he says the one word that for three years I have never wanted to hear.

TUESDAY

I am lying in bed. Rosza keeps bringing me hot milk. I imagine she thinks I am de-toxing. I force the milk down but the shuddering inside doesn't stop.

At night, when the clouds clear, enough moonlight floods the room to read by. The swaying branches stir the black milk lapping across the heated floor, making every object in the room tremble, as though Stefano's ghost is back but in a quiet mood, moving the furniture a few inches at a time. Maybe it is me. Sometimes I sit down in one chair and when I swim back to the surface, I find myself in another chair.

It is soothing now to sit staring through the window. People drift in and out, scrutinising me. Just like Anna, I hear someone say, and it seems to me that Pietr wears the same white look of shock for the rest of the day.

Later, an explosion of rage drifts down to me. I get out of bed carefully, my legs shaking. Pietr is arguing with Stefano, shouting on the walkway above my room. I have never seen him so angry. They go into the glass tower. The door is shut, the anger cut off.

Lying in my bed, I can't see the deserted ruins of Santa Margherita but I can imagine them: the broken buildings, the lonely graveyard. The planes landing at night, the wolves running up the hill.

It rains in fits and starts; the ashen sky shudders in the cold breeze. When I stand on the back terrace looking for Devlin, I smell smoke. Maybe it is fire caught in the broken stones on the jagged hill across the plain.

I wait for Devlin, but he doesn't come. There is no letter, no phone call. No message smuggled in. I am permanently cold, walking doesn't seem to help. I want to go to the hut but I am too afraid that the surveillance equipment is still there. I try to read poetry but the words are remote. They give me no consolation. Images of Devlin distract me, make me more nauseous. I say to myself, No coward soul is mine. I am still cold. Still afraid. I sleep a lot. I presume it is a result of the withdrawal. I am sluggish, disconnected. I tell myself that I don't mind that Devlin has gone, I don't miss him.

I wake one day to find a book wrapped in tissue paper on my bed. The pages are tied together with ribbon threaded through holes punched along the edges of two thin cracked sheets of wood; the wood has been painted red, roughly. It is the book that Pietr always talked about showing me but never did. Pages were missing. He said he didn't have the author's name. He had only flicked through it himself, he said.

I had been distracted, consumed by Devlin then. Now, I have time to study the black writing covering the yellowing pages. The writer is a Frenchman, a traveller, a writer. A poet. Heat runs through me; I forget my nausea.

There are maps, drawings of a burnt landscape, fragments of poems, diary entries. It is exactly what one would imagine an old, well-travelled diary would look like. There is no signature, only vague references to a provincial home, a farmyard. But when I see the name Verlaine, I immediately think I know the author. I tell myself that is wishful thinking. But I don't let the book out of my grasp. I sleep with it under my pillow.

I am in the back sitting room, reading Pietr's book. I have hidden it inside the cover of a bulky leather-bound edition of nineteenth-century love poems. Rosza sees the leather cover when she brings me my milk and gives it a disparaging look.

I study the maps. All are of Africa. This is a time spent in Morocco, at an old monastery which seems once to have been a fortress called Abu N'af. My French is rusty. I am painfully translating the diary segments. The poet seems to be in discussion with a slave trader. A Polish aristocrat. My translation could be wrong yet I can't bring myself to ask Pietr for a dictionary. I study the poet's drawings of the landscape, the waves of the desert, the plain beneath the monastery running across to a squat hill. The relation of the hill to the plain reminds me of something. It takes me days of reading to realise how similar it looks to Santa Margherita.

In the mornings, Pietr comes and sits with me. We don't talk about the present much. We talk about Anna. He says, 'She was a radiant little girl. But then all children are, before they inhale the rest of the world.'

He says, 'She was the best thing in my life.'

He brings me books on art and architecture, the international newspapers; an Aboriginal painting has sold for a million dollars. There is a picture in the paper and he downloads another from the internet. The print-out's tiny dot matrix can't disguise the glowing colours, the light shifting and lapping within each stroke. Even the smallest strokes hold sunlight.

'You're homesick,' says Pietr.

I swallow a wave of nausea. I am always sicker in the mornings. I refuse to consider what that means. I refuse to count back to Venice, to Devlin putting me up against the wall, running his hands over my body.

A bolt of warmth goes through me. But then the weight of absence comes back, like anti-blood, like poison. A tear, just one, runs out of my left eye and down my cheek. I think of Anna in the hospital. Pietr holds my hand and gives me a handkerchief.

SATURDAY

I am standing among the black trees below the back terrace of the glass house. The light from the candle in my unsteady hands turns the trees into crooked fingers. The early evening sky is purple, the low moon reflects off the strange new metal on my hand.

The house gleams, lit from within, a mindless diamond. Pietr's tower, usually dark at night, climbs into the sky like a glowing needle. Below is a vast black gulf; even the snow's light is swallowed, sucked across the plain into the ruins of Santa Margherita.

Childe Rolande to the dark tower came, I think to myself. I want the dark tower to come to me, I want to be swallowed. Night is a substance as water is a substance. Now that Devlin has gone, I want to drown in night.

The thought of him reminds me. I put the candle down, wedging it carefully into the snow next to my bare feet. A red web of dripped wax coats my wrist.

I move out from the well of shade. The moon's warm rays play over my face, falling into the two small bands of metal on my left hand. I try not to think of them as miniature electronic bracelets.

The night trees are glazed with stars, the night winds are talking to each other. I hold up my hands: a cold breeze travels over my fingers, under my nails. I can remake the wind, the stars, the trees, the water. I can build it.

I am having a conversation with Devlin. He is there, all around me, a substance like night is a substance, water is a substance. Like black smoke.

Let me tell you what I've been doing since you went away, I say to him. *I've been reading poems about blighted love. Revenge*, I say. *Poison.*

If you want to say something, say it, he says. *Don't use poems to frill it up.*

Do you know, I say, *that if you are poisoned by cyanide they find crystals in your heart?*

As usual, he looks at me as though I am mad.

The house seems to be growing, it is swelling with light, yet I know it cannot penetrate the forest. Only moonlight can do that. Pain prickles my skin. I feel pressure on my throat. I swing around but there is no-one there.

Water is the only substance that is renewed after use, I say to Devlin. *Water falls and vanishes and rises again. Tears flow backwards. Venice will rise again.*

Trust you, says Devlin, *to fall in love with a drowned city.*

Not fall in love with, I say. *In love there.*

Ghosts slip through the shadows towards me – there is a smell of smoke, of burnt winds. Ghosts are growing out of the black lake below. I imagine them breaking through the crust of ice, destroying the ripples of light patterning the silver surface, crawling onto the black bank, wearily climbing through the snow, the dead leaves, passing beneath the down-turned branches. They go around the hut, they never look back. They don't want to meet me but the wind will blow them here. It is inevitable.

No coward soul is mine, I whisper to myself, furiously. But the pressure on my throat increases. Maybe poetry can't save you, I think. Maybe all it does is make the awfulness slightly less awful. It can't truly console – it never did.

Pain prickles my skin again. Small dark shadows slip from branch to branch. I stretch out my arms. If I can become a shadow, if I can merge with the forest, I can erase myself. But nothing happens. The moonlight picks out the small black absences on my arms, the shackles on my finger.

I try to remember that morning but all I see are fragments of paper burning, words curling into trembling purple, calligraphy in flames spelling out some message I can't read. Writers and artists turned to ashes. Maybe I already knew what a terrible mistake I had made — out of anger, out of sickness. But for now, when I try to visualise the small church and the upstairs room with the buckled wooden floorboards and Pietr and the man in the black robe, all I see are books going up in flames.

I let my parka fall to the ground, pull off the silk jacket. The moon edges my arm in silver.

The candle goes out but the light from the glass house is bright enough to see by.

A black shape glides through the trees — not a man, not a wolf — something fluid like the mist across a toxic lagoon. A shape-shifter. I want to run but I am stiffening. I am turning to marble in the moonlight, into salt; the first stage of returning to the sea.

No coward soul is mine, I say to myself, thinking of Emily Brontë so bravely facing the death all around her. *No trembler in the world's storm-troubled sphere.*

The black shape surrounds me. The trees are engulfed by it as one of the unstoppable floods of the world is hurled at me: Noah's flood, the flooding of the Three Gorges Dam, the tsunamis. All the floods to come. It is arcing over me. I feel droplets of water on my cheek. I throw my head back and lift my arms.

Ice cracks and crunches. Pietr comes into the clearing, slipping on the snow despite his boots because he is walking fast. He picks up the silk jacket and parka, wraps them around me, kneels to put my shoes back on. I miss Devlin's shouts of rage. I want Pietr to say, *What the fuck are you doing?* the way Devlin would.

When Pietr holds me tight against him, I realise there is nothing there for me. He is like my brother, my uncle. A friend. There's no spark of insanity, nothing to make the giving up of self worthwhile.

He pulls my parka hood over my head. 'Winter was a bad time to cut your hair.'

'It was the kind of thing me and Anna would do. In our punk stage.'

His arms tighten around me. 'I couldn't bear it. Another Anna.'

'I'm not using,' I say. 'I don't know why I am like this.'

'Tell me what you need. I'll get it for you.'

I shake my head. 'I don't want to feel. That's what I need.'

'I'll get you Devlin.'

'No,' I say. 'He's poison.'

I gaze at the house swaying with light. 'I'm dreading the party.'

He says, 'They need to see you are with us.'

I nod, swallow the tightness in my throat, my stomach.

Noise swells in the background: the sound of cars travelling up the hill, doors slamming. Stars swarm. I try to watch them over his shoulder. The stars collect above the house and shoot up in two thin beams criss-crossing the sky. The beams go up into the heavens, gradually fading in the outer dark.

'Moonbeams,' I say.

'Lasers,' says Pietr. 'The guests are arriving.'

I am walking between earth and heaven. I see an open book: not my diary, the other book, the book with the cracked boards for a cover, the fine pen and ink writing, the delicate drawings of the desert, the small poems. The maps.

'In the end, there is always only the book, isn't there?' I say to Pietr as he helps me up the back steps. 'My diary, the Frenchman's book. All the books with maps inside. All the secret ways across the desert. But you knew that.'

He guides me across the back terrace. 'Yes.'

Fountains of light fall from the top levels of the glass house, shadows slide across them, laughter twining into the air, prisms of memories caught in the bubbles of champagne. I look across to where I imagine the dark tower of Santa Margherita is, eyeless and broken in the darkness. Then I look up at the glass tower. For a moment I am in dark water looking up at the sun. I am far out to sea . . .

Pietr is easing me across the threshold of the back sitting room. I put a hand against the doorway to steady myself.

'You know, from the sea, that tower would look exactly like – '

'Like what, my dear?' says Rosza, coming out of the light, bringing her own shadows with her.

She is smoking her thin black cigarette and holding a glass. It takes me a moment to register that it is a martini glass. She drains the glass and hands it without looking to the waiter hovering with a tray behind her. The muscles around her mouth are pinched white beneath the powder.

'I just found out,' she says to Pietr. She puts out her hand for another drink. She drains it without taking her eyes off Pietr. 'Stefano told me.'

'Of course,' says Pietr.

'You should treat Stefano with more respect.' She snaps her fingers at the waiter, who backs away.

'Why?' says Pietr. 'Did he give her the junk? Or did you?'

'Her choice,' says Rosza. 'She's *ofanculu* weak. Like – '

'If you mention Anna,' says Pietr, 'I will leave this house immediately. And never see you again.'

She gapes. 'I don't understand. How can you put her first?'

'I'm not putting her first. I'm protecting her. From you.'

I am confused. Pietr says to me, 'I did what you suggested. Family research.'

Rosza says, 'She's putting ideas into your head.'

'You can't touch her now.'

'She'll hurt the business,' says Rosza. 'You know there's something between her and Mr Devlin.'

Pietr says, 'Devlin's gone.' As he guides me past her, the light hits the diamond on my finger and patterns Rosza's face with silver. She blinks. 'You mongrel bitch – '

'Careful,' says Pietr. 'Behind you.'

Mitch says, 'This is a happy family scene.'

Pietr puts his arm around me. 'Always.'

Rosza says slowly, 'Signor . . . ?'

'From the Embassy.' Mitch turns to me. I put my hands behind my back but I know from the twitch of his eyelids that he has seen the diamond.

'Didn't I tell you?' he says softly. Then, to Pietr, 'When is the happy event?'

'We got married this morning.'

Mitch is still. 'Congratulations. I'll make sure Devlin finds out as soon as possible.'

'Where is Mr Devlin?' says Rosza.

Mitch dips his head sorrowfully. 'He had to take personal time.' He looks at me. 'He won't be back.'

Couples, mostly smokers, go past us to the back terrace. I see emeralds and rubies winking in the light, the oiled dead hairs of fox furs on over-tanned shoulders.

'The Iraqi Foreign Minister. And the Algerian Trade Secretary,' says Mitch. 'I'm impressed. That must facilitate trade routes.' He says to me, 'Your fiancé – oh, beg pardon – your husband is a very astute businessman.'

Pietr nods at a portly man standing by the wall. 'The Mayor seems lost.' He says to Mitch, 'I'm sure you would like to meet him.'

'I have met him,' says Mitch. 'But I'll join you. There's a little matter of deportation I need to discuss.' Pietr raises an eyebrow at me. I nod. He steers Rosza away.

Mitch extends his hand. 'Business before pleasure, I'm afraid.'

I reluctantly put my hand in his. It is dry and hot. Before I realise what he is doing, he reaches around me, picks up my other hand and examines the rings. I pull away almost immediately but he has seen the gold wedding band next to the diamond. 'Devlin will be pleased.'

'Fuck you.'

'Not very poetic.' He steps back. 'Well, clever you, buying

insurance. Everyone knows your husband has a dirt file in the event of his death. And clever Pietr, eliminating a potential witness. They don't believe drug-addicted wives in Italy.'

'Fuck you. That's repetition, parallelism. Poetry.'

'I hope you'll be happy,' says Mitch, 'knowing you ruined Devlin.'

He turns but I am already leaving. I blunder through the sitting room into the hall. A blonde woman in a black dress is carrying a tray into the dining room where couples are eating supper at the candlelit tables. The woman stops. It is Julietta.

'We need more champagne,' she says. 'Stefano says for you to get it. The door's open.' She gives me a little push. 'Now.'

As I go down the steps, the distances swell and disappear, the walls shimmer. I feel as though I am wading through strobed water; I put a hand against the wall to steady myself.

This is the bit I have to get exactly right. This is the end of the truth. Or is it the beginning? I know my recollections of that night are bad. I was sick, too sick to know how sick I was. I thought I was heart-sick but it was much worse than that.

I go down the last few steps, the concrete moving like sand beneath me. The door to the wine cellar is ajar. I am overcome with a terrible longing. I prop myself against the wall. There is a hole inside that needs to be filled. I try to remember some lines of poetry. But nothing comes to me.

Faint smoke in the cellar. I touch my inner elbow, feel the small pinpricks in my flesh. The miniature wells descend into darkness; I feel the pulse of my thumb, like that other pulse at my waist. I imagine the glint on the needle-tip, the way the light catches rainbows in the tilted liquid inside the glass vial. I try to hurl away the image, the taste, the smell. I know if I use again I will be killing myself – myself and my other self.

A thread of that now-familiar nausea curls through me. I lace my hands across my stomach.

On the perimeter of the pool of light near the door something moves. But there is no sound except for my own breathing. Whatever is there is holding its breath. I dread to think it is Mitch.

I begin edging along the wall to the door. Air whispers by me, another movement, the silhouette of a man. The door slams shut.

I put my hands up and meet a body coming towards me, driving me against the hard concrete.

'You're not getting away that easily,' says Devlin, and kisses me on the neck.

For a moment, I revel in the luxury of the full length of his body pressed against mine. I put my arms around his neck, I cling to him, I try to push myself into him, under his skin. His hands slide slowly up and down the heavy satin of my dress. He is luxuriating too, I can tell by the way his hands grip my flesh through the slippery material.

He says, 'Your surface is water,' his mouth at the base of my throat. He pulls me hard against him, kissing me so I can't move. My anger ebbs away. Stupid woman. He is running his hands up and down my arms, running up and down to my wrist, up, down. Up. Any moment now, I think. His breath is ragged, he is kissing me so I can't breathe. I don't want to breathe, don't want him to stop.

He says, 'I've been ravenous.' He kisses me again and again, takes my hands in his, raising them to his mouth as he says, 'I came to tell you – '

He feels the rings. His fingers go slack with shock. I push him away, slide from beneath him. Too late he grabs for me, his fingers slipping on my dress. I pull free, fumble for the switch on the wall.

He stands blinking at the sudden fall of light.

I back away, fast, so that the first of the wine racks is between us. They are shoulder height and heavy, the old wood knotted and black, but they will not be enough to stop him if this is the moment when he loses control.

He steps forward. Maybe the neon light overhead is flickering infinitesimally because he seems to shimmer as though he is a long way off.

He looks at my hand and aimlessly, as though they have only caught his eye because they are between us, at the bottles glinting sullenly in the light. He pulls out the nearest one. Brown paper is wrapped around the lower base, the wolf's head logo stamped inside a red circle. He turns the bottle over and over in his hands and grips it by the neck. The liquid, black through the dark brown glass, rocks back and forth, unsettled, unstable. I wait, wondering if he is going to use it as a weapon. Against me, against himself.

The silence lengthens, grows heavier. He can't ask the question.

I say, 'I'm married.'

His hands tighten on the glass. He holds the bottle, trying to keep the wine level, stop it from moving.

'Did you hear me?'

He puts the bottle carefully on the top corner of the nearest wine rack, on the very edge, so that half of its base is stepping out into white air.

'Engaged,' he says. 'We know Pietr bought a ring.'

'No,' I say. 'We were married. This morning.'

His eyes are completely black. There is no light there.

'It's not legal,' he says.

I shrug. 'It is to me.'

He makes a sharp wrenching movement with his hands as though he is tearing something in the air. The bottle sways in the current – he puts his forefinger against the base, holding it steady.

'I gave up drinking for you,' he says.

A jolt of rage goes through me. It burns any softness. All that is left is the asp of nausea twisting across dried earth and dead stones.

'I gave up poetry for you,' I shout. 'I gave you everything. And you totally betrayed me.'

'I never – ' He steps forward, letting go of the bottle, which crashes to the ground. A red river spreads across the flagstones, soaking up the brown paper wrapping so that the fibres collapse into a sodden dark pink mass. The stamped wolf's head nods at me as the liquid seeps across the floor, eddying around the jagged shards winking in the light and a small, shiny package.

As he crouches and carefully picks up the plastic bag, I come out slowly from behind the rack.

He lifts the bag to the light. I see the stones inside, the sparks of colour through the dull pebbly surfaces.

He isn't looking at the stones. 'I could leap up right now,' he says. 'I'm faster than you, bigger. I'll come through the racks. I'll jam the door. I can catch you and rip your throat out.'

'Do it then.'

He stands, shoves the bag of stones into his pocket and, very slowly, steps over the broken glass. He is little more than an arm's length away. This close, I am weakening already, my pulse climbing into my throat. I cling to the edge of the wine rack. I can't look at him but I know he is moving forward, warily. Soon he will be close enough to touch.

'You've got something to show Mitch now,' I say.

'I don't give a fuck about Mitch.' He is inches away.

'He said you'd left.'

He puts his hand next to mine on the wine rack. The skin is broken across his knuckles, there are bruises already turning purple-green around his wrists.

He says, 'They wanted me to alter my report.'

I imagine reaching out and resting my little finger between his first two knuckles. Some small gesture that he would remember later.

'I care as much about your report,' I say, 'as you care if another man asks the woman you're sleeping with to marry him.'

'I didn't expect you to goddamn marry him,' he shouts. 'What did you want me to do?'

'I wanted you to goddamn stop it,' I shout back. 'I wanted you to tell them all to go to hell, tell them I'm not the woman they thought I was. To take me away from this.'

He looks at me. I can tell he still doesn't understand. He reaches out and runs a hand over my hip, lingering. I slap him. I care enough not to hit hard but I forget about the rings. I cut him on the cheek. Blood wells up. He doesn't move; he doesn't try to staunch it.

'Now we're even.' He still thinks that we haven't gone past the point of no return.

I see the words coming, they are forming in the black air which is swirling around me. I can barely breathe but I know I have to say the words. Make him go away.

'Let's go then,' he says. 'I've got enough money, some friends. We might be okay – a good lawyer – '

'I'm not leaving Pietr.'

The black air is swirling around him now. 'But you can't stay married to him.'

'He stood up for me.'

'But that's – '

'You've known all along what my father did to my brother.'

'How could I tell you?' he shouts. 'Without you thinking I was trying to use you?'

I put my hands over my stomach. There are sharp jabs of pain as though I am being pierced inside. I hurt and I want to hurt him.

'He gave me a book,' I say. 'A book of poetry. A book beyond price. You and Mitch would never understand it.'

He puts his teeth together. 'Don't ever, *ever* equate me with Mitch.'

I nod, trying to breathe through the pain. I wonder if I am miscarrying but there is no sensation of liquid leaving me. I want someone to ask. I want Anna. For the first time in years, in my life, I want my mother.

Devlin says, 'Why didn't you?'

I breathe out, slowly. 'What?'

'Marry me.'

'You never asked me, Ash.'

'But you must have known.'

'How? I needed words.'

He is shocked. 'But I gave away so much.'

'All I got from you were absences. You knew about my father. You never told me. I could never rely on you.'

'Listen to me.' He holds my shoulders, turns me to face him. There is a moment when I sway towards him, when his hands move on my skin. Despite everything, in the middle of everything, I want him.

He takes a deep breath. 'If you sleep with him, I'll – '

'It's not like that. He says he just wants to protect me.'

'Oh fucking bullshit,' shouts Devlin. He looks around, grabs the nearest bottle by the neck and pulls it out onto the floor. He pulls out bottle after bottle from the rack, hurling them to the floor, the glass breaking and flying upwards, in wave after glittering wave. The smell of escaping spirits rises as sour as smoke. He grips the rack, shakes it so that it rocks back and forth, bottles chiming like bells. 'I think he bribed Mitch to show you my file.' He forces his voice down. 'Mitch would never usually show classified information to an outsider.'

'I don't care.'

'Pietr will do anything to get you.'

'How do you know?'

'I would.'

'But you didn't.'

His eyes are growing darker if that is possible. He is beginning to see now. 'So you're going to punish me. Out of spite.'

'I'm going to punish myself,' I say, 'out of guilt. How do you think I feel sleeping with the man who never told me who killed my brother?'

'How do you think,' he says, 'I could ever tell you it was your father?'

There is a sharp pain in my eyes. I don't even know what it is. I feel water leaving me. I start backing away from Devlin. 'I don't cry,' I say loudly. The snake twists in my stomach. I put my hand over my belly. I think about telling him. I think about his right to know. Then I remember what he has done. I feel my way around the wine rack. When I realise he isn't following me I stop, lean into the cold wood, the bottles pressing against my hip.

'You're sick,' he says. 'You've been using.'

I remember why I can't tell him. I can never trust him not to leave.

'The whole time,' I say. 'It was the only way I could get through sleeping with you.'

'That's a lie.' But there is a white line around his mouth, old insecurities being etched in. Bad memories from the bottle. Failures, humiliations.

'I pretended the whole time,' I say. 'I knew you'd sell me out. I had your file, remember? I knew – ' I am about to say the words that will make the final severing – 'I knew what you did to your father.'

'You – ' There is no word to describe the chasm I have opened up.

'Now you know how it feels,' I say.

He steps back. 'Go ahead and fuck him then. I'll leave you to the wolves. You deserve it.'

He walks away without looking back. I hear his footsteps, crunching the glass. A great coolness settles over me. I straighten, the wood rough and reassuring beneath my fingers. But before I can move, the lines of wood shiver. They dissolve in the thin white air. For the first time since my brother disappeared, I cry.

SUNDAY

I wake. It is raining: a clatter of gravel on the roof, hard chips against the window, the sense of the house swaying in the wind. The sound of voices receding, car doors slamming.

I am very drowsy but as I sink again, I see lightning flashes veining the horizon in silver, putting roots from the world in the sky down into the world of the earth. I see tornadoes spinning across the plain to Santa Margherita, giant whirlpools revolving around a black heart, churning up trees and dust and stones and bricks and wolf bones, passing across the black lake so that water flies upwards, the drops hanging in the air like blood. Threaded through it all is a sour smell, like sulfur, like burning gold.

I wake again or maybe I had never slept. The house is quiet; the room totally black. Then it fills with light but it isn't the soft translucence of the moon or the shivering yellow of candlelight but a harsh whiteness as cold as stone. There is silver at the centre and flashes of orange. Everything in the room is whited out. The light bursts through the French doors and sears my eyes. It surrounds me in the double lines and shifting shapes of blue and silver and shadow and light that are made when air meets water, when I swim in the pool and in that other dimension with Devlin, the one which fills every cell in my body with liquid colour.

I can't breathe. I think a plane is falling, is coming straight at me. The blazing light fills my eyes, my mouth, my ears. It is pure silent noise. It is coming from outside.

I lace my hands over my eyes, grope to the balcony doors and pull the curtains across. The light pulses against the heavy brocade, and a new sound of grinding.

I find my sunglasses, jamming them hard against my nose and cheek. Even then I have to cup my hands around the plastic as I open the door.

The grinding is much louder outside. It reminds me of the sound of the stone pestle on the ceramic bowl when I mixed paints as a kid.

Beyond the balcony the entire landscape is bleached into a map of extremes, just outlines now, every paler colour gone, as though in the flash from a cataclysmic bomb. The light obliterates the moon, the clouds, the stars. The sound is above me but closer than the sky.

Pietr's tower is lit from within. The curtains are drawn back and the glass tower, filled with light, rises into the sky. The heart of the light – a ball of pure silver – comes from the library, where the raised dais is. The vibrations in its turning break the white into distinct rays. Now that I see the tower revealed in its true purpose, I know why it has always seemed so familiar. I have lived on the coast, near the turning beams sent out to sea.

It is a light turning in a glass tower.

I wonder whether it is a warning or a welcome.

A hand drags me back into the bedroom.

Rosza closes the curtains, switches on the bedside lamp.

'There's a storm coming,' she says. 'Get into bed. You're sick.'

'Has everyone gone?'

'It's all over.' She looks at the half-empty glass of milk on the table.

I say, 'I didn't realise the tower was a lighthouse.'

'We sometimes put on the light to help the coastguard. It was Pietr's idea.'

My legs are trembling. Rosza helps me into bed. She says, 'I'll bring more milk.'

When she has gone, I lie for a moment, thinking. Then I get a towel from the bathroom and fold it up and put it over my stomach, under the sheets.

Outside, the light grinds its slow, relentless circles.

'I hope it doesn't keep you awake,' says Rosza, coming back with a cup on a tray.

She gives me the cup and sits in the chair next to the bed.

I pretend to sip the milk. 'Hot.'

'I micro-waved it, I'm afraid,' she says, watching as I raise the cup again. 'You don't mind that you're still in your same room?'

'Pietr's being very good about – giving me some time.'

She purses her lips. 'That's one way to see your situation.'

'He's a good man. He'll always do the right thing.'

'And you'll support him?'

'Yes.'

She shrugs and goes to the window. The moment her back is turned, I lift the sheet and pour the milk onto the towel beneath. When she comes back to the bed, I have the cup at my mouth and am tilting my head back.

'It wasn't as hot as I thought.' I hand her the cup and yawn. 'I could sleep for days.'

I examine the diary entry now and I try to think what happened next. There isn't too long to go to the end and I have to get it right. I think, I am sure, that I lay in bed and counted off time. To wait until the coast is clear. You always think in terms of water, I imagined Devlin saying.

I count to two hundred and go to the door. The floor is cool beneath my feet, chilly enough to keep me awake. On the landing, I hear a murmur of voices. Not many. I remember the staff was told to go home once they had cleaned up after the party.

I go back and pick up the wet towel, put on soft slippers that make my feet soundless.

The hall lights are off but there is enough light rising from the open door of the living room. I go down the stairs.

My legs are shaking; I hold tightly to the railing. I want to go back to my warm bed, to oblivion.

The wind hits the house. Rain is splayed over the glass roof; a broad shadow runs down the staircase wall.

Now I see my brother's face. I know he is not alive but it is no delusion. I understand that nothing else matters – not Devlin, not Pietr. I have a euphoric sense that I know what ails me and have the solution to solve it. No-one, not even Devlin, is going to stop me.

The fire is lit in the living room. Rosza stands with her back to it, drinking from a brandy glass. She is as coiffed as ever, still in her black gown from the party, but there is a smattering of rain on her shoulders and water drops gleam in her hair. Pietr stands by the terrace door. He has changed from his tuxedo into jeans and a jacket but he is soaked through. His hair is wet, the colour dulled. The world beyond the windows is pure white.

I stop next to the doorway, my back against the wall. The rise and fall of words becomes sharper. They are arguing.

Pietr says, 'You told me last time was the last.'

'You're living in a *fotutto* fool's paradise,' says Rosza. 'You think that woman, she will make up for everything. The people we work with won't let us walk away.'

'I can make a deal.'

'Deal?' Rosza starts shouting in Sicilian, harsh vowels burrowing inside each other.

'I don't speak that peasant language,' says Pietr, and for the first time I see how much he dislikes her.

'Oh, just like Czeslaw,' says Rosza. 'Above everyone.'

'I'd rather be like him than you.'

'Stop worshipping a *fotutto* book lover who never accomplished anything except running away. He couldn't even save himself to raise you.'

'Well, you saw to that, didn't you?'

'Don't blame that on me. The accident – '

'Another accident. Like the poisoned village. The ambulance driver's report . . . '

I edge into the room as Rosza throws her glass into the fire. The brandy flares purple above the logs; the cracking glass sounds like gun-shots.

'That woman put you up to it,' says Rosza. She turns the rings on her fingers. 'Or did Stefano say something?'

Pietr frowns. 'Why would Stefano say anything? He's your creature not mine.'

I see Rosza's expression of utter weariness. Or maybe resignation.

'I tried to be a good mother to you,' she says. 'I treated you as someone valuable. I made sure I didn't do to you what my mother did.'

'You treated me like a business partner,' says Pietr. 'You eliminated anyone who was a threat – not to me, to the business.' He pours himself a drink, downs half in a gulp. 'I need to know how far you have gone.'

Rosza twists her hands together. Behind her, the last blue flames flare.

She says, 'There's no proof of anything.'

I step into the room and say, 'There is proof.' I hold out the wet towel to Pietr. 'You should analyse this. I bet it is the same poison she used in the well in Santa Margherita.'

He is so surprised to see me that he doesn't move. He looks at the towel but he doesn't understand.

Rosza snaps her fingers. She says, 'Oh, she's mad.' Then her eyes turn inwards. She is remembering standing in my room. How fast I had drunk the milk.

Pietr is still looking at me as Rosza snatches the towel and throws it into the flames. She grabs his glass and pours the brandy over the sodden material. The falling liquid catches fire; a purple flame runs over the surface of the towel; purple and red blazes into the chimney.

I say, 'You have to get it back,' but Pietr is still, watching the remnants curling into ashes.

He says, 'She's promised tonight is the last time.'

I recoil. 'I thought you didn't know. Or were forced into it. The slave-trading.'

His head jerks back. 'Slave-trading? What are you talking about? It's helping people get into the country.'

'You know it's more than Africans being brought over.' I think of the cages I had seen beneath Koloshnovar. 'It's more than people-smuggling.'

He is shaking his head.

I say, deliberately, 'It's what your grandfather did.'

He says, 'It's nothing like that.' *Nothingk*. 'These people need us. It's domestic labour, construction workers.'

'How do you know?' I say. 'Do you talk to them in their cages? Do you find out what happens to them?'

'Oh, he would never get his hands dirty,' says Rosza. 'Even though he's lived off it all his life. He wanted his fine wines, his cars. Things he can't do without.'

Pietr is watching me. 'I left it up to you. You've got the book.'

Rosza raises her fist. 'That *ofanculu* black leather book. I should have burnt it years ago.'

'Red,' I say. 'The book with the red cover.' But they don't hear me.

'It was a reminder of my father,' says Pietr. 'You loved him.'

'I hated him!' shouts Rosza. 'I hated him because he never loved me. Even when my father threatened him. That *fotutto* Pole couldn't even pretend. How do you think I felt?' Her voice rises to a scream. 'Unloved. Unloved.'

Pietr's skin is as white as his hair. 'But you had his child – '

'That *minchia* of a monk!' shouts Rosza. 'All he wanted to fuck was a crucifix. He was a neuter, a nothing. In-bred blue-blood.' Her voice thickens. 'We had to boil shoes in winter when I was a child. Those pig-fucking rich move their chess pieces and we eat shoe leather and ashes.'

Pietr takes a step away as though he can't bear to be next to her. 'So you got pregnant to get Koloshnovar?'

She goes over to the sideboard, pours herself another brandy, throws it straight down. She wipes her mouth. Her hand is shaking.

She hisses, 'I'd fuck a wolf before I'd fuck a Pole.'

I look at Pietr's face and start backing towards the door.

Rosza sees me, shouts, 'How does it feel knowing you're surrounded by everyone involved in your brother's death?'

'No.'

'Oh, yes,' she says. 'Stupid Australian boy. Stupid foreigner. You come onto our land, you get shot. Or poisoned. That's the Sicilian way.'

Pietr rubs his forehead. There is a white sheen over his face. 'You should go now.'

I say to him, 'I'll never believe you had anything to do with it.' And I leave them.

I run across the hallway, out the front door. The rain has stopped; the entire world is filled with light, turning and pulsing and grinding, streaming past me to the sea. I wonder who is coming ashore.

Below, lights flare in the guard house. I run to the back terrace and down the steps. The forest sits, waiting for me. The hut, I think. I could change, try to reach Julietta in the morning. She might know where Devlin has gone.

On the back path, the air is white. As I reach the first trees, the grinding sound stops. The light is switched off. One of the shadows leaves the skeletal black outlines and comes towards me. In the last instant of illumination I see it is Devlin.

He grasps my hand, pulls me down through the trees. 'Run.'

This is it. This is the final thing I will write. The final truth of what happened. Or will I lose my nerve and try not to incriminate myself? Will I feel some misplaced loyalty? Will I try to protect the innocent? And the guilty. Will I prefer to slip away into the darkness, into the heart of the fire, with my memories intact? Carrying Devlin's heart. Carrying it in my heart.

We are running down through the trees, the branches breathing into the dark, the stars moving slowly. Behind us, I hear a sharp crack. Another one. It reminds me of the brandy glass exploding in the fire but this is a bigger glass, a bigger fire.

'Shooting,' says Devlin.

We don't stop. My slippers are soaked, I can no longer feel my toes. But I don't care. I keep running.

The wind swells again, the leaves stir restlessly. I imagine the sea whirling up its black points, its small angles of foam, trailing its dark-green dead hair.

We reach the road. It seems empty, a blank tongue in the dark. I assume we'll go to the hut but Devlin points at a square shadow which edges the road. 'I've got a car.'

He is unlocking the passenger door when the trees further along move out onto the road. Tall slender figures which merge with the macadam. I see woollen cloaks, feet bound with goatskins, the smaller humps of sleeping children. I see African faces.

A stocky shape surges out of the gloom. Stefano.

'Do you have a gun?' I say to Devlin.

'No guns,' he says.

I try to pull him away from Stefano. 'He'll hurt you.'

'No,' says Devlin and raises his hand. 'How long were you meant to keep them in the hut?'

Stefano eyes me. After a pause, he says, 'The buyers come tomorrow.'

'Keep them in the hut until then,' says Devlin. 'We may sting the buyers, too.'

Stefano nods. 'The deal is good?'

'Yes.'

Stefano puts out his hand. Devlin doesn't hesitate. They shake.

Stefano turns away.

'Stefano,' says Devlin. The other man stops, black and bulky. 'There are cameras in the ceiling. Keep one of those tapes for yourself. As insurance.'

We watch the group cross the road, a small dark stream moving over the white ground, past the lake. They climb the ridge and merge with the trees around the hut.

'Let's go,' says Devlin, opening the car door.

I am about to climb in. One more moment and I would have done it. I would have got in the car and driven away with Devlin. To a happy ending.

But a breeze passes across my face. I smell sulfur. Devlin says, 'It's nothing.' Across the car roof, he has the same look of resignation that Rosza had.

I clamber up the slope.

The silver quivers in the distance. Cracks sound and all the lights go out. The house sits in the black night but it is no longer silver. The shell is turning gold, tipped with orange from the flames burning below it.

I say, 'The book.'

'What book?' Devlin is behind me. 'Your diary?' He grasps my arm. I feel his wariness, I admire him for his bravery but it doesn't change what I am going to do. His grip tightens as if he already knows. 'It doesn't matter what you wrote. We're here.'

'I have to get the book with the red cover.'

'No.' Devlin drags me around to face him. 'This is our chance.'

'The book makes up for all the failures. It is the only pure thing.' I wrench myself away. 'I have to do something. I have to choose something.'

Minute chips of heat hit my cheek, burning cinders fall around me like confetti. I rub my skin. My fingertip is smeared black.

I say, 'I'm pregnant,' ashes in my mouth.

Orange flames are in his pupils. 'You're not pregnant. You're being poisoned.'

'Stefano told me,' he says. 'Rosza's been poisoning you. Almost from the start.'

'Why would Stefano tell you?'

'He cut a deal to save Pietr.' He takes a deep breath. 'You're sick. You know it's true.'

Ashes are in my eyes. 'You want it to be true,' I say. 'All you want is your own story. You never see the other stories around you.'

'For God's sake. After all the damage we've done to ourselves.'

'Why can't you comfort me?' I say. 'Just once.'

The hot air blurs. He is disappearing into a blizzard of ash. I taste dead buildings on my tongue, dead books.

He tries to put an arm around me. 'Be realistic,' he says. 'With people like us, do you really think – ?'

I shove him away. 'You're leaving me again.' His arms go slack. I shout, 'Why do you assume it is yours?'

'There's no baby,' he shouts. 'It's all in your mind.'

I put out my hands. I fill them with the falling fragments and rub ash all over my face. There is one last moment when I could have said the right thing. I could have said, It was always you. Right from the start.

Instead, I let myself drown in the bitterness. 'How can I ever trust you?'

I pull away and run up the slope and through the melting snow. I run across the burning ground and into the fire.

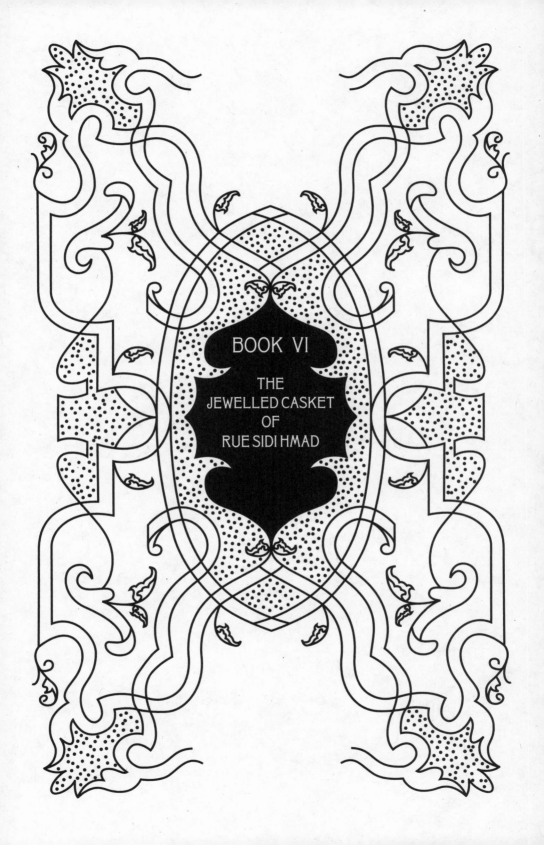

BOOK VI

THE
JEWELLED CASKET
OF
RUE SIDI HMAD

CASABLANCA, 1978

 There is no weather inside the walled city, thought Agnieska Walenzska as she stared down over the flat rooftops baking in the early morning sun. There are only temperatures of extremes, following their narrow track every day.

She sipped her mint tea and tried not to look for the stranger. The second round of morning prayers had just finished; an interim chant rose and fell in the distance. She rested against the window in the jeweller's shop; the wooden cross hanging on its camel-hair plait around her neck tapped against the sill.

On the next rooftop, men were up to their knees in the giant pots of dyes laid out in rows of red, yellow and blue. They walked in slow circles, mixing the colours in the pearl light, talking, gesturing. Nearby were their rolled prayer rugs, the tassels spilling like scarlet tears on the white stone. The voices travelled up to her; she could see lines connecting them to her, faint and wavering on the warming air. Beams of light, scrolled at the end.

In the corner of the market the grains and onions spilled out of their sacks next to the big earthenware bowls of chickpeas, the red and brown spices in their tall glass jars, the baby turtles pivoting around their own unsteady necks, sniffing the air, the snakes twisting in their wicker cages, the camels' eyelashes fanning across the bright blue glazed plates. The smell of dung and sweat and old fur and sour hard tobacco with the earth still in it. The thin skeins of flies rising and falling from the blood-stained goats' hooves hung on hooks; the antelope heads nodding in a line across the hot stone.

I won't look for him, she thought.

But still she scanned the crowds eddying between the canvas awnings and drifting along the stone arcade, all eager to shop before the heat set in: men in white cotton robes, rhythmically waving away flies with their plaited whips, poorer fellows in rough brown weave, women shuffling in their robes of black, viewing the world through the slit in the material which enveloped them. The bare-headed others were the foreigners: the hippies, the backpackers, the fair Scandinavians, the stocky tattooed British, the talkative Americans.

She always recognised her own kind, no matter how dark their tan, the way that every Arab knew what she was despite her dyed hair and the inked designs on her hands. This was the time the Europeans emerged, spilling out from dark rooms at the back of the shops after all-night sessions smoking kif. She knew those rooms: the low couches, the velvet cushions, the beads hanging on strings across the doorway. The charcoal would glow under the ornate chafing dish, there would be the smell of mint and goats' milk, and yellow dates still on the stem. The water pipe would sit in the middle of the room on its ornate silver stand, an octopus extending its black rubber arms. There would be nougat on the trays, rolled cigarettes, candles burning, the small deadly dark brown cubes on the silver platter. She could almost smell the lavender water. The bad memories.

She flexed her fingers so the tiny blue crosses tattooed on her knuckles swung through the warm air. She pushed back the black scarf around her head and put her hand to her left cheek, pressing in so the knotted flesh there was forced against a nerve. The real pain chased away the pretend pain and she flinched so convulsively that her long black robe dipped and swayed like a bell over the unpolished wooden floor of the jeweller's shop. A bell at God's bidding, she thought. She watched the crowds, standing in her pool of black light. But there was no-one who looked like the man who had followed her this morning.

The jewellery maker coughed behind her. He was a thin man, hollowed by age. She had known him for twenty years. When she first came to him, she had been strung out and shaking, scratching the pinpricks in her arms, trying to sell the first of her jewels. He avoided looking at her then and he avoided looking at her now.

He held a silver box studded with small rubies. The hinged lid was etched with triangles and spheres which looked elaborate but she knew were commonplace, a design to be had by anyone, dismissed by the craftsmen. She put down her silver and glass teacup and examined the casket carefully.

'To your specifications,' said the jeweller in French. He raised the casket on tented fingers, careful not to touch or be touched by her. Unlike the others. When she first arrived, the local men had no compunction about touching her. They all had the same expression: a curious, wary, waiting look. The look, she thought, that comes before the pounce. Their hands were cool as though night remained in their bodies but she thought the desert sun was so fierce that it had erased all emotion from their faces. When she walked through the market in those early days, with her blonde hair, her Western clothes, they looked at her from some quicklime hole, shouting up at her from some ditch of fire, *You want to make sex with me, Nazarene? Your husband is no good, ai? Weak benis. Many, many husbands is gay. Too weak benises. You make sex with me.*

Men, everywhere, all with the same watching expression, sitting in cafés side by side, not looking at each other, not talking to each other. A country with no women in its consciousness, with no care for its surroundings, the countryside filled with scrub and barbed wire, decrepit buildings. The ramparts like teeth, yawning over the huge wooden doors which separated the neighbourhoods. The trees gone long ago from all but the richest suburbs. The gardens reduced to small courtyards, tiny secret oases; a few palm trees and rocks creating shade on white stone, an unexpected nurturing constructed in small and humble shadows.

'It is because no one wants to look prosperous,' Jürgen had said, passing the opium pipe across. He had run his hand slowly against the nap of the purple velvet couch, spreading his fingers wide, leaving a smeared arc like an angel's wing. 'In case their neighbour becomes envious and tries to come and hurt them.'

A country where you had to fear your neighbour.

She took a square of paper from the deep pocket of her habit and placed it inside the casket. It fitted exactly.

'This is the shape of the book?' the jeweller asked.

She nodded. 'I attach the chain, where?'

He pointed to the hooks on the outside corners. He brought out a thick chain ending in a heavy cuff made of bronze. She clipped the cuff over her wrist and snapped it shut, and tried to pull it off. It slid down to the top of her hand but no further. When she tried to pull harder, it cut into her skin, leaving a red mark.

'Good.' She pulled again. The pain at her wrist chased away the pain inside her fingers. 'And the second box?'

He took the casket, his fingers arched, and disappeared into the shadows behind the shelves of leather goods and cheap coats. She thought, No man can afford to be the master of one trade in Casablanca. No woman.

She drifted back to the window, looked for the European. A donkey piled high with rolled-up carpets was sidling through the east entrance. The carpets were catching on the stone archway. The donkey's owner was shouting at two blonde women, sunburnt under their backpacks and singlets, who had stopped to take photographs; his curses had drawn the usual crowd of scrawny barefoot boys. She saw several she recognised, cheeky urchins who loitered outside the Mission. She ran her fingers absent-mindedly over the scar on her cheek, thinking.

The jeweller was back with a small plain wooden box. The lid sat unevenly above its brass clasps and she could see at once that it was too small. The book would not fit.

She shook her head.

'Why do you need this?' said the jeweller. 'To keep trinkets, your crosses?'

'I have only one cross,' she said.

He shrugged.

She picked up her glass and poured the mint tea into the box. Within a moment dark water began leaking from one corner. She thought, Why does it always come to this? She longed to be back in the desert, to be a speck of black in the eye of God. She dropped the box on the floor.

'Next week,' said the jeweller hastily.

'No.'

He raised his hands, palms upwards.

She shook her head. 'I need both. One is no good without the other.'

'Friday.'

'Tomorrow. I'm leaving for the desert.'

He drew away from her. 'The desert. Well, I will see.'

She pulled her scarf around her head. She had not dyed her hair recently and she knew that the pale blonde was showing along her hairline, enough to attract attention.

She went down the steps, past the dozen small staircases that ran off this main passage, up, down, haphazardly.

In the first months after her arrival, she was constantly lost. She was unable to visualise the streets which ran at cross purposes, the rooms which led off each other, stairs which ended in blocked door- ways or narrow balconies opening onto walls. All she remembered of those days was the smell of lavender water.

She went into the market. Above her, the soft grey marbled sky was settling and hardening into a sheet of pale blue. The moon still hung, a half-eaten ghost, above the stone ramparts; the wooden door which closed off this section of the neighbourhood was drawn back against the wall, its heavy brass knocker shaped like a fist hanging sullenly in the morning light. The houses on either side were windowless squares. There was faint music nearby, from another world: *She was a topsy turvy super curvy mega groovy love machine* . . . .

On the corner, she pressed coins into the creased brown palm of the thin woman who sat in the gutter with her packets of dusty paper handkerchiefs. A crowd of small boys streamed past her, making kissing noises, but when she straightened they saw the black robes and they fell silent. Across the road a group of men watched her with impassive faces. Poverty or desperation was no excuse for a woman to be on the street. She should be sitting at home, with her children, her relatives. Sitting behind tiled walls, behind her veils. Behind her markings of ink.

Agnieska was in the market, selecting hair combs, when she saw the tanned European again. He was at a stall across from her, pulling at a rack of clothes, holding up a T-shirt with the Camel cigarettes logo, pretending to look at it but looking over it, at her. She scanned the square. Decorated leather goods, brass trays, camel-hair mats, wooden bowls and coloured stone bracelets were laid out on rugs around the perimeter. Behind them, in the stone arcade, were the bread shops, the meat shops, the greengrocer with his wooden boxes of vegetables stacked around the doorway. The air smelled of cigarette smoke and spiralling wisps of mint. Beyond were more tourist stalls with their roughly stitched leather camels, mouths gaping at the twine suturing their bellies, sunglasses strung along wire, warm cans of soft drinks, boxes of cigarettes, some with water-stained corners, shawls from Kashmir. The first snake charmers were setting out their baskets, hissing at each other and their sleeping animals. The pigeon man, the boy selling cowry shells, the man who walked on glass, the thin child acrobats, were arriving. A drummer with matted black hair, naked to the waist, sat down and began beating a wild rhythm. The few women moved through, many with babies in slings across their backs. The fish would be sold later that night when it was cooler.

Her hands were hurting again. She held a butterfly-shaped hair comb up to the light, looked through the black teeth at the European. He had shiny dark brown hair pulled back into a ponytail. A beard or heavy five o'clock shadow – she couldn't tell from here. He was in his early forties, she thought, a few years younger than she. He wore a black T-shirt with jeans. She sensed he wasn't Polish: Albanian, Turkish maybe. Not Arabic. Or at least, not wholly Arabic.

The hair comb was made of oiled wood, she saw now. The spreading butterfly wings concealed the wooden teeth underneath. The colours and pattern on one wing did not match the colours and pattern on the other but the painted wood still had great vibrancy in its jumbles of reds and greens and blues and purples. It was small, with narrow teeth for fine hair. It was a child's comb. Maybe she could give it to Betsoul, to give to Meersun.

She paid for the comb and crossed to the south side of the market. Out of the corner of her eye, she saw the European moving parallel to her.

At the next stone archway, she turned sharply down a tiny alley. A skinny bare-foot boy stepped in front of her, chewing gum. He wore ragged shorts and half-heartedly held out his hand, not really expecting her to stop. She bent and pushed her scarf back so he could see the scar on her face.

'Can you understand me?' she said, asking first in standard Arabic. The boy looked wary. She tried Maghrebi Arabic. They would have problems communicating if he spoke a more regional dialect. Every other town – Tangier, Fes – had its own dialect, but Casablanca had been so buffeted by outsiders that the town's language was diluted and reshaped. She thought the locals now must feel like the Native Americans when they visited Las Vegas. Another construct in the desert.

The boy was fascinated by the scar – he couldn't help himself – he kept staring at it. She put her hand on his chin, forced him to look at her. 'Understand?'

He grinned. He couldn't help that either. 'Enough to do business.'

'Good. You know who I am?'

He nodded. 'The Mission Nazarene.' She led him to the stone arch, held him as they looked around the corner. The European was moving aimlessly back and forth.

'Do you see the white man?' The boy nodded. 'I need you to find out where he is from. But discreetly – secretly. So he doesn't know you are asking. Do you understand?'

She gave him some coins. 'More later,' she said. 'I'll meet you at Al Saad lookout.'

He took off.

She continued down the alley, finding the stairs, barely a foot across, cut into the dark brown rock. She climbed, gathering her robes around her, digging her fingers into the crevices to stop from falling backwards.

She came out on the upper street level. An opening between the shops looked over the houses which jammed against each other in endless pale tan rows and mazes, on and on to the blue-grey Rif Mountains. Irregular puckering in the sky hinted that the day could reject its relentless course, could rebel and add some unpredictability to the routine of an hour spent, like every hour, waiting for sunset and the cooler air.

A scorpion – dusted brown, innocuous – emerged from between the cracks of a broken pink stone jar lying against the wall. It walked sideways past her, following the glazed path of a lizard through the dirt. She breathed out and the scorpion swung to face her, its tail lifted. She stared at the fork at the end of the kinked plates. The devil's fork, the creature itself just a receptacle to carry spitefulness through the desert. It was born to strike at weakness: the exposed heel, the flinching sole.

She backed away. After a moment the scorpion lowered its tail, moved on.

Out there was the desert. The blank page waiting to be written, she thought to herself. The memories waiting to be unearthed like the water trapped deep beneath the sands, like the brown bodies thrown by the French into the wells to punish rebellious towns. The whole of the mind laid out in hills and fissures, dust and new growth. The desert as the landscape of all fears. A burial ground of lives waiting to be found. She visualised the hills with hard peaks that looked like the necks of broken bottles, the great boulders turned the colour of milk by distance and heat haze, the silence as vast as noise. In the desert, death has always already occurred, she thought; there is nothing to fear. She remembered driving into the desert, away from the red walls of the city, clouds of crickets enveloping her, her skin crawling from the drugs, sickness in her mouth, throwing everything she owned out the window. Everything but the book.

She had watched for sandstorms. She had been warned: that is when the Polisario, the Saharan liberation movement, usually strikes, in the shelter of a sandstorm.

She drove through the night and stopped a hundred miles from Abu N'af to scrape off the hot dust and dead crickets from the windscreen. The moon was still bruised in the sky, the sparrows burrowing into the evaporating night, sky and earth becoming one in a veil of pearl grey and dead silver, dawn as a half-erased dream. Her skin hurt from the brightness of the stars but the pain was gone from her hands. Her watch had stopped hours before. She threw it away and stood under the swelling fires of the sun and thought, I have fled Him down the years but here I am in the presence of all creation. I am in the presence of God. She imagined herself as a small black speck in the glowing ball. I am being watched by the eye of God.

Now, years later, she stretched her aching fingers. I have to get back to the desert.

The boy was in front of her, smug, bright-eyed. He took out his gum and held it while he recited, 'The white man's name is Stefano Tarfuri. A Sicilian.' The boy scrunched up his lips as though about to spit but thought better of it. 'He lives in the place called Trepani. His address is – '

She bent towards him. 'He told you his address?'

The boy nodded. 'I make good work.'

'Maybe,' she said. She gripped him by the shoulders and gave him a short sharp shake. The boy clapped his hands to his lower spine. She reached around him and found the brown leather wallet wedged into the back of his pants.

She opened it, saw the driver's licence, the identity card, the photo of the tanned European. His name meant nothing to her. *Trepani*. That was more familiar. She recalled the map she had carried twenty-five years before. Trepani. It was near the coast, she was sure. Near the mountain town which had been wrecked beyond repair when she saw it: its wells poisoned, its people gone. Santa Margherita.

There was little else in the wallet: money, a mix of lira and dirham, some scribbled notes in Italian. At the back she felt an opening in the cotton lining: tucked inside was a small photo of a woman, round-cheeked, dark-haired, unremarkable except for her marble-black eyes. Her eyes were all pupil, there seemed to be no lighter iris, no white. Not seemed, thought Agnieska. She put her finger over the face in the photo. She didn't look for a name on the back. She knew it was Rosita, the woman she would always blame for her brother's death, no matter what anyone else said.

She thought about keeping the photo, but even to hold it made her feel an accessory to murder. She gave the wallet to the boy. He took it, warily.

'You will return this to the man,' she said. The boy shoved his gum back into his mouth, chewed furiously. 'If you do not I will know.' She touched the corner of her eye, then her scar. 'I will see you. You know all the whites come together. Eventually. Do you know what eventually means?'

His mouth turned down. 'It means you will punish me.'

She straightened. 'Only if you do not do what I say. But if you do, you can come to the Mission tomorrow and get a pair of shoes.'

The boy stopped chewing. 'New shoes?'

'Almost new.'

The boy nodded, turned to run. 'I knew they wouldn't be new,' he said, but he couldn't hide the spark in his eyes.

Agnieska's home was a large room in a rambling house made up of half-levels and small staircases off an alley near Hafid Street. She shared the bath-room and the squatting toilet on the ground floor but she had her own enclosed courtyard which extended over the roof of the rooms below.

As she climbed the steps, she saw there were more gifts left on the worn yellow stone; small things, nothing expensive: wooden bracelets, a silk headscarf, a doll in a nun's habit made from rough black cotton.

The scrawny tortoiseshell cat was asleep on the scarf. 'Arthur,' she said in French and shooed him off. He gave her an offended look. She rubbed him behind the ears and wondered whether she could take him with her. Would he like the desert? Maybe he was a city cat. A desert fortress may not suit him. Abu N'af may not suit him.

Her neighbour, the ranting English poet, was shouting again, drunk, a stream of invective, his voice cracking. It was a steady harsh bellow which made her ears flinch. He cursed the city and everyone in it, cursed the desert and the plants and the water, cursed the surface of the wells. When he was sober he would say that was how he wrote his poetry, that out of the bile he extracted fragments that revealed his soul. But she thought that he hated and feared himself. She could recognise it.

'Monsieur?' she said in English, looking up to his balcony. 'Monsieur, what do you need?'

'Nothing,' he said after a while, but his tone was quieter.

'You know I am next door,' she said.

'No . . . ' He was uncertain.

'Yes, we wrote it down, do you remember? It is on a piece of paper, nailed on your wall.'

A silence. She heard bells in the distance, a mule braying. The rug-maker and his son passed the bottom of the steps, carrying the day's makings from the market, going home for lunch.

'Monsieur?'

'Yes,' he said. 'I see the note.' There was a long pause. 'I might have a lie-down now.'

'He's crazy, you know,' said a voice above her. Her other neighbour, the American girl, had come out onto the narrow balcony on the next level. She was smoking a cigarette in a black plastic holder, carefully using a tiny comb on her long false eyelashes.

'He can't stand being an outsider,' she said.

Agnieska shook her head.

The girl smirked and blew out a perfect smoke ring. 'You'll get him in the end,' she said. 'I know. He'll convert.'

'Why do you think that, my dear?' said Agnieska.

'You put the fear of God into me.'

'You wouldn't have stayed where you were,' said Agnieska.

'In the opium den, you mean,' said the girl. 'The devil's den.' She yawned and stretched. Her mini-skirt rode up, showing the red track marks on her inner thigh. 'Strange,' said the girl, 'how my friends all disappeared. Deported. Yet I was left.' She looked around her, bewildered. 'I don't know how I came here. I really don't.'

'It's just one step in a life,' said Agnieska. 'You won't look back now your friends have gone.' She picked up the cat and scarf and other gifts and opened her door.

The girl said, 'A monsignor' – she stumbled over the word – 'is here.' She lowered her voice. 'With another guy. Porky but charming. The other guy I mean.'

Agnieska opened the door and went into her room, which served as kitchen, living room and bedroom. It was sparsely furnished: two scarlet rugs on the tiled floor, a low couch, a few cushions. Next to the shelf with her cutlery, cooking utensils and the two framed prints was the potbellied Polish stove; its blackened flue climbed along the ceiling to escape through a grate over the far window. She used it as both cooker and winter heater. That was all she had of home now: the stove, the book and the dead flower.

Her bedroom was marked out by a thicker rug on the floor. Her spare habit and cloak hung on nails in the wall; her old blue suitcase held her few remaining clothes. Her bedroll was tied up in the corner during the day. A stone block was her bedside table; a place for her rosary beads at night. There was nearly nothing else left from Poland; she had sold the silver hairbrushes and cutlery over the years to buy extra food for the Mission, more shoes for the orphans. On the table now there was a blank space where her Bible used to lie.

Everything else that was valuable – the book, her passport – was hidden in the corner, under the rug, in a recess she had chipped out herself and covered with a fitted stone.

Through the window, she saw the buildings whitening in the morning sun. Voices came to her from the small courtyard. She touched the wooden cross around her neck and tightened the black scarf around her hair. Then she rubbed her hands to ease the pain and stepped out into the garden.

The Monsignor was sitting on the ledge of the small fountain, flanked by the palm trees in their terracotta pots. In the square pool, the water tumbled in uncertain rushes and odd beats of silence from the mouth of the stone cherub. Glass balls of light in water, she thought, travelling from the throat of God. The cherub's hands were clasped in front of its rigid tunic dress; its wings folded tightly. Usually it looked mournful. Now, she thought, it looked affronted.

Behind it, the rose vine struggled up the wall and across the frame laid over the bisecting walls. The lattice light fell on the Monsignor in stripes and crosses. She distinctly saw the shadows of crucifixes – black crosses flecked with tiny thorns – on the spreading white bowls of his cheeks. He ran his hand through the liquid silver in the fountain bowl, the great ruby on his finger moving through the water like the red eye on a fat white fish.

'Perpetual motion,' said the Monsignor in French, pointing to the wooden wheel and paddles at the back of the cherub. 'Very clever. We must enquire who designed it.'

Agnieska thought he was talking to her but a murmur in the corner made her turn her head. A small plump young man in his mid-twenties was sitting on the wooden chair in the shade. He had a sleek black moustache and was dressed in a white suit with a white hat in the American style. He bowed extravagantly when he saw her but, looking at the Monsignor, he did not speak. He stood, head slightly lowered, holding his white hat. She thought he was watching her under his eyelashes.

The Monsignor extended his hand without bothering to dry it. She bent and dutifully kissed the wet ring and withdrew, folding her arms into her wide sleeves. After a moment, she remembered not to look at him directly but dipped her head and rounded her shoulders.

'Very nice, Sister,' said the Monsignor, looking at the clusters of small pots, the blue walls, the green diamonds in the white-tiled floor. 'Women always have a knack for making pretty little corners.'

'It is our duty,' said Agnieska. 'The garden is the recurring image in the desert. An oasis from sin. A reminder of lost paradise.' She saw that the Monsignor's mouth had become a dark circle but she went on. 'It is the place of the first human bereavement. A heart like the heart of pure water inside a cactus. A heart filled at once with gods and demons.'

The Monsignor's companion lifted an eyebrow at the mention of demons. He put his hand up, to smooth his moustache. Maybe to hide a smile.

'Paradise,' said the Monsignor sharply. 'I hope you are not presuming . . . ' His voice ran away like water, as though her arrogance was too much for him.

She rounded her shoulders further. 'Never, Monsignor.'

He was staring at her intently. She saw the black sandals made of finest Italian leather, the solid gold buckles, the robes spreading like a dark stain across the tiles. She imagined the flesh spilling away beneath. These greedy men, she thought. Always less to them than meets the eye.

The faint creak of the fountain wheel ground into the silence. 'Good,' said the Monsignor. His hands were curled into fists on his knees. 'We are here for your well-being, child.'

She half-bowed and said, 'May I offer you mint tea? Grapes and dates?' He waved his hand dismissively. 'And your colleague?' She turned to the other man, who was still standing.

'Laforche will have nothing,' said the Monsignor. 'We will not be long.' The small man gave her a smile which turned in on itself at the corners. He bowed again, sardonically, and sat, putting his hat under his chair.

The Monsignor cleared his throat, a sound which made her think of rotting leaves in muddy water. 'Our paths may not often intersect,' he said, 'but everyone at the Papal Office watches over our hardworking brothers and sisters at the Mission.'

'Of course, Monsignor,' she said. She placed the fingers of her left hand on her cross, felt the reassuring roughness of the wood. The fine splinters pricked her skin. She pressed in. She said, 'I know that Ville Nouvelle is a long walk from Quartier Negro.'

The dark coin reappeared in his face. 'Your behaviour . . . ' His words boomed across the tiles. Laforche raised his eyebrow. The Monsignor frowned, gathered his voice, as though catching mud in a sieve. 'We are worried about you, Sister. Your health – ' he gestured at her misshapen hands – 'is not helped by the extra duties you have taken on.'

She lifted her head.

'Succouring the local women,' said the Monsignor. 'Clearly a toll on you.'

'Is the Church displeased?'

Laforche smiled. The dark coin in the Monsignor's face became a falling crescent. 'Of course not. But boundaries must be kept. For your own good.'

She waited. Laforche examined his nails. She saw they were polished; manicured professionally. A gold bracelet slid down beneath the starched cuffs, past the mother-of-pearl cuff links. He pushed it back, saw she was watching him and raised his eyebrow again.

She said to the Monsignor, 'I would not disappoint the Fathers.'

'Your way of dress offends,' he said. 'This robe and headscarf, not the veil and surplice. This shroud the local women wear.'

'The djellabah,' she said. 'It gives me protection.'

'Your habit should be enough protection.'

'Sometimes it is not.'

He breathed heavily through his nose but said, mildly enough, 'And the markings on your hands? There is no adornment before God.'

She looked at his gold buckles. 'I won't accept money from the local women. So they pay me with small gifts, services.'

He stared at the intricate circles and dotted stars etched on her wrists, the blue crosses on her knuckles. 'You cannot be inked like a native.'

'Are you telling me not to help them?'

'Our duty is not to encourage the more backward superstitions.'

She spread her hands. 'What can I do, Monsignor, if the women keep coming? They think I have luck with finding things. Small things, yes, but valued. I cannot turn them away. That would not be Christian.'

'Yes,' said the Monsignor. 'Well.'

'The Arab women will not come to the Church,' said Agnieska gently. 'Not after the revelations of Father Thomas's visits to Quartier Rouge.'

There was a small sound. Laforche's face was impassive. But she was sure he had sniggered. She wondered what he was thinking. The trickling water seemed louder — steel pins in the throat of God — drops here and there struck the wet air in hard blows. She saw a faint black shadow at the base of the cherub. The turtle with the scarred shell peered out. She could see its dark eyes, the small bubble at its mouth. One of her flock.

The Monsignor's flesh had finally escaped him. His robe slid over the stone rim into the water. A damp stain climbed steadily towards the red silk sash around his middle.

'It is still not known,' said the Monsignor sharply, 'how the Father's visits — ' He stopped, blew out his cheeks so they were shiny balls pricked with red. 'It seems strange that the Prefect was misdirected to that street at the very same hour.'

'It must have been God's will,' said Laforche.

'Don't be sarcastic, Laforche,' said the Monsignor, and for a moment the harsh flat vowels of the Bronx sawed beneath the phlegm. 'And now this,' he said to Agnieska. 'Your remarkable ability to find these things: a lost chicken, stolen clothing.'

Agnieska bowed her head. He must know, she thought. These ambitious public men always had minds like accountants.

But he said, 'I hope you do not think you are special in some way?'

She shook her head.

'Yet you set out to embarrass the Church?'

'No, Monsignor.' Her surprise was genuine.

'You give money, shoes, to the orphans in Quartier Negro.'

'Yes, but – '

'Why should we not think that you consider yourself above us? You no longer carry the Word. You have no Bible in your room. That alone could see you dismissed from the Church.'

She raised her head. At last, they had reached the heart of the matter. Had cut into the heart of the cactus. She looked at Laforche. She wondered whether he had been the one to rifle through her belongings. She said, 'I sold the book which tells me to sell everything and give money to the poor. So I gave the money to the poor.'

The Monsignor stared. Red rose in waves from his white jowls.

'Jesus walked out into the desert,' said Agnieska. 'He surrendered in the tradition of the desert fathers. He reduced himself to absolute poverty, made himself as blank as the desert, as the unwritten page.'

'How dare you lecture me,' said the Monsignor, his voice breaking up into choppy waves which became part of the loud rushing in her ears. But she forced herself to look at him and saw the sun had shifted; the shadows on his face had gone. She thought, Finally, you have come into the light.

She said, 'Jesus's body was his text and his visions in the desert were written on his body and in his heart. He became the living book. The only book that matters.'

'The Holy Book was not yours to give away, Sister,' said the Monsignor loudly.

Agnieska looked up to the sky; chalk marks smeared the flat sheet of blue. She bowed her head. She saw the crosses inscribed in the tiles in the floor. She was compelled to go on. 'In trying to be different I have become myself.' His knuckles were white on his knees. She said, 'I must shed my old identity.'

'You can't dispense what the Church decides,' said the Monsignor, his voice swelling.

'Saint Antony went into the desert and built the first great community – '

'There are protocols – '

'I cannot accomplish what I need to accomplish – '

'Devil talk,' shouted the Monsignor. He heaved himself to his feet. 'Devil talk.'

Blue shadows fell over the courtyard. Now the rushing water sounded like hummingbird wings in mist. Days I have held, she thought. Days I have lost.

'Know this, Sister,' said the Monsignor, beginning in a near bellow but quickly reining his voice in, so the noise descended like piano scales. 'Some say you have been given a gris-gris by these local women. So you are compelled to give away everything you own.' He raised a finger. 'Possessed.'

Behind him, Laforche frowned.

'Possession,' said the Monsignor. 'The only known cure is exorcism.'

'Dangerous,' said Laforche, standing up. 'The Van Kleipers tragedy, still in the news – '

'Silence!' shouted the Monsignor.

Agnieska shook her head at Laforche and said, 'I want to be known as Sister Antony.' When there was no sound from the Monsignor, she got up, slowly. They faced each other, she the taller by half a head, he oblivious to the wet robe clinging to his bowed and meaty thigh.

She wondered how he saw her, whether he ever pondered what she was like under her robe, whether he imagined her body. She couldn't believe that the black cloth cut off all imaginings. She wondered whether secretly it sent them crazy – these men who thought they ruled the world – this act of denial, of refusing to be viewed. Whether they hated the women who denied them, the way they hated the desert when the dust storms rose. Maybe wearing the robe, the shroud, was power of a sort. A refusal to interact.

She clasped her hands before her. 'I will be sure to apologise for my blasphemy,' she said. 'To Rome.'

The Monsignor gripped his ring. 'Don't even think of threatening me.'

'And to my family.'

'You gave yourself over to the Church. Your family cannot interfere in our decisions.'

'I'm sure they would feel it necessary to inform His Holiness.'

The wheel creaked in the silence. The Monsignor became aware of his wet skirt. He slapped at his leg, sending water drops flying. He straightened. 'You have ambitions. Why should the Church indulge them?'

She bowed her head. 'I am happy to stay here, working – '

He held up a hand. 'Don't bullshit me. You think you can do better. But there is no mission available. Fès, Rabat, Taghourit are taken.'

'I had hoped for a small – '

'No,' said the Monsignor. He stretched out his hand, admired the falling planes of light caught in the ruby.

'May I make a suggestion?' said Laforche. 'There is a derelict fort, a retreat for unfortunates, out past the Kabir plateau. A near ruin, early Islamic, maybe the Almoravids, but it has been occupied by the Spanish and French at one time or another. Now the Church has title.' He bowed apologetically to Agnieska. 'It is very isolated.'

'Isolated,' said the Monsignor.

'Isolated,' said Agnieska. She tightened the scarf across her face, withdrawing into its shadow. She thought of the way the turtle in the fountain withdrew into its shell. She tried not to smile. 'Oh dear.'

'I am sure it is possible for supplies to reach you regularly,' said Laforche. 'There has been talk of making the fort a rehabilitation centre. The King is very appreciative of our Casablanca drug clinic.'

'Such a long way,' said Agnieska, sighing into her scarf.

The Monsignor stared at her. 'I think I will think about this. It is far, you said?'

'Very,' said Laforche.

Agnieska sighed again.

'Yes, well,' said the Monsignor. 'We all make sacrifices.' He gathered up a fold of his black skirt and rubbed the ruby with it, watching Agnieska with unblinking eyes. She thought it was taking all his strength not to rip the scarf from her face. 'Perhaps you will fail,' he said. 'The times are in love with endings.'

'Maybe I should stay here,' said Agnieska. 'To learn more.'

'The Church doesn't take kindly to masqueraders,' said the Monsignor. 'Those without a clear conscience.'

'A clear conscience is usually the sign of a bad memory,' said Agnieska. She saw Laforche wince.

'You should learn humility,' said the Monsignor.

'You can teach me, Monsignor.' She stepped forward and dropped to her knees. He gasped and backed away from her but was trapped by the rim of the fountain. She raised her palms. His toes curled in his sandals.

She said, 'I know I have sinned. I should pay public penance. Saint John of the Cross was imprisoned for nine months – '

'I hardly think – ' said the Monsignor.

'Nine months in a cell with no room to stand up.'

The Monsignor dragged his sleeve across his flushed cheeks.

Agnieska said, 'I am not worthy. Maybe an iron box. In front of the Grande Mosque.'

'Enough,' shouted the Monsignor.

Agnieska said, 'Others could join me.'

He stared at her, breathing heavily. A thin hard word escaped through the rattling air. 'Mad,' he said. 'Mad.' He gathered his skirts and pushed past her.

She looked out of the corner of her eye. The Monsignor jerked his head at Laforche and turned. Laforche raised a forefinger at her and said loudly, 'You are a dangerous fanatic.'

She stayed where she was, hands clasped.

As the Monsignor stepped through the doorway, she heard him say, 'What is the place called again?'

'Abu N'af,' said Laforche. 'The Asylum at Abu N'af.'

Agnieska stood on the chair and looked over the courtyard wall and down to the street. There was a small café on the corner, a few chairs and tables on the pavement, lunch just being served. The smell of spiced chicken and roasted dates and thick silted coffee wafted up.

The Sicilian was sitting with his back to the wall, directly opposite the entrance to her building. After a moment, the Monsignor walked past, taking short angry steps, smoking a cigarette, his hand moving back and forth, pummelling the air. The Sicilian did not move. There was no recognition that she could see, no glances between the two men.

Agnieska rested her chin on the hot stone. The flies were easier up here and she lifted her face. The smeared blue was giving way to an uncertain white, the sky breaking up into torn paper.

The noon prayers began. She closed her eyes against the sun. Always music here, she thought, always a celebration of God. It should be enough but it wasn't.

The soothing repetitious phrases undulated through the bright air, climbing and falling, washing over the stone rooftops and patios, rooms within rooms, houses designed like puzzle boxes. Everything was designed to shut out the light: the narrow alleys, stairways, the material draped across doors and windows, the sheets hung over beds. Yet the rooms were never truly dark.

She opened her eyes and looked beyond the city, beyond the mountains, to the Western Sahara swathed in its blue veils. She remembered flying across the desert, low against the saffron moon. She flew over dark and jagged peaks, descended to the granite ground. She saw women walking in the shadows of their burdens, holy men moving backwards against the wind, their robes lifting as though plucked like flowers. I flew into the eternal silence, she thought. Landing, the plane's vibrations merged with the rising heat. Night and day were reversed here: night was solace in the desert, the bright day deadly.

Years later, when she had discovered what Father Thomas had done to Betsoul, she had taken the car Jürgen gave her – a small Renault so buckled with rust that the floor hit every large stone – and she drove east through twilight like a half-erased dream. When the car had inevitably sputtered to a stop, she had put the book and a canteen of water in her backpack and walked away into the desert, so busy looking up at the stars that she stumbled and fell over a small rock. Near her, a low-slung cactus sensed movement and wept white poison. She thought, Liquid can be a weapon in the desert.

She had walked through the spiralling heat. A yellow cloud passed across the broken-faced moon: a wheeling bowl of locusts. She saw the night trapped in hollows, felt every grain of sand beneath her. I have been blinded all my life, she thought. First by the counterfeit columns of my family. Then by the silk couches of the opium dens. And now by the hypocrisies in the Church I thought would save me. No God left even in a city of churches and mosques.

But here, a hundred other tribes surround me. I walk through an alphabet of sand, the vast silence of the desert cloaks me. The silence beyond the silence of death. She touched the scar on her left cheek. I see my way home between the dark marks left by the Mammon sun on my flesh. On the purity of the page. She kneeled by the pool in front of her, heat biting into her bones.

I see my way home.

Agnieska waited by the fountain, her hand in the cold water. She moved her fingers to try to encourage the turtle to come out. But it stayed, a shadow near the seashells which lined the white plaster. As she walked her hand over the tiled bottom, the blue crosses moving like pitchforks, she heard the front door open and close.

Footsteps – a man's boots – came across the tiles.

There was a pause. She knew why. He was smoothing his hair, straightening his tie. Then, the sound of whistling. The familiar notes: Edith Piaf's 'Non, Je Ne Regrette Rien'.

A shadow in the doorway. Laforche winked at her and went to his chair and picked up his hat. 'Yes, my dear Capitaine, I did not work hard to stay where I belong.' He flourished the hat at her. 'Especially not as a mere assistant director at an obscure Catholic outpost.'

She said, 'Will I get Abu N'af?'

Laforche sat down, took out a white handkerchief and wiped the dust off his shoes. 'The Monsignor would make you Pope to be rid of you. As we predicted.'

He looked at his shoes but again, she thought that he was looking up at her under his lashes. 'Your family must be influential. It would be easy enough for the irate priests to make you disappear into one of the brothels in Quartier Rouge.'

She said, 'My family has always ensured that in troubled times the Church's possessions are returned.'

'Blackmail,' said Laforche without surprise. 'Useful.' He put away his handkerchief and took a pearl necklace and a painted headband from his pocket. 'And they pay you to pay me to steal these objects?'

'The objects are always returned,' she said sharply.

'And your reputation enhanced.'

'For the greater good. No-one suffers.'

'Hmmm.'

'My family pays, for this.' She touched the scar on her left cheek.

'And they'll keep sending money to you, out in the desert?'

'They don't care where I go. The further the better.'

Laforche said, 'What a shame you won't listen to Piaf with me. What is good enough to be the anthem of the French Foreign Legion should be good enough for all. It is the message of the hours and the times: we must regret nothing.'

'You don't regret helping me?'

'I would have helped you just to see the look on the Monsignor's fat face,' said Laforche.

'He's a fool.'

'Even the broken clock is right twice a day.' He frowned. 'The Monsignor may be furious enough to go ahead with an exorcism. There is hatred there – '

'Hatred of women.'

'Or hatred of the future, his shrinking influence.'

'He knows the Church has always been a business first.'

'Even more so,' said Laforche, 'now the Americans have set up shop on Hafid Street. Casa is becoming a garrison town. Again.'

'And you spend your time dicing with legionnaires who look like criminals.'

'At least the legionnaires are too drunk to smoke kif. They don't hallucinate like madmen. Besides,' he saw he had creased the hat slightly in his hands and smoothed it out, 'I never realised how much I loved my country until I left it.' He laughed but the notes almost immediately collapsed.

'At 3 am when your heart is breaking loose, you surround yourself with the sounds of France,' said Agnieska softly, watching him.

He shrugged. 'All speech before *l'heure bleue* is lying. I still wake every morning in Rimbaud's city of black roses.'

'You would find your true self in the desert,' said Agnieska. 'All your false identities are erased.'

'The desert always smells of old rope to me.' He flicked a speck of dust from his hat. 'I have no desire to go beyond the south gate of Medina Ancienne.' He caught Agnieska's sharp look. 'Don't worry. I can still send your stores each week.'

He stood. 'Well . . . ' For the first time since she had met him, she saw he was uncertain what to say next. 'As a Moroccan I must tell you that it has been Allah's will we have conducted such good business. But it is my duty as a Frenchman to be gallant. So,' he bowed, with unusual awkwardness, 'I must say that if I was allowed a second wife . . . '

'Or could afford it.'

He smiled. 'Yes. Far more to the point.' His face settled. 'I'm sure the Monsignor is not serious about exorcism. But the Sahara is a chess board with everything painted white. To be out there in the vast empty – '

'The sacred empty.'

'*Le désert absolu*,' he said.

'Isabelle Eberhardt went into the desert when she was eighteen. She dived into it, without ropes, without maps, like the ancient well-divers.'

'Yes – but . . . ' He moved his hand aimlessly. 'What will you do out there?'

'I will begin a community.' She wanted to say, I will leave the technological marvels of the world and walk into the sacred empty.

There is no danger, I will be watched over, the way the eagle hovers over her young. But she knew he wouldn't understand. So she stretched out her hands: the slightly bent fingers, the enlarged knuckles, the bone showing white under the tanned skin. 'I have crystals in my joints. Yet the pain vanishes in the desert.'

'It is the heat,' said Laforche.

'It is a miracle.'

'The dry air is good for arthritis.'

'I see the desert blossoming like the blossoming of Jesus's love for his people.'

She could feel him withdrawing. This was a border he would never cross. He said, '*Le désert est monothéiste.* The desert is his own god. Whether we live or die is of profound indifference to the desert.'

'The desert is a place of wanderings,' said Agnieska. 'It knows we go there to find a home, a memory, a name. We take on other lives in the desert. Other identities.'

'New identities . . . ' said Laforche. 'The Church won't like that. The Americans on Hafid Street won't like it.'

Agnieska considered him. 'Are you working for them?'

He met her gaze openly. 'I already have one mistress.'

'Two,' she said. 'If you count the Church. Three if you include your wife.'

'Six if I include my children,' he said. 'You see? To avoid confusion, a man with so many masters must be honest.'

'Or exhausted,' she said.

He smiled, turned the hat in his hands. 'I will miss our conversations.' His voice was louder, rougher. She imagined him throwing out a rope, unwillingly. 'It is a pity you couldn't stay in Casablanca and start your own community like other women, by marrying and having children.'

'I will never marry,' she said. 'I want my family line to die out.'

As he turned to go, she said, 'Have you heard anything about a new arrival – a Sicilian? A man this tall, with brown hair, to here.' She gestured to her shoulders.

Laforche seemed genuinely surprised.

'Would your contacts know?' They both knew she meant the other players in the 2 am dice games in Quartier Rouge.

'I can make enquiries.' He said, looking down at his hat, 'Will you visit Betsoul before you leave?'

She kneaded the pain in her knuckles, pressing down on the blue crosses. 'I don't know.'

'Your intentions were good,' he said. 'It seemed a worthy thing, to be educated, to work in Father Thomas's house.'

She saw Betsoul's contorted face. 'To be taken from your family at the age of twelve, to be – ' She couldn't say the word. 'Your life ruined by a meddling Westerner. She hates us all. Rightly. She is reminded of it every day.' Agnieska saw herself walking through the labyrinth of narrow alleys to Rue Farouk, visualised placing the butterfly comb in Meersun's childish fingers. She saw the dark room with its low ceilings, the silent women endlessly sitting, Betsoul's remorseless eyes.

Agnieska shivered. 'You won't tell anyone when I am leaving? Especially Betsoul.'

'You can trust me.'

She stared at him.

His face twisted. '*Un coup de dés jamais n'abolira le hasard.*'

'Just let me get away,' she said. 'Into the desert.'

She left by the back entrance, a narrow passage which ran past the tiled bath-room. The house next door was so close that tiny flowers had managed to grow in the almost perpetual shade at the base of the wall.

She circled the block and came up beside the café, peered around the corner. The pavement tables were empty. The Sicilian had gone. She looked through the strips of beaded leather hanging in the doorway. She saw only a local standing at the bar, foot hooked up on the brass railing, bent over his espresso. The doorway light caught the mirror opposite him; rings of light were thrown across his face as he raised the cup.

She remembered the first time they had holidayed in Vienna. Her brother was fascinated by the white gloves of the traffic conductors, how the sun was caught in the silver buttons sewn on the inner cuff. Who would wear a button where no-one could see it? her brother kept asking. *Fools*, her father had said but her brother had a faraway look. Later she had asked him what he was thinking and he said, When the conductor raised his hand, hoops of light rose in the cloudy air, so the conductor would see himself reflected in the silver, in the eyes of the man in the button, and back to himself, again reflected, endlessly, in silver hoops of light across the city.

She thought the answer was an excuse, or only partly true. But they were close enough that she knew not to ask him, to respect the change that was coming over him which explained his frequent absences, when her father would shout with rage to know where her brother was and she could have said, but didn't, In the church at Przyznka.

Later, she would feel she knew the exact moment Czeslaw died. Crystals started growing in her hands, there was constant pain in her joints. Crystals in her heart.

She liked to walk around the city in the heat of the day. During the lunch hours, the crowds almost disappeared. The stalls closed up: their cigarettes and soft drinks and T-shirts and caps and elephants with sequinned eyes, all gone.

Now the old town was revealed in all its straight-backed defiance. Strange, she thought, walking through the zebra light of the narrow alleys, stepping across the gutter running down the middle, that in a land so changeable, so filled with the shifting curves of the desert, the occupiers felt compelled – or threatened – to build in squares, block upon block rising out of the sand, hunched into each other, back to back. Why not live in domes dug into the ground? Why not in caves like the miners in the Australian desert towns? The true desert dwellers adjusted their shapes, bent into the landscape. Bedouin tents swelled and billowed with the wind. Only shape-shifters survived in the desert.

People talk about the desert being barren, she thought as she walked the streets, seeing the children with staring eyes slumped by damp walls, the beggars curled on their sides, knees drawn up like shrivelled seahorses in the shadows. The dope addicts were the ones lying on their backs, their empty faces brushed by the tails of the hungry, ceaselessly roaming cats.

She thought, What is the difference between this – this wasteland of mazes and blocked walls and women sitting, their minds filled with fog, the fatalism of the poor – and the wastelands of the modern city, its hard lines, its neon, its empty parking lots, its bare rooms? The inner mind is lost in both, buried beneath sand.

She stepped back to allow the water man with his pony to pass, the bent tin cans clanking over the coat rubbed raw. This country is hard on animals, she thought. Hard on its people.

She remembered Laforche teaching her how to apply pressure on her knuckles, to relieve the pain, releasing the pressure only when she heard the tell-tale crack. He had said, smiling his sardonic smile, If you're poor in Casa, the only thing you're allowed to make an art of is dying.

Before she reached the Kabir Massif, before Jürgen's car had failed, she had been stopped by a roadblock. Soldiers in white uniforms and sand goggles, the flaps of their caps hanging over their necks, had surrounded the car, opened the boot. They were suspicious to find so little; just a woman, a canteen of water, an old book with a black leather cover.

The sky had been darkening, swelling like plums along the horizon. The soldiers weren't unkind; they told her to turn back. She looked at the landscape as it reared away in gritty planes. Symmetry in nature, a geometry imposed on man no matter how much he liked to think he was the one imposing the lines. Even a nearby road turned out to be the sharp curve of a sand dune, not a man-made thing at all.

The soldiers pointed to where dark purple-grey was soaking up the pale blue sky. The sun teetered uncertainly, the light breaking out in radiant lines from behind the Massif – lines reaching out from heaven. To her.

In Poland, she would have nodded, agreed to turn back. But now, looking at the desert, she thought, Entering the desert is like entering a book in which the story is narrated by your radical other. The deeper we go into the desert, everything that used to guide us is stripped away by the winds. We must go deeper into the hidden landscape, where black is white, night is solace, water is poison, love is hate. Deeper into subversion. Deeper into ourselves.

The soldiers stepped back. If you must go on, they shrugged.

You know there is no well until Tagherez? one said, waving at flies.

She nodded. But she remembered the book with the black leather cover and she thought, There is another well.

You should be careful, said the soldier. This route is used by smugglers and brigands. Make sure you are not mistaken for one.

I hardly think –

The government is interested in all approaches to Casablanca these days. You know Algerian Pour La Combat has been tracked over the border. They move at night through the desert and slip into the city and hide in the back alleys. Anyone arriving by truck, plane, ship, is searched now.

He stared at her with flat indifferent eyes. He said, During the day, they add twigs and branches to their clothes, they change their outline. They merge with the desert. They sleep dug in under boulders, grit in their mouths, the sun burning down. They survive on sheer will. Like tough desert plants. He squinted across the unyielding page of the desert. He said, Everyone is looking for an oasis.

Everyone who is not the government, she said.

Every Arab makes his garden an oasis, he said. Yet it is also the place of betrayal. He put up a hand to block the sun, opened his eyes wide at her in the shadow across his face. He studied her Western clothes and said, They have a new name for the brigands. Le terroriste. Born out of fire in l'Algérie. Maybe they will use Nazarenes or nuns to do their work.

She said, The nuns work for God.

Do they? he said. He looked her up and down. He said, *Do you?* The words hung in the air, like grains of sand. She wasn't sure whether he said the next words or she only imagined them.

He said, I think not.

Now, in the city where she had never found her true vocation, she turned down Hafid Street, past a man shouting into a phone in the wooden booth nailed to the wall, past another man sitting cross-legged in the shreds of clothes. He was eating couscous and dates from a blue-glazed bowl. In the shadow of his knee, a scrawny cat drank from a saucer of milk. She put coins next to him. He pointed at his small pyramid of rolled cigarettes for sale. She shook her head, saw the Sicilian coming out of the American building on the corner. The CIA building.

She squatted, drew her scarf around her face. In this position she looked like any Arab woman. My disguise, she thought. My protection. Safe in the loss of identity.

A man came out behind Stefano: a tall man with the greyish pallor of the businessman. He was followed by two children: a boy with pale hair, aged about twelve she thought, who stayed close by, looking around uncertainly while a younger child, a dark-haired girl, was drifting across the pavement. The men stood, talking.

The Arabs seated in wicker chairs behind the grille of the café opposite were glaring at her. She hunched her shoulders: shapeless, ineffectual, requesting mercy, insisting to be ignored.

For a time, after she arrived, she had tried to take on an Arab identity: she wore the burqa, she sequestered herself at home, she tried to be dutiful. Jürgen lay on the couch and smoked kif and looked up at her through a cloud of brown smoke and said, Your life is an extended suicide. He laughed at the posturing of the men in the marketplace, derided them for blaming their problems on the West, for controlling their women because their own lives were so beyond their control. Nothing is valued here, he said, unless it has value to someone else. Unless it is coveted.

She had tried to argue with him. Told him they had spent six years travelling the world: Asia, America. Didn't he want to know where he stood, what the rules were? If you behaved in the right way you'd be protected. He said, You're at the mercy of someone else's rules. When they change the rules or they discover you're a foreigner, you'll get raped. You're wrong, she had shouted. But of course he had been right.

The girl child was by the man huddled in his rags on the pavement. She stared at him, then she took the butterfly clip from her hair and kneeled and put the yellow plastic carefully next to the bowl. She extended her forefinger to gently touch the man's nose. The tall stranger looked over his shoulder and said roughly, 'Don't touch that,' in a loud voice. It took Agnieska a moment to place the flattened vowels: an Australian. By then, the man had picked up the hair clip, grasped the girl by the wrist and dragged her away.

The Sicilian strolled a few feet along the pavement, sat on a stone pillar, his foot swinging. He took out an apricot, began to eat it.

She had found it impossible to walk when she first tried on the burqa. She could barely see through the eyehole. Her sense of direction was gone, the material wrapped around her legs, tripping her. All she saw now was the ground: hard and stony.

Jürgen had told her about Michel Vieuchange, the Frenchman who disguised himself as a woman in a time when the French were much hated and who travelled in 1930 to the ghostly ruins of Smara.

Jürgen said, You could carry anything under a woman's robes. Books, make-up, guns.

The ability to take on different personas frees you, she said.

He looked at the blue robe, at the veiled and meshed eyehole. But this makes every woman the same.

Like the desert, she said. Everything real is beneath the surface.

You'll need to put corks in your ears to survive here, said Jürgen. For the dust. For the abuse.

Venturing outside the city she had met women who lived all their lives in the fields with their goats, only coming in for winter. Others walked for hours over the pale dusty stones each day to milk their animals, gather the fine hair. Some were veiled, some not. Yet, walking along with their milk pails, they had a status that made them untouchable, they had a job. They walked in clusters, they seemed united. Free. A ridiculous country, she thought, when women had to have a symbol, some article of clothing, to be protected. They had to be covered or they were just meat for ravaging dogs. A country of dogs.

The Sicilian was getting up. He spat out the apricot stone and came towards her.

She hunched into her robe. He went past, whistling under his breath, in short hollow-tinned bursts. She risked a glance. He was darker up close – something there, she thought, some trace of Africa – and stockier, with big hands, big knuckles. Peasant knuckles. There was a tattoo of a knife above his wrist; another – three crosses – on the veined muscle below his T-shirt sleeve. She saw comb marks in the shiny dark hair above the ponytail.

She waited until he turned into King Mohammed Boulevard. She followed him, keeping her head down, looking out from the shadow of her clothing. He wasn't hurrying but he wasn't shopping either. He didn't glance at the stalls on either side or at the hawkers who descended on him in small waves and trailed him for a few steps before they fell back. As though they were tethered to some invisible zone and could only graze for a few feet.

She remembered when she had emerged from the Massif, still shaking from what she had found in the caves. She had looked across the plain and seen Abu N'af on top of the hill, a light in the nearest tower. She had walked towards it through the sheet of dawn grey as the sun teetered on the edge of the horizon. The sky had been a growing quarrel but now it softened and wrapped around her. Scorpions moved away from her, the stony pebbles crumbled beneath her. She looked at the fortress on the hill, dark against the milk of the early morning. She was convinced she would reach Abu N'af, would find people, a way back to Casa.

The Sicilian turned, disappeared down an alley. She knew that alley. It led to a small square, enclosed nothing but a few silk shops, cafés. She would be in plain sight the minute she entered it.

She waited until a group of camel riders, angled in their long striped robes, also turned. She followed them through the shadows and slowed when she glimpsed the sleek ponytail ahead of her. The camel riders stepped into the sunlight. She pressed herself against the wall.

Far away, the first of the afternoon prayers climbed the air. The alley was airless; even the wall behind her pulsed with heat. Her hands were hurting, her elbows, her knees. Her heart.

She had a clear view across the square. The Sicilian stopped at a table. A man was seated there: tall, slender, in his mid-twenties. He wore a hat, was impeccably dressed in a white linen suit. A Viennese tailor; she knew the label. He wore sunglasses, it was hard to tell his features from here. He nodded at something the Sicilian was saying, not looking at him. After a moment, he took off his hat and ran his fingers through his hair. Even from this distance the colour was striking.

She turned and ran down the alley, blundering past a line of monks who stopped, recoiling as she ran past, the air full of nothing but the image of the man. Nothing but platinum silver filling the air.

The first thing she did when she reached her room was check the book. It was there in the recess, under the rug, in its ivory silk cloth. It wasn't enough for her distress but it would have to do. Her mirror image. She pulled off the cloth, held the book in her hands, ran her fingers reverentially over the cracked wooden cover, the painstaking lines of spidery French writing, the maps of the broken hills, the snippets of poetry, the diary entries. *1890. On Sitting With The Polish Traveller At Abu N'af.*

She had abandoned the car within sight of the Kabir Massif. On the other side, across the plain and the old road, was the shallow hill that rose to house Abu N'af. If the maps in the book were correct.

She had hoisted her backpack and walked through the warm blanket of late afternoon. She walked through soft sand and over hard earth, a mile of nothing but jagged stones which slid treacherously beneath her, a mile where humped sand trailed away from the south side of the trunks of pale green bushes with yellow flowers. Another mile filled with small black scorpions that raised their tails and circled her.

When she reached the base of the Massif, she looked for the boulders that marked the entrance. After nearly an hour, she was thirsty, her water was running low and she worried she wouldn't make it back to the car before dark. The maps in the book didn't seem to correlate. She wondered if the author had written in code. It would suit his subversiveness, she thought.

She saw two boulders set a man's width apart in front of a fissure in the rock wall. Behind one boulder, chipped low into the red-brown rock almost at the level of the dusty ground, was a tiny fleur-de-lis.

She went to the other boulder, crouched down. The light was slipping away, the temperature was dropping. She saw another carving.

She ran her fingers over the two letters etched there.

AR.

She looked at the empty desert and squeezed herself through the fissure.

By the fountain, Agnieska held the book with the red cover. The ripples aged her reflection and she saw what Abu N'af would do to her. Her hair would be rusted iron, her eyes would sink into her face, her hands would become permanently curled. She would have crystals in her joints, in her heart. She thought of the ulcers on her father's shins, the sores on his face, the froth like champagne foam falling from his open mouth. Anything but that, she thought.

She stood on the chair in her courtyard and peered over the wall. On the flat roof above the café she saw a woman rolling sheets by hand through a wooden mangle. Beyond her, the marbled sky slid down past the last scribblings of clouds. The afternoon prayers folded into themselves. There was a banging of metal poles and shouts as the night market was set up. She imagined the fish being unloaded and set on the hot stone in their wooden boxes: the long and silvery perch, the small bream, the chunky mullet.

A thin man with eyes too young for his lined face wheeled himself awkwardly down the street on crutches – two planks of wood – dragging his legs behind him. The sight reminded her that she should see Betsoul. She cracked her knuckles. After today, after the foreigners came to see her, as she knew they would, she would have to go to Quartier Negro. She cracked again; the pain was still in her hands.

She waved and the thin man's smile came up like the dawn of a new day.

There were some things she would miss. In the steel cities in Europe passers-by would look away from the crippled, flinch from the raving, the disoriented. Here, people considered mad or unwanted or an embarrassment in Europe were allowed to wander with respect, could sit in the sun, would be given coins by the locals. The ability to share wealth was regarded as the first step to holiness. She knew that only giving away her possessions had secured her place here.

When she thought of what she had seen in the caves near Abu N'af, she never ate more than she needed, never drank more than minimal. She lost weight. Before then, she imagined herself as stocky: square shoulders, big stomach. With her hands on her hips, her legs planted wide, she had been the true Polish housewife. Now, her body was withdrawing into itself: stretch marks where she had lost weight on her stomach, her upper thighs. Where she was eroded by what she had seen.

A chain of bubbles turned over on the surface of the fountain. The turtle climbed up the statue, half floating, half clinging to the bare feet of the cherub. The turtle's eyes closed, it swayed, held by the water. The wet mosaics of its shell were the colour of the desert at dusk.

She dragged the chair into the corner and sat in the shade. As always she had to hold the book for a few moments before she opened it. And this was a book she dared to open. She ran her hand over the red cracked boards which made up the cover. It didn't suit the words inside but its disguise was protection of a sort. This copy she had made of Rimbaud's book; this decoy to lure the thieves away from the real book.

Je suis un autre, she thought. I am another.

She opened the book.

At the beginning of the book, the traveller had written, *This is a story about maps*. When he steps onto land at Tangier, he is obsessed with maps, with keeping his bearings. Later that first night, he writes: *It is 3 am and my heart is breaking. I see arrows loosed into the sky. I never thought I would miss my country until I left it.*

Wherever the traveller goes there is always a wind blowing across the wilderness: occasionally benign, usually angry. The sirocco lifting up everything in its path as it sweeps across Morocco. The deadly sinoun — known as poison in Arabic — which carried locusts and bees safely within its yellow folds yet mercilessly choked goats and lambs. When the Libyan army marched into the Sahara to subdue the wind with drums and cymbals, the land appeared to quieten. But it was a deception, the traveller writes. *The winds always returned, driven to make men bow down before them. Storms are recorded when Moses ascends Mount Sinai to speak with God. There is rain, thunder, lightning, but there is also wind: whipping around Moses, clawing at his robes, trying to rip the wooden staff from his hand.*

You can escape Africa, the traveller writes, *but you cannot escape the winds. You can march east, deeper into Asia. But all you will find are the Indian winds: hot, red geysers which flee from the rain which never comes and boom among the trees as they flatten them.*

As the traveller comprehended the desert, he wrote, *The ones who went before me talk about the bowl of heaven, the sacred empty, the sheltering sky. But the sky is black beyond the clouds. There is nothing there, just black space pressing down upon us. Le désert absolu.*

He could see why men believed they found the sacred here. You had to believe if you survived the desert. The cost was too great. There had to be more than the great implacable uncaring of the wilderness. You must believe that your death mattered, that you were chosen to survive. If it was all random chance then the desert was just another place of contrary existence. Your life was a roll of the dice.

He walked for five days in a reversed world: of light that killed, night that comforted. Everything good was buried below ground, away from the light, closer to hell. He slept during the day and walked at night, trying to compose poetry, the words sliding away from him like sand running out of a sack, rushing away as they had for the past ten years. By the third day, the rushing sand was as loud as a waterfall. He was rationing his water by this time.

By the seventh day he found it impossible to think of anything but how long it was till his next drink. He had to write the times down on a piece of paper, a process which involved taking off his pack and kneeling and taking off his boots to air his hot feet and carefully pulling out his fob watch and then the paper and piece of charcoal he used to write and checking the time and carefully pouring the water out to the exact drop. Then replacing the flask and cup and boots and paper. A process which took half an hour. And then he was thirsty again.

By the tenth day he was turning to see if his words were lying behind him exhausted and sprawled. Those ferocious words, those deranged vowels. *A is a black corset gaudy with flies.*

When his water ran out, his words went too. His tongue was a dried sponge in his mouth, skin peeling away from his cheeks, his eyelids, his cuticles. There was sand in his ears, nose, the corners of his eyes. He saw the world through a veil. The sound of his knees hitting the sand was a torrent. He prayed, Give me back my poetry.

The gun-runners found him. They slung blankets between two camels and examined him in the shade, pulling at his mouth, his feet, as though he was a horse. They went through his pack, took out anything of value, compared the size of his boots with theirs. They found his diary; one of them read it out in slow hesitant French. The gun-runner stumbled over the copied fragments and, swearing, gave him the book. A knife at his throat, he read it out as clearly as he could: 'La traduction de Charles Baudelaire.' Baudelaire's translation of Edgar Allan Poe's *Eureka*. A journey to Etna to stand in the mouth of the volcano. 'Dissertation sur la poétique du feu.' An essay on the poetics of fire.

They gave him water, dripping drops into his mouth slowly, the camels' breaths making small fetid whirlwinds in the sand around him.

It was only when they reached the plateau and led him through the fissure in the rock wall into the milky darkness and he saw the ribbon of water bubbling up through the cracked black ground that he understood they wouldn't kill him. They dug at a certain spot and pulled out a cache of guns and strapped a bundle across his shoulders. They tethered him to the stirrup of a camel, a knotted whip hitting his neck whenever he slowed or stumbled. He imagined that death would come suddenly. He wondered whether they would waste a bullet. He thought not.

He began to recite his own verses, softly at first, and others: Verlaine's, Baudelaire's, Hugo's, his friends, his lovers, distant voices, songs of mists. The camel kept slowing at the sound of his voice, turning to look at him. The whip crisscrossed his neck, its owner laughed – the camel hates the verses, too – but he kept reciting, sometimes shouting, head thrown back to bellow at the sun. The laughter stopped. There was nothing but the shadows of dawn and dusk and his voice evaporating like water into the sands.

He knew what he would write if they let him live. He would write: *It is all an illusion. There is no test to face, no sacred challenge to overcome. Death has always already happened here. The desert continues on, beyond death, indifferent. The reality I see could be a dream which is dreaming me.*

And yet, I cannot resist. I must go on. I must conquer or be conquered.

Coming into Kufra they met a caravan train heading for Cap Juby. At nightfall he was led into a large tent with lion skins on the floor, ostrich feather fans waved by boys who didn't reach his waist. A Scotsman sat cross-legged and sour, barely looking at him as he translated the gun-runners' French into broken English. The Scotsman never asked about the ropes on his wrist. In the corner, a chimpanzee sat, resting its head in its hands, sighing occasionally.

When he woke the next morning, the gun runners, the caravan, the tent, all were gone. He was alone on the stony ground, dawn coming up, crimson along the rim. He lay on his back staring at the sky and saw a falcon spiralling towards earth, talons outstretched, disappearing for a moment close to the ground then rising, a small broken shape in its claws, trailed by the sound of shivering crystal: a bell tied to the falcon's leg. He heard a horse whinnying, men's voices.

He had barely taken a few rushed steps towards the men when he stumbled over a hard object and fell. It was a small gold cup, rubies embedded around the base. He used a sharp rock to prise out one of the rubies, hid the cup between his legs and set off after the hunters.

He traded them the ruby for water, two horses, a gun and a guide back to the Kabir Massif. He sold another ruby for a pen and paper.

After he made his map of the plateau, the caves, the secret trickle of water, he returned to Casablanca and went to a quiet café on Rue Sidi Hmad.

He sat down at a table on the edge of the market. It was early afternoon, the town was quiet, sleeping, waiting for sunset, the start of the evening prayers. A camel train was coming in, small dark bodies tethered by ropes, walking through the animals' dust. He thought he saw a face he knew but then one camel side-stepped into another, kicking backwards, and the train broke up into sandy clouds. The noise was overwhelming, it filled his ears, his soul. He wrote, *Sound is water in the desert.*

He opened his diary, read the first entries, the first line: *This is a story about maps.*

He thought for a long while. Then, beneath the maps of the journey through the caves beneath the plain to reach Abu N'af, and the notes on his meeting with the Polish slave-trader, he wrote, *This is a story about families.*

Agnieska turned to the last pages where the photo lay glued between two sheets of paper at the back. She felt its thickness through the cracking fibres. She considered removing it but told herself she had the original. It would be a warning to the men who were coming to steal the book. She kissed the red-painted cover and put the book away in the stone recess. She threw the rug over it. After today, she knew she would never see the book again.

There was a knock on the door. Agnieska got up, surprised that she felt so stiff. She had to think for a moment to remember her exact age. I am forty-seven. If Czeslaw was alive he would have been fifty.

There was pain in her legs. Too much sitting, she thought. This endless sitting of women, indoors. She wanted to rip away her robe, the roof, the city walls. She thought, Whatever happens now with the foreigners, I have to go. Tomorrow. All I have to do is survive until tomorrow. She took a deep breath and went to the door. She knew before she opened it what she would find. She had wondered for fifteen years whether they would come for her.

The Sicilian was outside. Without his sunglasses he had the kind of knowing black eyes that reminded her of Rosita. Rosza, she had insisted on calling herself, but Agnieska could never think of her as Rosza. After Czeslaw's death, the woman was always Rosita to her, always the harbinger of doom. This man had the same dead eyes.

The young priest in Palermo had said, There were bad rumours about that village. Stories about how they survived during the war.

Agnieska had imagined war-time starvation, being forced to live off horses and dogs. Everyone had to do it after the ferocious winter, the failed crops. The Russians. The partisans coming to hang traitors from street poles in the middle of the night.

The young priest had shaken his head. The entire village avoided starvation. That was what cursed them, those people in Santa Margherita.

She said to the Sicilian, *'Lei parla francese?'*

He said, 'Agnieska Walenzska?'

She nodded and he beckoned to the man waiting at the bottom of the steps. The tall young man with the platinum hair slowly ascended. He was a step below her when he removed his hat. She looked at the silver hair. It was almost but not quite the same shade as Czeslaw's. She supposed it was the Sicilian blood that muted the colour. She wanted to slam the door. There was no good reason he had come looking for her. Certainly no warm feelings, she was sure of it. But she had to know whether this man took after his mother or his father. As her fingers tightened on the handle, Arthur came up the stairs in a rush. She held the door open for the cat to run through.

'I speak French,' the young man said. His voice was precise, clipped even. A careful voice. Wary. 'You probably don't remember me – '

She said, 'You are Pietr. The son of Czeslaw.'

'Your nephew,' he said.

She served him mint tea, taking the small iron teapot from the shelf next to the stove. She remembered the ornate silver pot she had brought with her from Poland, the delicate Limoges china. Now her cups were glazed blue stone, stained around the bottom.

There was a pen-knife in the cutlery box, its serrated blade turned out. She glanced over her shoulder.

Pietr was sitting awkwardly on the low couch, his long legs drawn up. He had changed into a dark blue suit, a different shirt. He wore gold cufflinks and a heavy gold watch; he had a heavy gold signet ring on his forefinger. The Sicilian, Stefano, had gone outside to smoke. She saw him dropping ash in the fountain; Arthur sat in the corner's blue shadow, watching him. She hoped the turtle had hidden itself inside the base of the cherub, where it was hollow. Unsurprising that the Sicilian had gone straight to the statue. She touched the knife, felt the cold plastic handle, slipped it into her deep pocket. The Sicilian's eyes were too much like Rosita's. It wasn't the constant searching for the worst in the people around them that disturbed Agnieska: it was their expectation they would find it.

She brought the tea and gestured at Stefano. 'Your servant?' she said to Pietr.

'My mother's bodyguard, childhood friend, I don't know what you would call him. When my grandfather died – ' He stopped. She could see he was remembering he was speaking about Agnieska's father. Wondering how much she knew.

'In '63,' said Agnieska. 'He took nearly a century to die.' Like a devil, she thought.

Pietr made a small gesture with his hand, chopping the air, as though he had started to make a wilder movement then thought better of it. 'Yes, well,' he said. 'Rosza, my mother, bought land in Sicily near where she grew up; some coastal property, a vineyard. Stefano looks after it.'

'Santa Margherita,' said Agnieska.

He stiffened.

'I went there,' she said. 'To find out what happened to Czeslaw.'

Pietr looked down into his mint tea. A tremor ran across the inky liquid surface. She was reminded of a collapse of land, deep below.

She took a cup outside to Stefano. He was examining the statue in the fountain. This man, she thought, has some kind of sixth sense. Like a jackal or a wolf.

He straightened and thanked her. '*Merci*.' The word wrenched out of him. He hooked his thumb at the stone cherub. 'Shop?' he said in English, the last letter encased in wetness. Almost spit.

She said, 'I had it made.'

He nodded. 'Special,' he said, unblinking. A wolf, then, she thought.

Pietr was standing when she returned, twisting the signet ring. He took out a linen handkerchief. It was monogrammed: *PW*. Pietr Walenzska.

He slapped at the flattened clouds of dust on his dark trousers.

He said, again with that careful enunciation, 'How can you bear to live here? The dirt is impossible in an old city. One must change three, four times a day.'

'You need clothes the colour of sand,' she said. 'Robes not suits. You have to forget the straight lines of Europe.'

He raised his eyebrows. 'I couldn't imagine doing business in a dress.' He nodded through the window. 'I thought I would be impressed by the architecture. But these brick squares forced into the land – '

'The cities are like the desert,' she said. 'An illusion to stop the eye. To stop any coveting. Flat walls like a veil. Behind the walls, you'll find different worlds: gardens, hidden oases. Or maybe,' she tried for a joke, 'they don't want foreigners to dawdle in front of their gates.'

'I'm sure they hate us.'

'We've spent a century subjugating them,' she said.

'It's the way of the world,' he said. 'They lost.'

She tried to see if there was anything of Czeslaw's earnestness, his inability to smile easily, his permanent expression of puzzlement as though life overwhelmed him. She saw nothing of Czeslaw in this man, with his monogrammed cufflinks, his changes of clothes. He was staring through the window, down to the market. He tilted his head, listening to the men's shouts as they put up the night stalls. The way he stood now, the way he had held his hat, reminded her of Laforche.

He looked around, frowned. 'Have you been robbed?'

'No. Why?'

'You have so little.'

'There was little I wanted to bring from Poland.'

He shook his head, moved restlessly around the flat until he reached the old stove. He laid his hands on the black iron. A man who preferred to use his hands, to be on his feet, she thought. Not a talker. Not a writer. He ran his finger over the design stamped on the iron door.

'The family coat of arms,' he said. 'It's an odd place to find it.' He cupped his hand, let it rest there, like a man feeling the belly of his pregnant wife. 'Sturdy,' he said approvingly. 'You don't see it so much anymore.'

She thought, A man made happy by things. Not a man afflicted with internal demons. She said, 'You like fine things.'

'I like craftsmanship.'

'The true craft worker believes there is a sacred memory held in objects.'

He nodded. 'I like the honour of a name.'

'I wasn't thinking of names.'

'Tradition, then,' he said. 'I like the notion of generations living up to the standards of the previous one.'

'There are no names in the desert,' said Agnieska. 'We lose our identities here.'

His fingers curled. 'But we aren't in the desert now.'

'Aren't we?'

He looked at the plain cups and plates on the shelf and shook his head. 'And you brought nothing else from home?'

She pointed to the dried black rose in its glazed blue vase. 'From Koloshnovar.'

He slowly approached the shelf. She saw the rose as he must see it: a sad thing, dried to the texture of black crepe, the petals cracked and disintegrating, dust eating away at the leaves, the bent stem become faded green scaffolding. Maybe he thought she kept it for sentimental reasons.

'How old is this?' he said. She wondered whether to tell him the truth but he continued, 'How long since you left?'

'Twenty-five years.' His eyelashes flickered. He was calculating dates. 'The year you were born.' She wanted to say, 'But I've been back since then.' Instead she said, 'I never saw roses as black anywhere else.'

'Koloshnovar,' he said, and in another man she would have sworn he shuddered.

She waited for him to continue but he was moving again, staring at the two prints propped up at the end of the shelf.

She pointed at the first. '*The Temptation of Saint Antony* by Brueghel.'

'What a hellfire and damnation picture.' She watched him absorbing the image: the blank sky, the broken landscape, the tiny human, the winged monsters hovering overhead.

'Saint Antony confronting the fanciful monsters of his brain,' she said. 'They threaten to derange him with his own fears and lusts, obscuring the truth with their breath of fire, the way sandstorms obscure the desert.'

'All these old myths,' he said impatiently. 'They have no place in the modern city.'

'I'm sure the Church would agree with you.' She pointed to the smaller pen and ink sketch further along. 'But myths are part of history here. We back into truth through fables.'

He examined the image of the ruined town. The jagged silhouette was ringed by ghostly riders holding swords aloft. Their heads were covered against the harsh sun, so that only a gleam of light showed in their dark eyes.

'Smara,' she said, 'where the first peoples from the south settled. Before the Berbers on horseback, before the Almoravids and the Bedouins. For a thousand years Smara was in ruins but, so the legend goes, it was guarded by ghostly horsemen. They protected it until it became the centre for Saharan tribes as they fought the Europeans at the end of the last century.'

As always to her, the picture shimmered in its lines of pen and ink. She said, 'Michel Vieuchange, the Frenchman, disguised himself as a woman to cross the desert to see what he called mysterious Smara with its virginal ruins.'

'Another madman.' His tone incredulous.

She pictured vast skies above the great settlements of Nitria and Scetis. 'Everyone has their dreams of resurrection,' she said. 'And the desert is especially seductive. The blossoming of the desert is a sign of God's love for His people. Then we become true citizens of heaven.'

He frowned at the mention of heaven and said, 'Was Smara resurrected?'

'Until it was retaken by the French in '34. They had destroyed it in 1913. You can understand the bitterness. Why Vieuchange had to disguise himself to go there.'

'Everyone blames the heat I suppose,' said Pietr. 'The way the Poles blame their vodka or the rain or the Soviets.'

Agnieska said, 'It is the same the world over. One group has the power, the other the silence.'

'Poland is becoming a nation of sleepwalkers,' said Pietr. 'The old ways are going. We have moved our business to Sicily. If the Communists stay, well,' he shrugged, 'maybe it will not change so much. We will pay them. We'll keep the land. Eventually they will go.'

'You want to keep Koloshnovar,' she said. 'You love it.'

'I deserve it.'

He stared into the corner that was her bedroom, at the empty space on the stone table.

'I gave my Confirmation Bible away,' she said. 'I kept it mostly to remind myself of my childhood.' She said deliberately, 'With my brother.'

After a beat, he said, 'Maybe you are not as religious as you think.'

'I think I was hiding from God,' she said. 'The rituals of religion are like veils, they obscure the truth.'

He stepped away from her. 'Friends of mine, the ones I ski with at Gstaad, would say you need a weekend with EST or a good Jungian therapist. They would say you want to recreate your past.'

'If I wanted to recreate my past I wouldn't have come to the desert,' she said. Then she thought of the book, hidden beneath him. She said, 'Maybe I want to rewrite the past.'

'Maybe you want your childhood back.'

'My childhood was a disappointment,' she said. 'As my father kept telling me. But he was already aged and he wanted a dutiful daughter.'

She remembered as a girl – how old had she been? – she had gone around the house and taken the hands off the clocks and left a note next to each saying, *It is later than you think*. It had taken her all day. It was only when her father threatened to whip the servants that she confessed. How old was she? Twelve, thirteen. It was a few months after her first period. Old enough to know better, said her father, as he whipped her.

She said to Pietr, 'I was an angry child. And then I decided – what was that Viennese expression – the one they use for everything from a bad gas bill to Hitler taking over? *Das geht bei uns nicht.* "That does not go well with us." My anger did not go well with me. So I became a party girl instead. You mightn't know but it is a full-time job.'

'I know,' said Pietr.

She went to offer Stefano more tea. He had pulled his hair free and it hung, black and shiny to his shoulders. He looked her up and down. At first she thought he was trying, like so many others, to see under the black robes, imagine her inside her shadow. But his gaze lingered on her pocket. Before she could stop herself, she had slipped her hand in. She grasped the knife.

'Pietr and me, we do tour of city,' he said, and it took a moment to realise he was speaking in her own language. 'The guide, he said the women here carry weapons in clothes.'

She stared at him. 'You speak Polish?'

He lit a cigarette, cupping one hand around the flame as though he was used to wild weather. She saw the long black lashes, the blue shadow on his chin, the muscles in his arm rolling and flexing like waves under the inked purples and reds. A man of the sea, she thought. A man of water.

'Back home the padres carry Bible in one hand and knife in one hand.' He looked straight at her. 'I learned myself, to talk to Pietr. When he came back from Kolosh – ' He stopped and spat into the water. He crossed himself and took out the small gold crucifix on the chain around his neck and kissed it.

She stared at the bubbles of saliva broken by the falling water. 'You never went there?'

He raised his hand, his thumb pointing at her, the cigarette curled between his forefingers so the glowing tip was pointing inwards. He must feel the heat on his palm, she thought. It must be burning him.

Her fingers tightened on the knife. He set the nail of his thumb against his front teeth and flicked it out at her. 'I know your family.' This close she could see his pupils withdrawn: black points in the dark brown eyes. She looked at his inner arms: no noticeable track marks. A casual user then. A part-time drug addict.

He said, and she could barely hear him over the creak of the water wheel, 'If anything happens to Pietr, I will hunt you down like a wolf.'

Inside, Pietr was holding the tea but not drinking it, rocking the cup slightly.

'Stefano seems . . . angry.' She stared at the rose on the shelf.

Pietr laughed. 'He is still offended the tour guide told him not to lean against a wall. Some wall less than a thousand years old. Yesterday, to a Sicilian.' He laughed again, admiring Stefano the man of action. Of threat.

Pietr said, 'And he tried to drink the water.' He looked down at the black liquid in his hand. 'We are in the desert and the water tastes of salt.'

'Once this was all a giant sea.' She touched the cross at her neck and said, 'I thought you came here to talk about – '

'No.' He wouldn't look at her.

She said gently, 'Didn't you ever wonder?'

'Wonder what?' He put his tea down and drifted around the room, touching the wall now and again.

'No belongings,' he said, turning the signet ring. He looked around again, carefully; his knees bent as though he was about to get down and look under the rugs.

'No books,' he said at last.

'About Czeslaw – ' she said.

'No,' he said loudly. A shadow fell sideways across the tiles in the doorway. She had an image of Stefano: eternally waiting, his skin black against white walls, his head turned. What was he waiting for? Why did he wait?

Pietr said, 'It's the future that counts, the children.'

'Aren't children products of their past?'

He shook his head.

She remembered. 'You have a daughter.'

'Anna.' For the first time, the hard planes of his face relaxed.

He took out his wallet, passed across a photo of two little girls, both dark-haired, alike enough to be sisters. She pointed to the one in front who was looking directly at the camera: a pointed face, lively expression, laughing. A familiar girl; where had she seen her? Another girl – smaller, more serious – was behind her.

'This?' She pointed at the lively girl.

'That's her best friend. This is Anna.' He pointed to the serious girl.

She remembered sitting in the kitchen, the second to last time she had secretly visited Koloshnovar, her old nurse holding her hand. She was needed again, the nurse said. A new baby; Pietr a father at eighteen, his wife even younger. A good Polish girl. They had barely said two words to each other, said the nurse, rocking on her stool, wiping her nose on her apron. The Count and the Sicilian mother, they arranged it.

Pietr said, 'The marriage didn't last. I'm not proud of . . . ' He paused as though he found the word hard to say. 'My failure. But at least we parted as friends.' He held the photo carefully by its corners, on the white border.

'Since then you have searched,' said Agnieska. *Depuis ce moment tu fouilles.*

But he misheard heard her, thought the word was wandered. *Tu flânes.*

He said, 'The old ways which suited us so well won't look good to the new reformists. That is why we are moving the business to Sicily.'

'Sicily,' said Agnieska. She remembered the young priest watching her over his clasped hands, waiting for her to ask the question. She had smelt sulfur on the breeze. She thought of Stefano, waiting outside. She wondered whether he had taken out his knife.

Pietr said, 'You want your house back.'

'Is that what you think?'

'I would.'

'Koloshnovar.' She closed her eyes. It was a palace of rock in her mind's eye. 'I think I was the only one who ever loved it. Czeslaw couldn't wait to leave, my half-brothers despised it as a backwater, thought the shoe business was for peasants. My mother was constantly sick. She said the tannery smell poisoned her. But to me it was a magical place. A small kingdom. I never left it as a child. So when I discovered what was going on there, I couldn't bear it.'

'You ran away.'

'I ran away to find out what had happened to my brother.'

He didn't want to ask, she could see that. He said, fast, 'And did you?'

'Yes, I think so.'

He was moving around the room again. She waited for him to ask her the question he must have come to ask. But again, he didn't.

'I'd like to build a house,' he said. 'A house on a hill. Anna has never been strong. She likes being up high. Her friend has a house on the water in Sydney with fresh sea breezes.'

She sensed a displacement of air and light by the doorway. 'Anything that tears away the walls,' said Agnieska, 'is a good thing.'

He said, 'That is why I want the book.'

Finally. 'What book?'

'The Frenchman's book. The book my grandfather couldn't bring himself to destroy. The book my father took with him when he left. The book my mother used against my grandfather to get the estate.'

'The magic book,' said Agnieska.

He waved a hand irritably. 'The book of secrets.'

Out of the corner of her eye she saw the shadow growing through the doorway.

'The book of God,' she said. 'But your mother has it.'

He shook his head. 'It is gone from where she hid it. But she doesn't know yet.'

'She didn't send you here?'

'Stefano told me that you must have the book,' said Pietr.

Stefano came into the room, a black shape against the light. Nothing shuts out the light in the walled city, she thought, except for men.

'You should know,' she said. 'Your father didn't leave. He escaped.'

Outside, the flat planes of the sky were smudged, the haze soaking up the colour. She saw tracings of light through the grey, reminding her of that time she had walked through the caves, following the silver ribbon.

'My father ran away,' said Pietr. 'From his responsibilities. His name.' He picked up his tea, his shoulders rigid. The shadow that was Stefano slid along the wall.

'He was haunted,' said Agnieska. 'By what had been done in his name.'

'He had too much imagination.'

'We're all haunted. Everyone who reads the book.'

Stefano stopped. He crossed his arms.

She said, 'The book is no good to you.'

'I need it,' Pietr said, so low she could barely hear him.

'You think it is a weapon. But it is a weapon to be used against you.'

A black rage – a feeling from the old days – rose in her: sap spreading through tree roots, oil seeping across dry ground, lava spilling out of fissures; the air turned to smoke, heat, sulfur. She wondered what he would think if he saw the photo, if he knew what the book represented. Of how far people would go to get it. How far she would go against this stranger who came to take the one thing she had of value. This man with Sicilian diluting his Polish blood. A foreigner: easily made to disappear, no-one except the bodyguard to ask questions. Easy to pay a few dirham to certain men in the old medina. There were wells in cracked earth beyond the old town, dried black mouths which held piles of bodies.

She was back in the cave, the spear of light falling through the fissure behind her; the high cave roof rearing away into the gloom like a cathedral vault. She was following the butterfly markings on the wall by this time, drifting, letting her instinct guide her. The dark wrapped around her like a shroud. This was the only place, she had thought, where her father could not harm her. Ironic, really, considering what she would find.

Now she said, 'The book took me into the desert. I walked through an underground network of caves until I found a thin ribbon of water in the night.'

Stefano was watching her. Pietr looked impatient.

'In a dream?' he said.

'I was lost in the desert,' she said. 'I read the book by – ' she almost said the name – 'I read the book and it showed me the labyrinth that we all know and visit in our dreams. There were shapes drawn on the walls. Prehistoric elephants and giraffes crossing the Sahara, when it was a savanna. Lions, tigers. And animals with human faces. Then nothing for a millennium. It was only when I saw the butterflies that I saw the dates: 1886, 1897, 1910, 1921, 1944. 1960.' She closed her eyes, remembering. 'Butterflies drawn on the black walls. Drawn with rocks. Or fingernails.'

'The desert.' He stirred restlessly, muttered under his breath, the English shot through with raw Polish. *Vot the fok ist this?* Her father's phrase, when buyers of the African cargo lost their nerve or failed to pay.

She looked at his signet ring, the pressed clothes. She thought, We all veil ourselves in different ways. We're all caught between two worlds. She remembered Betsoul laughing at her, taunting her: You'll always be an outsider.

She was overcome by a sense of hopelessness so strong that it was almost like fainting. She thought, In Arabic there is a whole world of language just to do with the desert. The desert nurtures and cherishes its languages as a possession in its own right.

She said to Pietr, 'How could you ever think the writings of a desert poet would help you?'

'I can sell it,' he said. 'All those rock stars quoting Arthur Rimbaud, philosophers as gods, self-destruction as fashion. Jim Morrison, Bob Dylan, they've all made him the new seer, the man who started modern poetry. A book from him would be beyond price. The French alone would pay a fortune to get it back.'

She touched her cross. 'So you think the book is by Rimbaud?'

For the first time he looked unsure of himself. 'It has to be. Why else would my grandfather value it? My mother says it is so.'

She was silent.

'Is it?' he said. 'Is it not?'

The cross was cool and reassuring in her fingers. 'You should know it is an evil book.' She thought then said, 'No, it is a book which records evil.'

'It's mine,' said Pietr. 'It was my father's.'

Over by the wall, Stefano stirred.

'It was stolen,' said Agnieska, 'by your grandfather. Your father was taking it to France. To return it to the writer's family.'

'It's my inheritance. Mine.'

She touched the scar on her left cheek. 'I am owed something.'

'I thought you received an allowance from the estate.'

'It's hardly enough, is it?' He wouldn't meet her eye. She said, 'All the books in the world become sand in the desert. This book is by a poet. It would be justice to return it to the white page of the desert.' She was aware of Stefano wandering casually along the wall, sliding his feet over the tiles, stepping slowly on the rugs.

She said, 'Jesus walked into the desert, reduced himself to nothing. He made himself as blank as the desert. From the blank page you construct the poem, the way you make a garden in the desert. An oasis, a fragile tent of words. The dwelling place of the desert traveller, of the poet.'

Stefano spoke to Pietr. He had a deep voice in Italian, surprisingly melodious. There was no trace of the cracked hesitations evident when he spoke Polish. This was like the tolling of a bell. It was a voice a woman could fall in love with. She wondered about the photo of Rosza in his wallet. Was it given to him or did he take it?

Pietr said, 'Stefano says that whether we live or die is of profound indifference to the desert. It is like the sea.'

'You are a fisherman,' said Agnieska. 'You distrust anything to do with fire.'

Stefano muttered under his breath.

Pietr stood, adjusted his cuffs. 'I need to change. Come and have dinner with me.'

'And bring you the book?'

The shadow at the corner of her eye receded. Stefano was walking towards the window, across the rug in the corner. She could see by the way he moved that he was feeling the floor with his feet. He was approaching the recess where the book was hidden. The join was barely noticeable; it would be almost impossible to feel it through his boots. But he was moving more slowly. Somehow he had sensed something different in the floor.

She said, 'Once you read the book you'll want what I want.'

'What's that?' said Pietr.

She thrust her hand into her pocket, pressed her thumb against the knife blade. 'For the rottenness my father carried to stop spreading.'

He stared at her. His eyes were an odd colour: not Czeslaw's stormy grey but an ice blue muddied with shadows. Rosita's shadows.

Stefano hesitated as he passed over the recess in the floor. But he came and stood silent behind Pietr who, as though signalled, put down his mint tea. He flicked a speck of dust from his cuffs. Again, he reminded her of a younger Laforche, the man Laforche would have liked to have been, with enough money and a mansion in the country and a more welcoming climate. She could almost hear Laforche saying that he would have made a much better job of being an aristocrat than the aristocrats did.

Pietr said, 'So you won't give me the book?'

She said, 'What you will find there will horrify your sense of yourself.'

But he was already shaking his head. He wouldn't listen to her. She saw herself as he would: a dumpy scarred woman, old enough to be his mother but more easily dismissed. Maybe dismissed because she could be his mother. She was tired suddenly. She wanted to leave the city, all this pushing and pulling. She wanted open spaces and winds which caressed the skin, not the cuts from horsewhips held by syphilitic drunkards.

Pietr had forced a smile onto his face and was half bowing, a relic of some gallantry he felt obliged to make. She glanced at Stefano, expecting to see a smirk, some class-driven derision, but he wore an unexpectedly tender look.

She asked Pietr where he was staying. He named a hotel, one of the new foreign chains, in which every room was exactly as it would be in America. It had air-conditioning, he said; the bungalows in the gardens used the new Beani dome structure. She made herself look impressed and he said that Stefano had negotiated a very good rate. His tone was slightly defensive, as though he admired the bargaining but resented the need for it.

They went down the stairs without looking back and she thought how much she would have liked Laforche to have been there, hidden, watching. Deciphering the ways of men.

Early evening. The sky was a roughened blue-grey curtain, heavy and trembling over Rue Sidi Hmad. Women, their heads bare, were unpegging the laundry strung on lines across the flat roofs. This was the only place they could take off their veils, in their own small kingdom of air and light.

A red petticoat pinned at one end reminded her of Betsoul: rebellion hidden under black robes like the seeds of desert plants. The real world of women hidden.

The café was empty. As she turned away from the market, she heard the siren notes of the snake charmer's pipe. She imagined the animal being roused reluctantly from its sleep, beginning to sway. It wouldn't be able to resist. The pipe was like the call of the desert.

She found Laforche, smoking, his tie askew, in his cubicle. His desk was littered with papers. A magazine lay open, a picture of the desert with icebergs superimposed over it: *L'Afrique elle fait l'iceberg.* It half obscured a book cover. Camus, she saw, *L étranger.*

Laforche stood, tugging at his tie, but she motioned him down.

She said, 'If the image of the modern Arab is the Koran in one hand and a glass of Scotch in the other, what is the modern Frenchman?'

He sat down opposite her. 'Egoists with enough time to go mad on the beach,' he said. She put her hand on the icebergs. Even the photo cooled her.

'More ice marks found in the desert,' said Laforche. 'Strange to think all this once stood in Antarctica's place.'

'Fire and ice,' she said. 'Only a few degrees' difference changes one into the other.'

She sat up straight. 'I've come about shoes for one of the ben Asoub boys.'

Laforche cocked his head. She said, 'The mother with ten children in Quartier Rouge. The crippled one.' .

He looked puzzled.

'The pickpocket,' she said.

'Ah, I know. Well . . . ' He spread his hands. 'The minute you go the Church will reverse everything you've done.'

'I rely on you then.'

'Desperate woman.'

'Maybe I'll leave insurance. One of Betsoul's curses. Bury a pocket-knife clasped shut on a piece of paper with the Monsignor's name on it. Make him impotent. I'll bury it near a leaking well so that the water dissolves the words. The curse will remain, even if he opens the knife.'

'Sometimes I don't think you believe in religion at all.'

'Organised religion,' she said, emphasising the first word, 'interferes with discussions with God. I have never seen a dictatorship or corrupt society that didn't use organised religion to justify its possession.'

'*Mon Dieu.*' Laforche went to the door, closed it. 'Don't let the Monsignor hear you.'

She looked at him with amusement. 'Isn't he five miles away, in Quartier Nouvelle? The Western sector.'

'That's no protection anymore.' He kicked at the wall. Small spurts of dust and a crusted pebble fell out. 'Easy enough to insert listening devices from our new friends in Hafid Street.'

'The lizards and small creatures,' said Agnieska, 'they make tunnels between the loose stones.'

'Either way we are exposed.'

'You seem irritable. Or depressed.'

'Depression is merely anger without enthusiasm.' There was sweat in the grooves beside his nose. The small room was airless, facing a hot bare courtyard. He sat and unfolded his handkerchief, dipped it into the bowl of lavender water on the desk blotter and dabbed his throat, his forehead.

'You need plants,' she said. 'You need a garden.'

His fingers touched the water. 'You know drownings are the preferred torture of the CIA,' he said. 'So typical of the Americans. Even in the desert they must have the one thing that is the most valuable. Not ropes, not knives. Water.'

'So you still plan to leave tomorrow,' said Laforche. 'With nothing but your book of secrets.'

'Most women would call it a book of fears,' said Agnieska. 'A record of men's fears about women, fears about themselves. What they see in the night because they are so disconnected from nature.'

Laforche took out his cigarette case, offered her one. When she shook her head, he lit a small gold-tipped cigarette and blew a slow smoke ring, tilting his head back to watch it rise to the ceiling.

'You are right,' he said. 'I don't see lambs in the desert. I see monsters. Sumerian beasts, the chaos monster from Assyria. It is a wasteland for me.'

'You treat nature as fallen, the desert as a mistake,' said Agnieska. 'It is only when man loves the desert for what it is that the earth will be saved.'

Laforche said, 'Once they figure out how to mine the phosphates and iron ore in the Sahara the desert will become a strip mall. Like the icefields, like the jungles.'

'They'll never conquer the desert. The sandstorms will defeat them, the shifting ground. God will defeat them.'

'God?'

'Nature.'

Laforche said, 'Haven't the Americans made what they call a paradise in the desert?'

'Las Vegas.' She remembered seeing the tall buildings, the hotel that was a pyramid of glass and steel, all trying to reach heaven. She remembered driving down the main street, the endless blaze of light, the smell of money, the sound of the slot machines. The desperation.

'I would go to this Las Vegas,' said Laforche. 'As long as camels don't come into it. It is too undignified to ride a camel.'

He straightened the papers on his desk, wiped a curl of ash from the blotter. He said, not meeting her eyes, 'I must tell you, I may not be here for much longer.'

'You have paid off your debts?'

'Nearly.' Then, because he found he could rarely lie to her, 'One or two lucky dice will do it. And then I will return . . . '

'To Paris.'

She considered him. He had told her about his childhood: his father, the Paris banker, prosperous, with businesses in Casablanca and Rabat. 'A nice house in a respectable arrondissement,' Laforche had said, 'a pretty wife, a healthy son.' The family's life was ordered: every day the father returned at precisely six o'clock and went into his study for a whisky and soda or an aperitif before dinner. A pleasant routine.

Laforche had been a pampered child, allowed to play-act, have fantasies. He had been given an elaborate dolls' house, a mansion really, with stables and gardens and even a private zoo and a small lake. He stocked the zoo with beetles and ants, and the lake with tadpoles. The beetles often died and the tadpoles turned into frogs and hopped away but it had been his own little kingdom. Then, one day, his father returned home very late and spent a long time in his study. Dinner was delayed, the family waited. 'But when my father emerged,' Laforche said, 'he looked entirely normal. He assured us nothing was wrong and we ate and drank as usual.' The next night the father came home exactly on time. And the next. And the next. But that night, five minutes after closing the door, a gunshot rang out. 'Very odd,' Laforche told her. 'It sounded like a book falling. I smelled gunpowder for weeks.'

The family was bankrupt of course: a question of impropriety. Nothing proven but the suspicion lingered. Laforche had to leave school and go into the public service to pay off the family's debts. He had asked for a transfer as far away from Paris as possible.

She said, 'It is very respectable, to be the assistant director of the Catholic Mission in Casablanca.'

He grimaced. 'The desert is a tomb.'

She looked around the small office, the desk, the framed photo of King Hassan II on the wall. She said, 'For some.'

She thought that if she were in the desert now she would see the sun's beats gradually weaken until the misted air was the colour of a soap bubble. The wind would undulate across the pale earth in transparent eddies. The way she had seen the wind rising from the dunes beyond Abu N'af when she climbed to Rimbaud's tower.

She said, 'Do you hear the wind?'

'There is no wind in the walled city.'

But she had heard it. It would reach the city the next day. She would be travelling into the wind.

'I have a vision,' she said. 'Of a scarred and unrecognisable body. On it would be printed a text containing the ultimate answer, the way the desert is unreadable and yet contains the key to the restoration of shattered lives.'

'A man's body,' said Laforche.

'No, it will be a woman.' She looked at the inkings on the backs of her hands. She thought, It will be the reincarnation of the mad scullery girl who disappeared into the desert. Someone whose life created a text to be read the way the desert is a text. She touched her cheek – the old scar made by her father – and felt the throb of the newer marks on her back. The ones she had made.

'You are the key,' said Laforche.

'Not me but someone who marked herself in humility, not anger. Someone who knows that the desert is only as much a wasteland as the inner mind. She will come out of the desert the same way that Rimbaud came out of the desert.'

Laforche took her down to the first floor where two locals, watched by a black-browed nun, were sorting through the donation bins. Agnieska kneeled by the pile of shoes in the corner. She had persuaded a cobbler in Quartier Negro to donate an hour each week to fix the worst: to glue wood over the holes, remake the tongues with camel leather, plug the seams with tar. She found these abandoned shoes poignant: life reduced to a remnant of that part of a person most in direct touch with the earth. A man without shoes is a vulnerable thing. He will be cast out by the herd, left behind in the dust. The desert will defeat him. She thought of Rimbaud on his quest: trying to become a seer by entering into the sacred empty, risking madness by giving himself to the great silence. But when his leg ulcerated, he had to return to Europe. Without his feet he was defeated.

Laforche watched her as she turned over the shoes. He said, 'There is another irritant in the pearl that is our lives in Casablanca. Your nephew's servant – the Sicilian.'

She looked up at him, holding a child's ballet slipper, the pink satin tip smeared with red.

Laforche said, 'The CIA are so touching in their faith that their files will not be opened by illiterate cleaners.' He leaned against the window sill, looking down into the street. The shouts of the boys playing soccer floated up to them.

He said, 'The Sicilian has been buying brown opium. He likes to try it himself but these are large quantities. For business.'

'With Pietr?' she said.

He shook his head. 'With an Australian. Do you know him?'

'No.'

'The Australian has two children with him.'

She put her hand over the point of the ballet shoe, felt the comforting strength of the wood inside. Maybe it evoked her child-hood: the factory always in the background, the villagers walking to work, the smell of tanning leather. What she thought for years was the family business, until she discovered what the real business was. She wondered if Pietr had businesses within businesses, what his disguise was.

She looked at the shoes. Something hardy for the boy; big enough to grow into but not so big that he would trip and fall. She wanted him to have something formal that said: You are a man now. You have dignity. You have weight on this earth.

She chose a pair of lace-up shoes: British, black, the shoes to wear for work. The leather was stiff and smooth. Like Polish leather. She had refused to believe Czeslaw was dead until the young priest had shown her the shoes with the broken laces.

Laforche threw his cigarette out the window. 'What surprises me,' he said slowly, 'is the malevolence. There are rumours that you smoke kif and eat majoun. That you are mad.'

She looked at him. 'Because of my history.'

He said, 'Because a young fool got drunk while playing dice with the legionnaires and spoke about finding you eight years ago, curled up like a seahorse, bruises on your arms, brown powder around your mouth.'

'I relapsed,' said Agnieska, 'when I found out what Father Thomas did to Betsoul.' All that faith, she thought, gone: the time spent in the church's drug clinic after Jürgen left, the volunteer work at the Mission, the taking of her vows, the conviction that she had found a solution to the curse of her family. All erased by a few words. By the return of demons. 'I found out,' she said, 'and I returned to the opium dens in Quartier Rouge.'

'Your head fell back as I lifted you,' said Laforche. 'I saw tremors running up your neck. I wiped the powder off with my finger.'

'And the next day, I went into the desert. I found Abu N'af.'

She stood beside him. The last of the muezzin's calls began washing over the flat roofs and pink walls. As always when the voice lapped the city, disembodied, remote and unjudging, she felt calmed. As when she looked into bowls of water, the fountain.

'Drugs, alcohol, religion, poetry,' she said. 'All to obliterate the pain. Slow suicides.'

'Betsoul would say it is the words that kill,' he said.

She pressed her thumb into the blade in her pocket. 'Maybe asylums are all I'm good for.'

Laforche said, 'I think you should go tomorrow. There is a very good chance that they are embarrassed beyond civility. Beyond reason.'

They stood on the Mission's front step. A dog was barking nearby, a woman sobbing. Agnieska thought, Sobbing in her small sea of robes.

He said, 'You shouldn't walk alone, tonight of all nights.'

'I like to walk.' At night she could walk down alleyways as cool as streams and see into the small courtyards, the wooden benches with their high carved backs and their embroidered cushions lined neatly against the wall, the small brown finches in cages. Gardens shaped out of nothing but rocks and stones. Anything that changes its form has power.

He held her hand for a long moment and released it. 'I won't say goodbye.'

She said, '*Un coup de dés jamais n'abolira le hasard.*'

'A throw of the dice,' he said, grimacing, 'will never abolish chance. I will try to remember.'

When she left the Mission, the moon lay in the darkening blanket: broken-faced, a jagged fragment of light, as though seen through a cracked cup.

She remembered the inky blackness of the cave in the desert, the rock pressing down over her, the silence like a falling cloak and, as her ears adjusted, the small breathings, the displacing of air by small bodies. The seam of light which grew stronger the more she looked.

The cats were out, stalking the market, leaving bent and elongated shadows on the walls. She smelt fried eggs and onions, saw a man cooking on a steel platter over a kerosene flame.

She walked past the stalls, the men standing behind the racks of T-shirts with *Greetings From Casablanca* unevenly printed below the stamped silhouettes of a lone camel under a palm tree.

Occasionally, a woman sat there: small, hunched, light glinting on the stud in her nose. Frowning. All the women frowned in public. Frowns undercut by puzzlement, at the very now of their life, like the look on a horse she once saw being swept down a flooded river.

A beggar on the corner was selling paper flowers, the thin cardboard badly dyed and streaked. For a moment she saw the streets strewn with broken flowers, people crushed by falling stone and collapsed buildings. The future rose in front of her as a shrieking city of sounds, babble in the tower of Babel. There was no future for her among those for whom empty space was meaningless. She could see her life in the city going on and on, in a night which was always the same night. I am already alone, she thought. I've known that since the desert. She thought, Tomorrow I will go. No matter what happens tonight.

She stopped under a light strung from a wooden pole. Moths were dying in small tearless sparks against the bulb. She should turn here to take the boulevard to Pietr's hotel.

A group of shouting youths went past. She recognised the ben Asoub boy. He saw her and hesitated but he was with his friends; he didn't want to stop.

'I have your gift,' she called out.

He couldn't resist, he slowed.

'Tomorrow at the Mission,' she said.

He stopped, was drifting back.

She said, 'You can't give it to your family.'

His eyebrows shot up. It was a gift for him alone. He was pleased, she could tell by the way he leaned towards her.

'You can't sell it,' she said. He looked outraged, as though even to be accused of an impure thought was to be belittled. He was already trying on the adult masks of representation. No-one has a proper childhood in this country, she thought.

'I have a vision.' She saw Betsoul, like a flash of black fire in her eye. Maybe she was doomed to repeat her mistakes. She said, 'This gift will get you a job, do you hear me? You will support your family. Everyone will be proud of you.' Pride, she thought. Useless in itself but still a recognised commodity in the walled city. 'You can't betray the vision,' she said.

He nodded solemnly.

She could hear Laforche's voice. *Unscrupulous*, he was saying. His tone admiring.

There were birds perched on the telegraph wires. Night like water, the colour of the octopus eye, was stepping off into more night down the hill. A yellow tongue rolled up into the dark air. A pause then another flare further on. In the flash of light she saw the shape beneath, the tilted head. The flame-eater was practising as he walked to the night market.

She thought there was a fountain nearby, in a small square. She needed the sound of running water.

She entered the next alley. Night corkscrewed away from her. It was that peculiar moment of absolute stillness when every person vanished from the street. Deserted. Desert-ed. She thought of the cities she had known, the times when they were revealed as nothing but flickering neon and empty streets. That was the real barren mind, not the desert with its secret life growing beneath the sand. The city was bound by its lines and walls. But the desert was able to be transformed, the way Saint Antony built his community; the way a poet built a poem from the desert of the empty page. Conviction and faith transforming desolation, turning it into mystery and revelation. The barren wasteland inside the mind becomes a sacred place, she thought, the way that Saint John of the Cross transformed his own small cell into a marvellous garden of hope and optimism. She heard Betsoul laugh, a hard jeering sound, as she laid the scarf over the horns of the goat and raised her knife. You are deluded, she heard Betsoul say.

She walked through the falling cloak of night. At times, she wasn't sure if she was walking through the city or she was back in the desert. She thought – or was she reciting the words of the poet in the desert? – *It was a dream at times.*

I didn't know who I was. I heard His voice – I sang to myself – I recited poetry – I shouted into the wilderness – the sound echoed off the rocks. She was inside the cave yet the sky pressed down on her. There was nothing beneath her yet the stars in the map on the ground glowed fiery in their splendour. She was alone and not alone. A figure was ahead of her in the darkness, guiding her. But she knew that, in the end, the guide must be replaced by the follower.

Now she thought, Did I go mad there?

Outside Pietr's hotel, she looked at the square white balconies, the flags of America and France hanging over the entrance. The automatic front doors slid back and forth as people came and went. She saw the rectangular couches and glass tables scattered across the marble lobby. When the doors opened a pungent smell wafted out: a disinfectant. The smell of America.

Music see-sawed into the street; she couldn't even tell if it was Western or Arabic. That was the only thing that bothered her about journeying into the desert. She didn't mind moving into silence but she minded losing the music.

'It was a terrible house,' Agnieska said to Pietr, 'and yet somehow I loved it.'

She looked around what Pietr had called his suite but which Agnieska thought was a large white room with a bed in an alcove. The cold of the air-conditioning was amazing to her. The shock of leaving the warmth outside reminded her of those other times she had left the heat for the snow: to visit Koloshnovar, to search for her brother in Sicily.

A peacock came out of the dusk onto the narrow terrace, placing its feet carefully on marble the colour of clouds. The bird's dark flags of emeralds and sapphire blues swung behind it, merging with the muted garden. Even above the voices of the drinkers around the pool, she heard the soft swish of the silky tail and the click of claws on the stone.

The bird stopped at the glass door, dipped its head, nodding at them. Pietr got up and banged on the glass so the peacock jumped, its eye rolling as it retreated, offended, its tail colours streaming.

'Dirty birds,' he said.

She watched it sway along the concrete path, past the concrete domes which sat like fallen moons between the palm trees.

'A new invention,' said Pietr. 'Single-room apartments. Poured concrete hardens over a steel mesh skeleton and pressurised air. I would have liked to have stayed in one,' he said, his tone wistful, 'but apparently they were all booked out.'

Agnieska said, 'You should have been an architect.'

He picked up his brandy glass and sat on the couch next to her. 'There's no money in architecture.'

Agnieska said to him, 'Do you remember the hall at Koloshnovar? It gave me nightmares.'

He frowned, rolling the glass balloon between his hands. 'I remember the red wallpaper.'

'It was the long hall running the length of the house. It was lined with hundreds of heads, animals my father had killed. Thousands, it seemed to me as a child. Antelopes and zebras and lions from Africa, bears from Russia, wolves from Italy. Foxes, rabbits. After a bad day's hunting, he would go and shoot the ducks in the pond.'

'He was a man of his time,' said Pietr.

'Do you remember the death masks? His own father and mother, displayed there as trophies. As though by outliving them he had won.'

'He was proud. He believed in the bloodline.' He drank, a small amount, lifting his chin to roll the liquid on his tongue. He was not a drinker, she was glad to see. He had missed that addiction. She wondered what his obsession was.

'When my father was drunk,' she said, 'he would go and shout at the masks. A sea of bile running down the hall.'

'That was the red wallpaper,' said Pietr.

She looked at him. Maybe that was his obsession: keeping the truth at bay. She wanted to shake from him this – what? flippancy? deliberate detouring of the truth? In the desert you always zigzagged into the wind. But not here. She didn't have the time for detours. Maybe that would be what the desert would teach her. In that time-less place, she would give up her own obsession with time.

She remembered going back to Koloshnovar, secretly. The winter chill was a needle after the heat of Casablanca. She had stood in the snow, seeing the tracks of wolves, hearing the far-off howls. Someone had been breeding them – they had disappeared after the war, after the Russians had arrived with their tanks and hunger. Now they were back, maybe kept by some Politburo chief as trophy guard dogs. The money never strayed far from the top, no matter the government.

She stood in the rose plantation, saw the bare branches, imagined the buds in spring, only weeks away now. The roses would be grown in squares, arranged by colour, laid out like a patchwork quilt. There would be only one kind: the eighteen-point teacup rose so beloved by the Americans and English. The money rose. The famous Koloshnovar rose, grown by her grandmother to combat the stink of the shoe factory, the cheapening of her aristocratic name, so she said.

The pink roses had a sullen blood-red tinge, while the darker roses – the deep blues and purple – were streaked with black. Even before Agnieska knew what was in the fields, it made sense that the black soil around the house would be richer. The older servants crossed themselves whenever they went past the rose gardens. They wouldn't look at them on bad days – those mornings after a night-time arrival which, no matter how secret, everyone seemed to know of.

'My father,' said Agnieska. 'He was the only father you ever knew. Unless Stefano . . . ' She looked around.

'He's running errands,' said Pietr.

'That man would die for you.'

Pietr looked surprised. 'I wouldn't expect anything so feudal. I never met him until we visited Sicily.'

'After your grandfather died.'

'After my uncles lost the fight with my mother over the estate.'

'My half-brothers.' Miniature editions of her father, unable to comprehend that they couldn't win by shouting and bullying. Sitting in their smoking jackets, drinking, morose, the world passing them by.

'Stefano was always more like a bodyguard,' said Pietr. He took a larger mouthful of brandy.

Agnieska felt the weight of the objects in her pocket. She felt their coldness, their warmth. She wondered whether she would have the courage – or the anger – to use them.

'He seems devoted to your mother.'

'I'm glad someone is,' said Pietr.

He was watching her. Agnieska wondered whether this was his way of seeing where her sympathies lay. She thought of the first time she saw Rosita, the way she had come into the room. No-one had expected her to travel in her condition. But it was her condition that saved her from being killed outright.

There was a shocked silence when the butler led her into the smaller breakfast room. Fading laughter curled around her like charred fragments of paper as she planted her feet wide on the floor. A small squat girl in black. The folded arms should have warned us.

'My first impression of Rosita was that she was a witch,' Agnieska said to Pietr. 'Later I was ashamed of myself. It was because of the way she dressed in mourning for a man I believed she never loved. Or maybe I was jealous that she had had the last of my brother. I grew to admire the way she defied us. My brothers despised her, humiliated her, yet she never reacted, not even when my father picked up his riding crop and shouted, spittle flying from his mouth. Shouting at this dumpy Italian girl.'

'She knew she was going to win,' said Pietr.

'When my uncles left her in the catacombs,' said Agnieska, 'I thought she deserved the estate.'

'And now?'

The knife in her pocket was cold even through the thick material. But the other objects were small squares of pulsing warmth.

'I've tried to forgive her,' said Agnieska, 'for what happened to Czeslaw. The fact that I can't is my burden.'

'I wanted to ask you to come home,' said Pietr. 'You're the only one left now.'

She stood. 'There is no home. It is all ashes.'

She fingered the knife in her pocket and the wrapped pellets of tainted opium. It seemed so inevitable. She thought, I always wanted revenge.

Pietr was drinking. She was surprised to see the brandy almost gone. Maybe she had been wrong; firewater was his addiction. He said, the clipped evenness of his words beginning to liquefy, 'At a young age I learned my mother wasn't a source of comfort. By my early teens she was always the last one I called. That Viennese expression you used. That was my relationship with my mother. She did not go well with me.'

The shadows of the wood panels in the glass doors made large crosses on the wall. She wondered how surprised he would be if she told him what she planned to do. Which would prevail: Czeslaw's blood or Rosita's?

Agnieska said, 'We don't talk enough about demons in our society. I thought when my father died, the demon had died. Then I realised he had been replaced – by your mother.'

Pietr laughed but the sound turned into itself almost immediately.

'She bargained with my father to get the estate,' said Agnieska. 'She had something that Czeslaw was carrying. A photo in a book.'

'A book?' said Pietr. '*The* book?'

A breeze lifted the fronds of the palm trees in the huge pots outside. The shifting shadows of the trees broke up on the wall, turned the crosses into twisted vines. I think we keep entering ourselves, she thought, trying to change by layering ourselves with new experiences. With new people. Trying to beat back the dark emotions which are thrust into us. But it is like the way human flesh won't reject embedded coral. Our bodies sense that these dark emotions are living things; not to be rejected no matter how hard we try. We grow around the foreign object. But it is always there.

He got up and faced her. 'You want the book as a weapon.'

'If I wanted revenge I would have shown the book to the police. The African police.'

He looked uncertain.

She said, 'Haven't you heard the stories about me, as a child? The way I taunted my father.'

'You hate him because of this . . . ' Pietr gestured at her scar.

She put her hand over the dead skin. 'Mistakes are not mere chance. They are the result of repressed desires. That is what I learned here. What have you learned?'

'I learned you did take the book. I wasn't sure before.'

She said gently, 'You know there is a family tendency to steal.'

She gripped the pellet in her pocket. The blackness was burning in her hand. Was her anger enough? And then there was still the daughter.

She said, 'When my father met the Frenchman in the desert and heard his stories, of course he couldn't resist. My father was an educated man – he would have known who the Frenchman was. Remember: even the Nazis read poetry, worshipped classical music. It is one of the great ironies of history: the great art that moves men to tears at night fails to stop them massacring in the morning. The creative act will never abolish death.

'In the course of his wanderings the Frenchman had discovered many secret places. Places to hide. To store things.'

She saw her shadow rippling across the curtains. Shadows doubled the world just as reflections in the water doubled the world. But her shadow was small on the curtain: a small child falling on corrugated pavement.

She thought of the silence of water above a sunken tree, of ripples widening through the reeds. Sometimes she wondered how she could do it, live in a world where water was so scarce. Her memories of Poland were all of rain, water running down black stone.

She said, 'My father was a man who thought history couldn't touch him.' The edges of the pellet were softening as her hand heated it. 'I cursed him – did you know that? I cursed my father in the great hall in front of the family, the servants. I blamed him for driving Czeslaw away. And then I blamed him for whipping me. The whole hall was silent. Even the hounds stopped chewing their bones.

'My father called me mad, but in the desert madness is an asset. Once your mind has split and peeled backwards, then you can cope with the ultimate nothingness of it all.'

Her hand was cramping. 'Despair pushes you deeper into yourself, deeper into the emptiness; deeper into the desert. My mind lay open to the powers of the night.' She flexed her fingers and began to prise the foil wrapping off the pellet. 'I spent all my life in Poland thinking like a prisoner.'

Her thumbnail was catching on the foil. She had to take a breath, adjust her grip on the pellet. She said, 'Your grandfather accepted Rosita. He could see that they thought the same.'

'My mother told me it was blackmail.' He lifted the glass, drained the brandy.

'That too,' said Agnieska. She remembered the dumpy Italian girl shouting up from the black hole for them all to go except for the old man. He waved them back, his skin purple and red, and she shouted one word. The word. And his mottled skin floated on a sea of white, and he told them to bring her to the surface. The servants said they found butterflies drawn on the walls where the Sicilian girl had been standing. Butterflies or figures of eight lying on their side.

And then the girl was standing on the surface, blinking in the light: small, black-browed, relentless. She said something to the old man and he fell, foam in his mouth. And the girl put her hand over her stomach and Agnieska saw the gold band on her finger.

The old man didn't die. When the Sicilian girl gave birth to the baby with the platinum hair, he signed a new will giving Koloshnovar to the boy. Agnieska could remember her half-brothers – tall and thick-necked by then – kicking the oak panelled door of his bedroom. They wouldn't go to his funeral.

The pellet was crumbling in her hand. She used her fingernails to separate the small grains, felt the drug under her nails, she wondered if it would enter her bloodstream. She wondered if before the end Pietr would be honest about his father.

She motioned to Pietr to give her his glass. He looked at it as though surprised that it was empty. She went across, slowly, to the drinks table. With her back to him, she took the pellet from her pocket. She watched the small dark clots of powder fall onto the shining mirror at the bottom of the glass. She picked up the decanter.

She said, 'In my entire life I had no physical contact with my father. Maybe he held me as a baby. He would shout, at Czeslaw who was such a good gentle boy, *Du bist ein Puppenjunge*. You are a little puppet boy. One of his Nazi phrases.' The brandy was falling in streams of burnt gold. 'He was a cold unresponsive man. He had never been taught to give or receive affection. There was something in his own past. Before he went to Africa, he went over to Russia voluntarily. No-one would go to Russia voluntarily.'

The dark grains floated like ashes on the surface. Just as she was convinced they were too light, the alcohol filled the spaces within and they sank.

She said, 'Maybe my father was searching for something. The year before he was born, the Cossacks raided Koloshnovar. There were the usual stories.'

She shook the glass in her hand. The liquid swirled.

She said, 'From Russia he went straight to Africa. And you know what happened there. He met the Frenchman, the poet who had survived being lost in the desert. The man who created art met the man who created death. '

She stared down into the glass. There was no reflection. She remembered she had said to the Sicilian girl, 'Why did you come here?' And the Sicilian had said, 'We all go into worlds that have nothing to do with us. Worlds that are volcanoes to us. We suffer but it turns us into what we are.' And she had said to her, this widow of her brother, 'You did understand him after all.' And Rosita had hooded her dark eyes and placed her hands on her belly and said, 'First you dream, then your dreams die, then you die.'

Pietr said, 'My mother says you have an implacable will. She says you pretend to yourself it is fate. But it is your own will. You had a restless heart, she said, just like Czeslaw. There was nothing extraordinary about it.'

'Yes, there was,' said Agnieska, turning, the glass in her hand. 'The fact that we didn't accept it.

'Impossible dreams,' she said. She thought, There's a madness in us all. We look at the Polish army riding out to face the tanks, the sun glinting off the soldiers' silver helmets. We know they are doomed to failure. But there is something within us that if we were standing under the thin grey trees, our fingertips touching the yellow grass bending in the wind, we wouldn't call them back.

She came across the room and handed Pietr the glass. As he raised it, she found she couldn't sit next to him. She stepped to the door, looked at the garden.

'My father always liked his hiding places, his secrets,' she said. 'Something in his childhood, I think, some deprivation. That's why he liked the desert. You only survive by knowing secrets in the desert. Where to water your camel train. Where to hide supplies, your car, your plane. The desert is crisscrossed with the trails of travellers, desperately burying their planes and food and guns for a return which never happens.'

She looked at him, at his gold cufflinks, the immaculate shirt. A crease ran like a fissure across his cuff. She thought that, back home, he would not have worn a creased shirt.

Pietr raised his glass. He was drinking. There would be a slight interlude before the drug took effect. A time of delusion, of dreaming. Of revealing secrets. Before she decided whether to use the knife.

He was swallowing. She said, 'Why are you in Casablanca?'

'For the contacts,' he said. 'To promote the business.'

'Import and export.'

'Yes.' He raised the glass again.

'The shoe factory is no longer profitable.'

'No.' He was swallowing. His eyelids flickered. 'Too much competition. From South America. And now, Asia.'

'Contacts here. Pay-offs to the Americans?'

He started to speak, cleared his throat. 'Necessary expenses.' His eyes flickered again.

She sat next to him. 'You know you can make a fresh start with your next breath.'

He drew back. 'I don't want to make a fresh start.' He lurched to his feet, still holding the glass. He looked at the peacock swaying in its small sea of colours along the pale marble.

'I need the book,' he said, without turning his head.

'For a weapon?'

'We need the map,' he said. 'The family needs the map. My grandfather was the only one who knew. We . . . owe people for being allowed to keep Koloshnovar.' He raised the glass, looking at the liquid. From where she sat she couldn't tell if his hand was unsteady.

'The military,' she said. 'They need you to loot for them. They give you the information. You help them in the chaos of war.'

'What is looting?' he said. 'If you look at history, it has mostly been accident, blind chance. Sometimes, it saved the art. Look at the Ankara frieze: the Turks were using it as target practice. Big-city pollution is already eating away at great buildings like the Acropolis, pollution reacting with the limestone in the rock, weakening the whole structure. We only take what is unattended. We ensure its survival. If a country can't care for its art – '

'You pay good prices in wartime when people are desperate.' She waited. He didn't turn around. She wanted him to turn around. Why?

Maybe she wanted him to see the look on her face. She wanted to be caught. To be crucified.

'You pay when the victims of war need money, food,' she said.

'It is always about money. The rest is conversation.'

'You take their culture. You take them.'

But still he didn't turn.

She said, 'We can't steal to fill the hole in ourselves.'

He was immobile. She knew the words that would make him turn. 'Your father would never have condoned this.'

He leaned against the wall. 'What did he know?' he said loudly. 'What about wardship of our own history? His duty? Anyway . . .' He pushed away from the wall, stood, swaying. His forehead glistened.

'It won't last forever,' she said. 'All these black trades will be harnessed. Maybe for religion. Beyond the clash of countries, the clash of ideas. You'll become unnecessary to them.'

Pietr was drinking, fast. He drained the glass, grimacing as he put it down on the table.

'The dust even gets into the drinks,' he said. 'Miserable country.'

He approached the couch, walking as though his legs were cramped. She helped him sit, wedged cushions behind his back to keep him upright. She took his hand. He seemed unaware of her touch. She said, 'You don't want the book the way I want the book.'

'It's just a book,' he said impatiently. 'Photocopy it if you want to look at it.'

'I want to hold it,' she said. He tried to shake his head but his chin rolled from side to side. She placed her fingers over his pulse. The beat was fast, then slow.

'Scribblings,' said Pietr. He rubbed at his face. His eyes were almost closed. 'The words don't matter. It's the maps which are important. Maps are what save your life.

'What the French poet drew as he staggered through the desert,' he said, his voice slurred, the clipped edges lost. 'A map of undiscovered oases and water channels between the Kabir Massif and Kufra.' He rubbed his face again, pressing his knuckles in, leaving white marks. 'Maybe the ancients knew it was there. Some desert tribe which died out, taking their secret with them. If we find that vast underground sea it makes the desert open to traffic from the east.'

'There is no sea,' said Agnieska, speaking slowly and clearly so he would hear her. 'I was there – don't you remember? It is another excuse to attack the land: oil in the Arctic, gold in the ocean.'

He closed his eyes but she was sure that he was still awake. She said, 'You need to hear about my time in the desert.' She put her hand into her pocket, for the knife. 'You need to know what I saw there.

'You never asked me why I went into the desert. Maybe I didn't know myself. This was long before I had any thoughts of retreating permanently from life. But even then I wanted to go into a time of quarantine. Rehabilitate myself. I was sick: my hands were hurting, time was hurtling past me, people were turning into streams of light. I was already drying up, becoming a husk, already unable to have children even though I didn't know it. Maybe I suspected it.

'Maybe the decision to follow the clues in the book was a deception. Maybe I went into the desert to kill myself. I was already feeling fragmented, a bow of torn silver arrows, loosed from a wild heart.

'I followed the maps: yes, you are right. The book has maps but I don't know if you can read them. You have to be de-centred, to be peeled apart. You have to let the desert enter you before the book truly makes sense.

'There is water there, if you dig maybe there is enough to create a city. Maybe you can create another Las Vegas in the desert, a place where people shut out the light and go mad under neon. I don't think the desert will allow you, though.

'Isn't it perverse that only money makes men strong enough to face remorseless nature? But you don't want to know this. You want the story, the answers. The truth. Such as it is.

'So, let me tell you: I followed the thin ribbon of water through the network of black caves. I found the empty drums, I smelled petrol in the rusted metal. They were too big to have been brought through the crevice I had slipped through. So there must be another way in.

'I went on. The water was illuminated in the dark light, my fingers brushed against the wall. The darkness pulsed. I began to think that the whole head is a cave, the mind is a desert, a void waiting to be filled, a page waiting to be written on. I wondered if all this was a dream dreaming me.

'The caves reminded me of the catacombs at home, the labyrinth my half-brothers had put Rosita in. I realised now that she must have gone mad there. One could only go mad in a tomb or find God. And she was always too angry to have found God.

'There were odd marks on the walls: watermarks the colour of mottled bone, waves of forgotten seas, drowned reefs. The Sahara when it was covered by mile-thick ice; Africa where Antarctica is. Fire and ice. The desert is like the sea. Any borders are covered in sand or blown away. There are no countries, no nations, no different peoples in a sandstorm. You are either of the desert or you are not. But you don't want to hear this. Your breathing is slowing. You are slipping away.

'The first thing to tell me I had reached a place used by men were the iron rings hammered into the wall. I found what I thought were ribs buried in the dirt but which were the wooden planks of a cage.

'I saw a child's hair comb, the odd tip of an ivory tusk, a glint on metal that I thought at first was a sword. It was a machete, stained with darker patches along the blade. When I saw the eyeless skulls arranged in neat rows I knew it wasn't rust on the blade. And I knew I hadn't gone mad. I had been an accessory all my life to mass murder.'

Pietr was shaking his head, trying to open his eyes. 'There were no repercussions.' He was hard to understand. 'The police never turned up. There were no humiliations.'

'You didn't avenge your father's death,' she said. 'That is what eats into you.'

'It was an accident.'

Agnieska said, 'I talked to the ambulance driver – '

'I have a child now,' said Pietr. 'The past is no good to any of us.'

'Czeslaw was dead before the car went into the water,' said Agnieska. 'The marriage was a sham.'

'No,' said Pietr.

'The whole village was a part of it,' said Agnieska. 'The death of the old priest Dante was suspicious. What the villagers did during the war – '

He was shaking his head. 'No.'

Agnieska was exasperated. 'You're the last male. You could investigate.'

'No – '

'You have money, Koloshnovar.'

'Because she got everything,' shouted Pietr.

There was a silence as sharp as the pain in Agnieska's hands.

'He left everything to my mother, in trust for me until I am forty. If I don't do what she says, I'll be cut off without a penny.'

'Would that be so bad?'

He stared at her. 'I have to live. I have to . . . ' He struggled for the words. 'I have to maintain.'

'Maybe if you stripped away your possessions you wouldn't be so haunted.'

But his eyelids were dropping, his breathing was slowing.

'I went to the morgue,' said Agnieska. 'All the records had been destroyed, the original admittance forms. Even before she became wealthy, somehow she was able to do it. Some help she had. Maybe Stefano, some Mafia connection. But the Sicilians still respect family. So the ambulance driver talked to me.'

'I don't want to hear,' said Pietr. He raised one trembling hand.

She said, 'He told me that the villagers were there when the ambulance arrived: Rosita's father and his friends carried the body up from the lake. But in the morgue the blanket slipped off the body and the driver saw – '

'It's too long ago,' said Pietr. His hand dropped, his eyes closed.

She bent over him. His breathing was deep but rasping.

She said, 'Do you know what I saw, in the cave, in the desert?' She picked up his wrist. He had surprisingly broad wrists. She had expected Czeslaw's wrists: delicate and bony with pale blue veins. She pushed back his cuff and saw the tan line. A few days in the country and yet his hands were already a dark brown. So unlike Czeslaw who had never tanned, who remained almost translucent.

She gripped his wrist and shook it. She dug her fingernails in until she saw red half-moons in his skin. His eyelids twitched but he didn't move. She took out the knife.

She said, and she didn't know if she was talking to Pietr or to Czeslaw, or even Betsoul, 'Maybe I was in the cave for hours, days, weeks. I dreamed I stood on the riverbank and the wind swelled and the willows brushed my hair. I stared at the cages for so long they became clear to me in the light. The bones chewed by lions gleamed. The light intensified. The more I watched the more I could see. I saw all the way back – butterflies scratched on walls, ribbons of light, trees burning in the oasis, the sun glinting on the Polish cavalry – until the light grew so blinding that it consumed all colours. Everything turned to black. A light so pure it blinded me. A light that created pure darkness.

'I emerged from the cave into a place of no time and place. My eyes turned to stars. Mythical beasts rose before me: winged creatures, huge lizards, scorpions with mouths of black, sand vipers with eyes of blood, crabs eating turtles with their shells ripped off, every beast that my inner mind could conceive, every rotting smell. My face was bathed in an orange glow. I was in a ruined place, surrounded by ghostly horsemen galloping out of the sand. The sand itself was rising, being swept to heaven, revealing the barren earth.

'I was standing in a dead sea.

'I was silent in the void, contemplative before the infinite and the sublime. I became de-centred. I became wholly the other. I became at one with the desert.

'*Je est un autre.* I is an other.

'I saw the wind lifting the sand in the vanishing point where the land became the horizon. The point of absolute nothing, the point of absolute poverty. I had nothing with me now but the book. I saw there was nothing that separates us from the void but the word. And then out of the heat on the sand and the rocks, I heard the roaring of lions. I looked across the dead sea and I saw Abu N'af, abandoned on the hill.

'There was an old woman living in the ruins. She gave me water. The old woman had spent her entire life with her goats, moving west from Kabir across the rocky landscape. She said that her home was in her memory of her wanderings. She remembered the poet, the Polish slave trader, in the times when Abu N'af was a fort, a place for travellers to re-stock. The Polish trader would crucify runaways as a deterrent, she said. The orange sand was red sometimes.

'He had met up with the poet in Casablanca and stolen the book from him and returned to Abu N'af to explore the network of caves beneath the Massif. It became a place for him to store the goods smuggled up from southern Africa on to Europe and the West Indies sugar plantations. By goods I mean his lootings, his cargoes of slaves. People. Women, children, young men. Everyone else usually butchered in the raid. He used mercenaries, ex-soldiers, killers. Men who always gravitate to places of darkness in times of violence because they hate themselves.

'I saw that if I didn't save Abu N'af it would be buried by sand. I held the book and I thought, What is the dream but the erased book, the book that wants to be written, the book waiting to be written?'

'Do you have the book with the red cover?' she said.

Yes, she thought she heard him say.

Now there was only his ragged breathing and scrabbling from the peacock outside. She bent over him, lifted an eyelid, saw only white.

She wondered whether she should search for the book. Maybe it wasn't here. Maybe Stefano was stealing it at this very moment.

The knife lay on her palm, glinting in the light. It reminded her of the thin line of water leading into the blackness of the cave. She pressed her thumb against the blade, a slight movement. A thin wave of red rose up, a straight line. She turned her thumb and cut again so another line appeared at right angles to the first. A red cross on her thumb. She pressed her thumb against Pietr's forehead. He didn't stir.

She didn't think she could look at him; she considered standing behind him. She imagined holding him around the neck, the raised arm, the sudden swing. Like cutting hay with a scythe at Koloshnovar. But she was worried that he would wake up; the pain would be too great. She decided that cutting his wrist would be best; he would gradually slip further into unconsciousness. The death of emperors.

His pulse was beating in her hand. She felt as though she was holding his heart.

'I fled Him down the years,' she said.

She took off his watch and pinned his wrist against the couch. She still didn't know if she could do it. And then she remembered he had never asked her once about the men and women and children taken from their homes, bludgeoned into slavery. Her father's voice echoed around the room; the bored tone darkened the crucifix shadows on the wall: *The crying of the cargo kept us awake all night.*

Fury flared through her; the sun exploded over the desert.

She was in blackness but it was where she had to be. She lowered the knife.

Stefano's hand gripped her elbow so painfully the room turned white. Her fingers opened. He caught the knife and threw it across the room. His eyes dared her to go and get it.

He bent over Pietr, lifted an eyelid, checked the pulse.

'It's opium,' she said, 'to make him dream.'

'He already has too many bad dreams,' said Stefano.

He straightened, flexing his hands. She saw that he was deciding whether to kill her.

'One day he will want to know about his father,' she said. 'And I am the only one who can tell him.'

'You,' said Stefano and spat on the floor. 'I know your family.' He raised a finger. 'You're all destroyers.'

'It was my brother who died.'

'An accident. The car fell into the lake.'

'Murder.' She stood, to watch his reaction. To show she wasn't afraid. 'He had a bullet in his head.'

He wasn't surprised.

'You knew,' she said. 'It was you.'

'No.'

She was about to say the name. He said, 'It wasn't Rosita.' And she saw that he was more concerned that she didn't think Rosita was a killer. 'She loved him,' said Stefano and Agnieska saw how difficult it was for him to say it.

'Who then?'

'The fathers, the parents. They were already scavengers. They discovered he was rich, an heir to an estate. They forced him to marry her then they killed him and told her they would kill her.' He flexed his hands again, made them into fists. 'She went beyond reason when she saw his body.'

'And then the village well was poisoned,' said Agnieska slowly. 'Everyone died. Except you. Except her.'

'What did they expect?' he shouted. 'The things we saw during the war, the way they behaved. Children learn by example.'

'She poisoned the well before she went to Poland.'

'To be young, pregnant, misused. And then, at Koloshnovar – '

'They left her in the catacombs.'

'Pietr's uncles. Your brothers.'

'My half-brothers.'

'All from the same father. A murderer, like you.'

'Yes.' She said, 'That is why his bloodline must end.' She pointed at Pietr.

Stefano said, 'You think Pietr is Czeslaw's son?'

It was her turn to stare.

'But he isn't. He is mine.' Stefano looked down at Pietr. His eyes were shining black. He said, 'I've always tried to watch over him.'

Agnieska walked home through the city. The sky had tipped completely into its dark bowl. She took off her scarf; her hair was luminous in the darkness. She felt shadows behind her. Men standing in dark corners, staring at a woman alone. Men who prevented women from being alone in the landscape. Men who denied women contact with the great silence, the chance of the divine.

She walked and tried to imprint the streets in memories she could carry into the desert with her: the pink stone against the night sky. The lattices of shadows and vines. The broken pavement releasing cool secret air through its cracks.

Somewhere out there were Nitria and Scetis, the tomb of Saint Antony. Purgatory, she thought, the place of no place, the place of all evil and all hope of the divine. The place where Christ and Satan meet. *Le désert absolu.*

She reached the turn-off to Betsoul's alley. Metal groaned a few metres away. An old man was backing away from her, dragging the door by its metal fist, closing this section of the city for the night.

She imagined walking down the alley, through the unlit street, eyes watching her through the shutters, knocking on the painted wood door, saying hello to Meersun, looking over the head of the scrawny girl-child with the grey eyes to the circle of women sitting on the floor. The flames would rise, the orange light would be loosed across the uneven stone, over the blood as thick as soup in the wooden bowl, over Betsoul as she watched, unblinking.

Stefano hadn't bothered to replace the rug in her bedroom and it lay sprawled like a scarlet gash across the black hole in the floor. The book with the red cover was gone.

She took a hessian bag from her suitcase and filled it with a water bottle, a spare pair of sandals, the prints of Saint Antony and Smara. She left the black rose.

She looked for Arthur but he was nowhere to be seen. She went out to the courtyard. The turtle was drifting, its flippers moving slightly as though it was stroking the water. She wondered if she gave it to the ben Asoub boy whether he would take care of it. Unlikely – he would sell it at the first chance.

In the water, she saw the words. Matthew 11:7. *What did you go into the desert to seek?*

I go into the desert to make myself as blank as the page, as blank as the desert. To find and lose myself through self-abandonment to the needs of others.

But really all that is a lie, she thought. I fell in love with a book.

She stopped the turning wheel. The turtle sat on the bottom of the fountain, a shadow in the early light, and gazed up at her with great dark eyes. She kneeled and thrust her hand into the still water and reached down behind the cherub. She lifted up the false plaster bottom and pulled out the object wrapped in plastic. She didn't unwrap it. She knew exactly what was inside: the book with the black leather cover, the tissue-thin pages with the poems, the diary entries, the maps. The photo inscribed *Les fugitifs*.

She left a note for her neighbour, the drunken poet, asking him to take care of Arthur and the turtle.

Outside, the sky was the colour of milk. As she walked through the silent streets, the first call to the faithful began. She heard a lighter sound curled through the rising notes. She turned. Arthur was following her, his mouth open, mewling.

'Go home, Arthur,' she said in French. 'Go home.'

But he came to her and writhed around her ankles.

She said, 'Come as far as you want then.'

Even before the outer wall, she reached a place where the path was breaking up and crumbling. She put one foot in front of the other. A small wind lifted the sand; grains stuck between her toes. The wind was creeping inside the walled city. The desert was coming. But first she was coming to it. She put out her foot and started to walk.

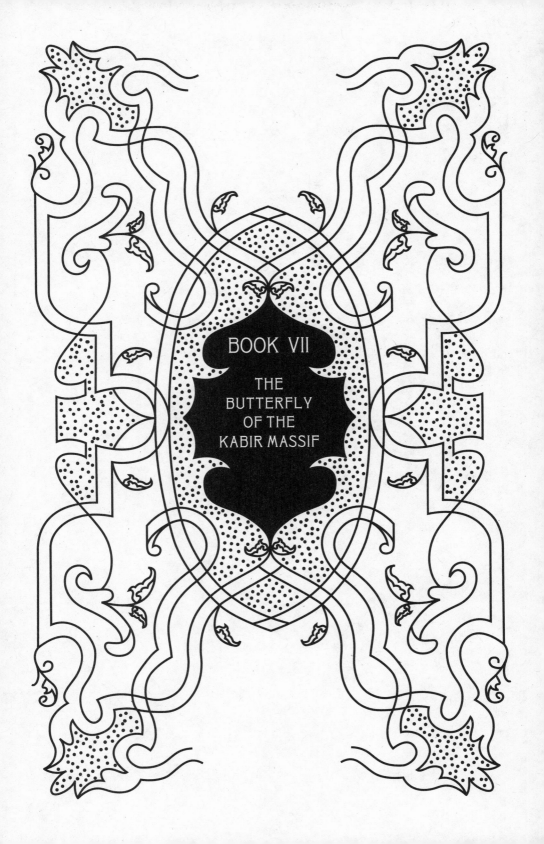

BOOK VII

THE
BUTTERFLY
OF THE
KABIR MASSIF

MOROCCO, PRESENT DAY

'Devlin, you fuck,' says Mitch. He climbs down from the helicopter. 'We found the Baghdad figurine you hid at Hafid Street. What else do you have?'

A spatter of sand rattles against my toes; the helicopter shudders in the wind. Mitch bends and walks out from the black blades slicing the pearl and blue sky.

He is close enough to see what I am wearing. 'Where the fuck is your tie?'

I look down at the robe Sister Antony has given me, the sandals on my feet. My briefcase sits nearby: alien, incongruous.

'You look like a peasant,' says Mitch. 'Or a terrorist.'

The heat expands; the horizon sways in the early morning light. The shadow of Abu N'af seems to shiver on the ground. Or maybe it is the poison in my system.

I stare past the helicopter and the edge of the plateau, down the rough road and across to the Kabir Massif, squat and blue-tinged on the other side of the plain. But the woman didn't go that way, Sister Antony had said. She went into nothing but sand rising and falling endlessly towards Algeria. Into the vast empty.

'I always knew you were susceptible.' Mitch rolls the word in his mouth like old Scotch. It is a crime, in his book, that a man would succumb.

More sand hits my foot. I flinch. There is pain in my tendon, below the ankle. Between the flashes of fire, my bones are turning to water. I need to get my circulation going.

Behind the Massif, the sky is a cupped shell opening along the horizon, veiling the burnt hole in its centre. The day is growing.

'I fell,' I say. 'Willingly.'

Mitch stares. He senses some biblical reference but he knows I am an atheist. It had been an unspoken job requirement: not to care. But I can see that he likes the concept of falling. A man who is already falling will be much easier to push. And it will always be his own fault.

'I'm here to clean up your mess,' says Mitch. Behind him, the pilot sits impassive in black sunglasses, trying to pretend he isn't listening.

Mitch says, 'There's nothing you can do to avoid punishment. So tell me where the woman is.'

'I quit. Or you can fire me. I don't care.'

'Oh, we don't want you to quit.'

More sand hits my foot, harder, scoring the skin. The helicopter rocks, the blades shudder. The pilot grabs the dashboard with both hands.

'You've got to make up for Borneo,' says Mitch. 'For your father.'

I have an image of the dark house, the open door, the garden path hard beneath my cheek.

'Borneo is the payment, Mitch. I don't owe you anymore.'

'Just give us the woman.'

'She's gone,' I say, pointing. 'Into the sacred empty.'

He takes off his sunglasses, squints to where the sun shakes on the horizon. Clouds of sand rise from the ground. The horizon is breaking up, becoming indistinct, like the blurred outlines of men in camouflage.

I put my hand over my watch, forcing myself not to look. My fingers tremble on the glass.

'Your helicopter can't fly in this,' I say. 'One grain of sand will bring down your fine machine.'

He is angry but he controls it. It is his most admirable quality.

'We'll get her eventually.' He examines me. He can't know every-thing – can he? – but he senses this is what I dread. The eternal wolves.

I take out the passport I had made in Casablanca and toss it to him. He catches it; his reflexes were always good.

He stares at the photo of the woman inside. The photo I know by heart now. He says, 'Who the fuck is Anna Walenzska?'

'That's the woman we've been chasing. Pietr Walenzska's daughter from his first marriage. It's all in the files.'

He blinks. He is trying to remember the reports. But minor details aren't his department. That is for grunts.

I say, 'Sister Antony is convinced – '

'Sister Antony is a nut job. She's Opus Dei or some camel jockey-version. She likes to whip herself.'

He is thinking, thinking. He is coming to believe that he doesn't believe me.

He says slowly, 'I think Anna Walenzska is dead.'

I pick up the briefcase. It is heavy in my hand – how had I carried it all these years? I remember flourishing it at Laforche as though he would be impressed by its titanium frame, its fingerprint-coded lock. Now, it reminds me of the beaten silver shell of Pietr's house. The silver mask he had erected around himself.

Mitch has tensed. He is wondering where my gun is. Or if I have a needle: small, sharp, silent.

I walk forward, put down the case, retreat carefully.

I say, 'You can see how alike the women are. Almost like sisters. But we've been following the wrong one.'

He frowns at the case but he doesn't pick it up. He says, 'Anna's dead.'

I should have known he would remember my reports. I try to clamp the desperation in my voice. 'What if the precious files are wrong? It's only words, easy to change. How did the woman get out of Sicily? I had her passport.'

'That fuck Stefano,' say Mitch. 'Tunisia is only a boat ride away.'

If I look at my watch, it will be a sign to him. It doesn't matter of what; he's trained to read everything into nothing. Devlin was anxiously checking his watch, he would say. Devlin was jittery, drunk, unstable, insane. Ask the pilot – he'll confirm it.

Soon the sun would break free of the milky horizon and surge up, shrivelling everything in its path.

My hands are shaking. I shove them into the robe's deep pockets.

'That bitch has made fools of us – of you,' says Mitch. 'If you can't finish it off there are plenty of Agency men who would love to take a crack at her.'

Maybe now is the time to bargain, to remind him about Hafid Street.

'She's an accessory,' says Mitch.

'She doesn't know it all.'

'She knows enough.'

That note in his voice again – something about this job makes him furious.

That mightn't be such a bad thing.

I nod at the briefcase. 'I've got Pietr's confession in there. When I went back into the house, he confirmed his daughter Anna had been staying there too.'

Mitch stares at me. 'But we never saw her.'

'She'd had a nervous breakdown. More than one. She was engaged to the woman's brother.'

He remembered that from the files.

'She was in seclusion,' I say. 'I listed her in my notes.'

We look at each other. We both know he's had people regularly hacking my laptop – in Venice, in Trepani. But he can't admit that here. He can't call me a liar.

He swallows down his protest. 'So the woman . . . ?'

'Could be anywhere. Maybe still in Sicily.'

He contemplates the helicopter, the puffs of red dust swirling over the black metal runners. Now I sneak a glimpse at my watch. One hour gone since I woke, maybe two since she went into the desert. I stare down the pitted road. Twenty minutes to the plain; an hour, maybe more, to circle the plateau and reach the desert proper. But the scorpion's poison in her system would have slowed her. She might have fallen. She might be crawling.

'I think this is all bullshit,' says Mitch. 'But forget that. What else did Pietr say?'

I am back in Sicily, smoke and steam rising through cracks in the floor. I heard hissing: the earth disgusted. Apocalyptio.

Red lace over the blue-veined marble. Reflections trapped in the shiny wetness: my face, the raised hand of the man lying on his back on the floor. In his red tributaries.

I kneeled beside Pietr. He was still alive. The gun was in his hand. His lips were blackened. He had put the gun in his mouth.

I looked across to the small crumpled heap in the black dress next to the fireplace.

It had been hard to make out what Pietr had been saying. I had done most of the talking.

But at the end he had turned his face very slightly so he could see from the corner of his eye. Looking at the shape next to the fireplace, he said, I never forgave my mother. I never could. It was in the blood.

I held his hand. After a while, he said the woman's name. He said, *My wife.*

We both felt my fingers tighten.

He said, I couldn't change for her.

I know.

You can change for her.

No, I said. I don't know if I can.

He coughed. His chin was shiny. He said – or was it me? – I was brought up to believe you had to be a bastard to get ahead. But ahead to what? All I had in the end was waking up in the middle of the night marooned on a white plain, a plain on which there were no footsteps other than my own.

I survey the desert. The sky is blown glass. Thunderheads distort the horizon, the sun flares in the red-grey mist. The land is rising to meet the sky.

'I told Pietr I wasn't a kind man,' I say. 'I don't do anything for free.'

'That's my boy,' says Mitch. He takes out a slim silver flask from his pocket, raises it to his lips, watching me over the rim.

I say, 'I presume the Americans aren't interested in Saddam's revolting collection of velour sparkle paintings and porn?'

Mitch lowers the flask, caps it. 'We're all on the same side here, Dev,' he says, quietly, pleasantly. 'You must have known we'd find the figurine in Hafid Street.'

'The minor figurine.'

He isn't surprised. I wonder if he has a briefcase of cash in the helicopter.

He says, still friendly, 'What else have you got?' We might have been old pals swapping golf scores.

I say, 'Two pieces. The gold falcon from the Royal Palace of Ur and a miniature of the goat guardian at Tel Halif.' I can almost feel the goat in my hands. It had been cut from the largest ruby I had ever seen, with beaten silver for a face plate and a rug of silver chain mail flung over the spine. The original was seven feet tall, created in the place where recorded history began. A place now sacked in less than ten years. Looted, vandalised, its excavation sites attacked with front-end loaders. Clay tablets taken from the museum of Baghdad: the first writings, many of them not even read yet. Civilisation unrecorded. History lost.

I say, 'You can have them back.'

'If we give up on the woman.' He sees my face and laughs. 'You're so easy to read, Dev. We all know you couldn't just fuck for your country.'

'Maybe I don't care about the woman,' I say. 'Maybe I just want to humiliate you.'

His face changes. This he can understand. This is what he suspected.

He says, 'We're trying to build goodwill here.'

'You're trying to reclaim moral ground after carnage,' I say. 'After looting by people who knew in advance. Who were tipped off.'

Mitch studies me. 'Our job is intervention or non-intervention. There's no middle ground.'

'There should be,' I say. 'The results are bad either way.'

'It's all adults here. Everyone over the age of twenty-one deserves what they get.'

'Not an entire people.'

He shrugs. 'Don't take it personally, Dev. Have some water.' He throws me the flask. 'You look parched.'

I am thirsty, I don't stop to think. I raise the flask, tip my head. Fire roars in my throat.

He says, 'Everything we do is for your own good, Dev.'

I cough and almost fall to my knees. The sky seems to darken, the sand is moving, shapes are rising on the horizon. A bird hovers overhead: not an eagle, a vulture. I squat and spit out the last of the Scotch.

'What's the matter?' says Mitch. 'Seeing monsters? Got the DTs?' He picks up the briefcase. 'You run away from everything.' He comes closer. 'Your father, Borneo.' He stands over me. 'You even went AWOL on the woman.'

I straighten and look down at him. 'You're Iago, Mitch. Filling your empty days with malice.'

He smiles. 'Who's this Iago, Dev? An informant? An imaginary character to justify being such a loser? You think she is on your side. But she left you, didn't she? And now you can't find her.'

The flask is cool in my hands. I pour a little into my palm and rub the liquid on my gums. I bare my teeth at him. 'I can't find her. And neither will you.'

He laughs. 'You know it will go on. Even without Pietr. It's too lucrative.'

'History catches up with all of us, Mitch. The world is too small a place now.'

He isn't listening. He has tucked the briefcase under his arm and is punching in a code on the locking panel. I watch him. It is the over-ride code. I know it well.

Nothing happens. He punches it in again. The locks don't open. He thumps the briefcase. 'Open it.'

I shake my head. 'You'll have to take it back. Get Grant on it. He's good.'

'How do I know you won't screw us?'

'Because I want you to leave me alone.'

His hands relax on the case. I know I have him. I look at my watch. I say, 'Both pieces are in a house on Rue Sidi Hmad. You'll have to go in during work-hours, there are tenants. The falcon is under the floor in the bedroom, the goat is in a cavity in the fountain statue.' I nod at the briefcase. 'The address is in the laptop. And details of the rest.'

'If we forget about the woman.'

'If you keep after her, well, she knows about the rendition site at Koloshnovar. The black box cells. The water-boarding. Just let her disappear quietly, Mitch. You got what you wanted.'

He is thinking. He is tempted. I have to make sure. I raise the flask, I take another drink. I let the liquid run down either side of my mouth. I see my face in the mirror in Borneo as the phone began to ring. I see Mitch's reflection in the mirror and I think, I hate you.

I say, 'Maybe I should be the hero here. Maybe I should use the insurance Pietr gave me.'

'Insurance?' His hands tighten on the briefcase.

'Pietr made his own tapes of what the CIA did in the holding cells at Koloshnovar. He was paranoid, apparently, after what happened to his father.'

Mitch says, 'You'll be crucified in a military court. Closed.'

I raise the flask in a salute. 'As you always say, you can't expect a drunk to behave rationally.' I tilt the flask over my mouth.

'Wait,' he says. He shakes the briefcase. 'It's all in here?'

'Plus a copy in safe hands. They know what to do if anything happens to me.'

'They?' He doesn't like the sound of that.

I want to say, Even you can't wipe out an entire village. But I don't. Just in case.

He thinks for a moment. 'You be where we can find you.'

'Sure, Mitch.' I drop the flask in the dust. I think of one last thing. 'Be careful of the old turtle in the fountain. It bites.'

I walk down the rutted road, his shouts folding into the dust behind me. I walk on and on, down and down. The last thing I hear as I pull the hood over my head is his voice. 'You'll kill her the way you killed your father.'

Or maybe it was, 'Everything we do is for your own good. You fuck.'

Sister Antony is waiting at the base of the plateau. She comes out of the entrance shadows, holding a backpack. When she sees me, she sets it down and says, 'Did he believe you?'

I have to rest against the rock. The trembling in my legs seems worse. Sister Antony gives me a bottle of water. I pour it over my face. I can still smell the Scotch.

I think of Pietr gasping out the co-ordinates of the safe in the basement office. 'Mitch wants to believe,' I say. 'But it doesn't mean he won't hunt for scapegoats. You, Laforche.'

'Laforche told me he can pay off his gambling debts now.' She doesn't sound surprised.

'You should leave with him.'

'Maybe.'

'You know they are closing this place down.'

'Yes.' The rock's shadow doesn't dim the hard grey polish of her eyes. She says, 'There is a place I always wanted to visit. The ghostly ruins of Smara.'

'At least you have the book. The magic book in your jewelled casket.'

'The book is the jewelled casket.' She raises her hand, flexing her fingers.

'Is it real?' I say. 'Is it by Rimbaud? Or by someone else?'

She turns her wrist, easily. 'There is always a book behind the book. Until eventually behind all the books in the world, we come to one man or one woman writing the book.'

'That's not enough,' I say loudly. My voice echoes against the black rock.

'Why not?' she says. 'We are the story being written. We don't know how it ends. That is why we keep looking. That is why we go out into the desert. We go into the white pages and look for traces beneath the black marks left by the noon-day sun.'

There is pain behind my eyes, the old anger. The old disbelief. I say, 'But the reality is the retired jeweller in Casablanca who says he sold you a box of nineteenth century parchment. Maybe your book is a fake.' I point out to the horizon. 'All of this is a fake.'

'Does it matter?' she says.

I drink some water and peer through the sandy mist to the shimmering folds of red earth. I see the tough pale plants, the lacework of low flowers, the cactuses burrowing under each other for protection, the broken question mark of a scuttling scorpion. It is familiar to me now.

'She preferred to go out into this,' I say. 'Instead of staying with me.'

'She was driven,' says Sister Antony. 'By lies and betrayals.'

'My lies.'

Sister Antony shakes her head. 'She was grieving. That is why she placed the scorpion on her face.'

'My betrayals.'

'She thought she had lost her life twice over.'

'I've failed at it all. It's been a nightmare, living this half-life.'

'Remember,' she says, 'Adam found Eve after a dream. Shared dreaming is the essence of humanity.'

'Shared.' I can't breathe. 'We have nothing to share.'

The Sister steps closer. 'Stop looking in the book of limits, the book of margins.' She takes my hand. It is so unexpected I can only stare at her.

She says, 'You need to look in the unwritten book.'

She gives me the backpack. 'Water. And a compass. You probably don't need it with all your fancy equipment.'

'I need it,' I say. 'I've left all my fancy equipment behind.'

I grip the backpack. 'I'm worried.' There is a tremor in my voice. I swallow. 'I've failed before. Everywhere I go there are – calamities.'

She touches the scar on her cheek. 'You will grow into speech through loneliness and suffering. Jesus began his work from solitariness.'

I can hardly process what I am hearing. 'But you can't think – I'm not Jesus, the woman is not Jesus.'

The muddy light coats her eyes now. Mitch could be right – her neighbour in Casablanca, the teetotaller poet, had said she had a taste for self-punishment.

She says, 'In the loneliness of the desert, we are visited by angels. I gaze out and see an immense flowering in the desert.'

'Do you really see it?'

'I see a silver lake and roses reaching up to the blue sky.'

I put my hand on the cool dark rock. 'You live in a tomb in the earth. Maybe what you see is a mirage of death.'

'You'll see it too,' she says. 'You will see lions in the desert. An eagle hovering overhead, protecting you like its young.'

'The only thing I'm likely to see is Mitch in his helicopter with machine-gun blazing.'

'You don't believe.'

'I – look, I'm sorry, but there are no lions in the desert. Wolves, I can believe.'

'You will see them.'

I heft the backpack but I don't put it on.

'You don't want to go out there,' she says.

'I may be a drunk but I'm not stupid.'

She watches me carefully.

I say, 'I don't know how much Laforche knows . . .'

She places her hands in her wide sleeves and stands, still and listening, in that way she has. I feel compelled to go on.

'There were incidents,' I say. 'Failures. One with my father, another in Borneo.' I find it hard to speak. 'There were deaths involved.'

'You drank firewater.'

'Yes, I suppose.'

'It burned you up.'

'Yes.'

'You want to make amends.'

'Yes.'

'Then you should go out into the vanishing point of absolute poverty,' she says. 'There will be pain. At first your body will be defiled. You will be alone. The desert will look on. It will not help you but it will not stand in your way.'

She hands me a square object; it slides through my hands like moon water. I catch it, remove the ivory silk. It takes me a moment to realise what it is.

'Rimbaud's book.' I visualise the bold inked writing. 'You can't give this away.'

'Yes. When you find Madeleine you will take her to the caves under the Kabir Massif. Use the caves that run under the plain to the Massif. She knows the way. You will give the book to a Moroccan woman called . . . ' There is a long pause before she says the name: 'Betsoul.'

'Isn't this part of your plan to save Abu N'af?'

'My plan was wrong.' Her face is shadowed. 'It is my fault,' she says and for the first time I see uncertainty in her face, anxiety in the hands clenching the cross. 'I needed to pay penance and I had given everything else away. Don't you understand? I had nothing else to give.'

'Why must sacrifice always come into it?' I say. 'What is it with you women?'

But she isn't listening to me. She has an expression of horror, seeing some horizon I can only imagine. 'I think I have done a terrible thing.' Her voice is a whisper. 'I saw a chance to wipe away my father's sins. My sins. Madeleine came to me for sanctuary. She needed to be hidden – '

'From me?' I can barely say it.

'When Stefano told her about me, she brought me what she thought was the real book, the book with the red cover that Pietr took from me in Casablanca. But that book was a copy I had made.

Madeleine brought me the book to stop Rosza using its desert maps for looting.'

'Why didn't you put fake maps in the copy?'

'All I cared about was being left alone, with the real book.' She shivered. 'I betrayed Madeleine. I stole from her.'

'Stole what?'

'A new book – ' Her voice cracks and she opens and closes her mouth as if she can no longer talk.

'Too many books,' I say, impatient. 'Too many lootings.'

She bows her head.

Sister Antony watches me as I place Rimbaud's book in my deep pocket. She says, 'Give the book to Betsoul. Tell her it is payment for the past week. Tell her she must give back what she stole from the woman.'

She holds out a dark wooden object. 'Give Betsoul this also.' It looks like a painted fang.

'I told her a lie,' says the Sister, 'because it was the only way to start a new community in the desert.'

'Lied to who?' I ask, not thinking, focused instead on what is ahead of me. 'This Betsoul?'

Sister Antony shakes her head. She says, 'First you dream, then you die.' She opens her hand. On her palm is a small wooden hair comb shaped like a butterfly. As I thrust it deep into my pocket, my fingers brush the torn-up fragments of the note the woman had left me. She had written, *When I look at you, I know the people I loved are gone. Five deaths are too much for one person to endure.* And she had fled into the desert.

I am drowning in desolation; I can barely hear what the Sister is saying.

'I was right about the book,' says the Sister. 'It is God's word. It created a community. I brought the book to the desert and people came and the desert flowered.' She closes her eyes. 'But I am not God.'

The sun sidles upwards. I am on the last stony piece of ground before the red dunes. Sand clumps around tough tufts of grass and dry squares of low-slung plants and squat bushes so faded they seem to lack all sap. I nudge a crouching cactus and white fluid spurts out from its thorny spine. The liquid disappears into the ground; within moments there is nothing but a white shadow on the rocks.

I walk on. Scorpions back away from me, their tails up. The further I walk the slower they are to move. A small dust-coloured lizard raises itself on stubby back legs and hisses at me. Its mouth is black as coal and its eyes are blood-red. It flicks its tail and disappears into a dust cloud of its own making.

My lips burn; I taste salt. I drink the water Sister Antony has given me and look back. There are no footprints yet I sense the ground has been altered, rocks moved, the air displaced. Those capable of reading such signs can follow me. But not Mitch. Not even Sister Antony, I think.

The land changes again. The rocks shrink to gravel, the plants descend into the ground. An occasional sand viper skitters in front of me but all life is disappearing. The dunes are tantalisingly close. For some reason, I am convinced that when she reaches the beginning of the dunes proper, she will stop. She will climb to the top of the first dune, to see the light on the horizon. All the paintings she loves have light on the horizon.

Sand is rising. An eddy dances on the same spot, turning and turning. The hot wind swings through the sandy mist, hitting my face, heavy with grit and salt.

A peculiar sighing rushes past me; the ground is breathing out. A long silence follows yet I feel rhythm in the silence, as though a pulse trapped in an invisible body is rapidly approaching.

I think: Now I am hearing the real silence of the desert. A silence filled with a thousand echoes: everything from the wind's idle stirring of a few grains on the top of the dunes to the distant whine eating up the side of the Massif. I hear the click of the beetle's barbed legs as it dives down through the sand. I hear drums, and yearning notes from a gramophone on the peaks. Is it Beethoven? Yes, poor Beethoven, trapped in his well of silence and trying to speak to God through his music. More voices, some from caves, some from tombs. Streamers of sound which float over the desert. And bells, I am sure I hear bells. And Laforche's voice: Mapmakers, criminals, suicidal poets, he is saying. Desert travellers are never city dwellers but nomads, ascetics. Behind him, Edith Piaf turns in mourning circles. And other voices: *In the dark, I wake on the white page of the desert* . . .

Laforche is saying, The desert is peopled with madmen, loners. The lost and those seeking to be lost.

I am all of those, I say to him.

You're a romantic with a streak of masochism, says Laforche. You always take the hardest way.

I am driven by self-disgust, I say. I refused her call and now all I have is the void.

First you dream and then you die, says Laforche.

I see clues: a smear in the dust between the rocks, a footprint pressing down the gravel. I am sure I am beginning to read the traces of the desert.

The voices, the sound of the beetles, fade into the great bell of silence. It seems that hour after hour I walk and the dunes are always the same distance ahead of me. Only the sky is changing: turning the colour of ash, tinged with the sickly yellow of the sun dying on the horizon, smelling of salt and smoke and dead flesh.

I am walking through a region of broken bones and crushed shells. The ground is growing lighter; the black rocks crumbling into grit are flecked by white and pink slivers of bone. I see a crab's claw, the chafed mosaic of a turtle's shell, cradled in camel skulls. Splinters of bone are caught between my toes.

I sit down to take off my sandal. The distance rustles as though a giant bush is being shaken. A yellow cloud detaches from the sickly sun and wheels back and forth across the sky. It turns towards me and blots out the light. The rustling grows into an endless whirring, the beating of a million tiny wings, the winds catching in barbed joints and searching antennae. The dark mass flies straight at me. A hot wind hits me, I feel drained and withered. I crouch on the ground, pulling the hood of the robe as far over my face as I can.

The whirring grows louder. It is a beating inside my head; my eardrums vibrate. Under the hood, the light has almost disappeared. Thunder booms. I peer through the dark grey light. The sky is the colour of coal seamed by silver; lightning flashes like the blinking of an eye. The ground is lit up and ahead, where the dunes rise like sculpted red waves, I see her walking away from me.

I release the backpack and stand up and the locusts hit me. I am knocked sideways, hurled along the ground, half dragged half pushed. My hood is no protection: the creatures fly in, scratching at my eyes, my cheeks, trying to climb into my mouth, my ears. They are climbing up my legs, under the sleeves of my robe, down my neck. The whirring is unbearably loud. I fling off the robe and run, naked, my hands over my face, into the dunes. When I feel real sand, not just grit, I hurl myself down and start digging. The booming increases behind me and there is the sound of a giant wave rising and rising. I grab handfuls of sand and pour them over me, I reach deep into the ground and pull myself forward. I dive into the sand.

I am in darkness. I roll and roll, corkscrewing into the sand, crushing the insects. The scratching and rustling on my body stops. Far away there is the sound of dogs barking then they too stop; the hammer blows of thunder recede. It is very quiet. I press my watch to illuminate it but when the light comes on, the panels are grey. I press and press. The panel flickers, the light goes out. I take the watch off and push it away from me. The silence and the sand fill my ears.

When I climb out of the sand, the sun is a spreading stain on the grey sky. Dunes rise on either side of me; it is as if an entire landscape has been created in moments. The crushed and stony ground is completely covered in sand.

My sandals have gone but I find my robe nearby. The book is still in the pocket, and something which jabs me between my fingers. It is the wooden hair comb. I am tempted to throw it away but I shove it back.

I walk in circles, digging in, trying to feel with my feet. I walk and dig but I know the backpack is gone.

When I climb to the top of the next dune, I am sure I will see Abu N'af but there is nothing: no plateau, no Kabir Massif, no blue mountains. Just endless sand stretching through the vast empty to Algeria.

I don't know how long I have been walking. The desert stretches ahead of me. I walk and all I can think is, I am so angry.

The sandy mist envelops me, red clouds roll over me, the dunes rear up shadowless, constantly shifting in the wind which wraps my robe around me. I do not know if I am walking up hills or down. My feet sink into the sand. The glazed and crumbling fragments of clay jars are scattered between rusting cutlasses, useless pistols, abandoned compasses, empty water bottles. Occasionally I think I see monks on the horizon moving slowly in a centipede line under a hunch-backed and pockmarked yellow moon. Sometimes I see lions, sometimes wolves. Sometimes a hot breath snorts behind me, there is a shuddering on the back of my neck. Objects which glint metal, statuettes made of mud, float around me, their sharp edges dissolving in the gritty air. I ignore them all. The huge silence cloaks me. I plod on.

The wind comes again. It is a lupine wind. Wolves howl within it. The sky dogs. My skin hurts but I no longer feel thirsty or tired.

Images from my past keep appearing and disappearing, rolling away like the white crests turning over in rough seas against the shore.

I can remember saying to her, What you do to your body is insane.

The light seeps away. I see windmills dark in a landscape of tormented rocks and boulders. Lacking water, lacking hope. Lacking the ability to cry, she had said to me.

In the wasted light, the earth falls away from all the other stars into silence. Day is reversed. I see the dying gardens of the star isle. Night slides into me; the breath from the moon's gaping mouth trails across the black sky.

Time goes by, the stars wheel across the sky. I am on my knees in the sand. Dark birds circle overhead. I know this barren landscape, I have been here for years. I know those serrated peaks, those curtains of clouds that hum in the air, that lightning which looks like flares over a battlefield, which turns the smallest plant into the huge shadows of monsters moving between the stubby peaks and the milky blue boulders. Wings beat above me and in the next lightning flash I see a bird in flames, spiralling into the dark clouds.

A grain of sand hits my cheek. I kneel and look for a footprint. There is nothing but a pool of black water.

I don't want to see but I must. There is a shape there. I am hoping beyond hope that it is her face – just to see her one last time. But of course it is not. I think, I am so angry.

I lean forward. I see my reflection.

I surrender, I say. I know you are indifferent to me. Borneo taught me that. You are beautiful in your sheer awful indifference, in your unattainability.

I take off my mask.

I am nothing now but sand and water.

Reveal the hard implacable truth to me, I say.

In the black pool the man who is me reaches out and writes a name in the water. Her name. And then he turns his back on me and walks away into a light which is so bright that it blinds me and the world turns to black.

I am on my back, drowning in light. The hovering birds beat their wings above me. A shadow moves across me, rain falls on me. There is a voice filled with silence and with light saying my name.

Listen, I say to the shape above me, we're lost.

We're not lost, she says.

I dig my hand into the sand, find a long curving piece of shell. I bring it to my wrist, begin to dig in. I cut downwards, following the vein, opening up the artery. The sky dogs howl, the book of the desert begins to close.

Listen, I say, save yourself. Open my veins. Let the blood out. There is water in blood. Drink it.

I press the sharp point of the shell in. There is pain then nothing. The shell goes in.

I hear all the other small voices of silence now. How can I not have heard them before? The voice of pure winds, the voice of the prince of rain.

I put my hands up to cup the rain and the stars.

There are books snowing from my hands, letters and words falling from my fingers.

If only you knew all I wished to say.

There is a long silence. I am looking out into the void and it is as I think.

I raise the shell to cut again and she says, *You are the poem being written.*

She is holding me, my head against her heart. I feel rain falling on me but it must be the touch of her hair against my cheek.

I am finding it hard to open my eyes against the white light but I do. The sun has burned a white hole in the sky. It is the moon.

She is lit up by light, the way light fills a hand with light. The way light fills the face in a certain position. The way that, in a certain position, a certain time, I would see moonlight fall into her shoulder.

Her eyes are blank, glassy. She might be blinded. Her lips move, she is tracing in the air with one hand. I make out the rhythms of the notes, hear the echoes of a tune.

She makes the same gesture I had seen her make in the sick bay at Abu N'af. Her tracings had been a silent symphony. She had been conducting in the air, to the words she was thinking.

I say to her, What is that song you are singing?

She looks down at me.

Is that a poem?

It isn't a poem.

What is it?

She hesitates.

I raise my hand to touch her face and see the bandage around my wrist.

She says, You are my lucky star, you glow for me from afar. Lucky, lucky, lucky.

A nursery rhyme.

Yes.

For some reason I think of Sister Antony.

I say, The Sister –

Her face hardens. She pushes me away.

She says, We have to go.

She helps me to my feet, gives me more water from her backpack. My legs tremble, my heart is shaking but I am upright. I stare at the water bottle.

So it was water then, I say. Not rain. Not tears.

No, she says, turning away. It wasn't tears. I don't cry.

I catch her by the shoulder, bring her closer. She doesn't resist. She stares at me with her furious blue gaze. The welts on her face seem faded, reduced.

It was never as bad as it looked, she says. Sister Antony got something, monk's bane, from a Moroccan woman who knows about these things.

More poison, I say. This is a story about poisonings.

No, she says. This is a story about families.

She turns and walks away, into the desert. She doesn't look back. I think she doesn't care if I follow her or not.

I follow.

A wind whistles nearby, cold air wraps around me. I don't know it if it is real or some reaction to the poison. Or fear. The light grows brighter. The landscape is bleached. I see only the shadows skipping between the dunes and her figure an unyielding silhouette ahead of me. I am being blinded by light. Soon there will be only her. Unless she leaves me.

I say, *We danced.* My voice is insubstantial, making faint black marks in the white air.

I say, louder, We danced together at the party in the glass house.

There is a pause. I wondered if she is so far ahead that she can't hear me.

No, she says. She had been deciding whether to answer.

Yes, I say. When I was watching you from outside the house. I came up out of the darkness, out of my cave, out of my well. I took your hand.

The ground feels hotter under my bare feet. Sand cuts between my toes. I say, At first we were awkward together. I said to you, Christ it's a waltz. I can't waltz. And you said, Neither can I. But can't we try together?

There is a rustling in the distance. The locusts returning. My feet flinch at the heat.

I never said that, she says. I already knew you couldn't be trusted.

I go on, And I held you and you said one two three and we moved off but in different directions and I said Oh, for fuck's sake and you laughed. You made some small step and somehow we synchronised, effortlessly turning. Your dress was emerald water in my hands and we turned through the cool air and we danced on wordlessly and I felt I was in a trance.

There is a very long silence. I hear wings beating above me again. My feet are burning. Something is falling on my face: powdery, hot. I press a finger against my cheek. Ash.

Silence. I think she has left me.

Eventually, when I have given up hope, she says, *You should have told me.*

The light goes completely. I am blinded. I fall to my knees. The rustling is closer. I cover my ears. Something: wings, nails, brushes my forehead.

I want to shout but I don't want to open my mouth.

I feel her hands in my hair, tilting my head, pulling my arms away. Liquid falls into my eyes; I smell lavender. A black mist covers my face. She is tying black silk over my eyes.

You're sand-blinded, she says. Keep your eyes closed.

She says, Hold onto this. She gives me one end of a rope. I feel her leave me. The rope tugs at me to follow her.

I touch the silk. I say, Just when I was trying to take off my masks. My mask of anger.

Your mask of power, she says.

My mask of weakness, I say.

The rope becomes slack. She has stopped. She says, I saw you as all-powerful. I felt manipulated by you. How can you think I would not?

No. It was you who had all the power.

All I had was silence.

No, that was me.

She says, We never connected right from the start. There is a great weariness in her voice. She says, When I see you it is the opening of a wound.

The sky presses into my eyes. I refuse to think it might be too late. A wave of the old anger washes up me. I thrust my fist into the pocket of my robe and hear a sharp crack. I have broken one of the comb's wooden teeth. I feel the splintered end with my finger, force the sharp tip under my nail. I remember the bone points filled with charcoal jabbing in under my skin in Borneo.

I say, *I'll never stop looking for you.*

The rope tightens.

We walk. My feet sink into the hot sand. Through the silk, I see a halo around a low moon. I see the sand lifting up in eddies which turn into shapes. I see animals pacing.

I see lions, I say. The rope slackens. I put my hand up to remove the silk blindfold but she says, Not yet.

She takes my wrist and leads me across ground which seems firmer. I dig my toes into the sand and meet stone. A rock looms: I feel a small outcrop covered in chalky earth and clotted sand. I pass from pure light into shadow. Just as the merciless glare recedes, I look back and see a lion, kneeling, its nose to the ground, digging into the stony earth.

She leads me deeper. It is cooler here. There is no wind. The air is heavy with salt and the sloping ground feels strange. After a moment it comes to me. The earth is damp.

Leave the blindfold on for a little longer, she says. She lifts my wrist until my finger touches rock. She says, Keep this wall on your right even when the path splits. It's part of a network of caves. It takes you back to Abu N'af.

And the other way?

She lets go of my wrist. She says, It runs through to Kabir Massif. It's the old watercourse that still feeds the well. She says, All of this was once a giant sea.

I pull off the blindfold. She edges away from me. With the light from the fissure behind her, I find it hard to make out her face, the expression in her eyes.

I say, Aren't you coming with me?

No, she says. Because all I want to do is hurt you. She reaches into her backpack. I see a black spine, a circle of light. An old camera.

I move towards her, slowly.

Don't, she says.

I put my hands up, palms towards her. I say, Why did your message say that five people you loved had died? There was your brother, Pietr, Anna —

And you, she says. It was only ever you.

But who is the fifth?

483

I lost you twice, she says. In the caves.

Her hands tighten on the darkness in her hands.

There is a glint of light. I say, Sister Antóny lied –

Stars stream from her hands. As she swings the camera at my temple, I shout, *I'll never stop.*

When I wake it is dark. I am back lying on the path outside my father's house, sweating alcohol, raising my head, hearing the shouts inside, the breaking glass.

I sit up. My temple and throat are wet. I mop at both with my robe. My pockets feel heavy: she has left me a water bottle and a candle and matches. I can't feel the book and the wooden comb. I dig deeper; they have slipped to the bottom.

I haul myself up and walk, my right hand on the jagged wall. I leave it up to fate whether I find the entrance or keep going, walking endlessly under the dead sea.

I don't bother to use the candle. My eyes adjust to the darkness. I sense light in the tiny metal gleams in the wall. The ground is nearly smooth, compacted by the weight of water. Or maybe by many feet carrying heavy burdens.

I feel dampness under my sole. There is still water trapped somewhere below. Water in the Sahara. Man only settles the frontiers for business. The desert would become a strip mall. Then I remember the sand lifting in spirals, the locusts. Even Las Vegas didn't have locusts.

I am sick suddenly, throwing up into the darkness. My bandaged hand is cramped, the side of my face spasms. Tremors wrack my body.

I dump sand in the direction of my illness and keep going. Surprisingly I feel better. It is as though my body is euphoric after expelling the poison. I am convinced that she hasn't left me, that she is ahead of me, watching out for me. The logical man that I had been would have said there is no evidence for this but I believe it. I am happy.

I say to the woman, I found you.

I say her name over and over again.

Finally, she says, and her voice is as weary as the wind trapped against the rocks, Yes, you found me.

The path slopes more steeply. The ground is grittier, my feet curl against sharper rocks. I feel the roof opening above my head, an eddying of air. I am still walking quite quickly when I hear the rustling. I stop, jam my back against the wall, pull up my hood.

I wait. The darkness swells.

I feel sound. I light the candle and hold it above my head.

The flame moves across the stirring, shifting bodies like light moving across the night sea. The black furry bodies sway, the hanging heads nod. Here and there a wing is half extended, an eye blinks red in the light. Bats.

I have just blown out the candle, the smoke hanging grey in the air, when another light flares on the opposite side of the cave. A figure in a robe waves at me. The light recedes. There is a stirring above me, a ripple across a pond. I press my face to the wall and edge sideways, trying not to make a sound. The rustlings and whisperings grow louder. I am sure the whole nest will come alive. I wait, rigid. The darkness pulses. The cave settles into silence.

Boulders block the entrance into the next cave. I pick my way carefully over the fallen rocks and find muddy ground and pools of water gleaming in low light.

The far end of the cave is illuminated. The robed figure is standing by a small fire which burns against the wall. The flames make shadows which climb the dark jags to disappear into the vaulted blackness.

The figure throws back its hood as I approach: a middle-aged woman, Moroccan. Her dark hair is flecked with grey, her brown skin is etched with glowing blue lines: blue flames lick the base of her neck, more crawl out from the soles of her feet; the backs of her hands are heavily inked in lines and swirls and circles. There is a sun image on one wrist, the moon on the other, writing in Arabic below each.

She watches me approach. Her eyes are grey around the pupil; the flames turn them orange in this light.

I say, 'Are you Betsoul?'

She waits. I wonder if she speaks English.

'I have something from Sister Antony for you,' I say, slowly and clearly. I put my hand in my pocket and take out the wooden comb and lay it at her feet. She doesn't pick it up but sketches a small gesture which reminds me of the helicopter pilot who brought me to Abu N'af. The gesture, rising then falling, can be read both ways: acknowledgement if you are a friend, feigned puzzlement if you are not.

I say, 'There was a woman with me. Have you seen her?'

Betsoul peers at my neck. She says, 'Someone cut your throat.'

I put my hand up, feel the crusted slash, see the dark flecks of dried blood on my fingers.

Betsoul points beyond the fire to a hollow in the ground filled with water and surrounded by a low wall of rocks packed in mud. Near the pool is a cleared space. A large flat piece of lighter rock lies there. There are odd shadows – almost stains – on the rubbed smooth surface. The stains remind me of Sicily.

On the rock a strip of black silk is draped across a pile of white animal skins. Next to the skins is a bucket of coals, a heaped camel-hair blanket, a knobbly chunk of metal which looks like lead, a dried branch with wicked inch-long thorns and a wide knife, almost a hatchet.

The skins stir, the black silk shifts and slips. It is a baby goat, asleep, the material tied across its small horns.

I am still staring at the goat when Betsoul says, 'Look at water.' Her voice is a deep, flat monotone.

'Look at water,' she says again and again, as though she is trying to hypnotise me.

'The woman,' I say.

'A ghost,' says Betsoul. She points to the pool. It lies like a dark eye in the flickering cave. I move closer. The water is thick, viscous, veined by some lighter liquid. I bend over it. I am worried that I will see – my father? my love? the bottomless well inside me?

'The spirit is released by the sound of the human voice,' says Betsoul. 'You have to say all you think and never dared to say.'

I put my hand into the pool. It is deeper than it appears. I kneel on the rim, thrust my hand further. The blue-black water closes around me. My reflection is the colour of sand. I see myself in the pub, drunk as usual, cursing my father to my new best friends, the same curses I had shouted at him as I left the house.

'What do you see?' says Betsoul. She flicks with her hand and dark grains fall on the fire. The flames flare turquoise; dark grey smoke rises. A heady smell, tarter than incense, fills the cave.

'Nothing,' I say. I withdraw my arm. There is a dented shadow in the water where my hand had been.

'Mirages,' I say.

'All you never dared to say,' says Betsoul, waving with her hand so the smoke writhes around me.

I say, 'When I was with her, the woman I loved, when her hair was too short to hide daggers or poisons, she would say that water is a kiss. She loved water, she loved to swim. She would say that we dive into rock pools like lives we never think we would encounter, shedding our skins, desperate to turn ourselves inside out. We want new masks, new identities, but all we can do is take another life inside us, like water.'

The grey smoke is hanging like a veil over me. I breathe in. I take my first deep breath in the desert, I fill my lungs with night. I breathe in the grit, the poisons. I inhale the fragments of a trillion words. I dream light and the horizon. I open myself out to the desert.

'What else?' says Betsoul. Her eyes are clouded moonlight.

'When I was a drunk,' I say, 'and I was a drunk for a long time, because the army won't tolerate questions or initiative but being a career drunk is no problem. Anyway. After yet another period of drunkenness, I was released into the care of my father. I told him I wasn't going back to the army. That I wanted – ' I can't believe I am saying these words out loud. 'I told him I wanted to be a painter. Of course we had a shouting match and I told him I wished he was dead.'

I stop. Betsoul throws more grains on the fire. The grey smoke rises.

After a while I say, 'I got drunker at the pub and was pathetically grateful when these three friendly guys gave me a lift home. Soon I was maudlin, regretted what I said; my father had never recovered from my mother's death. So I told my new best friends, Thanks for the ride, I'm going to make it up with my dad. At which point they hit me over the head, robbed the house and threw my pensioner father through a glass door. His jugular was cut and he bled to death an arm's length from me. They never found the guys.'

I raise my hand, the water swallows the reflection like black syrup. In the disappearing shadow, I see the light falling from the moon onto her shoulder in the night that we never spent together.

I hear her voice, 'All the pain in the world is swallowed by water.'

'Water aspires to death,' says Betsoul. 'Its first transformation is despair.'

She comes and stands next to me.

'Do you know what I see?' she says. 'I see Sister Antony taking me away from my family when I was twelve. To give me a better life in a good home, so she told me. To become civilised. To become a Westerner. To speak well, to be able to read all those Western stories that had nothing to do with me. I see myself being raped every night after mass by Father Thomas. I see myself pregnant at thirteen.' She turns to face me. She holds out her hand. In her other hand, I see the glint of steel. She says, 'I see you giving me what the good Sister owes me.'

I give her the book. I think she will examine it, read it, ask me questions. But she takes it from me without a word. She turns and throws Rimbaud's book into the fire.

I cry out.

She stands between me and the burning pages, the knife glinting in her hand.

She says, 'Western books have nothing for me, Nazarene.'

I look past her. The book has fallen open, the pages in the centre are orange and black roses on fire. Curling fragments tear away from the spine, sweep up to the dark roof. Words and letters fly into the night, returning to the desert which houses all the letters and all the words in the world.

I say, 'Everything is in the book. The maps of the Kabir Massif, the underground water.'

A charred fragment floats past Betsoul. She catches it and puts it in her mouth.

She says, 'Now we have it.'

More fragments rise and merge with the night; small voyagers from another century. His book was never ours to keep, Pietr had said. We weren't worthy of it.

The outer pages are burning now, the cover beginning to curl, turning shiny. The leather looks wet; it looks like black water.

I see the back pages pull away from the leather; they burn and float, revealing a thicker page: a shiny page of shadows and light.

'Wait.' I scoop my arm through the pool and throw myself next to the fire. I thrust my hand in its sopping sleeve into the flames. I catch the black page just as the glue melts and it begins to rise.

I sit back, charred remains eddying slowly around me. The shiny page is barely touched; the chemicals on its surface have made it harder to burn. I rub my wet sleeve over the blue flames at the corners. I lay the page on the ground in front of Betsoul.

'This is what everybody wanted,' I say. 'You can use this.'

The flames make the shapes in the photograph come alive and sway. Except that these shapes would never be alive again.

Betsoul falls to her knees and bows her head but her eyelids twitch and I see the gleam of grey. She can't stop looking. I don't blame her.

'Who is this man?' she points at the white man with the whip who stands next to the grim wooden structures.

'A Polish count,' I say. 'The grandfather of a man who has been working with the American military. The grandson is – was – allowing the Americans to use his airfield in Poland. To transport people.'

'Slaves?' She puts her fingers over the three darker shapes attached to the wooden structures. She puts her fingers over their hearts.

I wonder what she knows about the CIA's secret rendition flights. I point to the Pole. 'The Americans are going to be very embarrassed if their connection to this man is revealed.'

She covers the Pole's eyes with her thumb.

I say, 'Many Westerners will be very unhappy.'

She picks up the photo, clutching it as though she thinks I will rip it from her.

I say, 'I have my own photos. The grandson had cages in a cave below his home.'

She says, 'There are cages in the caves under the Kabir Massif. That is why your woman came here. She thought she would find the bones of her brother.'

My feet are aching again, my hands, my eyes. 'She will never find the bones,' I say. 'All the witnesses are gone.'

I look at the photo of the three African children being crucified on the wooden crosses in the courtyard of Abu N'af. I read the word written in white dust on their small chests. *Les fugitifs, 1890.* The metal nails in their flesh are almost as large as their wrists.

The book has finished burning. Ash is falling around us.

Betsoul says, 'You know your woman was swollen with sickness.'

'Sick from her time in Sicily,' I say. 'From poison.'

She nods as though satisfied. 'She was asking questions in Quartier Rouge. So I took her to the Kabir Massif. She became unwell in the caves and I helped her as only women can help each other. She would have died without me. Later, she imagined things that had never happened. She ran out into the desert. I couldn't stop her.' She watches me carefully. 'I sent my daughter Meersun out to find her and take her to Abu N'af.'

Ashes are settling on my skin. I see fragments of words, messages I have no tools to read.

'I do not know why,' Betsoul says, 'your woman came back here.'

'Last week?'

'A few hours ago.'

I am on my feet. 'But you said – '

'If you go now you will catch her.' She stands. 'Go now,' she says. Her voice is rising, her urgency infectious. 'You'll find her,' she shouts. 'You'll catch her. Go.'

I am already stumbling to the exit. As I climb over the boulders into the next cave, I look back and see her: an ageing woman half-veiled in a shroud of falling ashes.

The light from the fire guides me through the next cave. The boulders are smaller here. As the darkness falls, I light the candle so I can move more quickly. I am tensed, about to break into a half-run, when my foot crunches. More shells, I think, but instead find small bones. I have to look for a long time to make sure. Not animal bones. I see the graceful scallop of a hip bone, the archer's bow of a femur.

I lower the candle and see – at waist-height, at the reach of a child – the marking on the wall. It is a mark scratched into the rock by a human hand.

At first I think it is an infinity symbol. I bring the candle closer.

The light falls on the etched wings. A butterfly.

There is no logical reason for what happens next. There is no coherent link. There is only a wooden hair comb shaped like a butterfly and a butterfly cut into a cave wall.

I stare at the butterfly for a long time. I think about dates, illnesses. I think about poison. I think about the bottomless well that makes me drink, makes me do nothing but work. Always needing to be filled.

I look at the butterfly and I think, If I had read poetry I would understand.

Then I think, I do understand. It is in my blood.

I hear the beating of the drum, the frenzied cries, from the next cave. I step as quietly as I know how but my shadow on the wall must have warned her because she swings. She had been cutting the baby goat's throat on the sacrifice stone. She waves the red-tipped knife at me. The kid goat, shocked out of its drugged stupor, begins to crawl away.

Betsoul's face is pierced by thorns and covered in ash; she is the colour of ghost. She stares at me, rings of white around the rings of grey. She doesn't know me. She is shrieking in a strange dialect. She waves the knife back and forth but she seems unable to walk.

I back away from her. I scan the cave, searching for an adult body. 'Where is she?' I say.

Betsoul's gaze darts to the pool. I barely glance at it: it is too small.

'Where is the woman?'

Betsoul gapes at me. Her tongue is black. 'I told you,' she says, the words broken by huge gasps. She is coming out of her trance, she is hyperventilating. 'Gone to the Kabir Massif.'

I look around helplessly. Burning candle wax is hardening on my hands. I blow out the flame. There is nowhere to hide. I had been wrong. I turn to go.

'Don't kill the kid,' I say to Betsoul.

She puts her hands over her mouth. She peers down at the pool again. There are bubbles on the surface. More poisoned water, I think, just like Sicily. I move closer. Betsoul's panting fills the cave. What was the Sicily story? A poisoned lake, the mother covering up for the husband's murder by the village. Some old story, not relevant.

I stare at the bubbles. Poisonous gasses rising to the surface. Maybe it was sulfur, some unknown deposits. I had read that monks used to die of it. More useless knowledge. Monks' bane. Antimony, just another name for sulfur, pockets of it all across Sicily. Giving the land that peculiar smell. The odour of hell.

But there is no smell here.

I kneel on the rocky rim and pass my hand through the water, parting the heavy black surface. Nothing but a patch of pale sand on the bottom of the pool.

Betsoul is trying to speak. 'They owed me,' she says. She looks dazed. Saliva runs out of the corner of her mouth. 'I kept what she gave in the cave,' she says, gasping for breath. 'It was a just payment.'

I trail my hand through the water again. My reflection breaks up: I am an aging man, alone. Working myself into my grave. As I sit back, the water settles. A small clear bubble pops on the surface. There is no smell. Another bubble rises, then another. A chain of them now. Clear, pure, odourless. Oxygen.

Betsoul screams. The sound climbs, higher and high‹
vaulted dark, shaking the walls, the smoke, the air. It ›
beyond tabulating: every howl of pain collected, every cr‹
every separation. Ashes rain down upon us. Words rain
Endless grief. She screams and screams and it is everything ı
wanted to say.

I half-leap half-fall into the pool and reach down to the palε
square. I grab at the bundle in the camel-hair blanket. It is weighted.
The chunk of lead is tied to it with rope.

Betsoul shouts, 'We told her everyone was dead. So she went into
the desert. She's a desert ghost now. A ghost.' She shudders and is still.

I claw over the rocky rim and rip away the rope. The bundle
moves in my hands. I still think it is another goat, another sacrifice.
Images of birds on fire are in front of me. The flashes of light are so
bright as I pull and pull at the wet blanket that when I finally reach
the last layer, where the material is almost dry, I am so blinded by
flames and smoke and ash and old memories and all the thousand
failures of my life that I can barely see the baby girl with blue eyes
who lies there, reaching up for me.

ACKNOWLEDGEMENTS

I would like to express my deepest gratitude to Dr Sue Woolfe of the Creative Writing Program at the University of Sydney for all her support and encouragement during the writing of this book. *Notorious* was inspired by attending Sue's class; it would not have been written without her.

Thank you also to Gaby Naher, Sarah Thompson, Sue Britton, Lisa Thatcher, Ashley Burton, Mark Kosta, Scott Goddard, Nicolette Scapens, and to everyone at Allen & Unwin, especially Jane Palfreyman and Ali Lavau.

While the Arthur Rimbaud portrayed here is based on historical fact, and on the poet's explorations in east Africa and his writings (including variations of his famous phrase *'Je est un autre'*), it is important to stress that this story is a work of fiction, as are some of the names of villages and localities.

Many books of non-fiction and poetry were helpful in my research, including the lives and works of Emily Brontë, Stéphane Mallarmé and Robert Browning. The phrases 'night remained in their bodies' and 'walking in the shadows of their burdens' are from the memoir *Desert Divers* by Sven Lindqvist, while Devlin's recollections of his early army days are extrapolated from Henry Reed's poem 'Naming Of Parts' from his sequence *Lessons Of The War*. Sister Antony's recollection of her first meeting with the woman in the desert ('I am eating my heart. It is bitter but I like it because it is bitter and because it is my heart') are taken from Stephen Crane's poem 'In The Desert'.

The reinforced Beani dome which Pietr Walenzska so admires is based on the innovative concrete shell structures of Dr Dante Bini. The excerpt from 'i carry your heart with me(i carry it in' is reprinted from *Complete Poems 1904–1962*, by E.E. Cummings, edited by George J. Firmage, by permission of W.W. Norton & Company. Copyright © 1991 by the Trustees for the E.E. Cummings Trust and George James Firmage:

i carry your heart with me(i carry it in
my heart)

ABOUT THE AUTHOR

Roberta Lowing is a poet, author, and film critic. Her poetry has appeared in literary journals such as *Meanjin*, *Blue Dog*, and *Overland*, and her first collection, *Ruin*, was published in 2010. She was a film and video critic for twenty-three years and covered the Cannes and Venice Film Festivals for ten years, interviewing directors and actors and writing travel stories. She recently completed her Master of Letters at the University of Sydney. *Notorious* is her first novel. She lives in Sydney, Australia.